WARM BLOODED

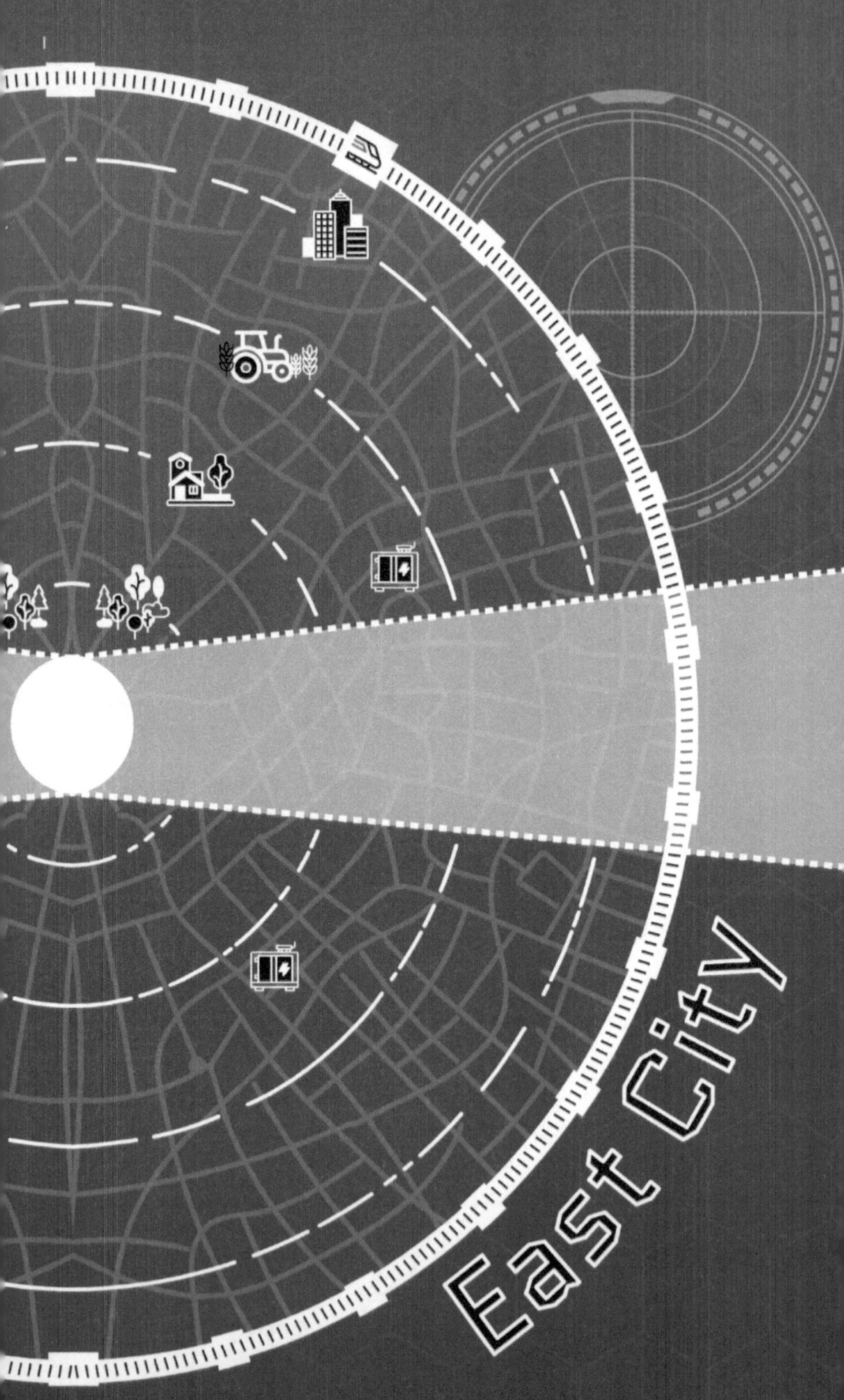

East City

East Technical Institute

1. Campus Main Entrance
2. Armorer's Lab
3. Gym
4. Field House
5. Jet Pad
6. Disaster Simulator
7. Power Gym
8. Service Entrance
9. Dining Hall

To Sam, who has seen every draft, every typo, and every tear throughout this process. I couldn't have done it without you.

And to Erin. Who read every single terrible story it took to get here. I wouldn't have made it this far if I didn't have you, and I'm happy to finally feel like I wrote you a story worth reading.

Book Cover by Mariska Maas.

Map by Loona Ginga.

Interior illustrations by Minikyu.

Second edition 2025.

ISBN: 979-8-9909492-0-1; 979-8-99029492-2-5

WARM BLOODED

BOOK ONE OF THE CARBON CHRONICLES

J GREENE

With Art by Mariska Maas,
Loona Ginga, & Minikyu

For the mental well-being of all readers, please find a list of trigger warnings below. If you wish to avoid any and all potential spoilers, do not read below the break. Please take care of your mental health; for detailed descriptions of trigger warnings you can go to my website, which will also have short summaries of what was important from each scene so you can skip over potentially upsetting moments without missing any critical information.

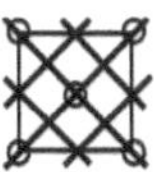

Trigger warnings: child abuse/neglect (mentioned/implied, not on page), comic typical violence, cults/extremist groups, death/death of a parent, discrimination based on appearance/abilities, kidnapping, gore (not described in detail, two instances), gun violence, language, murder, police brutality, terrorism. For more information on trigger warnings and summaries of scenes in which trigger warnings occur, please visit jgreene.ink.

0

Examination

"So, what made you decide to become a hero?"

The clock behind the therapist's head ticked angrily, counting down the long seconds it took him to formulate a response.

"Don't you know that already?" He winced at how rude it sounded. "I mean, the form said your mien was mind-reading, after all."

That earned a slow smile, one that promised she'd been answering the same question all day. It was almost jarring, seeing her without a mask on. Everyone else he'd dealt with had their faces covered, since the whole process had been shrouded in secrecy from the moment his first acceptance letter arrived. Indeed, this whole session— interview?— felt out of place. She— Reader, if the nameplate on her desk was to be believed— was dressed comfortably, in a large cardigan and slacks, round glasses perched on the end of a small nose. With the plush chairs and the tea she'd offered when he'd walked in, it'd felt more like a friendly conversation than a school-mandated psych profile to confirm prospective students weren't harboring any... unsavory secrets.

"It's a common misconception, don't worry." She spoke slowly, like every word was measured. "I can only read the thoughts you're *currently* having. I can't dig around in your mind to find the information we want, whatever the media might like to believe. But more importantly, I want you to tell me what you believe, in the words you want to use, not just the ones floating around in your head."

"Right, sorry." He fought the urge to fidget, the overly stuffed sides of the chair pressing against him in a way that wasn't helping his anxiety at all. His button up and jacket felt tight too, threatening to choke him. "I'm really sorry— what was the question again?"

"You really don't need to apologize. It's understandable that you're anxious." This smile was different from the first, less practiced and more genuine. "What made you decide to become a hero?"

Several different memories immediately crowded his mind, and he did his besttowere to shove them away by focusing on the simple truth.

"I want to help. And I feel like this would be the best way."

"Can you elaborate more on that?" The professional smile was back in place now, and he tried to ignore the way his heart skipped a beat. Had she seen through him already?

"I've done a lot of volunteering since high school, really just went wherever they needed an extra pair of hands." His mouth felt dry and his hands damp, but he pressed his palms together and continued. "I've worked with food pantries and firefighters, homeless shelters and advocacy agencies, but they're all just treating symptoms rather than fighting the problems at the root of it all. Most of the people we helped were mien-users, and usually with miens that were impossible to hide. More often than not they had been *targets* of the very attacks heroes are meant to stop. I might not have the strongest ability out there, but with the proper training, it could be something dependable, if not formidable."

Someday you'll be so strong that no one will be able to hurt you again.

He really hoped that she'd missed that, his left hand curling into a fist. She wasn't looking at him, her head down as she wrote something on the notepad on her lap. Maybe she really hadn't noticed at all.

"You speak of fighting against injustice at its root. Do you not think politics are better suited to that? Heroes come in once a crime has already been committed, not before."

"I think that should change, someday. It already is changing. Heroes shape policy whether they know it or not, because even the most stubborn politician has to bow to public approval."

"That's very true." She spoke slowly, her eyes slightly narrowed. There it was again, that subtle shift in personality. A moment later, gone. "Regardless, it's nice to see that not everyone accepts the world as it is."

It suddenly occurred to him that talking about changing the very profession he was trying to get into might have been a terrible idea.

"Yes," she said with a slow smile, "it was."

Mind reader. Right.

"But I suppose it does bring us to the question of what risks you think you're willing to take for this profession. Heroism is dangerous, almost by definition. And not only for you."

"I'm not worried about the personal risk, and the mandatory anonymity has successfully protected heroes' families so far. I don't see why it'd be any different for me." He forced the faces that swam behind his eyes away. It was fine, the chances that he got in were small, laughably miniscule. He didn't have to think about leaving them behind just yet.

"That anonymity is at a cost, you know." It was so strange, having someone respond to your thoughts.

"Yes." He hesitated for a moment, but this fear was easy

to shove away once he thought about it. They'd be better off without him. Or at least, there'd be fewer *graves* without him. "But for their protection, it's worth it."

"Are you sure you care this strongly about being a hero? Being removed from your family, never hearing your real name again, isn't that almost like dying?"

"I'm not afraid to die."

"You should be." She spoke with such grave sincerity he couldn't help but wonder what she'd seen to make her so sure.

"Like I said, I've done a lot of things in the past three years. Admittedly, only when I had the time, but I spent enough hours working side by side with folks trying to make things better to realize it wasn't *enough*. I know there are people out there who wanted to be a hero from the moment they knew they had a mien, but that's not me. I only ever wanted to make the world a better place, and everything I tried just felt like too little. This gives me a chance to do something, to fix things in a way that affects more than a tiny farming town in Korea that no one has ever heard of." He managed to not say that it could maybe make up for the things he'd done, too. "I know the problems that my community faces are smaller than most. And I know that there are solutions to them. But the world is a worse place than it was ten years ago."

"Things were bad before Satol too." She would know better than he would, since he'd still been a child at the time.

"Absolutely. But never before had everyone been able to point to one incident and say here is the reason that people who are different are dangerous. Here is the reason we can hate them. Shockingly little has been done since then to fix that, and what better way to start than with the people who fight them?" He hadn't meant to get worked up, but his chest was heaving up and down, half out of his seat as he leaned forward. He forced himself to sit back in his chair, not wanting to tower over her. "I know it's such a small chance, but it's one I had to take."

"You keep saying that. Small chance. *Miniscule* chance. You are aware that this is the *final* stage of the application process, yes?" When he didn't respond, she pressed further. "You've made it past the base screening, the four interviews, the physical assessment, the mien assessment, and now all you have left is this little discussion and you're in. I don't understand why you think so little of yourself when fewer than one percent of applicants make it this far."

You're too weak.

Maybe if he didn't respond to the voice, she wouldn't notice it either.

"I... I honestly never expected to make it to the first interview, let alone the physical tests." He folded his hands, pressing the palms together hard. "I don't think I ever dreamed I could make it this far."

"Why is that?" She leaned forward herself now, abandoning all pretenses of only being casually interested. He hadn't failed to notice her eyes drifting to his hands and he resisted the urge to tuck them under his legs.

"It's like I said. I didn't have this dream as a kid, the dream of being a hero. I didn't need to be in the spotlight or be famous. I was happy, with my family, living a simple life. But things... changed. And it's not safe for people like me, people like that kid that was taken. I don't mean to disparage the profession, but it feels increasingly like heroes want to be heroes for the fame and fortune more than they want to help people. If there was a chance that I could make sure at least one hero out there was looking out for the people and not themself, I needed to."

The memory of a hero just like that flitted across his mind, a flash of bright blue in front of a burning sky.

"And yet that doesn't mean I don't feel like somewhat of a

fraud. Like I'm stealing an opportunity from someone who has dreamed about this for years, who really wants to be here, and instead it's just... me."

"But *you* really want to be here." It was a statement, not a question.

"Yes, more than anything." He looked down at his hands again. "But I don't know if I'm the right person. I'll never know."

"Then why are you here?"

"Because if I believe that everyone deserves a chance to go for what they believe in, that applies to me too." He managed to look her in the eye now, at least. "Maybe I'm being selfish being here, sitting in this chair at the end of the road when millions didn't make it this far, but I'm incredibly grateful for this opportunity. If I somehow make it, I *will* work my hardest every single day to prove that I can do this, not only to everyone at the school who gave me the chance at a dream, but also to myself."

The clock chimed quietly behind Reader, and he blinked. He hadn't realized the hour was passing so quickly; it'd really felt like no time at all.

"That means we're done, but fear not, I got what I needed." Her gentle smile was back as she stood and walked him to the door. He really couldn't believe she was a licensed hero since she hardly came up to his bicep. Then again, his head was nearly at the top of the door. "It should only take a few minutes for them to process the paperwork, please take a seat outside and they'll call you shortly."

He could only nod, his tongue not remembering how to form words. He'd been far too casual, hadn't he? He'd forgotten his plan entirely; forgotten to try and present the strong hero image he'd wanted to. His heart sank as he realized this was where the road was going to end. Part of him wanted to fight, to beg for more time to make his case. Because suddenly, with a sharp pain building in his chest, he became aware of just how badly he wanted this.

But the door shut in his face before he could even figure out where to begin pleading. He blinked at it dumbly before moving to sit down, not wanting to make an ass out of himself in front of the other prospective students behind him.

This wait was possibly more painful than the first had been. When he'd arrived early that morning, some childish part of him had clung to the hope that he'd excel at seeming confident and pass with flying colors. To prove that he had a real hero's attitude and wouldn't be daunted by anything they could throw at him. And yet all he'd managed to do was show all the confidence he lacked, so now he was just waiting for the inevitable polite rejection, the tiny sliver of hope shriveling up in his chest.

Knowing he'd failed didn't make the waiting any less agonizing, though.

"Number thirteen?" A gentle voice called from the receptionist's desk, and he stood up woodenly, feeling as if his head was made of cotton. It was convenient they'd given him a slip of paper with his number on it; he'd started the whole process with a number somewhere in the two million range and he wasn't sure he would have remembered the new one otherwise.

"There you are, hard to miss, aren't you?" The receptionist was wearing a surgical mask too, but her eyes were crinkled into half-moons as she smiled up at him, holding out a folder with an E embossed on the cover. "You're all set, have a lovely rest of your day."

He accepted it with a slight bow of the head, deciding to not open it immediately and instead tucking the folder into his bag. They'd already had to deal with enough sobbing people that morning; he refused to add to that tally. But cry he would when he knew he finally had to let go. After all, there was only this one shot.

There wasn't any privacy immediately after exiting the building either. Somehow word had made it to the press that this was the location of the final interviews. They filled the sidewalk and even dared creep into the flower beds that lined the path, faces peeking out from behind snow covered bushes. Flashes left him blinking stars from his eyes and he hugged his bag tightly to his chest, not willing to risk any of them getting their hands on it. His destination was in sight, a car meant to take him to the train station parked just past the curb, and he took a breath before wading into the sea of bodies.

As he towered above the reporters, head and shoulders free of the crowd, they sent their photography drones up in front of his face instead. Robotic voices chirped away with rapid fire questions they must have known he couldn't answer. Hands were waved in front of his face by the more aggressive journalists, and it took the driver of the car to shoo them away before he could safely close the door.

And then he was alone, or as alone as he would be. The train home would be filled with people at this hour, so if he wanted to open it, now was the time. Yet he took the folder out with all the care he might a poisonous snake, resting it on his knees hesitantly like he expected it to turn and bite him. Abruptly, the air in the car felt too stuffy, the mask on his face too scratchy where it pinched on the bridge of his nose. This was too much. Tears were beginning to prick the corner of his eyes and he hadn't even *opened* the damn thing yet.

No, he wouldn't cry. This driver must have been going back and forth to the train station all day carrying crying passengers and he wouldn't add to the poor woman's troubles if he could help it. No, he could do this. He could.

He flipped the folder open.

And stared.

One of the reporters must have stolen the real folder, or

maybe his whole backpack, and substituted it for this fake one. That was the only explanation. In the crowd, though he'd kept it tight to his chest, someone must have gotten it. A light sob startled him, and he realized that despite all his best efforts, tears were running down his face.

"I'll give you some space." The driver moved to close the window between the front and the back of the car. He reached a hand out to do what? Stop her? Apologize? But the black glass thudded into place, leaving his own incredulous eyes staring back at him.

There had to be some kind of mistake, right? This couldn't be real.

Otherwise, how could there be a bright green "ACCEPTED" stamped across the top of his paperwork?

He read it. And reread it. And reread it again. He held the paper up to the car's interior light and squinted, waiting to find a flaw in the watermark pressed into the paper that would indicate it was in fact a forgery, that it wasn't a real, official document. He flipped through the other pages in the folder, but none of them took back that word. None of them began with "we regret to inform you" or "unfortunately" or "sincerest apologies." Instead, there were only congratulations, instructions, and a new name.

1

Arrival

As Kirin strode off the train, he stretched his arms overhead and surreptitiously looked around. The station was empty, save for the people who'd taken the same late night direct as him. There were only a handful of them, all walking swiftly toward the exit, walls lighting up wherever folks passed by. His eyes trailed the final passenger as she passed out of sight, the walls dimming to a peaceful glow where they curved into the distance. When he moved forward even slightly, they brightened again, helpful directions flooding to fill the ceramic white. It was reassuring that they reacted to proximity alone, since it meant anyone tailing him would find it far harder to hide.

There were only two ways into the city, by train and by plane. Plane was far more expensive, since there was no official airport within the island's bounds, but in just a short week, it would be the only route. Though East City had been nearly docked on the shore of Japan during his final interviews— frustratingly close at hand and yet he wasn't allowed to set foot on the man-made ground— now it was testing the very limits to which the shifting train tracks could reach. The electric rails were able to reach hundreds of kilometers off the coast when needed, but now, almost a quarter of the way through the year, the island was about to push beyond the train line, out into the open sea.

But for the next few days at least, the train was still the main way into the city, and the one his instructions had required him to take.

Hello, Hero Trainee.

We congratulate you again on your acceptance to East Technical Institute's Hero Class of 2084. Please make your way to campus no later than one week before the start of term— which shall begin on March 15th— without being followed or intercepted. As secrecy is one of the most important requirements for the program, any student who fails to arrive on campus without being spotted will have their acceptance rescinded and will be escorted from school grounds immediately.

The belongings you sent ahead will either be waiting at your dorm or returned to sender. Students with conditional acceptance must lose (an) additional pursuer(s) to receive their orientation packets. The tickets enclosed in this letter must be used.

Mien regulations are to be followed at all times. No mien usage will be allowed unless students are on school property and/or have a special use license. Any students found to be in violation of local and national mien restrictions will be brought to the proper authorities.

Good luck.

This newest communication from the school had arrived only the day before, but that wasn't unusual. The less time the information was out there, the less likely it was the press would find out. Or so the school claimed.

Trading in the tickets had been a risky play, but seeing the desolate state of the station, he was convinced he'd made the right choice. The tickets *had* been used, albeit to purchase another, but anyone following him now would stand out, since his footsteps echoed alone in the passageway to the street.

When he arrived at the end, he was rewarded by his first real look at East City.

It was best viewed at night, he suspected. In the dark, the whole city turned into a map of neon lines, ads for everything from techware to TV shows beaming down from skyscrapers that looked too fragile to stand. The city seemed awash with glass, reflecting a familiar hero as she flashed across screens in her iconic bright blue.

He jumped as the room started to move, a wall rising up behind him as the floor began to descend from the top of the wall. The train station was at the very edge of the metal behemoth that served as the boundary of the city, keeping even the tallest of waves from reaching the people inside. Fifty meters tall, the wall curved at the top, leaning over the buildings like a closing hand. Yet it was closer to a beating heart, housing most of the critical life-sustaining equipment the city would need: water purifiers, water pumps to keep the plants on the streets alive, the main hydro-electric generators that supported every building on the island. True, there were backup generators farther inland, marked even in the dark by glowing red fences, but it was on the outskirts that the main power was concentrated, for in the center was the reason the island existed at all.

Though it might seem strange, to those who didn't know, that the tech center of the world had a forest at its heart, the trees served a very practical purpose. For nestled in the very middle of the park was East Technical Institute.

It was one thing to see it on a map, but looking over the expanse of the city, so quiet but so *alive*, Kirin felt his heartbeat quicken. Would he make it there without running into anyone? Or would he be sent home without catching a glimpse of the school? He'd be beyond disappointed if it was the latter, since photos were only allowed at the edges of the tech section, and none within the hero. But no, he *would* make it. He'd prepared well enough.

Now that Kirin was halfway down the wall, he could see in more detail. The skyscrapers that had peeked out above the rim of the wall weren't near the edges of the city, the buildings directly below him seeming far more like homes instead of businesses. The windows were all dark, no screens projecting from their sides, and the small gardens and trees that dotted the streets seemed comforting, if one managed to ignore the looming wall just at the end of the road. Power gyms began to stand out to him too, the squat and stout buildings hiding between structures of glass and metal. They looked the same here as they did everywhere else, sturdy things of concrete instead of steel, with ads that promised incredible features within.

When the elevator docked at street level and the windows opened into a door, he almost hesitated to step out. It still felt like a dream, an impossible goal. But he was here.

The lights overhead flashed once, prompting him to move before the elevator headed back up. The neighborhood was quieter down here than he'd expected it to be, but his shoulders moved marginally away from his ears as he heard the quiet hooting of owls and other hints of animals rummaging around in the night. Though East City had been created by human hands rather than the march of time, it was a functioning ecosystem in its own right, with farms scattered across the island to provide both produce and protein should the city ever become disconnected from the outside world.

Hiking his bag more firmly on his back, Kirin set off at a brisk pace.

His plan wasn't complicated at all, with the only real stroke of brilliance being his decision to change the train he arrived on. The subway would require ID to board, the personal vehicles would require digital payment from an account with his name on it; the only safe way to make it to the school without any record of his arrival was to walk.

He wasn't upset about it. Once classes started, he expected he'd be far too busy to go out and see the city, so now he took the chance to experience it. Albeit darkly.

Once he moved out of the shadow of the wall, the paths brightened considerably, closed storefronts still illuminating their windows in the hopes any late night viewers might be enticed to come back in the daytime. Some were still open— mostly late night convenience stores and one or two old-fashioned arcades— but the majority only presented the illusion of a well-populated district, all the inhabitants long fled from the glowing façades. Kirin kept his pace swift as he moved through the shining beacons, feeling all too exposed as the lone person passing through the streets. It was nearly bright as day here, and it made him feel like there were eyes on his back as he headed resolutely toward the center of the city.

It took the better part of an hour to leave the glowing entrance to East City behind, but unfortunately the new section he found himself in was more heavily populated. The buildings around him rose to peer back over the wall, the windows looking like eyes with living shadows for their pupils. Trolleys zoomed past on electric tracks near silently, his only warning to get out of the way was the tell-tale blue glow of the line ahead of the tram. These were working people milling about around him, if their tired eyes were anything to go by, and none spared Kirin a second glance as he cut through. The non-attention almost felt forced, like none of them dared look his way. He kept moving.

Though the majority of the population lived on the outer

edges of the city, there were large, sprawling houses to be found on the island, midway between the park and the outer wall. It glowed here too, but not with bright screens. Instead, it was the dim glow of electric barriers that butted right up against the street, promising anyone who dared trespass on these expensive properties would be met with a swift and painful punishment. While the earlier sections had glowed with reds and blues and whites, the shields all flickered a sickly yellow. The ugly discoloration would be almost invisible during the day, yet in these neighborhoods it was the only source of light in the darkness.

Kirin didn't linger there, either. It took another hour to pass through the homes of the well-to-dos, and he didn't slow once to look around. He wanted to be far away from the wall when morning came, though he knew that he couldn't make it to the school until dawn at the earliest. The park would be closed until the sun was back above the horizon, and he wasn't sure he could convince the officers patrolling within that no, he really *was* a prospective student, or had been, until he'd been caught.

Rather than try his luck in the park, Kirin's feet took him to a squat building that looked identical to the power gyms near the edge of the wall, only twice the size.

Though it wasn't officially confirmed by the city's government, anyone who knew how to read a map— or even *look* at a map— could see that East City was comprised of several concentric circles. The closest to the wall was the cheapest, as the space just inside the barrier felt horribly ominous indeed. It was typically inhabited by the smallest and sleaziest shops the city had to offer, as well as the most affordable houses. Packed apartments started to appear at the edge of this circle, feeding the human needs of the next.

The second circle was filled with smaller companies, or even some larger ones that catered to a poorer clientele. These spaces were seen by nearly everyone who entered the city, and more than one company had recorded a sharp increase in name recognition once they'd gotten real estate on the outskirts of East City.

After them came the "short" circle. It was only called such because there was a conspicuous lack of skyscrapers or packed apartment buildings; only single-family homes or farms filled that ring. Farmers were surprisingly prosperous on the island, likely because those who had taken the chance and moved forty years before had exclusive access to rich patrons, at least for nine months out of the year.

The houses that existed in the third ring were home to the employees of the last ring. The final divider between the city and the park was full of giant techware companies like Futurus or Begin, heroes who had largely retired from government work but still contracted themselves out privately, and— most important to Kirin— cutting edge power gym developers.

Pre-paid card in hand, Kirin's mask hid his smile as the door chimed and let him into the biggest power gym he'd ever seen.

The power gyms were old fashioned in many ways, including their name. *Mien* had been in use Kirin's whole life, the term gaining popularity due to the oft-repeated myth that the powers people were born with somehow reflected their personalities. There was no scientific evidence to support the claim— though that wasn't *really* surprising since nearly every country in the world had unilateral bans on mien research— but the term had stuck.

No matter what they were called, Kirin would love power gyms anyway.

His gym at home had seemed massive and impressive, with a man-made pond in the center and different types of terrain in the quadrants surrounding it. There had been precious few private rooms to rent there, and the main gym was so small it was common for multiple people to team up to work through the larger scenarios together. But this... this was something else entirely.

When Kirin entered, he was surprised to see that the floor was smooth, unbroken concrete for the full length of the ground floor. To the left, elevators waited to bring patrons to level upon level of private rooms, which were all currently glowing green to show they were available for purchase. The ceiling was made of glass and let in the starlight, but none of that was what drew Kirin's eye. No, it was where the floor had ripped itself up and been remade into a forest.

There was someone in there practicing, but he couldn't see much of them at all. They were a blur between trees that sprung into being as they passed through, only to immediately recede into the floor the moment they were gone. No wonder the space wasn't decorated with anything; it *created* what it needed and then reset to let the next customer have the exact conditions they wanted.

Though Kirin's fingers itched to go to the scanner by the door and see what the computer could come up with for him, he forced himself instead to go to the bank of elevators. He rode to the top, picking the farthest room from the entry, as if that made it less visible that the space was occupied when the whole exterior was glowing red. Hopefully, whoever was training in the main hall would be too busy or too tired to notice they were no longer alone.

When he entered the practice room, he was surprised to see that there was a window, and even more surprised that it actually opened. He stuck his head out, as if those extra few centimeters could give him a new perspective on the dark mass of trees just across the street. There was still plenty of time until daylight, giving him just under four hours to figure out how to break into the most secure school in the world.

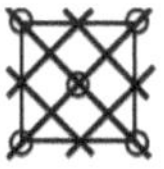

Kirin felt absolutely ridiculous hiding in the woods until someone crashed into him.

His immediate thought was that he'd failed. While he was hoping the school would take the technicality of *using* the tickets as he had, he was less confident that they'd accept that he hadn't been *seen* just *run into*. But that hope was rekindled the moment his assailant sighed.

"Does this mean I don't get in?" As she spoke, she came slightly more into focus, which helped Kirin realize it wasn't just the light filtering through the trees that made her appear fuzzy. That early in the morning he'd thought maybe it was just his eyes being tired, but no, it must have been her mien.

"Not unless I fail too." Kirin debated getting up from the ground, but he'd been sitting so long he felt like he'd fall over if he tried. It didn't matter in the end, as a moment later she was crouched on the ground next to him, regarding him with large, dark eyes. They were the only thing about her that was truly visible, even the black mask over the bottom half of her face somehow looking blurry.

"Great! I take it you have a plan to get inside?" Her eyes became crescents as she beamed under her mask. "I've been circling for at least an hour, and I agree this is best spot for it."

She'd been there an hour, when it wasn't yet six. Kirin's heart soared.

"You swapped your tickets too?"

"Oh, absolutely. I'm pretty stealthy, but if you know what you're looking for I can be easy to spot, even in a crowd." Watching her shake her head was odd, like his brain was stuttering over the image of her. The more he looked, the less he saw, somehow. Her hair had seemed light in color and straight when he'd first seen her, but now, down in the underbrush, it seemed dark and curly. Her skin too seemed darker now, but almost dappled, shifting as she moved. Even her clothes were hard to identify; if he was pressed, he'd say she was wearing casual athletic clothes, like she was simply out for a jog.

He'd perhaps been looking for a moment too long since she raised an eyebrow.

"If you keep staring at me, I'm going to punch you." Her tone was playful, but he didn't think for a moment she wouldn't follow through.

"Sorry it's just—"

"Hard to look at me?" When he winced, she laughed, quietly, yet genuinely. "I know, I know, you wouldn't have said it like that, would have said something like 'it's really not that bad,' or whatever. But that's the easiest way to put it, and it's true, so what do I care?"

"You can't turn it off then?"

"Not even for a second." There was the smallest hint of sadness in her words, and she looked down. Without the steadiness of her gaze, she really seemed to fade into the ground around her. The seconds stretched longer, the wind and the birds the only sounds in between.

"You really think they'll accept it?" Her eyes reappeared as she looked back up, head tilted to the side in confusion. "Swapping in our train tickets, I mean."

"It's a *bit* late to be worrying about that." There was humor in her voice as she nodded towards the wall. "Instead, we should be worrying about how to get around *that*."

It was a shame that he'd been attempting to come up with a plan for the last thirty minutes with absolutely no luck. The metal was solid and unbroken, too thick to smash through, too thick to melt. Or ten years ago Kirin would have said it was too solid to melt. Now, he wasn't sure if anything was.

"You don't happen to have a map, do you?" She held up her school-issued phone, shaking him out of bad memories. "I took the battery out of my phone when I got the letter, didn't want them tracking me."

Kirin rummaged through his bag a moment before he found the paper map he'd printed before he left home. He hadn't gone so far as to remove the battery entirely, though his cell phone had been firmly turned off before he'd boarded his train, the map printed so it could stay off until he arrived.

"Ha!" The woman's exclamation was loud enough that it displaced a bird sitting directly above their heads and they both flinched. "Sorry. I just realized why the letter was worded the way it was. It said school *property*, not just on campus."

She held out the map for him to see and pointed at a thin line that was nearly invisible within the shaded trees.

"The school owns the area of the park immediately around it. Miens are fair game within a dozen meters every way." She stood up, eyes narrowing as she looked at the wall. She crept a few steps farther forward, Kirin hurriedly closing his backpack as he tried to follow her quietly, feeling rather bullish with the amount of noise he made. "How thick do you think that wall is?"

There was an odd undercurrent to her voice that he couldn't identify.

"A meter, supposedly. Maybe thicker."

"Hm."

"If we head back toward the main entrance that way—" Kirin pointed in the direction the woman had been headed before she tripped over him— "there's a service entrance door. It's currently guarded by two people, but even if we get them to move, the whole wall is shielded. It's the only way *through* the wall I've found, not that it's highly promising. I was considering climbing a tree and just trying to jump over."

"All the trees are cut back from the wall a good couple meters; you think you can make that jump without getting a running start?" She tapped her fingers along her chin. "No, the door's the best option by far. And only two guards you say?"

"Yeah. I'd guess they're students since they don't seem much older than we are. And because one of them was juggling knives made of ice when I passed by."

"Hm." She turned to him and smiled, her face coming into focus for just a minute to show the way her eyes crinkled around the edges. "Good thing there are two of us, then, isn't it?"

As Kirin stumbled over another root, he was forced to acknowl-edge that running through a dense forest was a stupid idea.

It had been a simple plan, just the way he liked it. The woman would make enough noise to get the attention of one of the guards and pull them away, and once they were out of sight entirely, Kirin would do the same for the other. Once they felt like their respective guards were sufficiently far away, they'd double back and go through the door. *How* they'd get through the door was still unclear to Kirin, but his new companion seemed assured she'd be able to get it open. And Kirin didn't have any better ideas, so he'd agreed. Anything was better than the utter boredom of sitting in the woods and staring at a wall.

Now, bolting back towards the door, he was forced to con-sider that sometimes simple and idiotic were synonyms for a reason.

Firstly, he didn't know why he hadn't bothered to consider that his guard would be *fast*. The goal had been to stealthily and steadily lead them away, to save energy for the final sprint backwards, but the man who was following him was quick. Kirin's only saving grace was that the man had no idea where to look, really, and was sweeping in wide arcs while Kirin stumbled his way out of their path. He'd only just managed to creep away from his pursuer and realized how much distance he had to cover, which made him abandon all pretenses of stealth and run flat out. If he tumbled and twisted his ankle, well, that would just be deserved.

Secondly, he'd trusted a complete stranger. A complete stranger who— for all he knew— was already a student at East Tech and messing with him. Even if she wasn't, how monumentally stupid to trust some random person with his entire future. His own failure to come up with a plan was an indictment, not a reason to accept help. Well, that wasn't entirely true. He *had* thought of a plan, since the shield wasn't a problem, but the entire solution was simply punching the door until it crumpled, and while he'd never been to college before, he suspected property damage wasn't a great way to start the year.

His musings were interrupted by his sudden arrival back at the service entrance.

It'd taken the better part of ten minutes to shake his guard, but he'd made it back in under one. The other guard had failed to re-appear which meant the woman had upheld at least part of her end of the bargain, though the door in front of him remained stubbornly closed.

He took a deep breath, feeling the cloth of his mask pull tightly against his cheeks. Up close, the door didn't look all too sturdy, but the yellow sheen over the top promised that getting to the door would hurt. For most people. But his stores weren't where he wanted them to be, and if it took more than a few hits to deal with the door, would he have enough left to pass through the shield fully? *Would* the school be mad about him ripping a hole in their wall, or would just failing be worse? If he couldn't do this, he'd have to go back home, and he didn't think he could face his mother knowing—

The door swung open in the middle of his spiraling. There she was, her strange out-of-focus appearance feeling out of place in the morning sunshine.

"Shit, I forgot about this." Her eyebrows drew together in concern. "Maybe we could—"

A shout from somewhere on her side of the wall drew her attention, her head snapping to the side. It was the only opening he needed, and he let his mien wash over him, hurriedly stepping through the doorway too. His mask suffered from it, sliced along the sides, but he was already pulling out another when she turned back around.

"How did you—" She stopped herself and shook her head. "Right. Not allowed to say."

"Will you *shut* that door?" A man was running toward them, waving frantically. "Very good, you made it in, but now *close* it so other people can use it."

Kirin stepped around the (much) shorter woman and shut the door, bowing his head slightly in an apology.

"See? First it was just you, now him." The man sighed and pinched his nose, aging in front of their very eyes. Gray appeared in his short brown hair and bags under his eyes as he muttered something that did not sound happy under his breath. When he finally removed his hand, he didn't seem annoyed any longer, just tired. "Alright, now that I can stop that, let's get both of you to check-in."

With considerably less energy than he'd just used to yell at them, the man turned and slouched away.

Kirin and the woman looked at each other before she had the good sense to hurry after him, having to jog slightly to keep up. She wasn't just short by Kirin's standards, he realized, as it took him two whole steps to catch up with their guide. She was just... small.

When the man didn't offer any conversation, Kirin took the opportunity to look around campus for the very first time.

They were in the hero section, as far as he could tell, since the dorms were off in the distance to the left, behind a secondary shield. Past that slice of the campus would be the tech section, the only area where photos were allowed at all. No one had ever managed to leak images of the hero side, or even draw a map of it, though it looked almost... ordinary.

The buildings weren't covered in screens or tech, favoring ceramic panels on all the smaller halls, almost looking like seashells someone had dropped in the grass. A large gym sat directly across from them, with enough glass to make up for the lack elsewhere, but Kirin's attention was mostly caught by the giant, concrete block that took up the entirety of the back half of campus. It *had* to be the school's famous Disaster Simulator, which was a power gym the size of several city blocks. There was also an ordinary power gym— he could see it peeking above what he assumed were the lecture halls— but it looked tiny in comparison.

It was strange how a campus built all at once could feel so haphazard, with meandering paths between randomly placed buildings. The common areas were heavily planted with flowers and bushes and trees, providing relief from the now fully risen sun. As they walked, he thought he spotted picnic tables nestled in shaded coves, which felt somewhat antithetical for such a tech heavy school.

In addition to the smaller footpaths, there were two main thoroughfares here, with evergreen trees planted on either side of the wide walkways. One headed towards the regular gym, parallel to the path they were on, and the other, perpendicular to it, to the monolithic structure at the back.

"Thank you, by the way." The woman stuck a hand toward him at an awkward angle, since she was standing on his right. "I didn't want to introduce myself in case everything went horribly wrong, but I'm Ness. Couldn't have made it without you!"

"Kirin." Something about the name seemed vaguely familiar, but he couldn't quite place it.

"Nice to meet you." She shook his hand enthusiastically. "Think we're the first ones here?"

"Close." Though he showed absolutely no signs of interest, the man leading them was clearly listening in. "One beat you here. Arrived middle of the night."

"That was allowed?"

"He used the tickets. Didn't use his mien till he arrived on school property. Didn't get caught. Those were the only rules." They'd arrived at the gym rather abruptly, and the man only faced them when he pulled open the door. "If you followed those, you're in."

The gym was rather disappointing. It was, simply put, a gym. The door had opened onto a basketball court, with a few rows of bleachers lining the edges. East Tech's colors of gold and blue were striped around the walls, and windows looked down into the space from the upper floors of the exercise rooms. In other words, it could have been any gym, from any number of colleges across the world. The only thing out of place was a woman sitting at a table a few paces inside the door and looking rather bored.

Surprisingly, Kirin recognized her.

"I've got two for you, Pressure."

"And so quickly!" She practically leapt to her feet, nearly knocking the table over in the process. A quiet *"tch"* sound came from the bleachers, and Kirin looked over to see that there was in fact someone sitting there. He was quickly distracted again by Pressure, who was flipping through the folders on the table.

"Can I go now?" The man that walked in with them looked even more tired than he had before, like merely being in the presence of such energy was exhausting.

"Really Shifty? You don't want to meet my new students?"

"That's not my name." With that Shifty— or apparently *not* Shifty— left.

"Sorry if this is rude, but aren't you the therapist from the psych evaluations?" Ness was both blunter and braver than Kirin was. It was true though; she *was* the same woman from then, albeit in athletic wear instead of professional. The brown hair was the same, even still pulled back, with the familiar discerning brown eyes and slightly amused set to her lips. The glasses were gone, admittedly, but there was no mistaking her.

"Yes and no." Pressure handed each of them a folder with the logo of East Tech on the front. "I *was* the person you spoke with, that's true, but that's because I like to get a feel for potential students before Reader gives their official report. They're the real therapist— and the dean of the school I might add— but they watch from a distance so I can ask the questions I want to, with a little guidance to get the answers the school needs."

"How far can their mien work from, then?" Kirin hadn't meant to speak out loud, but sometimes his thoughts forgot they were supposed to stay inside his head.

Happily, Pressure didn't seem bothered.

"I think you know I can't *really* answer that, but you'll find that it's both more and less than you think." She winked as she shooed them away. "Now go read through all that, and I'll have Shifty come back and walk you to the dorms once a few more of you arrive."

The dismissal happened so quickly that it took Kirin's brain several seconds to catch up and get him moving. He hurriedly inclined his head before following Ness, who was headed for the bleachers.

"She's... different than the first time." Ness said once they'd taken a few steps.

Kirin offered a noncommittal grunt in response, too busy flipping through the papers they'd been given. He was so focused he almost entirely missed the person who'd come down from the bleachers to block his path.

"Change your fucking hair." The man who stood in front of Kirin had his eyes narrowed and arms crossed, looking absolutely *pissed* about something. The scowl on his face and his relatively impressive height probably would have made him intimidating to most, but he was still only at Kirin's shoulder. However, Kirin was much more focused on the fact that the man seemed to be wearing a necklace made of actual *fire.*

"Sorry?" Kirin finally registered that the man had said something to him.

"Your hair. Dye it a different color." It was said with utter authority, his chin raised slightly as if to *dare* Kirin to say anything.

"Are you with the school?" Even as he said it, Kirin knew that this was just another student, since they looked about the same age and from the folder half hidden by his tightly crossed arms.

"Black is my color." He ignored the question.

"But... your eyes are red?"

"My hair, dumbass." It was such a deep black too, like ink, shaved down the sides but long enough that curls formed on the top. His skin wasn't light, a warm brown, but it looked almost pale in comparison. It probably should have drawn Kirin's attention more, but he was distracted by the startling crimson of the man's eyes, made even more brilliant by the fire reflected in them.

"Oh, right, it's almost the same shade as *my* eyes!" Kirin scrambled for something to diffuse the situation.

"Wear fucking contacts too." And with that he stalked off, done with the conversation. He didn't go very far, just back to the bleachers, though he did pointedly look at Kirin while he turned off his hearing aids. It seemed that in his mind the conversation was over, and he wanted to make sure Kirin didn't try again.

However, there was nothing else *to* do for the moment. Ness hadn't bothered to intervene with their argument— was it an argument when it was so one-sided?— since she had her head buried in the papers from her folder. Kirin had followed her and sat down, trying to do the same, yet his head didn't want to process the words. Besides, it was little more than a dorm assignment and a detailed map of campus, the first he'd seen that had anything shown inside the wall. He gave up trying to read the denser papers after a few minutes, instead his eyes roaming to the angry man. He was similarly just sitting there, though his gaze was firmly fixed on the ceiling, ignoring everyone else. After a few more minutes of sitting in boredom, Kirin stood up and walked the few rows over to where the other man sat.

We seem to have gotten off on the wrong foot. Kirin signed. *I don't have any plans on changing my hair color, but we could maybe work something out?*

The man's eyes widened fractionally before snapping back to their angry squint.

Fuck off. At least he responded. And what luck, he knew international sign too. Sure, they all *spoke* the same language, since it was an admissions requirement, but sign wasn't, and the man could've known any of the hundreds of variants throughout the world. Surely, he hadn't been forced to teach himself through online videos like Kirin had, though.

I'm Kirin. Kirin had hardly finished spelling it out when he was greeted with a loud "*tch.*" Undeterred, he kept at it. *And you are?*

You'll find out soon enough. Kirin could've been mistaken but it seemed like the man had tensed up slightly. It was impressive that he could seem *angrier*, but he managed. Deciding that line of conversation was fruitless, he tried a different approach.

Must have taken a lot of gym time to be able to control your mien so minutely. The fire necklace— choker? It almost looked spiked from the way fire skittered out from his throat in places— didn't appear to be coming from any bit of technology that Kirin could see, so it had to be the man's ability.

I have a fucking license for it. Didn't need to go to a fucking gym. Again, somehow, Kirin had picked a bad topic.

Special licenses for personal use are really rare, aren't they? It's pretty impressive to get one.

Don't need to be impressive. Just need to have fucking money. Kirin's practice speaking to people in sign was limited, but the way this man could imbue contempt into the signs was impressive indeed. It was like he threw his words like weapons, intending them to keep everyone else at bay.

I'm sure that's not true. There're a lot of people with a lot of money who're arguing for the legalization of mien use for everyone, and I don't believe they're doing it out of the goodness of their hearts. Seems more likely they just couldn't get a special use license on their own.

No shit. With that, his very eloquent conversation partner decided to look in an entirely different direction, and Kirin finally gave up. He made his way back to Ness, who'd put away her paperwork in favor of staring fixedly at the doors.

"It's been thirty minutes since we arrived and still no one else has." She didn't look at Kirin as she spoke, but her words were too loud to just be to herself. "I suppose we were quite fast."

"I think entirely avoiding the people who were supposed to be tailing us helped." Kirin shrugged. "We still weren't the first though."

"What train did you come in on?" Ness suddenly turned to him, her face pensive.

"I got in around midnight." Kirin said carefully, remembering that several other trains had arrived around that time. She couldn't figure out where he came from if he only told her that. They weren't supposed to say anything about their past lives, not where they were from, not how many siblings they might have had, not what their parents did for work, nothing.

"I bet we all did." She nodded, not caring that he'd mildly side-stepped the question. "If I had to guess, we all traded in our old tickets for new ones on the express. All the express trains arrive at midnight, then eight, and then four."

"It's just about six thirty now." Kirin went to check his watch, only to realize the band must have snapped when he used his mien, since it wasn't there anymore. He settled for squinting at the wall clock across the room. "The original trains should've arrived at just after six."

"I guess it did take me a while to make it here." Ness chewed on her lip. Kirin hadn't even noticed she'd taken her mask off until then.

"It'd certainly be a bit awkward if it was just the three of us in class." Kirin took a guess as to what she was thinking, and even if he hadn't gotten it right, it still got her to smile. In the brighter light of the gym, he could see that the shifting quality of her face hadn't gone away, but it was less prominent. If he had to describe it, the best way would be that the edges of everything fuzzed out, like his eyes were trying to focus on something that wasn't there. Her appearance had changed slightly again, her hair, cut just above the shoulder, was now closer to the color of the wood bleachers, her skin darkened slightly to match the floor. Her facial features were harder to pinpoint, but her eyes still appeared large and dark.

He realized he was staring again and looked away. Luckily,

she'd resumed her own vigil watching the door and didn't notice a thing.

"If you three want to head out to the dorms to unpack, feel free." Pressure's voice carried over to them. "Reader just patched through, you've all passed. You can find the access code to the shield and your IDs in your folders. The IDs will get you into the dorms, just make sure to close the door behind you so no one else follows you in."

There was a pointed edge to her voice, though Kirin wasn't sure why. The black-haired man was already on his feet, eager to move. Kirin went to follow him when he noticed Ness hadn't stood up.

"You going to wait here?" He was weighing whether he should stay with her or not when she stood up, shaking her head.

"I'll see everyone once they get here." The sentence felt like it wasn't meant for him, this time. She shook her head again and suddenly her smile was back, bright as ever. "Might as well see where we'll be living."

2

Introduction

Kirin had little frame of reference for what a typical college dorm might look like, since he'd never been in one before. Even so, he was fairly sure they weren't usually like *this.*

The building was organized in two, with a larger first floor than the ones above. The left half was the same as the upper floors, Kirin assumed, with four dorm rooms lining the back of the wall, and a common kitchen and bathroom. There was a living room, though this one certainly was bigger than those on the higher stories, as it bled into the longer one-story section to the right. All that seemed relatively standard— if not much nicer quality— but the one-story section, the same width and length as the apartment block, was filled with a training room.

It was fronted with glass, so that those in the common area could see inside. The glass was thick, likely because the back wall was lined with weaponry, from relatively medieval looking swords to modern laser guns. These were locked in place with a keypad on the far wall, though there was a second panel close to the door that promised the innocuous concrete floor was just as programmable as the power gym he'd seen, if not more.

"You. In." Kirin turned to find the angry man from earlier pointing at him.

"Sorry?"

"We're sparring. I win, you dye your hair a different fucking color." Without waiting for a response, he headed straight to the door, pulling it open. Kirin stared after him open-mouthed, glancing at Ness for help. She didn't offer any, instead curling up in a chair with a perfect view. After a moment, Kirin dropped his bag and went in after him, intrigued.

"What do I get if I win?" The man's head snapped back around at the words, as if he hadn't really expected Kirin to follow.

"You're not going to." He was already punching something into the computer's system, too quickly for Kirin to follow.

"If there's nothing in it for me, why would I bother?" Kirin moved back to the door, feigning disinterest, but he was curious how it would go now. Surely someone this abrasive must have an immense amount of power for his personality to be overlooked during admissions.

"My name."

"Hm?" Kirin genuinely wasn't sure he'd heard correctly, since the man had mumbled.

"If you win, I'll tell you my name." The black-haired man moved into a half crouch, computer beeping as a timer appeared, counting down from ten. "You in or out?"

Kirin rolled his shoulders, moving back toward the center of the room, settling into his own stance instead of responding. His eyes weren't fixed on the timer, instead focused on his opponent, whose ring of fire betrayed his excitement by growing brighter and brighter until the clock hit zero.

He didn't see the other man move, but heard the sound, magnified in such a small space, and threw himself to the left just in time. He'd thought he'd had nothing left, but the sudden shocking attack forced his body to move and the skin on his right arm crackled, freezing in place to block the heel of the other man's shoe as it came down hard on his forearm. Extra carbon came from somewhere and he ripped through his shoe as the skin densified and hardened into pure diamond. The force embedded his foot into the floor, stopping him from getting pushed back any farther.

The man used Kirin's arm as a springboard, flipping backward and landing in a crouch, half hidden in the smoke. Kirin hesitantly glanced at his arm and nearly sagged in relief; even in his panic he'd managed to keep the top layer of skin the normal color, though it had scraped off slightly in spots, revealing the glittering below. He released his breath into the air, the visible shine dulling to his usual tan.

Despite using his mien without any chance to recharge his store of carbon dioxide, Kirin found that when the next attack came at his knee, he was able to crystallize again, easily, and though his leg was frozen in place, he nearly managed to grab the back of the man's neck, only to be blasted with heat as the ring of fire expanded to cover it. With his seemingly inexhaustible— for the moment— reserve, he grabbed on anyway, his fingers turning to diamond not even a second after he made contact. There was no fear of anyone seeing anything with the smoke filling the room, after all, and diamond couldn't be hurt by fire.

Before he was able to throw his opponent to the ground, two hands grabbed his right arm; he could only see metal rings clash together before another explosion rent the air and he was thrown back, though his stiffened hand meant he brought the man with him. They crashed down together, Kirin belatedly turning his hand back before the flesh underneath could start to blister. Diamond was immune to fire, but it *was* an excellent conductor of heat, and his skin and muscle underneath were vulnerable.

His opponent made a sound halfway between displeasure and approval and rolled backward, away from Kirin, now very much on guard. The room was almost entirely filled with smoke, and Kirin breathed in, finding his carbon reserves filling rapidly. Maybe that was it, then, the smoke being richer in carbon than the air. He found himself smiling. He could do this all day.

The feeling seemed to be mutual as another blast alerted him to his opponent's movements, seconds before he felt hands grab at his face, the man having gone *over* his head, trying to throw him off balance and knock him to the ground. Kirin hardened his feet again, his head pulled back, but he remained standing. He swung blindly behind himself, managing to land a blow on the other man's ribcage before he was met with an explosion of heat and the contact vanished again.

They circled each other, and Kirin found his wild grin mirrored by his rival. The power gyms could simulate combat quite well, but he'd never actually been allowed to fight another person using his mien. And, as it turned out, there was a world of difference between the two.

Another wave of flames came, but no blows, the smoke now making it almost impossible to see the other man, his black clothes melding into the darkness. Kirin's ears felt clogged with the sudden silence, the hairs on the back of his neck standing up, waiting to see where the next attack would come from. He kept his body low and his hands in front of him, hardly breathing to not disturb the smoke.

He felt the barest whisper of movement from behind and turned as quickly as he could, only to be met with a punch to the face. He hadn't had time to harden so the hit was good, though he managed to stiffen his neck, so his head didn't even turn.

"Is that all you've got?" The man hadn't moved his fist, so the corner of Kirin's lips brushed the knuckles as he spoke, unable to keep himself from smiling.

Rather than being discouraged, this seemed to give his challenger more determination, and the rings clicked together again behind his elbow, creating another blast that forced the man's arm forward, causing Kirin to stumble back a step.

It was at precisely that moment when the computer projected a large red X between the two of them.

"Conditions for forcible end of combat reached. Please vacate the room and allow cleaning procedures to commence." The robotic voice was oddly cheery. Kirin blinked and looked over at the black-haired man, who had fallen to the ground from the force of his own swing.

"Call it a draw?" Kirin offered his hand to help him up, but the man swatted it away and got to his feet on his own.

"Anything less than an all-out victory is a defeat." Kirin could've sworn, however, that the crease between the man's eyes had lessened slightly. However, it was back in full force once he looked through the window to the common room.

"Ah." Kirin looked over to see several new faces staring at them in interest, and he waved awkwardly back at them. This wasn't exactly how he'd wanted to meet his new classmates, but at least Ness looked amused.

"Bastard." It was said less like an insult and more a way to draw his attention to the other occupant in the room, who was now by the door. The smoke had cleared largely, especially with the door open and the fans going, but it was still hard to see what he was finger spelling. *I-f-r-i-t*.

And just like that he was gone.

Ifrit, huh. Kirin smiled to himself. Named after a fiery demon. A good fit.

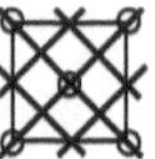

A loud knock on the door woke Kirin. He hadn't realized he'd even fallen asleep, but after the stress of getting to campus, sparring with Ifrit, and the lack of sleep from the night before, he'd just touched the mattress and passed out. His room was partially unpacked around him, the only thing that still needed doing was putting the sheets on the bed, which he'd foolishly decided to do after taking a short break.

Judging by the position of the sun in the sky, it'd been several hours, too. He sighed and scrubbed at his face tiredly. It still hadn't been enough. He really should've forced himself to sleep at the gym instead of thinking just meditating would be fine. If he'd had to go straight into classes, he surely would've fallen asleep at his desk, and that was not the first impression he wanted to make. He'd already been slightly rude to his class-mates when they'd tried to talk to him after sparring, too busy trying to go after Ifrit, to find out how *exactly* the man had managed to control his body when moving at explosive speeds, and where he'd learned such good form while fighting, and when they could spar again.

Another knock came and his eyes shot open, remembering why he'd been awoken in the first place. Quickly, worried that it was important, he walked over to the door, patting at his head absently to put away any stray hairs.

It was not important.

"Oh, tall *and* handsome this one. Write down 'potentially charming enough to kill.'" A flame-haired person stood just outside the door, with Ness and someone else close behind. The person who spoke had clearly been the one to knock, since she was closest, but the others crowded in too, peering unabashedly into his room.

"I'm going to guess something strength-based, if the muscle is anything to go by. Is that going to be your actual guess Phoenix?" A tall woman with dark hair and ochre skin was taking notes on a pad, flashing Kirin a smile as she finished writing. When she moved, he caught a glimpse of gold on her ears, which matched the bars in her eyebrows.

"I got to see him fight earlier, so Yantra could be right. If not strength, he's definitely sturdy." Ness didn't seem ashamed of trying to sneak a glimpse of his room. She was squatting, trying to look around him, and Kirin noticed that when she moved, she was notably easier to see.

The woman noted down what Ness had said.

"Phoenix, any *real* guesses?"

The person in the front— Phoenix, apparently— stood on tiptoes to get as close to his face as possible. She was still a good bit away, but the intensity of her gray-eyed gaze was such that he felt distinctly uncomfortable.

"Uh, can I ask what this is about?" He leaned away as best he could, looking to Ness for help for the second time that day.

"Ugh, I think you're right Yantra, probably something strength-based." Phoenix sighed and dramatically leaned against the doorway, looking defeated.

"There're quite a few people here now, and we figured we'd all have to say hi sooner or later, so we're starting from the top and working our way down." Ness explained.

"But introductions get boring fast, so we're also trying to guess what everyone's miens could be." The woman with the notebook— Yantra— closed it and smiled at Kirin again. She seemed nice, at least. But—

"Aren't we not supposed to talk about our miens? I thought there was a pretty clear note about that in the acceptance packet." Kirin frowned.

"That's true!" Phoenix spoke up, past disappointment forgotten in an instant. "But we're not going to ask you to confirm or deny anything. Simply taking a wild stab in the dark, completely baseless guess on what everyone can do based on first impressions."

"If it's based on first impressions, it's not baseless, firstly, and secondly, I did have some information so mine wasn't baseless *anyways*." Ness corrected. From the time of day, they could only have met a few hours before at the earliest, but Ness already sounded world-weary as she corrected Phoenix.

"Semantics aside, your name is on the door, but we won't be getting to mine for a while, so I'm Yantra. Officially Bhuta Vahana Yantra, but that's a bit long to say all the time, so just Yantra's fine." The dark-haired woman waved, pen still in hand.

"Ah, nice to meet you." Something about the name seemed familiar, though he wasn't sure why.

"So, you joining us?" Phoenix was suddenly all business, the change in her personality almost startling.

"Um, sure?" Kirin looked back at his unmade bed but decided that would be a problem for later. He did want to meet his classmates. After all, he couldn't have any friends outside of school anymore.

Not that he'd really had friends before.

"Let's go then! To the fourth floor!" Phoenix dramatically pointed at the elevator and started to march off.

"Wait, shouldn't we ask him if he wants to come?" Kirin pointed at Ifrit's door, which was just one down from his own. The only other named room on their floor belonged to Phoenix, he suddenly remembered.

"Ah, our very angry floor-mate." Phoenix didn't sound particularly annoyed, instead almost fondly reminiscing. "We stopped by his room first. I've never heard someone curse that many times in one sentence. I need to get a counter to see what the ratio between curse words and non-curse words is when he speaks."

"You'd need two counters." Yantra pointed out.

"Tragic, I know." Phoenix called the elevator, putting a hand to her head and swooning against the wall. "Alas, the pains I go to for true scientific methodology."

"I'm beginning to think your mien has something to do with being overdramatic." Yantra chuckled, twirling her pen between her fingers.

"I cannot confirm nor deny."

The elevator dinged and they piled in, fitting easily. The elevator was wide enough that Kirin could stretch out both arms and not touch either wall, and just as deep. If his math was right, there could be up to nineteen students in their class, considering the empty room on the fifth floor, and certainly even a full house of twenty would have fit easily into the compartment.

"Fourth floor." Phoenix called out as the elevator doors shut and they began to move, Kirin leaning against the back wall as they went down. Ness and Yantra were chatting as Phoenix hummed off-key, all three seeming entirely relaxed and friendly with each other. Kirin wished he felt the same, but the feeling of discomfort was already creeping up the back of his neck and he'd only been introduced to *two* new people. He had just enough time to consider that he probably should have said no before the elevator opened onto the floor below.

"Has everyone made it up yet?" Kirin asked as they walked out. "I saw some people earlier, but I've just been holed up in my room."

"I would say there's probably... ten people so far? Not entirely sure, which is part of the reason we're doing this." Phoenix walked backwards as she talked to him, heading for the door farthest from the elevator. There was a stairwell this end of the hall, and a door that said "Wyrm." "That's a very unfortunate name."

She knocked anyway, Kirin feeling awkward as they all stood in silence.

"Must not be here yet." Yantra commented, making a note on her pad. "Or was spotted."

"Probably has some kind of lizard or dragon-like mien, though." Kirin said absently, thinking of how Ifrit's power was quite similar to what he'd expect from the legendary demon. It apparently wasn't an obvious thought, however, as the other three were looking at him like he'd said something odd. "What?"

"It's a myth!" Yantra suddenly snapped her fingers. "Kirin, you just might be onto something."

"Still lost here." Phoenix said. Ness nodded in agreement though her eyes were squinted in concentration as she thought it over.

"Usually the names are pretty self-explanatory, yeah?" Yantra was already pulling out her phone. "But this year they're not just words that vaguely describe what the hero's mien does. Instead, I think they're matching us to folklore."

"I did think that spelling of worm was weird."

"It's Norse, apparently." Yantra informed the group. "A name for dragons, usually ones that are venomous and have no legs."

"We'll have to be on the lookout for a classmate who's trying to bite people, then." Phoenix said dryly. Though admittedly, Kirin thought, that wouldn't be the *strangest* mien he'd ever heard of.

"It might not be so cut and dry as that. After all, there are several different associations with different animals, yeah? Like a phoenix, right? It's most closely related with rebirth, but also fire and the sun." Yantra gestured at Phoenix. "If we're guessing for you, it could be something to do with controlling fire, or creating fire, or creating sunlight, or healing yourself when injured, etc. It gives us a general theme to work off of, but not a clear picture."

"I'm still confused why they want our names to indicate anything about our abilities when it might be safer to just let us pick regular names." Kirin sighed. "I mean, we're not even supposed to talk to *each other* about our miens, all so fewer people know how they work."

"I don't think anything about what we're going to be doing is safe, bud." Phoenix patted his shoulder and started heading to the next door, knocking on it before the rest followed.

"It could also be slightly misleading strategy, yeah? Like I said, there are a lot of associations with some of these, so depending on how the mien presents, it could be fairly easy to misdirect people into believing it works one way instead of another." Yantra tapped her pencil against her chin.

"And for some of us, it's already obvious as is." Ness walked past the door that Phoenix was waiting at, since it had her own name on it. Seeing the name spelled out though, did make something click for Kirin.

"Ness... like the Loch Ness monster?"

"Oh!" Phoenix tapped her nose and pointed at Kirin and then at Ness. "You're right!"

"I was really hoping no one was going to make that connection, but my luck never was that good." Ness sighed as she knocked on the only other labelled door on the floor. "I don't have much hope that this Naddāha's here yet, or at least they weren't right before we started."

"Damn, I thought there were more people here than this." Yantra frowned. "Should we wait a bit and then go around?"

"I think there are a few folks below us, or at least I heard some sort of commotion a bit ago. But I'm still unpacking, so either way works for me." There was something odd about Ness's expression as she spoke, but it very well might have just been that Kirin couldn't see her face fully. Especially since it had gone slightly more transparent as she spoke.

"Nonsense, we're already through a few! Yantra, look up that last name and we'll see if we can't guess something while we head down." Phoenix encouraged them, punching her fist in the sky and shooing them all into the elevator.

"Naddāha, huh." Yantra said the name aloud as she pulled up the holo screen from her phone. "Ah, I assume it's En-Nad-dāha... oh that could be fun."

"What's the story?" Ness leaned around Yantra, peering at the screen. A wry smile slowly spread across her face.

"Best known for luring men to their deaths in the Nile, apparently."

"That seems a little too specific to be their mien." Kirin thought about it for a moment. "That would be interesting though."

"Have you no manly pride?" Phoenix raised a hand to her head again, feigning outrage.

"I'm just saying! Being able to draw people to you. Perhaps not the death part, but it would make it far easier to get into close combat fighting, particularly when you have enemies that are long-ranged or winged..."

Kirin looked up to see Ness making a face that clearly showed she was trying not to make fun of him.

"What?"

"You're totally a fan boy, aren't you?"

"...no?"

"Oh, he is!" Phoenix had joined in. "You aren't in one of those mien appreciation groups, are you?"

"No! I just... I was a mythology kid, you know? There are so many stories out there, right, about people or gods or spirits, and I don't know… I just thought maybe they weren't all super-natural, maybe they were just like me." Kirin could feel the tips of his ears burning.

"Oh!" Yantra perked up. "Oh, me too! I especially had a whole drawn up thing on Amba and how they could have been the same person in the same lifetime as Shikhandi and their mien just needed fire to active. We'll have to compare notes some-time, I *love* to hear other people's theories."

The elevator opened just as Ness and Phoenix managed to synchronize eye rolls.

They did find the source of the noise rather quickly.

The scene on the third floor was… entertaining, in Phoenix's words. There were three people in the room: one was blind-folded, with a guide cane next to her, hands up placatingly, one lying on the floor entirely unmoving, and the third was walking straight forward angrily, as the floor seemed to *move* underneath him, keeping him in one spot.

"I told you it was an accident!" The blind-folded woman was protesting. "I'd talked with Kapre and they said they were going to their room so I wanted to get a look around at where all the furniture was but you walked in right as I took it off!"

"You used your mien on me! Only fair that I get to use mine!" The man was dressed in all black, but blinding light was emanating from his palms, so hot that the air above them shimmered.

"I guess we have at least one of them figured out." Phoenix muttered out of the corner of her mouth.

"Should we be concerned about the body on the floor?" Kirin asked, nearly at the same time.

It was at that moment the body in question jumped up, the floor stopped moving underneath the black-clothed man and he lurched forward, and the blind-folded woman smacked him in the head with her cane.

"A thousand apologies, this wasn't how I wanted this to go." The blind-folded woman offered their group a shy smile, ignoring the man now rolling on the floor holding his head. They made an interesting pair, her all pale and light, him dark from his hair to his clothes. "I assume you were coming to say hello?"

Kirin fumbled for words, while the rest of his group still gawked openly, except for Phoenix, who appeared to be trying very hard not to laugh.

"Ah, yes! We're just seeing who's around." Ness managed to find her words before he did, giving an award winning attempt at a smile, which only seemed the slightest bit forced.

"And trying to guess everyone's abilities!" Phoenix chimed in.

"Well, I suppose I'm incredibly easy to guess, what with the blindfold and the name." The woman waved at her face.

"I take it you're Medusa?" Ness asked.

"That's me!"

Kirin was momentarily distracted by the man getting to his feet.

"And you are?" He quickly walked from the elevator to put himself firmly between the man and Medusa, right past the short person who'd originally been on the floor. They were still looking around and blinking slowly, as if they weren't quite sure what they were seeing.

"Kuafu." The man hardly looked at Kirin, trying to find a way around him instead, eyes darting to all sides. His fingers were twitching, though the light had ceased.

"I think you've managed to capture the sun this time, though." Yantra had a hand on the short person's shoulder, but was listening in. "Does it not hurt? Sorry, I suppose you can't answer that."

He seemed taken aback, finally straightening fully out of his crouch and his shoulders moving away from his ears.

"You know the story?"

"Mhm! Or more accurately, I heard it used to describe some-one and looked it up ages ago." Yantra wandered closer and attempted to casually put her arm on Kirin's shoulder, though he was far too tall for her to do so comfortably.

"It is admirable." Kuafu seemed entirely relaxed now, nod-ding.

"We good, then?" The blind-folded woman peeked around the pair, though the thick white gauze over her eyes made the movement pointless. It was quite firmly in place too, Kirin noted, pulled tightly around the bridge of her nose and pinned into her wavy brown hair. He couldn't tell much more about her features, considering the fabric covered her face from her eyebrows almost all the way to the bottom of her nose.

"Apologies." Kuafu sounded incredibly sincere, belying his earlier anger. "I overreacted."

"It's alright! It's definitely disconcerting, so I get it." Medusa offered a quick thumbs up and a smile.

"Can you really turn people to stone? That feels a little... on the nose. And he doesn't look like stone to me." Ness gestured to Kuafu. He certainly didn't, with dark hair and dark eyes. Ifrit might have something to say about the hair color, Kirin thought.

"I believe I'm not supposed to say." Medusa spread her hands in a shrug.

"I could believe it, particularly coupled with the blindfold. But that leaves how the floor was moving..." As Yantra trailed off, all the eyes in the room were drawn to the previously prone person.

They were on the shorter side, with long dark hair that was pulled up into twin buns, though a few chunks had fallen out and were hanging over their face. They had light taupe skin and deep brown eyes, which were still struggling to focus.

"Are you alright?" Ness was closest to them, passing a finger slowly in front of their face that they failed to follow.

"Give me... a few moments." Their voice came out croaky, as if they hadn't had anything to drink in a very long time. The words were slurred slightly too, slow and quiet.

"Take your time." Kirin moved closer, mentally going through the checklist for a concussion. But indeed, a few moments later and their gaze was much clearer.

"It does take a moment to come back, particularly..." Their voice trailed off. "Never mind that."

"No worries." Yantra was at Kirin's elbow again, peering at their face. "Better for us to guess anyways! What's the name?"

"Kapre."

"I don't know that one." Yantra pulled up her screen again, scrolling through results quickly enough to make the words blur for Kirin.

"Tree giants. Big, hairy, smoke a lot." Kapre gave a slow smile.

"None of that aligns with what we just saw." Ness looked over at Phoenix, as she was usually spear-heading the charge, but she'd been suspiciously quiet. The second Ness located her, her whole face fell into disapproval. Kirin followed Ness's gaze to see what Phoenix was doing.

The frown was easily explained as Phoenix was attempting to take off Medusa's blindfold sneakily, her hands hovering just above the fabric. Having been caught, she quickly moved away, and looked off in the distance innocently, miming whistling the whole time. Medusa had clearly noticed, but a small grin quirked her mouth instead of annoyance.

"Maybe we were wrong about the naming convention." Yantra didn't seem convinced by that explanation.

"Can you show me one of those articles?" Ness was at her side, trying to read, and Yantra slowed her scrolling. After a few seconds, Ness nodded. "I think I got it."

"Are you going to share?" Phoenix was suddenly interested

again, popping over to the group and leaving Medusa alone for the time being.

"No, I don't think so."

Phoenix wilted, but quickly moved to trying to figure out what Ness had spotted by squinting at the screen herself. Kuafu was trying very hard to appear disinterested, though Kirin didn't miss how he snuck over to try and read too.

"Do *none* of you have your own phones?" Yantra finally closed the article and threw up her hands. "Make your guesses now, I hate having everyone crowding around me."

Ness and Yantra dissolved into bickering and Kirin watched as Phoenix crept back over to Medusa, while Kuafu was apologizing profusely to Kapre for the inconvenience. Despite the rowdiness of the crowd, Kirin felt a slow smile unfurling on his face. In this bigger group, he could almost disappear. The chaos and arguments even felt familiar, just like home. Right about now it would be dinner time, everyone gathering around the table as one of his younger siblings lured their mother out of her office for just a few minutes to eat food...

The smile faded.

"Alright, alright, let's keep this moving!" Phoenix was suddenly shooing him towards the elevator. "We've got two more floors to cover before we're done!"

Kuafu tried to go back to his room, but Phoenix grabbed one arm and Yantra the other and he was half carried into the lift, Medusa and Kapre following without complaint. If Kirin thought Phoenix's distraction meant he could slip off unnoticed he'd been wrong, as Ness corralled him into the elevator before the door closed. With such a large group now, it was very loud as they went down, so he wasn't surprised when one of the occupants on the next floor was waiting for them as the doors opened.

"Did I miss something going on?" A very pale ginger woman

was standing there, her head cocked slightly. She was near covered in freckles, sturdily built, and had her long hair pulled up and away from her face.

"Aha! A clean slate." Phoenix pointed at her and nearly shouted. "Place your guesses before we find out the name!"

"I'm going with something strength related." Yantra looked their newest member up and down in a way that made her blush all the way to the roots of her hair.

"Maybe something auditory?" Kirin offered.

His guess was perhaps in poor sportsmanship, as he'd noticed the earplugs she was wearing. The way her eyes flickered to him and narrowed, he suspected he'd gotten close.

"Hm, I think Yantra might be right though." Phoenix was first out into the hall and was circling around the woman, tapping her chin thoughtfully. "She's quite muscular. Though, I'm inclined to think that's from hard work and not just unnaturally bestowed gifts."

"I'm with Kirin." Ness appeared at his side, or perhaps she'd been there the whole time.

"I will also stick with the tall man." Kapre did have to look up significantly to see Kirin's face, as they were standing right next to him.

"Two for strength, three for auditory, any other takers?" Yantra looked at Medusa and Kuafu.

"My guess will be more random than most, but for the sake of fun, I'll go strength as well." Medusa leaned on her cane, not seeming upset at the prospect.

"It was clearly written in our introductory packet that what could not be understood from basic observations of our miens should remain a mystery." Kuafu was standing rigidly, a sharp contrast to Medusa's casual posture. They were the last two out of the elevator, which promptly closed behind them and began to move. It was heading down, Kirin noted, and wondered offhand if that meant one of the empty doors they'd passed would be filled.

"We've already got a strong clue as to yours, as well as the angry guy on the top floor's. Kirin's wasn't super visible, but some of us got at least a little hint. Hell, most of the schedule says mien practice anyways, so we'll find out a lot of each other's abilities the longer we're here." Phoenix put an elbow on Kuafu's shoulder leaning closer to him. "What's a little friendly guessing between classmates?"

"We should not—" He was cut off by the elevator opening.

"TIEBREAKER!" Phoenix immediately ran to the new person, hair flying. She ended up having to back away just as quickly, to avoid getting skewered by some large and rather impressive ram's horns. That appeared to be solid gold.

"Well, that name suddenly makes a lot of sense, but also is incredibly on the nose." It was the ginger woman who spoke, nodding to herself. "You must be Goldhorn?"

She was certainly right about the name being very literal. Goldhorn was about Yantra's height, not accounting for the horns. They had tanned skin and long blond hair so pale it seemed to reflect the gold from their horns, which started just above their ears. Evidently, they'd just arrived, as they were covered in dust and sweat, the dust providing the only spots of color on their black hoodie and jeans.

"Yes, and I while I would love to do introductions, I *do* need to take a shower first." They briefly nodded their head to the group before hurrying off to the room that was second from the end. The door closed a second later and the whole group broke out into conversation.

"I suppose, for some people, they cannot hide their mien, so it matters not if it is discussed—" Kuafu was trying to rationalize his ability to participate.

"Is there really a creature from mythology named *Goldhorn*, or do we think they just made up a new name since they couldn't find one?"

"I *told* you; you have your own phone too!" Yantra's protestations were contradicted by her pulling out the holo screen as she looked it up.

"Do you think the horns are made of actual gold? Or is it like an aesthetic thing?" Phoenix mused.

"I'm sorry, they had a *literal gold horn*?!"

"I don't think it was an aesthetic thing, they were wearing all black otherwise." Ness decided.

"Alright, it is in fact a mythical creature, and yes, it had gold horns."

"I feel like that's not the whole story, though." Ness had moved before she spoke and was now next to Kapre, who jumped at her words. If Ness noticed the reaction, she didn't comment on it. "Is there more to it?"

"Some plants grew from its blood, and it got incredibly powerful from eating those plants." Yantra summarized out loud.

"Hm."

"You need to stop noticing things if you aren't going to share with the class. It's not polite." Phoenix pouted.

The creak of a door opening startled everyone into silence, and they were greeted by a figure shrouded in shadow standing in the doorway of the second room.

"Could you be a little quieter? I'm trying to meditate." The voice was quiet, hardly audible.

"Sorry! We'll move to the next floor." Phoenix shot the owner a thumbs up, hardly having done so before the door closed. The nameplate read "Enenra."

"Onwards!" Phoenix whisper-yelled, moving toward the elevator before pausing to check the first door. "Clid-na?"

"It's pronounced *Clee-na*." The ginger woman corrected, waving her hand in front of the sensor to open the elevator doors.

"My room."

"And should we check the one at the end of the hall before we go?" Ness pointed out.

"It's empty, at least for now. Name on it was Impundulu, if I'm saying that right." Clidna shrugged. "I didn't have a moment to look it up."

"Enenra appears to be a type of yokai made of smoke." Yantra announced, Phoenix hanging over her shoulder to read. "Impundulu translates as 'lightning bird' and I'm sure you can all guess what it does."

"I didn't get a good look, but Enenra didn't *appear* smokey." Ness's nose wrinkled as she thought.

"That's all it really said about them online," Yantra said as the doors opened onto the final floor.

No one was immediately in the common area, the training room still filled with a projected X as a robotic arm scrubbed soot off the glass wall. Phoenix didn't spare a glance to the side though, marching all the way down to the farther door.

"That one's mine, try the next one." Yantra made it there before Phoenix did, though, so she knocked for a change.

"Antaeus." Phoenix read the name aloud as they waited, but it seemed like no one was there.

"A Greek giant, who was the son of Poseidon and Gaia, and could renew his strength by touching the ground." Ness was faster than Yantra that time, and she knew it, from the way she flashed a smile to the taller woman. "So presumably someone very tall?"

"If we hadn't found you upstairs, I would've guessed that was you." Clidna lightly punched Kirin's shoulder as she walked past with the group already moving to the next room.

"Aïcha Kandicha is a Moroccan legend in which she appears in various forms, but usually as a beautiful woman with hooves. She seduces men so she can kill them or drive them mad."

Yantra read, once it became apparent that she wasn't there yet.

"Oh, we've got two of those." Phoenix nodded sagely. "I'll make sure to befriend them both."

That left one room unaccounted for, the one nearest the elevator.

The door swung open after Phoenix's first knock, and Phoenix said something snarky to the inhabitant, though Kirin missed it. The woman who opened the door was a good head taller than Phoenix, taller even than Goldhorn had been. There was a prominent scar around her throat, but Kirin's attention was mostly drawn to how she seemed to be studying him, like she could see *through* him, her eyes knowing. There was an eerie stillness to her as well, like even the wind wouldn't blow and disturb her.

"Yantra?" Phoenix was prompting for information on the name.

"Adlivun are the spirits of the recently departed in Inuit tradition." Yantra spoke softly, reluctant to believe what it implied.

"I'm very much alive, if that's what you're all worried about." Adlivun smiled, amused. She didn't look at all how Kirin might imagine a ghost, with long, black hair and chestnut skin, bright brown eyes the color of amber.

"No, we've been trying to guess everyone's miens, but yours is... trickier." Ness was biting her lip. "Maybe invisibility? Something to appear like she's dead?"

And just like that, the room devolved into conversation again, everyone discussing exactly *what* power could be related to death. Phoenix was dragged away from the door and into a heated argument with Yantra and Medusa, who seemed to think that she'd know more. Adlivun stared over the heads of the crowd right at Kirin, her gaze a little sad. There was also something else there, something in the way her eyes flickered just off to the side of him, almost like she felt too guilty to look at him fully. But after a few moments, her resolve hardened and she started to move toward him with purpose, like she had something to say.

Maybe it was just from too many new people, maybe it was just from an exhausting day, but for whatever reason Kirin was filled with a horrible sensation of dread as she moved closer. So horrible in fact, that he fled.

He didn't even take the elevator, since Adlivun had been standing in the way. He'd been at the back of the crowd anyway, and the stairs were behind him, making it easy enough to sneak off before the main group noticed he'd gone missing at all. As he climbed, he tried to banish the lurking sensation that Adlivun *knew* something. Tried to ignore the whisper in his brain that asked if maybe she could *sense* death, and knew it surrounded him like a familiar shroud.

He didn't have the energy to make his bed, cursing his earlier self for not taking the time, instead flopping down onto the bare mattress and staring at the blank ceiling. Ignoring her expression for a moment, Kirin's brain latched onto the scar on her neck, displayed almost proudly, or at least, unabashedly. He hadn't expected that here. East Tech was usually so particular about the image heroes were allowed to have, and any sign of weakness— or simple proof of their fragile humanity— was frowned upon. This batch of trainees, with Medusa's blindfold and Ifrit's hearing aids and now Adlivun's scar, there was something different here. He just wasn't sure what, yet. Or how he fit into it.

He sat up suddenly, realizing something. For the bottom four floors, the names were arranged alphabetically by the Latin alphabet. Starting with A and up to W, each floor followed the pattern. Each floor except this floor. On Kirin's level, it was him, closest to the stairwell, Ifrit in the middle, and then Phoenix closest to the elevator, but still with an empty room between. Why that was the case, he wasn't sure. At first he'd been thrilled to have the top floor, glad to be out of the way and with the best view off his small balcony. But now it felt... othering. Like he'd done something wrong and needed to be watched.

He chewed on a snack and tossed the wrapper into the trash can, lying back down with a sigh. He'd expected the classes to be the most exhausting part, but in reality, this just might be worse. He'd always found it easy to make friends in school, but only during classes. After the day was done, he'd be at work, where he didn't have to be so worried about what everyone thought until he got home. He'd hoped maybe his classmates wouldn't feel the need to socialize so much so quickly, but his options were to form friendships now or have none for the next two years. He wasn't sure which was more daunting.

It hadn't even been a full day, but he already felt homesick. It was... strange, being here alone. There were things that were familiar, it was true, but for the most part his room felt sterile, foreign. He'd brought a few books, his guitar, and of course his clothes, but everything else was new, from the laptop that sat on his desk to the trash can he'd just thrown his wrapper into. Even with more furniture than he'd ever had before, the room felt empty.

Kirin's eyes flickered to the corner of the room, to the air filter over the vent and the fire detector by the door. They were all easy places to hide a camera, and with the school-issued phone and laptop, the way his things had obviously been searched before they'd been placed in his room, he wouldn't put it past East Tech to have bugged the dorms as well. But he couldn't hide it forever, and there was a good chance the footage wouldn't be good enough to see details anyways, so he reached into his pants pocket and pulled out the one thing he absolutely wasn't supposed to bring. A photo.

It was old, and hadn't appreciated being shoved in a pocket, a last minute decision when he'd been headed out the door. But it was the only photo that'd ever been taken of his family in full, all seven of them, and part of Kirin needed it. To remind himself both of why he'd come here, and why he shouldn't have.

"Hey dad." Speaking to the photo wasn't much different than speaking to his father's grave. At least this held some semblance of humanity, his father's face frozen into a smile instead of cold gray stone. "I know you thought that this would be the wrong path, that this was the worst possible choice. But I'm here now. I need to do this, for the little ones. You never really got to know them, but they're just like mom, you know? Which means I needed to leave, to make it safe for them. I don't think... I don't think what we used to do would work anymore."

The photo didn't respond.

"I don't know how this is going to go, but... if you can hear me at all, I just don't want you to be mad at me." Kirin swallowed. Though the sun was just starting to go down, he tucked the photo underneath his pillow and curled up to go back to sleep. "Please don't be mad."

3

Other

Kirin's plan for his first official day on campus had been simple: go for a jog around the outskirts to get some sense of how big it was, map out the path to all his classes, and maybe try to go into the city to buy some things to personalize his space. He'd thought it'd be easy to stick to such basic goals, but apparently, he needed to start factoring the human tornado that was Phoenix into his planning.

"Since we were the only people at check in yesterday, that means other classes should be arriving starting today!" Phoenix had said, ambushing Kirin as he'd exited the bathroom. "Since we're here first, that means we have the chance to scope them all out before the school year starts!"

Which had led to a handful of their classmates and him sitting in the grass, in view of the entrance gate on the tech side of campus. Phoenix had rounded up everyone who'd been awake, shepherding them out the door with almost practiced ease, phone in hand.

"Half of us didn't arrive until the afternoon, what makes you think we need to be out here *this* early?" Yantra was bleary-eyed, apparently having been woken up by the commotion, rather than having been awake before hurricane Phoenix blew through.

"Because these students aren't being tested to enter. They just get to walk in." Phoenix hadn't taken their eyes off the gate, their whole body turned away from the group and straight at the visible shield. It wasn't a standard one— of course it wasn't, how could the impressive East Tech have something so simple for its main entrance?— but one that glowed blue and then gold, a sheet of color that blocked the opening in the wall. They could see straight through to the road that curved up to the school, but anyone on the outside would only see a block of color and not a hint of what lay beyond it. At least the edges of the wall were decorated, lending the steel a less ominous cast. The gate was flanked by two piers, the school's motto sunk into the side: saving those who need to be saved.

"How do you know that?" It was one of the later arrivals who spoke up, a dark-skinned man with sky blue eyes. Phoenix had introduced him as Dulu, but it was only when Yantra scolded them for giving everyone nicknames that Kirin processed he must be Impundulu, though he didn't seem very birdlike at all. True, he was tall and willowy, but he had close-cropped black hair and open, soft features that were far from hawkish.

"Because I overheard *him*." Phoenix nodded toward Ifrit, who was sitting with rigid posture a few meters away from their group.

"Find another fucking spot to sit." The words should have been difficult to hear, considering Ifrit hadn't turned to look at them when he spoke, but he nearly yelled them.

"Overheard him *when*? And who was he talking to?" Ness asked. She was seated between even more people Kirin hadn't met the day before, a short man with curly brown hair and a Mediterranean complexion, and a woman whose most notable quality was she appeared to have *goat hooves*. Kirin had seen both of them leaving their rooms on the first floor as he followed Phoenix, which meant they had to be Antaeus and Aïcha. Aïcha's name made more sense than Antaeus's, who hardly looked like a big, strong giant. Their other man-killer classmate, Naddāha, was certainly quite pretty with wavy black hair, rich wheat-colored skin, and deep green eyes. Kirin wasn't sure if she was "seduce a man to death" pretty, but admittedly, he wasn't really the target audience.

"Oh, he went to bug Pressure about it just after dinner yesterday." Phoenix airily waved a hand.

"I saw him leave through the common area, but I never saw you come down." Ness frowned.

"You're not the only one who's sneaky."

"What did he ask Pressure about?" The last of the faces Kirin didn't recognize spoke up. She was seated next to Kuafu, her dark, curly hair the only common point between them. She'd already been with the rest of the group when he'd arrived, so she had to be Lilin— the name on the empty room on Kuafu's floor— but she didn't look the way he'd expect for a demon of the night, dressed in bright colors and with a friendly smile. If anything, Kuafu's name seemed better for her sunny personality.

"He was asking when the— and I'm quoting— 'group of pretentious assholes' would be arriving." Phoenix snorted.

Kirin glanced over to see if Ifrit was particularly irritated with everyone talking like he wasn't sitting *right there*, but much like Phoenix, his whole attention was focused on the gate.

"How do you make the leap in logic from 'pretentious assholes' to 'allowed to arrive on campus without an obnoxious test?'" Yantra suddenly seemed more awake.

"My natural genius. No, I asked Pressure about it because he told me to, and again, I quote: 'fuck right off, nosy bastard.'"

"And Pressure said..." Antaeus prompted.

"She said that typically a group is let in as legacy admissions or relations. Additionally, the school does give *priority* to the children of donors. These students have usually been allowed to develop their miens under retired heroes who function as licensed trainers and often are far more accustomed to the life of a hero than, say, the average person. As such, they are granted immediate entry to campus upon acceptance." Adlivun spoke up for what Kirin thought might have been the first time that morning. Despite how physically big she was, with how still she sat, Kirin had nearly forgotten she was there.

"Yeah." For the first time Phoenix took their eyes off the gate, turning to looked at her. Adlivun met their gaze levelly, dark eyes meeting shocking gray. "Exactly that."

Phoenix looked like they were going to ask her how *she* knew that, but then everyone's attention was shifted back to the front gate as a quiet hum announced the arrival of a car.

It was a large van, not one of the small sedans that had picked Kirin up for all his interviews, enough room to seat at least ten. If this class was to be the same size as his, there would have to be at least two cars. And indeed, the second pulled up just as the passengers from the first began disembarking.

It was shocking, to Kirin, how everyone who piled out of from the vans had the same presence. Overwhelming. Powerful. Proud. *Heroic*. Not a single person among them had any visible physical differences, just clean, unbroken skin, toned muscle, and determined faces. Already they had the eyes of professionals, calm and alert, and only a little haughty.

"I hate them." Phoenix decided as the second group was filing out. "Also, do they all have matching outfits? Is there some uniform I wasn't made aware of?"

"It's techware." Yantra somehow already had the outfits in question pulled up. "The sort of thing all the companies that exist on the islands make. Helps with muscle strain, minor defensive capabilities, can record and report on vital signs, etc."

"Were they expecting to be ambushed on the way to campus?" Ness asked dryly.

"I suspect they were hoping to make an impression." Adlivun's face was mostly hidden by her mask, but the wrinkle that appeared between her eyes coupled with the disapproving tone made it clear what she thought about them.

"That they have." Antaeus muttered.

Their group was far enough away, up a small hill, that their conversation couldn't be heard as the new class passed through an opening that appeared in the gate, but they were certainly visible to those arriving. If any of the new students saw them, however, they didn't react at all, instead marching eerily in sync toward the far side of campus, where check in had been.

A flicker of movement in the corner of his eye was all the advance warning Kirin got before he was flying to his feet and grabbing Ifrit's arm before the man could make it more than a few steps.

"Don't." He wasn't quite sure what he thought Ifrit's plan had been, but from the angry set of his shoulders, the way the fire around his throat was flickering, Kirin was certain he didn't want to find out.

Ifrit wrenched his arm out of Kirin's grip but didn't move to go intercept the other class again, his eyes flickering briefly back to where the rest of their classmates sat. If Kirin wasn't mistaken, the expression that flitted across his face was something akin to concern.

"At least one of you charity cases understands how this works." A drawling voice from behind Ifrit called out. "Keep your temper and you just *might* make it past the first semester."

None of the students were looking their way, all eyes forward as they headed into campus, but several were snickering. Kirin couldn't pick out which person had spoken— they really did all look alike, didn't they?— and quite honestly, he didn't care.

"Ah, sorry, didn't want any of you to show up to the check in all messed up! That would be pretty embarrassing." He gave a bright smile that was hidden behind his mask, grabbed onto Ifrit's arm again, and practically *dragged* the other man up the hill.

"Dude." Phoenix was waiting for him, arms crossed. "Why didn't you *let them fight?* Sparks here would have at *least* given them a run for their money, and I didn't wake up this early just to watch them *walk!*"

"You knew this was the plan?" Kirin was still holding onto Ifrit, but the shorter man seemed too shocked to react, at least for the moment.

"I didn't *know*, but I had a suspicion! And now this was all practically for nothing. If I wanted to see rich assholes just existing, I would've stayed in and watched TV." Phoenix sighed.

"I think it's probably for the best we don't pick a fight with the people who bought their way in. That kind of connection runs deep, and I didn't give up my entire life to get here just to lose it because of one hot head." Dulu, at least, seemed as angry as Kirin felt, standing to his full height. It put him almost eye level with Ifrit, who met the glare with a slight raise of his chin.

"There should be another class coming today too, not just those bastards." Ifrit finally said something after an awkwardly long staredown with Dulu. "They should be here any fucking minute now."

An uneasy silence fell over the group, no one quite sure how to respond. Ifrit's shoulders were hiked nearly to his ears, though only Dulu was really looking at him at all. Ness was staring out after the newly arrived students, and most of the others weren't looking at anyone.

"Think we can still guess their miens, even from the back?"

Yantra pulled out her notebook, brushing a loose strand of hair out of her face as she did.

"Does money count as a superpower?"

"Might as well, apparently."

The bubble of tension popped, and then they were all staring at the retreating backs of the other group, Phoenix commenting that at least one of them had slits in the back of their suit. As the attention shifted, Kirin was left alone at the back with Ifrit. Ifrit turned as if to leave, but Kirin grabbed his wrist.

"I don't think you're allowed to fight people from other classes, man, and even if you were, maybe *don't* pick a fight first day. Your actions reflect on all our classmates, so please don't mess this up for them. Okay?" He spoke softly, not wanting Ifrit to feel like it was an attack.

"I won't fuck up anything for anyone. We're only judged on our own merits, no one else's." Ifrit wrenched his arm out of Kirin's grasp, crossing his arms over his chest. "And *they* need to know not to look down on us."

"Gonna be honest, I don't think they even know we exist."

"They do." Ifrit seemed so sure of it.

"I'll take your word for it." Kirin clapped him on the back, perhaps slightly too hard as it made him flinch. "Just... *try* to think about how your actions impact us all, okay?"

"Fuck off." Ifrit struck out from the group, away from the entrance entirely. His footsteps seemed to head for the retreating class for a few moments and Kirin thought he'd have to chase after him again, but a second later his path veered right, toward the dorm.

It was only after they'd both vanished from sight that Kirin remembered to wonder how Ifrit had known they were coming in the first place.

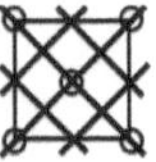

Kirin was about ready to give up. He'd been at it for an hour, but it seemed so pointless. Was it really so impossible? Was this really how it was going to be? Why was there absolutely *no* privacy on such a large campus?

The awkwardness of Ifrit's reaction had seemed to linger, and Kirin excused himself from the group on the grounds of needing something to eat— which wasn't completely wrong— and snuck back to the dorm. When he made it to the top floor, it was just in time to see Ifrit slamming the door to his room, the lock clicking loudly in the empty space. The kitchen was stocked with plenty of staple foods, and he quickly made himself lunch, packing it away into a small container with the hope of finding somewhere private to eat. That had been his mistake.

The small garden space in the center of campus? Filled with a group of what he assumed were upperclassmen. The area along the wall? Shielded so that no one could even get *close*. An empty classroom? Since classes weren't in session until the end of the week, all the school buildings except the gym were locked up tight. The common area in the dorm? It seemed like everyone who hadn't been grabbed by Phoenix was congregating down there.

Eating in his room felt depressing, but honestly, he just wanted a few minutes to himself. Living with four siblings in a small house should have accustomed him to being surrounded by people, but there were plenty of woods and hills that he could run to if he wanted to be alone there. Now, he would apparently need to ask for a pass off campus— as he'd been so rudely informed by a guard at the entrance— if he so much as wanted to go running in the park just outside the wall, and those passes wouldn't even be granted for months.

He'd ended up back in the common area on the fifth floor, Ifrit still very much ensconced behind his own door. Phoenix likely would be coming back soon, but for the moment it was almost private, almost quiet, if not for the rhythmic thud from Ifrit's room that promised he was listening to music with a good drumline.

And yet he'd hardly been there for a few minutes when the elevator doors opened. He sighed, expecting to be overrun by Phoenix's energy, but instead was met by someone he didn't know yet and immediately assumed to be Wyrm.

The man was tall, with pale skin and blond hair pulled up into a bun, though his most striking features were the bright orange spikes that protruded from his shoulders and down his arms, little chips of rust-colored scales dotting his face like freckles. His fingers ended in what looked like talons, and when he opened his mouth to speak it became obvious that his teeth were razor sharp too.

"Are you Kirin?" His voice was gravelly, like his throat was rubbed raw.

"Yeah, and you are?"

"Wyrm." Though he was standing nearby, Wyrm didn't try to shake his hand; Kirin absently wondered if he *could*, without stabbing someone. "One of the professors asked me to grab you. You're wanted downstairs."

As Kirin moved to get up, he noticed Wyrm moving to Ifrit's door.

"They need him too?" Any hope Kirin might have had that this *wasn't* about the morning's attempted meeting fled.

"Yeah. Phoenix was downstairs already, but him too." Wyrm knocked with the back of his hand, not curling his fingers into a fist.

Kirin's heart sank further. Would he get kicked out before he even attended classes? That would be... embarrassing.

He didn't wait to see how poorly Ifrit would react to someone knocking on his door, but instead took the stairs down to the first floor, trying to burn off some of his anxiety before he got there. It'd be fine, they probably just wanted to reaffirm that they shouldn't be talking to other classes. Yeah, that was it.

He was, of course, wrong.

It wasn't just him, Phoenix, and Ifrit who were needed, but Dulu as well, and a shorter woman with cropped black hair and almond eyes. Pressure was standing at the entrance to the dorm, wearing casual athletic clothes and bouncing impatiently on her feet. She didn't acknowledge Kirin's arrival with anything more than a nod, staring back out the doors as if looking for someone.

"Any idea what this is about?" Kirin asked Phoenix, since they were standing close by.

"Not a clue." Phoenix didn't seem concerned, instead giving Kirin a wide smile. "But I did remember to look up your name this morning after you ditched us."

Kirin internally groaned. He'd been quite pleased that no one had done so while he was there, but it should have crossed his mind that someone would later.

"I'm going to assume it's the mythical version, considering your neck's a normal length. Well, that plus Kapre said they saw you fight and mentioned nothing about giraffes."

"It's not really a unicorn." He cringed at how defensive he sounded. But it wasn't *his* fault that the immediate first article that came up said it was just an "Asian unicorn," despite the two creatures having almost no similarities at all.

"I read the whole article; did you think I wouldn't?" Phoenix feigned offense, and Kirin pointedly refrained from saying that yes, he would indeed have assumed Phoenix only read the first few lines. "Gotta say though, it wasn't super helpful. Though if you *can* turn into different animals, or even just one chimera, that's pretty cool."

Kirin was spared the need to respond by the arrival of Ifrit, who had apparently also decided to take the stairs and *kicked* the door open once he reached it. Arms crossed over his chest, he looked ready for a fight, eyes searching the group for any challengers. Wyrm was right behind him but made considerably less of an entrance by taking the elevator.

"That's everyone!" Pressure clapped her hands together and waved for them all to follow, offering no explanation for where they were going. With a few confused glances, they all went after her. Despite her being shorter than almost all of them, she set a fast pace that had them all scrambling.

"Do you know what this is for?" Kirin asked Wyrm, since he'd been told to get everyone.

"I couldn't tell you." Wyrm's voice sounded just as torn as it had before. He didn't appear to be in any pain when he spoke, but the rawness made Kirin want to wince. "She caught me while I was outside and sent me ahead to try and grab people."

Kirin nodded absently, suddenly paying more attention to where they were headed. It wasn't toward the gymnasium like he'd thought they might, nor toward the hero section of campus at all. Instead, they seemed to be heading to the research and development half.

East Tech was best known for having the only licensed hero program, but it wasn't the *only* program offered. In order for new techware to be developed, and especially anything to do with mien-related tech, a company needed to have licensed researchers, who in turn needed an accredited degree. The only places that offered accredited programs were the Cardinal Islands, including East City.

Indeed, most of the student body for the school wasn't in the hero track, but rather the tech, which was still difficult to get into. Unlike the hero program, the tech course wasn't fully funded, and lasted seven years, in contrast to the short two for heroes.

"Put a mask on, all of you." Pressure had already put one on herself, pausing the group at the digital gate between the residential and tech sides of campus. The barrier itself was hard to see, only catching the light so often, but Kirin knew from that morning that it looked completely opaque on the other side. The tech section was much more modern than the hero side had been, the buildings all glass and steel, and now that it was into the afternoon, there were dozens of people milling about, just on the other side.

Pressure was already punching in the code as Kirin fixed the straps around his ears, nervously making sure none of his hair had gotten caught in his mask. The fact that no one outside of the hero program was ever supposed to see his face again was... going to take some getting used to.

He wasn't the only one who felt uncomfortable, a muscle in Wyrm's neck visibly tense. The rest of their classmates and even Kirin could look like the rest of the people milling about in the tech section, but Wyrm's spikes stood out, especially vivid against his pale skin and hair. People did stare as they walked by, many edging slightly farther from the group than was strictly necessary.

"Is the orange natural or did you do that yourself, so it'd look cool?" Kirin tried to distract him from the staring faces.

"You think it looks cool?" Wyrm looked a little surprised at that, his eyebrows raising more when Kirin nodded. Over the edges of his mask, his cheeks had gone slightly red. "Oh. Yeah, it's natural."

"That's wicked, dude. You think you'll go for orange as your color, or something else to compliment it?" Kirin subtly swapped sides with Wyrm, so now Wyrm walked alongside the buildings and Kirin faced the people moving about.

"I'm not sure to be honest; I want to talk with the marketing people here to try and find something that wouldn't be scary to kids. I know I'm a bit... much, but I think if I play it right, it could be something fun rather than terrifying, you know?" He'd clearly put a lot of thought into it already, and Kirin felt his lips twitch with how excited Wyrm had gotten.

"I definitely think you can do that."

"I was originally leaning toward something dinosaur themed, maybe? My little— I mean all the little kids I know love them. Only issue is I *really* need to make sure no kids try to touch the spikes..." Wyrm seemed to realize he'd been rambling, and his eyes creased in an embarrassed grin.

"Can't you cover them?"

"It's not really that easy." Their group was coming to a halt in front of a large glass building, the closest one to the campus entrance, in fact. Out of the corner of his eye, Kirin could see the gate change color, gold fracturing into blue until it was the same shade as the spring sky. "Though I suspect that might be why we're here."

"Alright you lot, once we head in, you'll be asked a ton of questions." Pressure had stopped at the door, holding onto the handle with one hand as she addressed them. "Answer them as best you can, and don't worry, this'll be the armorer you're paired with for the entirety of your school career. Likely your professional one, too. You can tell them anything."

With a flourish, she opened the door.

"Let's get your orders in now."

The building was just as impressive inside as the outside had implied. The door opened onto an atrium several stories tall, filled with robots buzzing around with materials to deliver to labs. They filled the air, darting down hallways that stretched as far back as the eye could see. Screens flickered a few meters above their heads, listing room numbers that were flickering from green to red as Kirin watched. A central hub of screens was surrounded by a group of people, one woman swiping through photos of researchers in long white coats. As she tapped on a button, another room lit up red.

Kirin realized he recognized the people standing behind her as they approached, just as he heard a loud *"tch"* from Ifrit.

"I believe my class is the only one permitted to be suited today." A monotone voice came from the woman at the screen, her eyes never even looking up. She was dressed in a hero costume of dark blue that complimented her bright azure hair. Her mask covered the top half of her face, blending seamlessly, somehow, into her perfectly slicked back ponytail. Kirin was surprised to recognize her, even more surprised since Majesty hadn't been active in the past eight years. Yet she looked every bit as severe and intense as he remembered from her TV appearances. Perhaps even more so, since alone she couldn't be compared to her more impressive peer.

Pressure, on the other hand, hardly looked like a hero at all. Her hair was up in a bun that was already losing pieces, her clothes cheap and comfortable instead of a military grade suit. But the presence she exuded and the sudden steel in her eyes left no one wondering who would win in a fight.

"Ah, Majesty, I think you'll find that I *did* put in a request for several of my students who need more custom work." The way she said the other woman's name made Kirin's toes curl, and from how his classmates slightly leaned back, he suspected he wasn't the only one feeling that way.

"We still have first pick."

"Then pick." Pressure's voice was cold, and if looks could kill, Majesty would be bleeding out on the floor. It hit him, very suddenly, that Pressure's very position in the school promised she was a licensed killer.

Majesty appeared to be fighting between the desire to take her time out of spite and the flicker of fear that crossed her face. Her fingers hesitated over the screen for just a moment before she minimized the images she'd been browsing, and selected rooms seemingly at random.

"Was that so hard?" Pressure accessed the console and started reading through, pointedly taking a much longer time than Majesty had. While she read, Majesty was leading her class away, though she glanced over her shoulder once as if to check that Pressure wasn't following. It seemed like her fear had won out, but the students she was corralling didn't appear to feel the same. Kirin really did have to agree with Ifrit's assessment of them as pretentious, because several of them were staring at Pressure like she was dirt under their heels. If she noticed, she made no comment on it.

"Kirin, come here." Pressure waved him forward without turning around. "You're planning on staying a close range fighter, yes?"

"Yes ma'am."

"Mm." She selected a room from the list and held up his phone— when had she grabbed that?— which chimed. "This'll let you in the elevator. It'll take you where you need to go. Wait just a moment; I'll have you go with Ifrit, you'll be heading the same way."

The dismissal clear, he stepped to the side to let the shorter man through. Ifrit wordlessly handed over his phone, Pressure already clicking a name from the list.

"You don't have to listen to anything they say. They don't know shit about you." Pressure didn't look at Ifrit while she spoke, and Kirin pointedly started staring at the ceiling, feeling like maybe he shouldn't be hearing this. "Tell them what you need and leave."

Ifrit nearly slapped the phone out of her hand in response.

"I already fucking know that." Without waiting for confirmation that he was set, he turned on his heel and beelined to the elevator, Kirin belatedly running after him. The doors were nearly closed by the time he reached it and he had to shove his arm in to make sure he didn't get left behind. Ifrit didn't acknowledge him as he pressed his phone to a scanner, the elevator already starting to move. Kirin rushed to do the same, not sure if it did anything at all.

"Have you... been here before?" The speed they were rising was shockingly slow, especially considering how state of the art the rest of the building was. Kirin was tapping his fingers along his arms impatiently as the floors counted by.

Ifrit only responded with a grunt, and a quieter one than Kirin had expected. He hazarded a glance over at the other man and was surprised to find him staring at the ground intensely, his shoulders so tense that Kirin wasn't sure how the metal rail didn't just snap between his hands. And for some reason he was holding his breath.

"You can breathe man, it'll be fine." Kirin was well aware that he had no idea what he was talking about, but he should still say *something*. "We'll be in and out."

Ifrit shot him a look that was more confused than angry, but before he could say anything, the doors opened. He blinked at Kirin once, twice, and then he was gone, down the hall in an instant. He didn't even bother to check his phone for the number, disappearing into a room only a few doors down the corridor before Kirin had even taken a single step.

His own assigned room was blinking farther down, and suddenly his mouth felt dry. There was nothing to be worried about. It was just... well he didn't know what it was, but it was going to be fine. Yeah.

The door opened before he could gather up his courage to go in, and he was rather surprised to see a dark-skinned and bright eyed man who looked to be several years younger than Kirin was. He'd clearly been expecting Kirin— or at least expecting someone— as he was greeted with a gigantic grin and hands dragging him inside, the top of his head hitting the door frame as he forgot to duck.

"Sorry about that! This is just terribly exciting. Feel free to sit anywhere!" The young man was certainly enthusiastic, pulling out a chair, notebook, and pen in the span of two seconds. The room looked like a cross between a lab and a workshop, a large scanner in the back corner and several prototypes of something on a workbench near the window, which looked out onto the atrium. There were neatly labeled racks of chemicals, but also welding equipment and scrap metal tucked into crisply labelled cubbies that ran along all four walls. In the middle of the room was a drafting table that was covered in sketches, though half of the designs were covered in text so dense Kirin couldn't make any sense of what the drawings themselves were.

A high pitched whine startled Kirin back to the present and he found the man wincing to himself, pulling out a wrench to adjust one of the braces on his legs as he sat.

"Sorry, these are in dire need of a tune up, but I can never find the time! Nerves got severed, so it was a whole mess of trying to get them to interface with my— never mind that. The main problem is if I try to move too quickly it overloads the processor and— I'm starting to do it again, apologies. The short of it is if I move too quickly, the electronics get *loud*."

"It seems like the best bug to have out of all the options." Kirin couldn't get himself to sit down, not that there was another seat to be found, and leaned against the drafting table instead.

"Oh, certainly! There were a lot worse possibilities when I— well, that's not what we're here to talk about." He rolled closer in his chair, needing to crane his neck all the way back to look

Kirin in the face. "Your mien. What does it do?"

Kirin knew to expect the question, but he still froze up for a moment, the old, practiced answer bubbling to his lips. Yet this young man was looking at him excitedly, expectantly, like a kid about to get candy, and the pure joy of his expression eased Kirin's worries enough to free up his voice.

"I can turn all parts of my body into diamond, provided I have enough carbon dioxide in my system." He spoke slowly, the words feeling odd as he'd never really said it aloud before. A voice in his head whispered *foolish*, but he ignored it.

"Does cellular respiration not provide enough?"

"It would, over time. But diamond is so dense that the amount of carbon required to, say, fully change my finger, bone and all, would take me a week to build up. Most of my store comes from the air I breathe in, and how much I can save depends on the air quality." His throat felt dry, and he coughed in an attempt to clear it before continuing. "Rural areas have far less carbon in the air from density of people alone, not to mention any industrial byproducts. It's only been a day since I've gotten here, and with the city being as heavily populated as it is, I've noticed I gain back what I use much faster."

The man started scribbling quickly, his hand moving so fast it seemed to blur.

"Very interesting. Does it have to be inhaled? Could you eat something high in carbon and absorb what you need from that?"

"I can't say that I've tried to eat graphite or anything, but from regular foods I've never noticed a difference."

The pen scratched away.

"And do you breathe out carbon dioxide or oxygen? Do you need oxygen or does your body subsist on carbon alone? Or do you simply not need to breathe out at all?"

"If I'm trying to conserve how much carbon I have left I tend to hold my breath for longer, but I'm not sure how much good it does. I've never tried to hold my breath indefinitely, so I'm not sure there, but I definitely don't know if my lungs process things differently. No doctor's ever commented on it." Kirin pointedly didn't mention he'd stopped going to the doctor regularly when he was seven.

"Can you metabolize carbon monoxide as well?"

"I'm not sure."

"We'll have to test that." The man muttered more to himself than Kirin. "In your request form, you had noted you would prefer full coverage. I'm happy to do so, but is that strictly necessary?"

Oh. *Oh.* This was about his hero *costume*. Suddenly everything that had happened in the past week felt more real. The request for costuming requirements had been part of his first application, months ago now, and he'd almost forgotten about it entirely.

It took him a moment to come back to himself and remember there was a question in there.

"It's..." Kirin took a minute to try to figure out how to say it, his father's words already trying to crowd out his thoughts. "I thought it might be better to keep as much of my skin covered as possible so it'd be harder for opponents to counter it. Diamond can stop fire for a moment, but underneath it the flesh will burn. Figured the less information they had the better."

That was plausible. The man tapped his pen to his chin, considering the half-lie.

"Can you stop bullets?"

"I can't say I've tested it in real life, but in simulations, yes."

"Interesting." He wrote something down on his pad. "I would, then, deem it necessary to inform you that you're likely not turning into diamond, exactly, but rather some other carbon composite structure."

"Oh?" It'd certainly passed for the real thing before.

"While diamond is the *hardest* naturally occurring substance, it's still a crystal. It's brittle, and especially on a large scale would be prone to shattering. The scanners might have misinterpreted the data and incorrectly played out the scenario, but I'm inclined to believe that it didn't, which leads me to believe that diamond seems... implausible. No, I'd guess it's an as-yet unknown structure of carbon, something that is both hard *and* tough, though what that might look like... I'll have to run some tests." He'd gotten up from his chair, pacing back and forth in front of the table. "Have you noticed issues with heat conductivity before?"

Kirin thought back to the day before, of Ifrit nearly scorching his hand.

"Yes, definitely."

"Intriguing." He stopped pacing directly in front of Kirin, gray eyes flashing. "May I see?"

Kirin swallowed, suddenly wishing he owned more long sleeved shirts instead of the high necked tank tops that filled out most of his wardrobe. He'd known that coming here would require him to expose his mien but it was still jarring to just... be asked by someone.

He fought down his anxiety and changed his whole hand, the right one, and held it out for the scientist to examine.

"That is, forgive me for being so casual, so *cool*." He was openly grinning, pulling a small flashlight out of his pocket and shining the light at Kirin's now entirely crystallized hand. "I see why you would assume that it's diamond; it has fire and everything! If you'd be comfortable with it, I would certainly love to see how it tolerates stress and force, so I might be looking to sit in on some of your training sessions."

"I tend to stay pretty covered when I know I'm going to be using it, I can't promise you'd see much."

"This is quite enough for visual observations of the effects; I would rather like to know how *much* you can withstand. It's really a shame that I can't get a sample of this material to see what other properties it might have." And he did seem genuinely crestfallen at the thought, brows sinking in disappointment.

"Do you... want a sample?" Kirin asked.

"Can you change things you touch as well?" The scientist perked right back up, pen and paper at the ready.

"No, not at all." Kirin released his hand, and it faded back to smooth skin, pulling out his utility knife from his back pocket. Before he could question himself, he pricked the tip of his right pointer finger and cupped his other hand beneath. Into it, fell a tiny diamond. "But if I was using my mien on any part of my body and it gets removed, it stays that way. As luck would have it, that applies to blood as well."

"Incredible!" The man took the small sample with shining eyes, quickly putting in into a petri dish. "That is really and truly remarkable. It seems, then, that your cells have a default on/off state, and it takes further instruction to reset. Interesting."

"Is that a large enough sample, or do you need more? I've been told I've got plenty of blood to give."

"With our scanners, this should be more than enough!" He really was beaming.

"Do you need anything else from me?"

"Oh, gosh, sorry, I just got so excited. There are a few more questions I'd like you to answer, particularly now that I have a better sense of what you can do. Firstly, are there any areas on your body where your abilities don't work?"

"Only my teeth, from what I can tell. Admittedly, I've never tried to do anything with my eyes or brain, and quite frankly I don't plan to."

"Any reason?"

"When I crystallize any part of my body, I can't move it at all. I don't know what that'd mean for my brain, considering diamond has high electrical resistivity. Never seemed worth the risk."

"I can't fault you for that, though I am curious. I take it you'll need reinforcement around the joints then, assuming you'll need to keep those as flesh to move. That should be easy enough, if we're going full sleeves and pants. The teeth might be trickier, but I've already got an idea for the mask, if you need carbon. We'll set you up with a carbon filtration mask, I think, which will actually aim to draw in more carbon from the air, as well as having carbon charges you can use as needed."

"If you're thinking of doing charges rather than canisters, would it be possible to include oxygen ones as well? I was just thinking of fire victims, and how helpful it is to have fresh oxygen on hand. I'm fairly immune to smoke myself, only the heat is a problem."

"We should certainly check to see if carbon monoxide works with your mien then, because that would be just as valuable as the durability you gain. Someone able to go in and fix gas leaks without any fear? That's a valuable thing with so many cities struggling with archaic energy grids." The man wrote that down on his pad, nodding to himself. It was just a casual observation, but somehow it made Kirin's whole chest warm, thinking that even *if* he was terrible at all the other hero work, he could still help somehow. Speaking of archaic though—

"Is there a reason you're writing everything down on paper? Wouldn't it be faster to dictate it to the computer?"

"Security measure. We have some truly remarkable cyber security, but it's still harder to walk into this building than it would be to hack into the server. While I'll need to design some components of this suit digitally, that'll only be saved to my personal desktop, not the server, and only physical backups, nothing up in the cloud. If anyone wants to try to find out the miens of the incoming class, they would have to physically break into every office of every single person assigned to each of you. That's why they only ever give us one hero to work with at a time, all data wiped if they decide to go with someone else." It was impressive how he could write and speak at the same time.

"Is that really a risk? Someone trying to break into the system?"

"Oh, absolutely. On the more innocent side, it's those reporters you'll see flocking the school constantly. At worst, it's some villain who got it into their mind that they can take down someone just by knowing their mien." The scientist finally put down his notes, shooing Kirin over to the scanner in the corner of the room. It booted up instantly as he stepped on, a miniature 3D version of himself appearing almost immediately above the scanner's controls.

"Can they? Take people down just by knowing their miens, I mean." Kirin tore his eyes away from his own tiny face and looked at the man. He looked so young, with an almost gleeful expression on his face as he watched the readings come in.

"With the numbers I'm seeing, I'd be surprised if *anything* could take you down. You're built like a tank!"

"Thanks?"

"Do you have a color preference? Fabric?" The scan seemed to be complete, or at least the light beneath Kirin's feet shut off. The man was already moving again, pulling a file off his desk.

"I don't particularly, no." Ifrit's face flashed across his mind. "Not black."

"They don't let anyone do black, too villain-esque."

"Hm."

"I'm sure the marketing team will pick a color scheme eventually, so for now I'll leave it just as the color of the material. If you have any strong feelings later on, we can certainly change it." The man looked at the scan one last time and frowned. "I know about the hand and the surgery, but do you need any protection on your back and shoulders?"

"Ah, no."

"Then why—"

"From when I was much younger. Is that all?" Kirin was suddenly very eager to leave.

"If you have any weaknesses, you need to tell me. The whole point of this is to compensate for any areas of concern, but I can't do that unless you tell me what those are."

"I understand that, and I appreciate it. But that's not a weakness, just a mistake. And one I won't make again." Kirin flashed a smile that was still hidden by cloth. "So long as you get me carbon, I'll be indestructible."

The scientist seemed unconvinced, his lips pursed. But, mercifully, he let it drop.

"I'll need you back for a fitting in a few weeks. And if I discover anything from scanning the sample you gave me, I'll let you know that too." He hesitated for a moment and then held out his hand, which Kirin shook. "I look forward to working with you."

"I'm very excited to be working with you too. And I can call you..."

"Oh! Sorry, got over excited, how foolish. It's Nwabudike." He looked like he was on the verge of saying more when Kirin cut him off.

"Pleasure to meet you!" With a wave, Kirin walked out the door, inhaling sharply once it closed behind him. His shoulders sagged slightly before he realized he wasn't alone.

"Ah, just finished?" He hoped his voice didn't sound as shaken as he felt. Ifrit was staring at him from down the hall, leaning against the wall, his brow furrowed. Instead of a response, he turned on his heel and headed toward the elevator, pressing the button instead of calling out the floor. Kirin followed him in, wondering if he'd been waiting. It certainly didn't seem like he'd just finished.

"Kind of exciting, huh? I didn't think we'd be doing this stuff for a while, especially considering we'll have physical training and might learn new things about our own abilities. Wonder why they want us to check in now." He felt like he was searching for something to fill the silence, as Ifrit obviously wouldn't. "Also, it's kind of strange how not the entire class is here, isn't it? There's a good number of us, but not everyone. I was trying to figure out why on the way over."

"It's the people who have longer lead times." Kirin was surprised to hear that Ifrit's voice almost sounded calm. "Whose costume'll take longer to complete."

"Oh. Oh, yeah, that makes a lot of sense!" The doors slid open before Kirin could try to puzzle out why Ifrit had suddenly changed his entire personality. The crease between his eyes was gone, the fire around his throat swayed almost lazily, and his eyes looked peaceful. However, when Kirin, still wrapped in his own thoughts, failed to move—

"Are you fucking coming, dumbass?" The furrow was back, as was the attitude.

"Yeah, sorry!" Kirin hurried after him, shaking his head. There'd been a moment there, just a flicker, where some dim memory tried to break forth, but as the elevator doors closed, it was gone.

4

Settling

THE REST OF THE week passed without incident, and Kirin settled into a routine, almost. In the morning, he sat with Phoenix, though this was less of a choice and more of a kidnapping. Other hero classes were still trickling in, and Phoenix had taken to staking out the gym, with however many of their classmates they could scrounge. They'd started bringing other things to do, since these hero students faced the same test they had, and arrived in unpredictable waves, sometimes hours apart. Over the course of the week, Kirin watched Lilin knit no fewer than three scarves, Aïcha finish no fewer than fifteen books, and Wyrm finish enough paintings to give every person in their class one for their dorm rooms. Kirin considered bringing his guitar, but he never could get himself to, instead opting to leave after an hour or so to go get food. The timing worked out just right that he'd get back to the dorm to see Ifrit finishing cleaning the kitchen, the smell of spices heavy in the air, and though Kirin attempted to speak to him every time, Ifrit only ever responded by disappearing back into his room and slamming the door.

That left the rest of Kirin's day free, which usually meant combing through his textbooks and trying to get a head start on his notes. The font in them was so tiny it made his head swim, and he was glad of the free time now to try to stay afloat once classes started in earnest.

Whenever his headache got too great, he'd find himself outside, exploring campus. If he went past the barrier separating the dorms from the tech side, he needed to wear a mask, so he'd spent the first few days only in the space the dorms carved out between shields, happily succeeding in finding some hidden spots that didn't appear to be claimed by anyone yet. However, it only took so long to explore every inch he could, so later in the week he found his footsteps straying through the shields.

The whole campus was sectioned in three, technically, one portion for the tech department, a middle slice for the dorms themselves, and the final and farthest back section for the hero course. The dorm he was in was right on the edge of the hero portion, closest to the wall as well. His balcony faced toward the park, just peeking over the metal barrier, which was much nicer than staring at the blurred-out shield. That would feel too much like a cage. It was bad enough that they had to wear masks if they were outside the dorm or hero section, making Kirin feel like he was being watched whenever he was outside.

There wasn't much to explore in the dorms, as his key card only allowed entry to his own. There was the garden, directly in the middle, but that was always full of people, almost every single bench occupied. He'd yet to find a spot where there wasn't *someone* within hearing range, if not within sight entirely. The same was true in the main cafeteria building, which seemed more fit for a shopping mall than a college.

Dozens of different stations filled the inside, with every type of cuisine imaginable. The building was four stories tall, with the capacity to seat nearly ten thousand, though Kirin had no idea how many students there actually were. Despite never being close to reaching max capacity, Kirin had yet to find a time when it wasn't exceedingly loud inside, voices filling the open space to make the crowd seem greater than it was. Since they had to have their faces covered in common areas, he'd expected to not be allowed inside, but there was a small cordoned off hero dining area. He'd gone in there once, on the first full day, and been met with a bunch of cold stares from Majesty's class. He hadn't been back since.

The tech section was another beast entirely, being the closest to the public sphere. Classes hadn't started, but there was already a near constant stream of people that would be coming and going in the afternoons. Some would be outside researchers commuting in, but most would be students and staff, as well as the exceedingly wealthy clients that could afford to have a licensed East Tech technician fix their tech woes. Even amid the crowd, Kirin sometimes thought he could spot the prospective hero students making their way to the farthest reaches of campus. If he found her, he'd ask Ness if his suspicions were correct, and he was right more often than not.

He never stayed long in the tech area, always feeling like the mask on his face painted a target on his back. He wasn't the only person with their face covered— a mix of surgical masks, veils, and high fashion headwear kept people from being easily recognized— but he still felt like it marked him as a potential hero student too easily. The reporters which had been absent the first few days were now out in force, kept just outside the gate, though they were persistent in bothering anyone exiting if they'd seen any would-be heroes. He walked through as long as he dared, yet by the end of the day he always found himself in the hero section.

There were plenty of students and staff milling about, but the relative quiet was reassuring. There was the power gym, of course, and every so often he could hear the sounds of combat from within. The one time he'd tried to enter he'd found his ID wasn't authorized to do so, and it was the same for the building he was most excited for: the Disaster Simulator.

From his schedule, he knew it was where they'd be conducting Rescue Operations, the only combat class on his docket for the first semester. Mien Practice was to be supervised— heavily, he'd been told— so it was understandable that the gym was locked up tight, but he'd hoped to sneak a peek at the DS. Up close, it looked even larger, taking up the entire length of the hero section. Tall as his dorm, and yet it looked entirely unassuming, a monumental block of concrete that might as well have been pulled straight out of the ground. The entrance looked laughably tiny in comparison to the larger mass, which had no windows decorating the façade.

The other buildings almost felt like they were the odd ones, white ceramic panels, glass, and steel. As far as he could tell, these were professor offices and debriefing rooms, since none looked large enough for a lecture hall. On his schedule, all the lecture classes were even in the tech section, only practicals on this side of campus. Whatever they might be, the smaller buildings were locked just as tightly as the rest, with his ID only accessing the regular gym near the edge of the residential section. He only ever saw his own classmates there, and a few other students who he suspected were fellow first years. Happily, he didn't recognize any from Majesty's group, which hopefully meant he didn't need to start tagging along every time Ifrit went to work out.

Kirin had begun taking longer and longer to wander around the campus, because at the end of the day Phoenix would be back in the dorm and dragging him into some level of chaos. That night, the last night before classes, it seemed like it'd end poorly. Because, somehow, Phoenix had convinced Ifrit to join.

His immediate impression that it'd be tiring to try and make friends was both accurate and not. No one knew each other, and the things that he'd always had to skirt around in conversations were off limits anyways. There could be no discussion of where they lived, or what they'd done outside of school, or how many siblings they had, or what their parents did; all the questions Kirin didn't want to answer were never broached, all the things he wanted buried firmly locked away by a simple signature on a line. While it was a benefit to him, a lot of conversations died off fully before someone could think of a new safe topic to pick up.

Yet despite it all, they got along shockingly well. The silences never felt awkward because they were understandable, a fact Kirin still found surprising. And even if he ducked out when everyone else was still hanging out, no one seemed to mind much at all, and still greeted him just as warmly the next day.

That night, he found himself wedged between his two floor mates, Phoenix talking animatedly while Ifrit had his arms crossed over his chest, glaring at anyone who dared make eye contact. Lilin was having an in-depth discussion with Antaeus about what the best type of tea was, of all things, when everything went to shit.

"Wow, they really do let anyone in here." A mocking voice called from the doorway, startling Wyrm, who'd just walked in. Half the room hadn't even noticed the new arrival, too caught up in their own conversations, but Ifrit sat up stiffly, the only time he'd moved since he'd sat down.

"Sorry, are you supposed to be in here?" Wyrm had only just taken out his headphones, clearly not having heard what was said.

"Just having a look around." The intruder wasn't alone, three others waiting in the doorway behind her. She was tall, lean, and everything a hero should look like. The only thing that didn't quite match was the coldness in her blue eyes, even when she smiled. Ifrit was on his feet before Kirin could stop him, hackles raised.

"You got something to say, *Bia*?" Ifrit had a muscle twitching along his jaw, eyes narrowed. Kirin stood up slowly, not wanting to startle the other man, who seemed to barely be holding himself back. The room around them had gone quiet, tense.

"And what is the world coming to? A whole class filled with monsters." The woman— Bia, apparently— clicked her tongue in disappointment. The people behind her laughed, one of them openly staring at Wyrm, who looked away, his face burning.

"Please, you're just fucking upset that you're not even close to being the strongest student this year." Ifrit sounded almost... relaxed. Like this was something he'd expected, and now that it was happening some of the anxiety faded. "Jealousy isn't a fucking good look for a *hero*."

Kirin didn't see her move, but Wyrm was suddenly flying at the wall, Ifrit blasting forward. The whole class was on their feet, but few moved forward, unsure of how to help without being in the way now that Ifrit was in the midst of their attackers. There were only four interlopers, but they'd been prepared to fight.

In the split second that Kirin hesitated, Ifrit had grabbed Bia by her midriff and thrown her over his head, back towards the door. Kirin ran and caught Wyrm, hardening his chest; none of the spikes penetrated his flesh, but they did rip open the front of his shirt. Phoenix was on their feet, having vaulted over the back of the couch, heading for the door, a knife in their hands appearing out of nowhere. But it was Dulu who made it to Ifrit first.

The other three people had just entered when Kirin's ears popped, the front half of the room suddenly filled with enormous, snow-white wings. They stretched a good five meters in each direction, effectively hiding Majesty's students from view entirely.

"Let's think about this." That was all Dulu managed to say before the wings were forced to curl around him and Ifrit as a barrage of ice flew at the pair. It looked to be coming from the man on the left, his fingertips covered in frost. A stream of smoke appeared behind him, converging into the short-haired woman with almond eyes— Enenra. She struck the man hard enough in the back of the head that he fell to his knees, her whole head fuzzing back out into air as the woman behind him attempted to hit back, passing harmlessly through.

Perhaps it was good that her ears weren't solid, because a second later Dulu and Ifrit were collapsed on the floor, covering theirs, but that lasted only a moment when Clidna opened her mouth and *screamed*, the glasses on the table shattering as she countered whatever attack was making Ifrit rip out his hearing aids, blood spraying as he tossed them away. He was up a moment later, Dulu still dazed.

It was Kirin's turn to take up position next to Ifrit, the tears in his shirt not large enough to give anyone a clear view as he crystallized his whole chest. The ice man was back on his feet, but his attack bounced off Kirin harmlessly, as he held his hands up placatingly. It didn't seem to stop the onslaught, just focused it on him enough that Phoenix was able to grab Dulu and Ifrit, pulling them a few meters back. One more second and everything... stopped.

"There you are." The words weren't meant for Kirin, but Phoenix. They were crouched, one hand on Dulu's shoulder and the other on Ifrit's. For once there was no smile on their face, only rage. "We heard there was a healer in this little reject group."

Phoenix didn't respond, but stood, warily. Kirin's eyes flickered to Ifrit; Kirin had assumed they were coming to pick a fight with him, specifically, but Ifrit looked unsurprised that wasn't the case.

"Did you just come to confirm that? There are easier ways, like me breaking your nose and then fixing it so I can do it all over again." The knife that Kirin had seen Phoenix with earlier had vanished, but he had a nagging suspicion it wasn't far out of their reach.

"We came to recruit." Bia seemed unconcerned about Phoenix's rebuke. "You're wasted here, and healers are always useful."

Kirin didn't turn around, but he could feel the confused looks being traded behind him. He wasn't following what they were talking about, and he knew he wasn't the only one.

"'fraid you're gonna have to explain that a bit more." Phoenix moved so they were only a few steps behind Kirin.

"You can switch classes up until the semester officially starts. Didn't think there was anyone worth taking until now, other-wise we would have come sooner." Bia crossed her arms over her chest, looking at her watch. "We don't have all day. Are you coming?"

"Listen, maybe it's because you *are* as dumb as you look, but I'm going to spell something out for you nice and slow: if you wanna make friends with someone, this is *so* not the way to go about it." Phoenix nearly rolled their eyes out of their head. "Really? How'd you think this was going to go? You just roll in here, attack the *only* people I've been hanging around and think 'oh gee! They'll be *super* stoked to join us!' Like did you not workshop this plan or..."

Bia curled her lips in an open sneer.

"Do you not know how any of this works? Gods, this really is made up of fools and backwater hicks, isn't it?"

"Apparently. But I'll take that to a pretentious bitch like you any day." Phoenix stepped up, nose to nose with Bia now. Kirin saw something flicker in Bia's eyes and reacted just in time, practically throwing Phoenix behind himself. Somehow, he had the instinct to dig his heels in, which ended up being fortunate as the hit to his chest rattled the windows, but he didn't give a centimeter.

"I'm going to have to ask you to leave. Now." He spoke quietly, hoping not to betray the tremor in his voice. Rage was burning low and hot in his stomach, and if he had to fight, he was going to throw at least one of these people through the window.

Bia was looking at him with sudden interest, less concerned that her attack hadn't done a thing and more intrigued.

"I don't know you."

"And you're not going to."

"Oh please. All it takes is one of us saying you were the ones attacking, and you can all kiss this sad little pipe dream goodbye." The confidence in her voice brokered no doubt that she would lie. "I'm not leaving without a new healer on my team."

"It'd be tragic, then, if someone had a recording of how this all really went down then, wouldn't it?" Yantra had a holo screen circling her eye, the tell-tale red light blinking. "I do doubt you'll face any real consequences, but they can't do a damn thing if we've got proof we did nothing wrong. None of us attacked you with our miens, only defended, which— since we're on school grounds— we're allowed to do. You blatantly attacked. Shame we can't have socials. This would make a lovely insight into how this school is run, hm?"

Bia sighed, as if this was a minor inconvenience. She really didn't seem angry. Somehow that made Kirin even *more* incensed.

"Why do I even waste my time trying? Come on then, the garbage stays." And like this had all been a casual conversation, she turned and left. One of the three with her lingered back, the woman who had tried to hit Enenra, glancing toward their group like she was going to apologize. But instead, she turned on her heel and followed her classmates away.

Kirin put his arm out to stop Ifrit from following, though the angry part of his brain also wanted to go and demand a fight.

"Okay. I definitely hate them." Phoenix handed Ifrit his hearing aids, joining Kirin in staring at the retreating backs. At some point during the short fight, it'd started pouring rain. They then startled like they'd remembered something. "Oh shit, Wyrm, you good?"

"I feel like my ribcage is cracked." Wyrm hissed between his teeth as he tried to sit up. Kirin hadn't even noticed that he'd fallen to the floor. Phoenix offered a hand to help him up and Kirin opened his mouth to suggest that maybe it wasn't a good idea to move him just yet, but when their hands made contact, Wyrm gasped. He dropped Phoenix's grip and pressed both hands to his chest. "It's... fine?"

"I'm good at what I do." Phoenix did help him to his feet then, narrowly avoiding getting a bright orange spike to the face. "I just hope we don't need it all the time."

"They won't come back." Ifrit hadn't moved from the doorway, hands curling and uncurling as if he was still debating going after them. "Classes start tomorrow; they can't fucking do anything now."

"Why bother, though? I know healers are exceptionally rare, but it doesn't matter who's in what class, right?" Clidna was helping Dulu to his feet, his wings having vanished again.

"They just want to keep anything helpful for themselves." Ifrit nearly spat the words.

"I sure do love being talked about like a commodity." Phoenix said dryly.

"I think he's being serious." Kirin's voice was soft, his eyes following the ring of fire around Ifrit's neck.

Ifrit himself finally turned to face the group, silhouetted by his own flames against the thunderstorm outside.

"We're all tools now. That's what we signed up for." He raised his chin. "And it's best you don't fucking forget it."

5

Start

It was not a fortuitous start to the semester that Kirin nearly missed his first class.

It wasn't really his fault, honestly. After the assholes had unexpectedly swept in, caused chaos, and just as promptly left, everyone in the dorm was rightfully shaken up. Ifrit had made his dramatic pronouncement and then immediately fucked off, leaving them with more questions than answers. In some attempt to cheer the class back up, Yantra had made a poll titled "what's wrong with the rich bitches" in which everyone submitted an option. When he finally made it back to his room long after midnight, "daddy issues" was winning.

Going back to his dorm hadn't magically made his brain shut off unfortunately, and he'd stayed up for several more hours, staring at his ceiling and wondering why It would matter which class someone was in. Ifrit knew, of that he was sure, and Kirin just had to figure out how he could get the man to explain it to him.

Given how overly tired he'd been, Kirin had missed his first alarm. And the second. And the third. It was only after the fourth time it went off that he'd awoken, less to do with the alarm itself and more to do with Ifrit slamming his door open and yelling at him to turn it off. Even in his half-asleep state, Kirin hadn't failed to notice that Ifrit seemed to have just woken up too. They'd been almost in step together as they raced across campus silently, just making it in the door for their morning lecture before the clock turned. Kirin sighed when he saw his name light up green on the roster, moving to find a seat as the professor began to speak. He didn't appear to notice their almost late arrival, which was unsurprising, given the size of the room. A large semi-circle, the students were all seated in tiers, Kirin and Ifrit standing on the tallest level looking down at the professor who stood directly in the middle at a podium. A holo screen curved above his head, switching from the class list to an image of a hero in a bright blue suit, her familiar piercing gaze sweeping over the audience.

"Kirin!" Phoenix was whisper-yelling, waving him over to one of the few empty seats left along the back row. Most of their class was seated there, though Kirin thought he could spot Adlivun and Antaeus closer to the front, Goldhorn unmistak-able in the first row. Ifrit apparently planned to stand the whole class, already having flipped open a notebook and taken out a pen, but Kirin tugged on the sleeve of his sweatshirt and inclined his head toward the others. Ifrit looked annoyed, and a little surprised, but he followed when Kirin headed over.

"Thought you weren't going to make it." Yantra tilted her head back to see them, her black hair spilling over the chair and revealing an impressive number of piercings and a scar that went straight back from just above her ear. "If you're going to sleep in, pass one of us your phone, that's how they do attendance, apparently."

Kirin just nodded and sat down, getting out his own note-book. Out of the corner of his eye, he saw Ifrit hesitate before taking the seat next to him.

"...now how long ago did the first heroes appear?" If Professor Kushim expected a response, he certainly didn't wait for one. "It was over fifty years ago, following the AI collapse. Now, I assume everyone in the room is familiar with the prevalent conspiracy theory that one was the result of the other, but I will remind you that there is no logical way a computer program could have altered the genetics of humans worldwide, especially once the world went dark. There is already plenty of speculation on what could have caused such a leap in evolution, indeed and such a random one too, but this class is the *History* of Heroics, and not the *Theory* of Mien Origins, so we will be putting any discussions of that to rest now.

"The first decade after the appearance of superhuman abilities was, understandably, chaotic." The image on the screen behind the professor changed, showing the desolation of what used to be the United States of America, now the First Nations. "Without regulation, free usage of these unknown powers caused the collapse of many countries, and rocked the world to its core, so soon after the ability to freely share information was sabotaged. There are records demonstrating that many countries thought this was a problem unique to *their* region, due to the simple fact that they had no evidence to the contrary."

"*Problem.*" Naddāha scoffed at the word quietly, Kirin only hearing because she was sitting directly in front of him.

"According to the overwhelming amount of data, we can say that miens appeared in all areas of the world almost near simultaneously, which has impeded efforts to find an inciting incident.

"Immediately, there were calls to study the abilities that appeared, but louder still were the cries against the use of human experimentation, even for observation. Those with miens were understandably reluctant to reveal their abilities for fear of being taken and used in inhumane 'scientific studies'— we will cover these in more detail in chapter thirteen, especially the implanting of monitoring equipment in a number of young people without their or their parents knowledge or consent—which worsened the ability of all communities to understand the scope of what the world was to deal with. It wasn't until after an international treaty was signed by over 140 countries to completely eliminate and criminalize experimentation on or about any powered individual that we truly began to see the expression of miens flourish."

"I mean, not really." Ness shushed Yantra, who stuck her tongue out.

"Our earliest estimates put the occurrence rate of miens at approximately ten percent. For each decade that has passed since, it has increased ten percent more. Now, you should all note that it has increased ten percent *of ten percent* every decade, not an additional ten percent of the population have presented miens."

"Say ten percent more," Clidna muttered, adding to the freckles across her hands as she clicked her pen open and closed.

"Therefore, as of today, the official estimated mien population worldwide is sitting at just sixteen point one percent. We do assume that there are a number of people choosing to not report their abilities, as well as some who are simply unaware that they are powered. It is assumed that the true number is closer to twenty or twenty-five percent, but that is beside the point.

"What we will be investigating for the next few months is how the profession of heroics sprung up, what frameworks there are, and how the public perception of the term hero has changed in the past half-century. I'm sure you've all done the assigned reading that was supposed to be completed before today's class, so this should all be review, and yet I fear much of this will be new."

Kirin found his eyelids drooping as the professor continued to speak. It wasn't that he *wasn't* interested in the lecture, but he had indeed read the textbook, and this was covering the exact same information. Besides, even *before* doing the reading he'd known everything in the chapter. All that combined with his lack of sleep was proving to be a lethal combination. Before he could fully drop off, Ifrit kicked his shin.

"... the quiz." The professor was speaking, but Kirin was frowning at Ifrit. The other man wasn't even looking at him, instead hunched over his own notes, surprisingly focused. Kirin was actually a little worried he might be *too* focused, his necklace of fire sparking dangerously close to the sheets of paper. Not having the energy to argue, Kirin tried to pay attention to the lecture, but it wasn't long before the droning was starting to get to him again.

"...licensing. An imperfect solution, perhaps, but it was all the countries could agree on at the time. Mien usage was restricted to specially designated gyms, which were rated to withstand earthquakes and bombs, as well as on personal property, with restrictions." Professor Kushim cleared his throat, though Kirin wasn't sure why. His voice had remained the same monotone drone the entire lecture. It had to be some kind of talent, or maybe even a mien, to be able to speak so flatly without any inflection. That or simply a new form of torture, particularly when his lecture was at eight in the morning.

Kirin's eyes had hardly closed when he received another, more forceful, kick.

"...need to remember." If anyone else noticed Ifrit drilling Kirin in the knee, they weren't saying anything about it. On Kirin's left, Phoenix was fully passed out, snoring softly. Other members of their class were doing similarly poorly, and it wasn't just them either; the whole lecture hall was barely staying awake, with almost half of the heads in the crowd down on their desks.

Ifrit, however, was scribbling frantically, as if he could keep himself awake by writing down every single thing that the professor said. Kirin's own notes were pretty poor, considering how much of the lecture his brain had simply filtered out. He made a mental note to *always* make sure to get enough sleep before this class, or he'd flunk out before the second semester.

"If you told the politicians signing East Technical Institute's charter into law that fifty years later the system would still be in place, they would likely think you were lying. There was little to no confidence that all the countries of the world would stand by and watch mien users consolidate on one location, with only one licensure path, but yet here we are. Why has this exclusivity survived for so long? Especially after the creation of the other Cardinal Islands?

"Well, that is a simple answer. When there is only one track for heroes to come from, it is incredibly easy to confirm that licenses are valid and that your countries newest hired hero is up to standard. Should the dam break, should even one new school appear, dozens would, instantly, and it would take time to figure out which are good or not. Crime is up, everywhere, and it greatly helps response times for the police to know someone is a criminal by virtue of checking one database, instead of hundreds. This is why prohibitions on cybernetics have become locked in place, because it muddies the waters of enforcement."

It was lucky that Kirin wasn't actually taking notes, since he'd just crushed his pencil in his fist. He tried to focus on cleaning the dust off his notebook, but the professor's voice filtered in anyway.

"It is even more important for heroes to make these snap decisions, and mien restrictions serve to help a hero decide between an innocent and a villain in the heat of battle. A moment's hesitation could cause the loss of a civilian, or even a comrade. We can look at Force, as an example." The screen changed, showing her, though Kirin knew that costume by heart. Force wasn't large, but her presence was unmistakable. The photo the professor used was one of the more popular ones, where the hood to her bright blue jacket was down, her brown hair whipping out behind her. She hovered in the air, eyes focused on the camera. "Force has the lowest rate of civilian casualties out of any hero, currently active or retired, and that is most likely tied to the fact that she also has the highest kill rate of any hero."

There was another snap as a second writing instrument died, but this time it was Ifrit's pen that suffered. Black ink now stained his fingers, dripping slowly onto his notes. Kirin pulled some tissues out of his bag and offered them to Ifrit, who shot him a look that fell halfway between angry and confused. Once the worst of the ink was sopped up, Kirin swapped the now dirty cloth with a new pen, which Ifrit picked up delicately, like it might bite him.

"That leads us to our first homework assignment." Kirin nudged Phoenix awake, so at least he'd *hear* what they were assigned, though Kirin doubted he'd remember it. "By next class, write a two thousand word essay on the appearance of mien-users in society, and what factors led the international community to create East City, and by extension East Tech."

The whole class rose almost at once, all eager to get to the door. Despite having been seated in the backmost rows, their section was stuck for several minutes as people rushed by. Kirin checked his phone as they waited, shocked to see that their first class had lasted the entire class period. He must have been asleep for a lot longer than he'd thought. Ifrit had slipped out before the crush of people, so Kirin hadn't even been able to scold him. Though, maybe he'd just been kicking aimlessly in an attempt to stay awake and not even realized he'd been hitting Kirin...

"I know we're not supposed to record the lectures, but if they're all that boring I might just have to and watch it back on two times speed." Yantra yawned. "That was *rough*."

"We all have ethics next, yeah?" Phoenix peered over Yantra's shoulder to look at her schedule. "Boo, you're not in our seminar."

"I think we're all broken up." Ness appeared at Kirin's elbow, and it was only with conscious effort that he didn't start in surprise.

"Hm, who's got Wright?"

A few voices spoke up in agreement, but far fewer than Kirin had expected. It was in one of the tech buildings, so he should've expected that it wouldn't only be hero students, but he'd held out a little bit of hope that it might be. Wearing the face mask didn't bother him physically, but knowing he couldn't take it off made it feel suffocating. Particularly with so many people around.

"Looks like we're with you." Lilin's eyes creased at the corners as she looked up at Kirin. Enenra, the woman with cropped hair and almond eyes, Kuafu, with his hair half covering his face, and Goldhorn, with their hair pulled up and back so severely it seemed to be pulling their brows upward, were standing behind her, obviously waiting.

"Do any of you know the way? I meant to find my way through campus, but I mistakenly believed we were not to go to this section, and never explored here." Kuafu looked pained, like he was admitting to something horrible.

"I walked around, it's just a building over. We'll make it with plenty of time." Kirin shouldered his bag and started forward, since the tide of students had ebbed. The others followed him without comment, which felt shockingly quiet compared to the stream of chatter Phoenix always tried to keep going. In fact, they'd almost made it to their next class before anyone spoke up.

"If any one of those assholes from yesterday show up again, I might just hit them on sight." Goldhorn didn't sound angry, and that was more concerning, since they didn't sound like they were joking either.

"It would reflect poorly on the class to cause a scene." Kuafu, on the other hand, sounded upset.

"I agree they'd deserve it, but it'd still be bad if the school found out about the incident at all. We didn't instigate, and yet I don't doubt they'd find some way to make it our fault." Lilin opened the door to their classroom, ending the conversation there.

It was arranged in a rough U-shape, with two rows of desks that sat two each. Many of the chairs were occupied, with a few desks empty at the far side of the room. There were several people Kirin recognized from Majesty's class, but none of the four who'd attacked. He breathed out a tiny sigh of relief before it seized in his chest; if they weren't in this group, were they in the session with Phoenix? Or worse, Ifrit?

Lilin seemed to mirror his thoughts and frowned as they all sat, Goldhorn with Enenra, Lilin with Kirin, and Kuafu by himself.

"I'd almost rather that they were with us." She spoke softly, apparently not wanting the other tables to hear.

"Everyone knows not to make trouble, it'll be fine."

"You're sure of that?" She sounded skeptical and it almost made Kirin bristle in response, despite having the same thought only a moment before.

"Yes, we all know the consequences."

"Hm." There was a question behind her eyes, yet she just

pulled out a notebook instead. As confident as Kirin had sounded, he could feel the worry building as he realized it would be another two hours before he found out if anything *had* gone wrong. The professor entered, and he sighed to himself. At least the anxiety would keep him awake for this class.

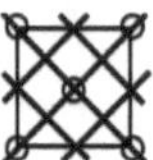

"It was like winning the world's worst lottery." Phoenix was complaining, loudly. The entire class, more or less, had met up for lunch, mostly because they had to. The hero dining area had been full, so they'd all slowly made their way back to the common area of the dorm, where they'd discovered which of their classmates had indeed ended up with the worst of Majesty's class.

"How'd our edgelord do with that?" Clidna asked so dryly it made Kirin choke on his food.

"Mm, if looks could kill, we'd all be giving statements right about now. But apart from muttering an impressive array of curse words for the entire length of class, he was fine." Phoenix waved his fork dismissively. "He's surprisingly studious. I'm really hoping he'll let me borrow his notes because I was *so* not paying attention."

"After all the effort to get here, you're not paying attention?" Adlivun was smiling to herself, as if there was some joke that everyone else was missing. Phoenix didn't have an immediate rebuttal to that, instead choosing to shovel food into his face. "Our professor was rather... unenthusiastic about his own subject though. I have to give credit to Ifrit for finding anything worth writing down from the lecture."

"It's a seminar, shouldn't it be a discussion?" Medusa asked from somewhere to Kirin's right. He was sitting at one end of a now very long table, since they'd pushed together all the available ones in the common area to have enough room for everyone to sit together.

"Did your section make it that far? Ours simply got lectured on what ethics *means*." Phoenix sighed. "We have to write on essay on that very topic, but the only thing that's coming to my mind right now is boredom."

"We just had a discussion about the same." Medusa smiled. "Though we also have to write an essay."

"I was really hoping that none of us would have those pricks, considering there have to be other times that class is offered. It's required for both hero and tech students, and there are—as far as I can tell— only three sections during that time slot." Yantra speared a potato with her fork like it'd personally offended her.

"If I had to guess, it's probably just hero students in our sections." Clidna looked up to a bunch of questioning eyes. "I mean, the professor said a *lot* of stuff, but it was all the 'responsibility of power' and 'understanding the ethical implications of the *entire* situation before taking action.' Nothing at all that would be applicable to developing tech. Would have expected *that* lecture to focus mostly on 'please don't create AI that wipes out our entire technological system again.'"

"To be fair, the tech companies specifically *don't* use AI." Yantra shrugged.

"You know what I mean. Something, something, technology should be used for the benefit of the people without doing harm, etc."

"If you're right, then there are a lot fewer hero classes than I thought there'd be." If Kirin's math was correct (which it very well might not have been), with thirty students per session that would mean there were only five other hero classes.

"Could just be that they're pushed back to one of the different semesters this year, but it's so hard to say when East Tech refuses to give any statistics on how many hero students it has at a time." Yantra talked with her hands a lot when she got annoyed. "I get the whole need for secrecy, but I think the most nerve-wracking part of waiting for acceptance was not even *knowing* what the chances were."

"I think it might be worse to know though, considering they *do* release how many applications they receive, and it's always well into the millions." Medusa had already finished eating but seemed content to sit and chat. She'd changed her blindfold today, and this one was patterned with oak leaves and ferns that complimented the chestnut color of her skin.

"I was convinced I wasn't going to get in regardless of numbers, pretty sure knowing the odds would have made me not bother applying at all." Kirin shrugged.

"Really?" Ness was sitting across the table from him, but he'd forgotten she was there. It was through a tremendous force of will that he didn't startle; Clidna and Phoenix, who were directly next to her, didn't manage to hide their surprise so well. "You seem the right type for it."

He wasn't sure what to say in response, though Antaeus spared him from having to find words.

"I agree with Kirin, I think I would've been scared off. I was really surprised to hear back at all; I'm still not sure I'm not dreaming!" Antaeus was directly to Kirin's right, made to seem even smaller by comparison. His curly hair only came up to about Kirin's shoulder when sitting, his elbow when standing.

"Oh, I feel that." Ness bumped her glass against his, sighing. "I had a brief glimmer of hope that maybe heroes weren't so homogenous as they seem, but seeing the other classes... I think we're the odd ones out."

"I mean, that was obvious, wasn't it?" Yantra tilted her head.

"The entire time the school's existed it spat out heroes that looked identical: tall, but not too tall, muscular, but never intimidating, powerful but visibly *human*. Like Force was barely taller than average, and she'd blend right in on the street. I've never even seen them turn out a hero who didn't have a so-called natural eye color, let alone any real physical difference."

"They all but vocally say anyone with a disability can't get in." Clidna spoke quietly, one hand absently touching her earplugs.

"I don't know if I expected it to be different here, but I did kind of hope, you know?" Kirin hadn't noticed the conversation ebbing, but it had quieted enough that Wyrm, who was sitting close to the center, had been able to overhear them. "If not open acceptance, just less fear. Guess we haven't quite proven ourselves to be the good guys yet, but still, the school at least thinks we could be."

"Wish we could shove it down those assholes' throats that us even *being* here means the school decided we're just as good as them." Clidna's voice was much firmer now.

"I'm sure we'll get a chance to." Kirin said, more confidently than he felt.

"And we'll blow them out of the water when we do." Phoenix smiled, showing his pointed teeth.

The more Kirin thought about it, the more he *wasn't* sure that would be the case. There was a schedule posted on the side of the power gym *and* the Disaster Simulator, showing when each class would be allowed in, and it looked like they'd only be going one at a time. Combat wasn't even on their schedule yet— though he knew there would be since he'd had to fill out a waiver for expressly that purpose— but he hadn't the slightest clue when. If Phoenix knew, he hadn't bothered to share that with Kirin, and the only other people who seemed to know anything about the school were Adlivun or...

"Pst, hey." Kirin tried to get Ifrit's attention, but the other man was pointedly ignoring him. "*Hey!*"

At the overdramatic whisper-yell, Ifrit gave him an eyeroll, which was at least an acknowledgement that he'd heard. That was more than Kirin had gotten in the last five minutes, so he counted it as a win. It seemed like this first anatomy lecture was going to be a syllabus class, so Kirin had taken to reading the textbook, but that had bored him after the first hour, and his mind had latched onto the lunchtime conversation instead.

"When do we start doing combat, do you know?" Kirin leaned closer to Ifrit, who gave him a vaguely disgusted look and leaned backwards.

"Why the fuck would I know?" Ifrit turned his eyes back to the lecturer, shoulders pulled up nearly to his ears.

"You seem to know a lot about this place. I don't really know why, and I don't really care, but I *am* curious why another class would be trying to steal one of our people."

Ifrit looked surprised for some reason, his usual frown absent for just a moment.

"No combat till the end of the first year." Ifrit had turned to face the front again, and barely moved his mouth as he spoke, making it feel like the words weren't coming from him. "Don't want anyone trying to fight each other when they don't fucking know how their miens work yet, right?"

"And the classes?" Kirin prompted. Ifrit shot him an angry look but continued.

"Think of it less like a class and more like a squadron, dumbass. Use your head. We're all stuck together, all the time, of fucking course we're going to know about each other's miens.

The fewer people who see us in action, the better. Might as well send us out together so shit can get done without worrying about who's looking."

Kirin leaned back in his own chair and thought about it for a minute.

"Having Phoenix, then, means we have a built-in safety net for all our live missions." He drummed his fingers on the table. "That is useful."

Ifrit only offered a grunt in return, standing up. Apparently, Professor Harvey could only stretch a two-page syllabus so far. Kirin had been impressed she'd managed to pull it for more than thirty minutes, let alone an hour and a half.

Ifrit seemed content to run out the door immediately, like he'd done in their earlier classes, but Kirin had prepared for that and had already swung his bag over his shoulder and matched pace, waving at their classmates as they passed. Not everyone was taking anatomy, which was the first time there was a difference in their schedules. And apparently, the only difference. Wyrm, Dulu, and Goldhorn had been sitting just a few rows behind Kirin and Ifrit and looked surprised to see them leaving together.

"Any chance we'd get to do joint training or something so I can actually kick one of them in the face?" Kirin asked.

Ifrit made a vague, choked sound, which concerned Kirin for a moment until he realized the man was trying not to laugh. Ifrit managed to contain all but the smallest of chuckles, which came out as a wheeze.

"Got it, comic violence is what it takes to make you laugh." Kirin nodded sagely as he tucked his hands into his pockets. "Can't fault you for that, it *is* a classic."

"I'm *not* laughing." Ifrit managed to get the angry crease in his forehead back with impressive speed. "I just... didn't expect that from you."

"Hard to expect something if you don't know someone, isn't it?"

"You're in a hero program. Aren't you supposed to be a fucking saint or something?"

"You're also in the hero program."

"I'm... an exception." Ifrit looked even more annoyed to admit it.

"I don't think that's true."

The whole time they'd been talking, Ifrit had pointedly not been looking in Kirin's direction. At that, however, he fully started staring, the lines in his brow softening to allow confusion to flood his eyes.

"They did make us all do a whole psychiatric exam before letting us enter. I don't think you're a bad person. Maybe just a little rough around the edges."

"A little?" Ifrit said dryly.

"Just a little." Kirin smiled, though Ifrit wouldn't be able to see it behind his mask. They were rapidly approaching the barrier between the tech sector and the dorms, most of their classmates far behind.

"Then you're even dumber than you look." Ifrit started walking faster, as if he could lose Kirin that easily.

"What can I say, intellect isn't my strong suit." He threw an arm around the shorter man's shoulders, cheering internally when Ifrit seemed too shocked to throw him off immediately. Maybe it was just that, or maybe there was nothing more to say, but the rest of their walk back to the dorm was silent.

6

Practice

KIRIN MANAGED TO WAKE up for his alarm on the second day of classes, or rather before it. Mondays would be a relatively boring slog, all lectures and general education requirements, but Tuesdays he'd been looking forward to. Because on Tuesdays, hero training would truly begin.

Ifrit and Phoenix appeared to share his feelings, as the three of them exited their rooms at the same time, though Phoenix was bleary-eyed and pulling himself to the coffeemaker with some urgency. None of them spoke at all, each wrapped in their own thoughts until it was time to head out. Newly caffeinated, Phoenix was practically vibrating with excitement, and while Kirin wasn't quite as hyperactive, he certainly felt the same. Ifrit had even abandoned his trademark scowl for an expectant smile, though it felt more like a smirk.

Their IDs hadn't been working the day before to get them into the Disaster Simulator, but when Yantra tried hers, the doors popped open, and the entire class rushed in to get a glimpse.

Kirin knew he was in a building, but it looked like he was instead in a walled off section of the city, with bright blue sky sparkling overhead. Mock buildings filled out fake city blocks, six stories tall, some of brick and mortar, some of steel and glass, all laid out in neat rows. If he squinted, he could see the too-sharp edges, the way materials met, proving that this was printed material, not real construction. As he walked through the door, he could see coiled hoses with adaptable nozzles overhead, which could reconfigure the space into whatever it needed to be.

"Hurry in, don't stand there gawking." Their professor was waiting down at the "street" level, a good several meters below the entry door. A raised platform ran all the way around the perimeter of the building, or it seemed to, as it vanished behind the constructed neighborhood. Yantra headed down first, the rest of the class quick to follow, but Kirin hesitated at the top of the stairs.

"This is..." Ness trailed off, just to Kirin's left.

"Intense." He finished. She gave him a relieved look, the two of them alone at the entrance for a moment. Kirin had walked next to Ifrit the whole way there, but he'd surged ahead with the rest of the crowd, now waiting in front of the professor. When Kirin's eyes found him, he absently noted that Ifrit *could* in fact smile. It was only brief, a flicker of joy as Ifrit looked out at the mock city, and then Ifrit's eyes were drawn to Kirin, and the smile slid away.

"Yes, yes, it's all very impressive. You'll have to adapt quickly to new environments, no matter how wondrous they might seem, so focus on taking in the important information first." If the schedule hadn't shown her name clearly, Kirin wouldn't have recognized Phantasm. She wasn't in her typical black and white uniform, dressed instead like she was about to head to a business meeting. After seeing Majesty in her full costume, it was jarring to see Phantasm without her face covered, and she was younger than he would have expected from photos. It *was* somewhat surprising that she was here, though, unless Kirin's theories about her mien not only creating faceless shadowy phantoms but *also* copies of herself were true. Majesty had almost made sense to see at the school, since she'd been out of public eye for years, but Phantasm was— as far as he knew— still very much active. "Since you're all here early, we may as well not waste a moment. Do you all know your rank?"

There were noises of assent from the group; they'd woken up the first morning of classes to a screen outside the training room displaying the current class rankings. Clicking on a name would bring up more information on what assessments had been performed and how everyone had scored. So far, there was only one assignment, which was simply labelled "arrival," and Kirin had figured out from his own rank that it was simply the order in which they'd arrived on campus. Naturally, that meant the person in first was—

"Does that mean I go first?" Ifrit strode forward, his eyes flashing. The momentary grin was gone entirely now, though his usual scowl hadn't replaced it. He looked shockingly calm, the most relaxed Kirin had ever seen him, his eyes scanning the scene in front of him.

"Not quite." Phantasm smiled, bright teeth against dark skin. "Top five, come forward."

Kirin stepped forward; Ness right next to him. They were third and second, respectively, Yantra next at fourth. Coming in fifth was Adlivun, her long hair pulled up into a bun for training. She seemed on edge, which was understandable. Kirin couldn't say he was calm either, but he was mostly *excited*.

"Today, you five will be destroying as much of this built environment as you can." Phantasm waved behind herself. "You'll have only ten minutes; feel free to work together or try to go off on your own. I'll give the five of you five minutes to discuss a strategy, and then a buzzer will sound. The rest of the class will be waiting along the rim. There's a barrier that prevents any debris from falling along the walkway, so you needn't be concerned about hurting anyone. This 'town' is completely empty as well."

Before Kirin could ask any questions, she was shepherding everyone else up and away, and a large countdown clock appeared in the sky overhead.

"I'm not good with destruction, I can tell you that right now." Ness shook her head. "I won't be much help here."

"A good plan would be to scout out the area and see if there are any weaknesses we can exploit, any water mains or pressured piping that we can disrupt to create widespread damage quickly." Yantra was scanning the buildings behind them. "I can say right now there's electricity, but I don't know about other utilities."

"There's running water." Adlivun said. She hadn't bothered to look at the buildings, leaving Kirin to wonder how she knew. "I can't say how it's supplied, but it's there."

"Kirin, do you have any ability to gather information or are we leaving it to me?" Yantra asked.

"I can bulldoze but that's about it. If you give me any structural weak points that'd be great."

"I can do that."

"And you? Is there anything you can do to assist?" Adlivun directed her question to Ifrit, who'd been standing with his back to the group, facing the false city.

"You assholes don't have to do anything." He didn't turn around. "Just stay out of my fucking way."

The buzzer sounded before Kirin had a chance to respond. A large explosion shot Ifrit into the sky, a continual stream of fire trailing after him as he landed in the furthest reaches of the simulation, another large explosion leveling the buildings around him.

Kirin's attention was brought back to his immediate surroundings as wires shattered the window in front of his face, shooting towards Yantra who looked thoroughly unconcerned. They began winding around themselves, weaving a pattern that he couldn't follow until a giant snake formed, his height or maybe even taller.

If he thought that was going to be the most disturbing part of this exercise, he was wrong. Next to Yantra's robot was yet another writhing shape, three meters tall and made of what could only be described as thickened air. Or maybe *viscous* air was a better way to put it, as it seemed like water sloshing up the sides of a container, but *wrong* somehow. The air around the now solidly human shape chilled, and though it had no face, Kirin felt that if it looked him in the eye he would drop dead on the spot.

"I'll go right. You three go left." Adlivun's eyes, usually the color of tilled soil, were now milky white. She seemed to be able to see despite her pupils and irises having vanished, or maybe the *thing* with her was seeing for her. When the creature formed a fist and slammed into the side of a building hard enough to make bricks rain from the rooftop, Kirin flinched despite himself.

"Kirin, there are steel posts in the corner of each building that seem to hold most of the structure. They look pretty sturdy—"

"I got it. I'll head straight. You two take left." Some of Kirin's eagerness returned and he took a deep breath in. Knowing that training began today, he'd been storing, and had plenty of carbon reserves. He let the transformation wash over him, everything but his joints and face turning to crystal. His hair stiffened around him, sharpening itself into points and he forced himself to hold his breath even as he broke into a run. Dislodging those posts wouldn't be easy, but if he took out at least two he could bring a whole house down.

Maybe he'd underestimated his own strength, or overestimated the sturdiness of the columns, but when he ran into the first, his arm sheared clean through, the floors above groaning. He heard glass shatter and his run turned into a sprint as he grabbed a chunk out of the second column, crashing through the window on the other side and rolling clear of the building just in time. The steel twisted in upon itself and screeched as it collapsed, the building tilting forward and across the street into the next structure.

He swapped sides of the street, ducking through the narrow alley between to tear out the rear posts of that house, it toppling and taking out one, two more. A hydrant was sitting innocently next to a lamppost; a quick kick shattered the enclosure and water fountained high, flooding the street, seconds before he sent the lamppost down into it. He punched a hand through the post and ripped out the wires, tossing them into the puddle he'd made. The electricity flowed through the water quickly and set one of the buildings still standing ablaze.

Kirin felt himself smiling. Oh, this was going to be *fun*.

It was eight minutes in when he crashed into Ifrit. Or, more accurately, when Ifrit crashed a building into him.

Kirin hardly had time to register the smattering of bricks that were coming, hardening his face to shield his nose from breaking. That was quickly the least of his concerns, as an entire wall was ominously leaning his way, almost perfectly centered on where he stood. Ifrit saw him far too late, his eyes widening as the collapsing façade allowed them to see each other, but that didn't stop him from trying to dart around and shove Kirin to safety.

Ifrit had just reached him as the first impact hit Kirin's back, hand outstretched. Instead of letting himself be moved, Kirin grabbed Ifrit by the wrist, releasing his mien on his chest and arms, and pulled the smaller man in, covering Ifrit's head with his own. He was running low on carbon now, particularly after his run there, but he found that extra from somewhere, holding on long enough to keep them both safe until the last brick clattered off his hair.

"Sorry, didn't mean to get in your way!" Kirin said sheepishly as his muscles returned to normal. "Got too trigger happy, I suppose, and didn't notice the explosions ahead."

Ifrit didn't say anything, just threw Kirin off of him and took a few steps back. He was breathing heavily, covered in dust from his own progression through the buildings. Kirin's eyes flickered to the timer above and saw that they only had a few seconds left, not enough time to do much else. Feeling rather awkward, he rocked on his heels until the buzzer sounded.

"Let's head back to the start, yeah? I've left us an obvious trail to follow." He offered Ifrit a smile, trying to appear much more relaxed than he felt. He really hadn't *meant* to get in the way, but sounds didn't travel well when he had a giant rock around his ears.

Ifrit still didn't respond, though he did start heading back towards the entrance without turning around. Kirin's heart sank as he looked at the man's retreating back, but as he started to follow, he realized just how *much* damage he'd done, and his mood lifted just a hair.

Ifrit had leveled almost the entire rear section on his own, razed so completely that Kirin could see the back wall clearly at eye level, the rubble so fine it looked like the ground was covered in gravel. While the destruction Kirin had wrought was not nearly so complete, he'd created a large swath of precariously tilting— or outright fallen— buildings, sparking wires, and flooded streets. The path back to the entrance was clearly marked by his passage, and he followed Ifrit back with a slight smile on his face. He'd done better than he'd hoped to, but *damn* if the angry man wasn't incredibly impressive. Maybe a month ago that would have felt daunting, but right then Kirin could only think about the fact that he'd fought that same man to a draw.

Phantasm was waiting for them with the rest of the class. The screens showed camera footage of the arena, painting a clear picture of who'd been most successful. Adlivun looked to have made the most progress after Kirin, with Ness and Yantra having ruptured what looked like the water main along at least three blocks. All three had made it back first, and Kirin was incredibly glad to see that Adlivun's creature had vanished again.

"Wonderful job you five, we can start the lesson proper now." Phantasm clapped her hands and walked into the newly destroyed town, turning to face their class. "This class is a practical, where we will focus on physical skills, abilities, and decision making. Today, we're starting with what will likely become the most familiar environment to you all: a destroyed residential area. Unfortunately, most villain attacks do occur in mixed-use residential areas, with shops below and apartments above. The typical situation is that a low-level criminal got desperate— or dumb— enough to use their mien for a small robbery, and things escalated. Why do you think that might be?"

There was silence for a moment as people considered.

"They didn't realize the extent of their abilities." Dulu had his wings out already, curled around himself, but as he spoke one twitched slightly.

"That is correct. Villains are often lower-class citizens who've fallen on hard times and are reacting as they feel there is nothing else they *can* do. More often than not, these will be people who have never been able to afford to go to a power gym, and certainly they do not own their own property. It very well might be the second or third time they've ever used their mien in their entire lives. It's much, much rarer to find a villain who has experience with their own abilities than one who does not.

"That's not to say they're not dangerous, however. If any-thing, they are *more* dangerous. An enemy who does not know what they are going to do next is impossible to predict. These villains have the benefit of inscrutability since even *they* don't know how they'll react." Phantasm's shades began to form behind her, just shadows really, made out of living darkness. Out of the corner of his eye, Kirin saw Adlivun stiffen. "This is not, as you will see, a combat class. All we care about for this semester in regards to low-level villains is the sheer amount of destruction they can cause, and what that means for our job."

The shades slipped away, farther into the town and out of sight.

"A good portion of your fieldwork will ultimately be search and rescue. For these low-level 'common' villains, a single hero is often more than enough to subdue them, so the rest of the heroes will be searching for survivors. That's what we'll be doing today." Phantasm waved a hand and another shade appeared, which turned immediately and phased through the rubble blocking entry to the closest building. "I'll now ask for a volunteer to go retrieve that shade."

A few hands went up hesitantly, but Kuafu's hand shot up straightest and highest.

"Ah, perfect." Phantasm motioned him forward, gesturing at the building. It was four stories tall, with the first floor entire-ly cut off by the collapsed concrete. Kuafu stepped forward, hands heating, then paused.

"Is there a problem?"

"I'm not sure how the building is still standing when there

appears to be significant structural damage. If I force my way through, I'm concerned it will collapse." Kuafu was scrutinizing the destruction, as if it would tell him which pieces were safe to pull.

"Wonderful! That's what I was hoping you'd realize." Phantasm clapped her hands again. "There's a general misconception that most of our work is brute force, violence without thought or discretion. In actuality, as the first responders on the scene, we must assess the situation, adapt to the environment, and create a planned response. Heroes typically have the highest authority in an emergency, so many will be looking to you to dictate what is to be done."

The class nodded, but several among their number looked uncomfortable with the notion. Wyrm, in particular, had his lips pressed into a thin line.

"We'll have you break into teams of three, each tasked with retrieving one 'civilian.' Once you've removed them from immediate danger, they'll dissipate, and you may meet back here. For this first class you may ask me any questions you like, but after today, you'll be on your own. Experience will be your best teacher in these situations, and you'll be far less likely to repeat a mistake if you see the consequences of it firsthand." She looked around the class, and when no one had any questions, she pulled up a chart on her phone, organizing them into six teams. "Find your teammates and then head in the direction indicated on your phones. You're free to begin once you arrive at your respective locations."

Kirin's teammates found him first, since he'd still been trying to find his name on the list. He'd been paired with Naddāha and Antaeus, the three of them walking off in relative silence, rubble crunching quietly underfoot. They were headed into the section that Adlivun had destroyed, and Kirin felt the hair on the back of his neck stand up as he thought of the *thing* that had caused the destruction. It didn't help that they were very much alone, having long since lost sight of any of the other teams.

"I suppose we should come up with a plan?" Antaeus spoke up hesitantly. His curly hair was pushed out of his face with a brightly colored headband, which seemed so out of place in the eerily quiet and desolate town.

"My mien isn't terribly helpful for this type of thing, so I'll be relying on you two. If it was a real civilian, maybe, but this isn't my forte." Naddāha shook her head, her dark hair swinging as a curtain around her face. She was even shorter than Antaeus, which meant Kirin towered over the pair. "I can hazard a guess as to what Kirin can do, but it's hard to know what we *should* do if I don't know what we *can* do."

"Guessing just based on the make-up of the other teams; you don't get any larger." Kirin said to Antaeus slowly, trying to form a plan in his head. The small man didn't respond, instead walking slightly off the path to a large chunk of concrete.

"I'm not allowed to say, but I can *show*, since you'll see any-ways." He explained, touching fingers to the stone. Immediate-ly, it rapidly shrunk in size, from near a meter across, to just a few centimeters siting in the palm of his hand.

"Can you do that to yourself?" Naddāha asked. Antaeus's eyes flickered to their surroundings, as if checking for cameras.

"No." He answered, slowly.

"Can you do that to someone else?" A plan was forming in Kirin's head, or the outline of one, anyway.

"Yes."

"That'll be our key. If Naddāha's okay with it, we could have her head inside and see what the conditions are. If we're feeling really confident, she can stay there and monitor how it's look-ing, but that's an unnecessary risk, in my opinion. Antaeus, you can start shrinking the rubble trapping the civilian, and I'll serve as a physical jack post to hold up the structure while you create a large enough opening. Then Naddāha can pull the civilian out." He looked up, both to get his companions' reactions, and because his phone had stopped directing them, meaning they'd arrived at their rescue. The remains of a building stood in front of them, the first floor made entirely impassable because a neighboring building had fallen directly in front of it.

"That sounds reasonable." Naddāha looked to Antaeus to confirm, and he nodded. She then turned back to Kirin. "Are you sure you can hold the up the whole thing? And how will you get out once we're done?"

"I can hold it." On that, he was confident. "Once everyone's out, we can prop up the opening with rubble or other things nearby and I can just slide right out."

"How long can you hold up an entire *building*?" Antaeus looked a little concerned at the idea.

"As long as we need me to."

Kirin was suddenly incredibly grateful for the long lunch break that was built into their schedules. It had taken a *long* shower to get all the dust out of his hair, and his shoulders were still stiff from a house bearing down on him. The class period hadn't been over by the time they'd rescued their civilian and returned, so Phantasm had them hauling rubble until time ran out, claiming it would be something they'd need to do to clear space for paramedics in the field. Kirin had thought he was in rather good shape, but after carrying chunks of concrete for the better part of an hour, he was beginning to feel like he was not nearly in shape enough.

After showering and changing he'd hardly had time to get

food before they were heading back out for the Rescue Operations seminar. He only saw Ifrit as they were approaching the building, the other man not having been seen in the dorm at all. He'd showered somewhere, his hair still damp.

"What do you think we'll be doing for this?" Kirin asked, having sped up to stand next to him. Ifrit only shot him a withering look and walked faster, leaving Kirin slightly puzzled behind him.

"What'd you do to piss him off?" Naddāha was suddenly at his elbow, peering at Ifrit's back as he disappeared through the door.

"I don't think he's pissed off, he's just... cranky." Kirin frowned.

"I can promise you; he's *really* pissed." Naddāha patted his arm and moved into the classroom, a few students passing by before Kirin shook his head and entered. He ended up taking a seat next to Medusa, who gave him a smile before turning her attention to the professor.

"Sit down quickly, the sooner we start this the sooner we get out." It was the tired looking man that had led him and Ness to Pressure when they'd first arrived. Though Pressure had called him Shifty, the schedule said his name was Shifter. He didn't look much better than when they'd first seen him, but he was at least marginally tidier, wearing a sweater vest and slacks, his short hair still unruly but looking like there'd been an *attempt* to comb it.

"We'll start with reviewing the results." Shifter pressed a button and a holo screen turned on, ranking the teams from one to six. Kirin's team had managed to be ranked number two, and Kirin found himself smiling, almost unable to believe they'd done so well. But it faded almost immediately when Kirin noticed that Ifrit's was dead last. Kirin shot a glance at the other man, but his face was inscrutable, or at least it hadn't changed from his usual scowl. Maybe that was why he was so on edge.

"These scores are based on several criteria. Firstly, how much risk there was for the civilian. That should always be your top priority: not making the situation worse. Secondly, time was and is a critical factor. If you have injured people in a wreckage, a few minutes may mean the difference between life and death. And thirdly, we'll be assessing your actual actions. Are you performing things well? A plan is only so good as its execution. We'll go from the worst team to the first team and assess what could have been done better, what mistakes each team made, and what went well, if indeed anything did."

Shifter pressed a button and footage began playing on the screen. There was no sound, but it was obvious that Ifrit and Kuafu were arguing, Phoenix trying to step between the two and being pushed aside. Kuafu was putting his face right in Ifrit's the words lost as Kuafu's back was to the camera. Not even a second later he was flying, Ifrit having backhanded him, powering the hit with an explosion. Phoenix ran after Kuafu, who was sprawled on the ground unmoving.

Ifrit unleashed a large blast, sending the entire front of the partially collapsed building up in the air, moving at a speed that turned him into little more than a blur. He was back in frame in a heartbeat, the shade in his grasp.

The video froze on that image, Ifrit's face set with cold anger, Kuafu on the ground, Phoenix looking back over his shoulder, eyes wide, at the destruction.

The room was silent, all the class except the members in question turning to look at Ifrit, who held his chin high, his expression unapologetic.

"What went wrong?" Shifter asked calmly.

"What *didn't*?" Phoenix spat. He looked angrier than the other two, pointedly not looking at either of them. "We hadn't even begun before these two were at each other's throats."

"Poor cooperation, then." Medusa had watched the footage on her phone, but her blindfold was now firmly replaced over her eyes.

"It seems like an incredibly risky move to *explode* an already unstable building, particularly when you know there are civilians inside." Naddāha nearly snorted, exasperated that she even had to point that out.

"I'm not so sure about that." Dulu spoke up. "It was hard to see, but it looked like the building was already starting to move, in which case the only course of action would have been to move quickly, and if you can physically get in and out fast enough, it wouldn't be absurd to prioritize getting to the civilian over attempting to do so carefully."

"Now, what do you think they were arguing about?" Shifter's face was unreadable.

"Ifrit noticed the building was falling and wanted to go in, but they wanted to move with more caution." Kirin said. He felt red eyes looking at him.

Instead of responding, Shifter pressed play on the video again.

"...act now."

"We have no information! There is no reason that we must work with such urgency!"

"It's starting to come down! If you hadn't stuck your fucking hand through, we would've had more time, but you had to do that and now we have maybe a minute, tops."

"The proper procedure is to—"

"Fuck that! If this wasn't a test, I wouldn't even be talking to you right now, I'd be goddamn *doing something*."

"Forgoing the proper protocols is how we cause trouble, but you'd already know something about that, wouldn't you?"

Even knowing it was coming, Kirin winced as Ifrit's hand connected with Kuafu's face. Knowing where to look, he did see the line of the roof start to sag before Ifrit destroyed the entire façade. Shifter didn't pause the video this time, and they saw Ifrit shoot out of the building, which collapsed behind him. The rubble from the explosion landed neatly on top of the decimated structure.

"We obviously missed a few seconds of action before this footage began. Why do you think that is?" Shifter looked around the class.

"Because heroes are usually first on the scene and any reporters or onlookers wouldn't arrive until later?" Lilin suggested.

"Exactly. Though it is infuriating, image is everything in this profession. We walk a fine line between being admired and being feared, and part of the job is ensuring that we present a clean image to the public. Attacking your coworkers, even if it is in the people's interests, is not acceptable." Shifter's eyes flashed with something akin to rage. "We will ask, in the future, that this doesn't happen again."

Ifrit held the professor's gaze for a moment, a muscle going in his jaw. Kirin thought he was going to refuse to agree, but the proud expression grew closer to shame, and he gave the smallest, almost imperceptible nod.

7

Mien

KIRIN TRIED TO FOCUS. He really did. But it was incredibly hard to do so when an explosion was happening just behind his head.

"Can you remind me why we're doing this?" He finally gave up and turned to Ifrit, who didn't even look at him.

"I don't fucking know. If you don't like it, go complain to Pressure and leave me alone." Even with the curses, his tone was less irritated than usual, perhaps because he was focused intently on sending blasts with precision. That had been Ifrit's only instruction for the day, to narrow down the shape of the explosion, sending it in an almost perfectly straight line. He'd been at it for two hours already, a line scored into the ground in front of him.

"Like, I was expecting it to just be so that you'd have to practice not hitting *me*, but your control is way too good for that to be an issue." Kirin took the shots to his head without issue, cheating slightly and not dropping his power in between while he chatted.

Ifrit did shoot him a look out of the corner of his eye, the next explosion slightly wider than the one before. He swore under his breath and pointedly looked away from Kirin, who sighed and returned to his position opposite the angry man. Kirin let his power wash off, waiting for the red blinking light to give him the slightest warning before the next hit would come. It blinked once and then fired, the skin toughening just as the rubber ball connected. He smiled, let it drop, and waited again.

They were the only two paired up so closely, though they had been told expressly— and with a knowing look— that they weren't supposed to be training on each other. Everyone else was spread out around the power gym, some of their class-mates hardly visible with the varied terrain. Kapre was closest; they were working on shifting the ground around their prone body to move it.

Kirin was fairly certain he could figure out their mien, espe-cially combined with the footage from Rescue Training. They could control the ground that they stood on, at the expense of controlling their own body. From his vantage point, Kirin could even see that the soles of their shoes had been cut away, presumably because they needed contact with the ground for their mien to work.

Aïcha he could see clearly as she ran up yet another hill, leaping from one to another, hair floating like a cloud behind her. She was wearing shorts to train in, showing unabashedly that it wasn't just goat hooves she possessed. He wasn't sure if the goat legs were the extent of her mien or if there was more; there was a certain unearthly quality to the way she moved, and she almost laughed as she scaled peaks that stretched to the ceiling.

And, for the first time, he managed to catch a glimpse of Lilin's mien. She was about halfway through the room, him and Ifrit positioned at one end of the gym. When she reached out her arms, darkness boiled outwards, cutting off the sights and sounds of the others. It looked like it had physical weight to it, cascading down from the height she stood upon to crash against the shine that Kuafu was producing. The small, dark man was standing in a sphere of light, fighting against the encroaching shadow, but every time he failed. As time wore on, he seemed more exhausted than she did.

Wyrm was Kirin's favorite to watch, though. As much as he seemed shy and introverted, once he pulled himself to his full height, he was formidable. His hair was pulled out of his face, his lips pulled back as he concentrated, revealing pointed teeth. The big man seemed to be practicing fighting with the extra spikes on his shoulders, tearing through chunks of rock that would sizzle behind him. There was certainly some kind of acid on them, perhaps the reason for their odd color—

Thunk. Kirin winced as one of the rubber balls hit him in the forehead.

"Focus, dumbass." Ifrit seemed to have eyes in the back of his head, as he hadn't turned around.

"I'm *trying*, okay? But we haven't gotten to see what everyone can do yet, you know?" Kirin set his feet and focused on the machines in front of him. Another blinked red and he let his power sweep across the top of his leg, just before the ball hit.

"Don't pay attention to them. Only look at what you're doing." Ifrit had to yell to be heard over his explosions.

"When else will I get the chance to though?" Kirin sighed.

"You'll find out during Rescue Operations." Ifrit had finally stopped shouting, as the screen overhead flashed for a fifteen-minute break. Most of the class could be seen immediately dropping to the ground, Lilin's hair falling down the side of the hill as she lay sprawled out and breathing heavily. Ifrit, on the other hand, simply took a few sips of water before moving into stretches.

"Hm." Kirin was tired, but he was also excited enough to not want to rest, instead joining Ifrit. Hours into practice and he was doing far better than he'd anticipated, his carbon reserves still a long way from running out. It helped too that he was only focusing on isolating areas of his body instead of full armor; a single use of that could deplete his stores in seconds.

"Stop looking so disappointed; it's annoying." Ifrit threw his water bottle at Kirin's face, but Kirin easily caught it.

"How do you think Medusa and Naddāha train?"

"Who?" Ifrit looked genuinely confused.

"Medusa? The one who wears the blindfold? And Naddāha—she was in my group earlier. Dark hair, green eyes?" Kirin explained patiently. He was less than surprised that Ifrit didn't know their names; the man hadn't spent any time around their classmates if it wasn't required for classes. Or if Phoenix hadn't somehow bribed him out.

"I suspect like fucking everyone else." Ifrit shrugged, unconcerned.

"We're not supposed to be practicing on each other yet, so I don't know how it'd work though." They could be practicing with simulations, he supposed, or perhaps they'd just be stuck doing research into what their powers could do? Kirin knew they were in the gym, far on the other side, but it seemed silly to have them sit inside and read.

"What do you mean?" Ifrit had stopped stretching and was giving Kirin his full attention now. He always did that, Kirin was realizing, focusing all his energy on one thing at a time. It was part of the reason that he came across as so intense.

"Weren't you watching the footage from class? Medusa can effectively freeze a person in place, and Naddāha pointedly said that her mien wasn't going to be helpful for the rescue mission but would have been if there was a real person inside. My guess is that hers also effects other people in some way."

"Huh." Ifrit thought on that for a minute. "You're not as idiotic as you look."

"Thanks? You gotta work on how you compliment people dude."

Ifrit didn't respond, his eyes narrowed as he looked across the field. Kirin followed his gaze and found that he was staring at Enenra, who was so far away that she appeared even tinier than usual.

"She turns to smoke, right?"

Ifrit's eyes slid to him almost guiltily, as if he'd been caught doing something he shouldn't. The borderline embarrassed expression surprised Kirin enough that he laughed.

"Hey, I'm not judging. I'm definitely doing it too." Kirin smiled broadly. "It's funny though, how much she looks like Ness from a distance, especially when she's using her mien. They both go... blurry."

"And they both have trouble coming back." Ifrit grumbled.

Kirin hadn't thought about it, but now that he did, he realized Ifrit was right. Enenra certainly seemed less substantial now than she had at the beginning of the day. She could disperse herself entirely, from what they'd seen, but returning to a solid form seemed much more difficult for her. Or at least it took a lot longer.

"I didn't even notice. You spot anything else?"

"A whole fucking storm rolls in every time Angel over there pops out his wings." Ifrit was nodding towards Dulu, who did look rather striking. The bright feathers stood out against his dark skin, making him look like a classical portrait in black and white. For most of their practice time, he'd been focused on starting and stopping in midair, constantly passing by overhead.

"I guess it *is* raining."

"They're tucked away now; the storm will have passed by the time the break's over. Notice when he takes them back out and you'll see I'm fucking right."

"I wasn't doubting you."

"Horns works with plants."

"Goldhorn? I mean, that one was obvious though, wasn't it? Even someone as stupid looking as me could notice that." Kirin had just meant to tease him lightly, but the way Ifrit tensed up made him stumble into his next words. "But yeah, definitely unexpected. I can't tell how they're doing it either."

They were both quiet as they watched Goldhorn, who was nodding as Pressure said something to them. They were standing close enough that Kirin was able to notice the bright spot of red on their palms. That was odd, considering none of them were fighting each other. Goldhorn was bleeding though, a small stain left behind as they wiped their hands on a towel.

"One of those fucking types." Ifrit said it under his breath, but Kirin heard.

"What type?"

"The ones that you'd think were magic if you didn't fucking know better." The timer went off, indicating that their break was over. Ifrit got to his feet and hesitated. After a moment, he offered a hand to help Kirin up.

"I think we could all fall into that category." Kirin accepted, pulling himself up to his full height, now looking down at Ifrit.

"Not you." Ifrit had turned away, setting his stance to resume. "I'm going to fucking figure out yours."

Thunk.

A ball hit Kirin in the back of the head, but he didn't bother to turn. Instead, he found himself staring at Ifrit's back, disinclined to look away.

"Yeah," he agreed, "I'm going to figure you out too."

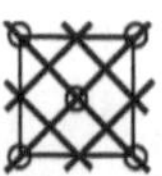

Ifrit made dinner for their floor that night. Kirin suspected he wouldn't admit to it even on pain of death, but how else had a bowl of food appeared outside his door? It was rice and some kind of grilled meat, and Ifrit was, surprisingly, sitting at the counter eating the same thing, the back of his neck faintly red.

Phoenix noticed Kirin first, waving far too enthusiastically from the couch.

"Blasty made us food!" She nearly spit food all over the floor as she yelled.

"Keep your mouth closed as you chew." Kirin gingerly picked up his bowl and closed the door, feeling somehow like if he moved too quickly, he'd scare Ifrit off. There *was* another chair directly next to the man, but that felt too personal right now, particularly when Ifrit's body language screamed "get away." Kirin opted for leaning against the wall, tentatively taking a bite of the food.

"This is really good man, thanks." He flashed a smile at Ifrit, who only glanced his way before stuffing his face more. The tips of Ifrit's ears were noticeably red, however, and Kirin suspected it wasn't from the spice of the dish.

"If this happens too often, I'll become a snob and be completely unable to eat the campus food." Phoenix sighed, placing a hand to her head. "Also, you being nice is weird."

Ifrit's shoulders bunched up nearly to his ears, his fork slamming against the counter as he stood up. Before he could open his mouth, Kirin place his hands on the shorter man's shoulders.

"That's a rude thing to say, Phoenix. Particularly when he also did the dishes." Kirin sat down between Ifrit and the couch, his arm still around Ifrit's shoulders and dragging him back down to sit. "Speaking of: next time you're cooking, let us do the dishes, okay? Especially after training. I was so tired I didn't think I could even shower, let alone cook a whole meal. We can help out, you don't need to do everything."

"What makes you think there'll fucking be a next time?" Ifrit had finished his food and stood up with his bowl, but Kirin swiped it and stacked it under his own.

"*If* there's a next time, let us do the dishes, okay?" Kirin asked innocently. Ifrit looked like he was going to try and take the bowl back, but then decided against it, throwing his hands in the air.

"Whatever, dumbass." With that, he fled into his room. The beat of loud music could be heard seconds later.

Phoenix and Kirin looked at each other, a smile tugging at Phoenix's mouth. She lost it second later, nearly dumping rice into her lap as she laughed.

"Oh, I probably was too mean to him. I think he was genuinely trying to say thanks but is way too proud to say it in words." She wiped a tear from her eye, smiling broadly. "What are we going to do with him?"

"Thank you? For what?"

"On the way back from training, he looked a little unsteady on his feet. I think he pushed himself too hard. I just healed him a little, that's all, didn't think anything of it. But when I came out of my room, poof! Dinner." Phoenix chuckled, turning back to her food. "Acts of service with that one."

"I'm just lucky to get some then." Kirin took another bite of his own food, savoring the way the meat melted on his tongue. "This is genuinely so good."

"Nah, I think for you, it's an apology." Phoenix waved her fork in the air, making little airplane noises. Kirin waited a moment, but she didn't elaborate.

"What for?"

"Oh, the building thing yesterday."

"Why would he have to apologize for that? I got in his way, and it was fine in the end."

"But if it hadn't been you, it wouldn't have been fine, would it? You weren't watching the cameras; you didn't see how panicked he looked when he realized you were down there. After you guys got out, I genuinely thought he was going to cry. He looked so upset."

Kirin looked at Phoenix to see if she was joking, but she seemed as serious as she ever was. His eyes then drifted to Ifrit's door. Perhaps "stay out of my way" was his way of saying "stay safe."

8

Outside

It wasn't until almost halfway through the semester that they were allowed to go out into the city. Kirin had been waiting for the trip, finally ready to get rid of the clinical feeling that clung to his room, but with midterms right around the corner, he found himself dreading the lost studying time more than anything.

"I'm not letting you skip." Phoenix was dragging him through the first-floor common area, Yantra pushing him from behind as well. Adlivun was walking alongside them, looking amused, not helping, but not interfering either.

"If he doesn't want to go, don't make him go! We'll have more opportunities in the future." Dulu was standing by the door checking his phone, Ness, Naddāha, and Medusa with him. And, surprisingly, Ifrit.

"It's not that I don't *want* to, but—"

"But nothing! You've been studying every waking minute you're not in the gym, and don't think I haven't noticed you've been skipping your morning runs to read the history textbook." Phoenix put an accusatory finger in his face. "You need a break. You're coming, and that's final."

Kirin looked at Adlivun for help, but she pointedly avoided

his gaze, instead finding something endlessly fascinating about her backpack strap.

"I have to do laundry?" He tried.

"Should have done that with everyone else the other day, but no, you were *studying*." Phoenix started pushing him out the door, Yantra giving one final shove before peeling off to wait for Ness. The rest of their group filed in behind them, chatting as they walked through campus.

"I can't believe they made us wait so long to get passes. Campus is great and all, but I've been getting stir crazy." Ness stretched her arms above her head as they walked, the motion making her slightly more visible than usual. Kirin had noticed that, over the weeks; if she moved, or spoke, the shifting quality of her appearance settled, if only for a moment.

"I'm just excited to get some new clothes. With all the strength training Pressure's been having me put in, my shirts have gotten shockingly tight around the shoulders." Naddāha tugged at her top, which was— presumably intentionally— ripped, but even still it looked tight around her muscles.

"What about you, Ad?" Phoenix smiled brightly at the tall woman, who had learned to stop questioning the nickname.

"I just wanted to see the city. Unsurprisingly, I've never been, and I didn't get a chance to look around on the way to campus." They passed through the first gate, their masks already up.

"We're just going to head straight for the arcades." Dulu high-fived Yantra as he spoke. Kirin had been caught in a tournament between the two *once*, and had left after Yantra threw a shoe at Dulu's face. Which, apparently, was not the worst thing that had ever happened when they started getting competitive.

"What're you up to then?" Kirin asked Medusa, who'd fallen into step beside him. Phoenix and Ness he knew were joining Naddāha in shopping, though he suspected the more brightly colored pair didn't usually buy from the same stores that Nad-dāha did.

"I'm sticking with Adlivun, she's going to describe things to me as we walk." Medusa shrugged. "Plus, there's a good chance that after school we might end up working in the area, so it'd be nice to familiarize myself with it when there isn't an emergency at hand."

"That's fair enough. I guess I didn't see too much either, even though I got in so early." Kirin shot a glance at Ifrit, but the man didn't offer a reason why he was tagging along. Though less dramatic about it than Phoenix, he also seemed like he'd climbed out of a grave every morning, so it was surprising to see him up and about so early.

"What about you, Kirin?" Medusa always turned to face whoever she was speaking to, even if it didn't matter at all with her blindfold on. For discretion's sake, she'd used bandages that were close in color to her skin, with sunglasses over the top. If he only looked out of the corner of his eye, he might miss it entirely.

"I wanted to get some new sheets and maybe some stuff to decorate my dorm, but I didn't really have a set plan. Was probably going to swing by a grocery store too, just to get some snacks."

"Ifrit, where are you going? I didn't know you were even tagging along." Medusa was more diplomatic than most of their classmates when dealing with Ifrit. Everyone else usually left him well enough alone, though others (Phoenix) loved to prod for a reaction.

"I just fucking need groceries. I can go by myself." Ifrit never helped his case much. While he wasn't throwing a fit about walking with the group, he was hovering a good few paces back, arms crossed over his chest and glaring at anyone who looked at him.

"We need to stay in pairs man, but it's alright, I'm going that way too." They all had to swipe their IDs at the main gate of campus, the final barrier between them and the rest of the world. Despite the nagging feeling he should be back at the dorm studying, Kirin felt a little thrill of anticipation. Even if it *was* just to the grocery store and back, he was looking forward to seeing the city in the daylight, to seeing how different it was from his home.

Ifrit looked slightly affronted, but, happily, he didn't argue any further. The entire group was clumped together until they left the park, anyways, as there were no subway stops within its borders. They walked in silence, Phoenix too tired to keep up their usual stream of commentary, the sun barely peeking over the horizon. Leaving so early had been a conscious choice, not one that the school enforced. First years weren't allowed off campus until they had "acclimated to school life," which the school deemed to mean mid-semester. This fact, however, was well known to many of the paparazzi around the area, and later in the day they could expect to find a few cameras lying in wait, hoping to catch the first shots of the new heroes.

The sun was well up by the time they made it to the edge of the park, and suddenly Kirin felt unbearably awkward. The rest of the group had shot off almost immediately, leaving him and Ifrit alone. He'd forgotten to check where the grocery store was, so he stood there, rocking on his heels, until Ifrit sighed.

"It's this way, dumbass." He strode off in the same direction Naddāha's group had gone, hands shoved in his pockets. It was the first time Kirin had seen him in anything other than workout clothes, but, he thought as they walked, it was incredibly on brand. Cargo pants, a jean jacket with a couple dozen patches, dark boots— even the fire ringing his neck seemed to fit in.

"Sorry, thanks! I wasn't going to come today, so I forgot to look at directions." Kirin smiled sheepishly.

"Why weren't you going to come? Aren't you one of those fucking social butterfly types?'

"Ah, just nervous about midterms. Studying is... hard."

They'd made it to the subway, which was somehow still packed despite the early hour. Tired eyes greeted them as they got on, squeezing into an empty corner of the car. Ifrit seemed uncomfortable, the lines of his neck pulled taut, and Kirin shifted them as subtly as he could so that Ifrit was in the corner, and he was standing between him and the people filling the standing room behind them.

"You don't have to do that." Ifrit wasn't stupid, however.

"I know dude, but you seem... you know. Like you're not exactly a people person."

Ifrit snorted at that, but his posture seemed to relax a tiny amount.

"What stop did we need again?" Kirin craned his head to see the screen, which was at the level of his forehead.

"It's not for a fucking while, don't worry about it yet." Ifrit leaned against the wall, giving himself a hand's breadth of space. They were really shoved in there, the fire around Ifrit's neck casting light on Kirin's shirt. Kirin wanted to back up, to give more room, since he'd seen how Ifrit seemed to hate having people so close to him. He barely tolerated when Kirin would put an arm around his shoulders, but the doors opened and even more people flooded in, pressing Kirin even farther into the corner with him.

Ifrit didn't react at all, except to extinguish the fire, sighing a little when he did.

"I never realized that could turn off."

"You wouldn't, only time I ever do is when I'm asleep."

"Why's that?"

"Don't want to set the fucking sheets on fire, now do I?"

"Oh, oh that makes sense."

They lapsed into silence, Kirin feeling awkward yet again.

"Why's studying hard?" Ifrit asked suddenly.

"Hm?"

"Fire-hair bitch was right; you've been studying all the fucking time. What do you mean it's hard?" Ifrit was looking directly at him now, having to tilt his head up to do so, since they were so close. The train rocked and Kirin reached up to brace himself against the ceiling, trying to ignore the burning in his cheeks from the intensity of Ifrit's stare.

"I, uh… it just is?"

"You might be a dumbass but you're not an idiot. What are you having trouble with?" Ifrit cleared his throat and looked off to the side. "I could, you know, help."

Kirin felt his brain stutter for a moment. Ifrit, willingly offering to hang out with him? Unprecedented. But…

"I appreciate it, but I don't think it's really something you can help with."

"What do you mean?" Ifrit narrowed his eyes, like Kirin had just issued a challenge.

"It's just the history stuff. They don't have an ebook for it, and the font is so small, and, well, I'm dyslexic. It just takes a while to get through, that's all. I have my notes, but usually reading through the textbook is the best thing since I can't record the lectures…"

Ifrit was staring at Kirin like he wanted to hit him.

"It's fine though! I knew there wouldn't be any accommodations if I came here; no accommodations in the field so none in the classroom and all that. It was my choice. That's why I've been studying so much, you know? I have a bit of ground to cover. I tried to get ahead before the semester started but I had to re-read a bunch of it since it'd been a while and that's been taking forever. Sometimes even trying to take notes is… hard."

Kirin nearly bit his tongue to get himself to stop rambling, hesitantly bringing his eyes back down to Ifrit, who still looked vaguely murderous.

"I can just read the chapter out to you, dumbass." The shorter man grumbled. "And this is our stop."

Ifrit pushed past Kirin to exit the train, Kirin standing stunned for a moment before he gathered himself and turned and ran after him.

"You really don't have to do that for me!"

"If I wasn't willing to do it, I wouldn't have fucking offered, shithead." Ifrit's ears were vaguely red, his hands balled into fists. But his expression wasn't angry anymore, more... uncertain. And perhaps a little embarrassed.

The protestations on Kirin's tongue died out as he realized he'd never heard Ifrit offer to hang out with *anyone*. And that uncertainty suddenly looked a lot more like worry.

"I'd really appreciate it, if it's not a problem for you." Kirin gave Ifrit a smile, which caused the man to "*tch*" and look away.

"Of fucking course it's not. But you better ace your exams, dumbass, if I'm spending time helping you."

"I will now! So, where are we headed?"

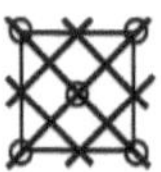

It was at the grocery store, of all places, that things went wrong. Ifrit was shockingly subdued as they went through stores to pick out décor for Kirin's room, insulting his choices the entire way but not with any real malice. Kirin was figuring out that the curse words were simply the only adjectives Ifrit knew. Ifrit had led them to a large grocery store that seemed to have everything they could ever possibly want, though they were currently in the spice aisle, Ifrit scrutinizing several different jars. They had been there for longer than Kirin had spent picking out posters, but he wasn't complaining. It felt... nice. Normal, even.

It was only natural that he fully put his foot in his mouth and ruin it.

"While we're here, should we also go pick up hair dye?" Ifrit had finished picking out his spices, their shopping basket full, and Kirin figured he should remind the other man before they headed to the check out. Judging from how the fire ringing his neck exploded outward abruptly, it wasn't a welcome change in topic.

"The fuck are you talking about?" The angry tone was somewhat counteracted by the clear worry on his face.

"Um, well, your roots are showing a little. I noticed on the train." When Ifrit's face grew even stormier, Kirin held up his hands placatingly. "Hey, it's alright, I need to re-dye my hair too!"

Ifrit looked like he was about to say something in response, when suddenly the hair on the back of Kirin's neck stood up. Before he could even process what he was doing, Kirin shoved Ifrit behind himself and took a punch to the shoulder.

Even without using his mien, Kirin was sturdier than most, hard pressed to be thrown by anything short of a gunshot. Yet a single punch found him bleeding, crashing back into Ifrit, whose eyes were wide with shock.

Somehow, Kirin managed to stay on his feet, eyesight blurred slightly as he tried to focus on the person who'd just hit him. All his eyes could pick out for a moment was the color orange, until he processed that if he hadn't moved, that punch would've taken Ifrit in the head. Anger snapped his vision back and he found himself face to face with a hero.

Reverb was the name, if he wasn't mistaken, which explained why the hit to his shoulder had also shredded parts of his shirt, and a non-insignificant amount of his skin. The hero had the top half of his face covered with his bright orange mask, his mouth set in a grim line, eyes still locked on Ifrit.

"Step away from the man." Reverb had his hands held up, palms out, ready to send another pulse to whoever was in his way. He was smaller than Kirin might have guessed from watching him fight on TV, but not by much. Ifrit's height, no, even less than that, and his costume clearly had plenty of padding to shield him from the blowback of his own strength.

"He has a license." Kirin was fighting hard to keep his hands at his sides, already failing to keep them from curling into fists. He'd noticed the stares as they were walking around, noticed the whispered words as eyes jumped to Ifrit's neck. Someone had called for help; there was no other reason that a hero would be inside an otherwise calm store.

"Bring it out." Reverb didn't put his hands down, glaring at the pair of them.

"It's in my back pocket." Ifrit had his hands up behind his head, looking, if anything, bored with the situation. The first time Kirin felt like man's brusque attitude might have been entirely deserved, it was gone.

"Get it out."

"So you can deck me for 'moving suspiciously?' No thanks." Ifrit didn't move. Reverb didn't either, the moment stretching out between them as other eyes peeked in from neighboring aisles.

"I'll get it." Kirin muttered, if only so he was occupied. "Which pocket?"

"Back right." Ifrit didn't react as Kirin fumbled for it, his hands shaking slightly. The adrenaline had worn off, the pain in his shoulder reminding him of another day, another time he'd been bleeding onto the floor.

"Here." Kirin held out the wallet to the hero, who shook his head.

"Open it."

Kirin fought the urge to roll his eyes and opened the wallet, the special use license the first thing visible. He held it up, but Reverb seemed unconvinced.

"And ID?"

Kirin looked back at Ifrit, who finally showed some emotion, irritation crawling over his face.

"It's under the flap."

Kirin flipped up the license, under which was Ifrit's university ID. It was more secure than a state one, which they weren't allowed to have anyway. Reverb finally seemed convinced and lowered his hands.

"Keep a better reign on your temper, next time." He straightened and walked away, leaving Kirin gaping after him.

"I'm going to go hit him." He said aloud.

"No, you fucking aren't." Ifrit finally looked angry, but a wave of sadness passed over his face. "It'll be worse if you do. Besides, we need to get you a new shirt now, unless you plan to bleed all over everyone on the way back."

Kirin quickly clamped a hand over the cut, remembering the hit had sliced open his shirt, and ripped it a good bit down his back. It'd been warm, that morning, so he hadn't bothered to bring a jacket. Luckily, at least, his hair was down.

"Maybe you'll finally wear something other than those stupid high-necked shirts. Like seriously, who the fuck owns that many of the same thing?" Ifrit's heart didn't seem in the insult, even less when he looked up. "Or whatever. 'S not the worst look."

Kirin offered a smile, forgetting for the moment that Ifrit couldn't see it. They'd lost their audience, at least. Considering how unperturbed Ifrit was, Kirin was certain this was a common occurrence for him. Ifrit's distaste for his own name suddenly made more sense.

"They really treat you like a demon, don't they?"

Ifrit's head shot up, before he started, of all things, taking off his jacket.

"They treat anyone who looks different that way. Not that you wouldn't know that." Ifrit took off his shirt and handed it to Kirin, who took it almost in shock. The black fabric hid the blood from his hands well, though he didn't move to put it on. Ifrit had put his jacket back on, buttoning the front without looking at Kirin. "You need hair dye too, yeah?"

"Uh, yeah."

"Bandages first. Then we can buy whatever fucking bullshit you needed."

"Ifrit?"

"What?" Ifrit looked up at him, his eyes betraying the fact that the irritation was only an act.

"I do get to give you shit for yelling at me about my hair when yours is also dyed." He couldn't stop himself from grinning as he spoke.

"At least mine doesn't look like fucking *tinsel*, asshole."

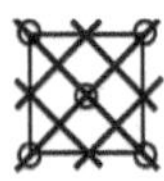

Ifrit hadn't let him carry a single thing on the way back to the dorms, insisting that he could carry everything until they got to the infirmary. The cheap bandages they'd found at the store were soaked through by the time they arrived, the nurse tutting as she took them off to clean the wound. Ifrit had been waiting by the door at first, tapping his foot against the ground impatiently, but as the nurse unwrapped it, he got pale and rushed off to the dorm to put their food away. It didn't take the nurse much time to re-bandage his arm, and, in that time,

Ifrit had yet to reappear, leaving Kirin to walk back to the dorm alone.

They'd snuck in the back way, eager to avoid the photographers camped out at the front gate, and though Kirin had refused to admit it to Ifrit, his shoulder *was* bothering him from walking the long way round. So much for only the gen ed classes being difficult; if his shoulder didn't heal up within the next two days, he'd need to be worried about the physical exams as well. The wound hadn't seemed deep, but the vibration had torn apart the skin, feeling like a friction burn on top of a cut.

When he stumbled into the common area, he was immediately accosted by Phoenix. Ifrit was hovering in the background, his face worried.

"I leave you alone for *four hours* and you've gone and done this." They rested a hand on his arm, and he felt the wound start to itch fiercely, the sensation almost more uncomfortable than the pain. It was gone in a moment though, leaving his shoulder feeling entirely back to normal. Having a healer *was* useful, wasn't it? "You know, after all these weeks, I was beginning to think you couldn't bleed at all."

"Without my mien, I'm just a person, like anyone else." Kirin shrugged. In truth, the only lingering discomfort was the pull of the bandages on his skin.

"Why didn't you block it? I feel like you'd get a pass being a hero student and all." Aïcha asked, her gaze almost accusatory.

Kirin didn't get to respond however, as Kuafu bristled at the question.

"*Because* we're hero students, we don't get to shirk the rules any more than anyone else."

"But it's in self-defense, surely that's allowed." She cocked her head slightly, now watching Kuafu carefully.

"No, never."

"Even if it would save a life?"

Aïcha's eyes found Kirin again, and suddenly, he felt like the room was too hot, her gaze too piercing. There was no way she knew.

"Even then. We follow what the law says, even to our own detriment. Once you decide to make your own moral compass, you can excuse anything. *Everything*." Kuafu's voice was getting louder, his hands clenched into fists. "We are not gods. We are not infallible."

Aïcha shrugged, not looking chastened at all. Kirin, on the other hand, found his mouth quite dry.

"I, for one, think people have a better idea of what's right and wrong than any god. But then again, I'm an idiot." Phoenix breezed through the room, patting Ifrit on the shoulder as they passed. He flinched and stalked off somewhere. "Kirin, you could be a god though, with all that muscle."

"Don't you *dare*." Kuafu had moved, suddenly up in Phoenix's face. "We are *not* almighty."

There was something in his voice that gave Phoenix pause and they regarded the man with a cool gaze, as if appraising him. Kirin found himself between them before he knew what had happened. For a second time that day.

"They didn't mean it, they're just joking." He held his hands up, placatingly. "I certainly don't see myself that way, and I don't think anyone else does either. We're all just trying our best, okay?"

Kuafu didn't seem appeased, but at least less angry, now that the object of his ire was out of sight. He gave a curt nod and walked off, just like that.

"You're ruining all my fun today." Phoenix sighed. "First Ifrit *willingly* calls me, asking me to come back here for your dumbass, completely immune to any prodding, and now you take away my next form of entertainment? Cruel."

"Phoenix, he cares about that, for whatever reason. Mess

around with breaking rules, that's fine, but lay off the things they care about, okay?" Kirin ran a hand across his face. He really should have just stayed in to study, shouldn't he? But then, if he had, what would've happened to Ifrit. The anger bubbled up in his chest again, remembering the disdainful eyes of Reverb, willing to kill Ifrit for raising his voice.

"I'm not going to be the one comparing us to gods in a few years, you know." Phoenix was speaking softly, maybe in response to Kirin's face, or maybe just to show that they were being sincere. "It's better he gets used to it now, when it's not coming from a screaming crowd."

"Then say it plainly, like that. He doesn't get it otherwise. Not everyone's so good with words and people like you are." Kirin didn't wait for a response, heading for the elevator instead of the stairs for once. He was tired already, but he needed to save at least a little bit of energy for dealing with someone else who was terrible with people.

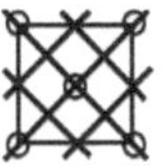

Ifrit came to him, surprising them both. Kirin had stopped in his room first, looking to change into a clean shirt now that Ifrit's was stiffening with dried blood. It only went down to about Kirin's navel, anyways, so he'd kept the now ruined shirt on underneath. He'd only just finished changing and had been wondering if there was a way to ask Ifrit if he was okay without offending him, when there was a knock at his door. He opened it to find Ifrit standing outside, textbook in one hand, shopping bag in the other, looking uncharacteristically anxious.

"We fucking studying, or whatever?" There was still the proud set of his jaw, now visible since he'd abandoned his mask, but the challenge in his eyes was gone, his fingers tapping the edge of the book.

"Yeah. Yeah, we can study." Kirin didn't move from the door-way, still somewhat bemused. "But we don't have to, you know, after—"

"You were all fucking worried about losing studying time this morning." Ifrit's hand tightened around the book. His eyes flickered to Kirin's shoulder, unspoken worry in them.

"Yeah, you're right. Let's study." Kirin stepped back, allowing the shorter man into the room. Ifrit shuffled in quickly, as if expecting the offer to be rescinded. His eyes roamed the room, not that there was much to see.

"I expected you to be messy." There was a note of almost disappointment in his voice.

"Can't really make that much of a mess if there isn't anything in here to start." Kirin shut the door, suddenly feeling awkward. It occurred to him that Ifrit was the first person he'd had in *his* room, usually he went to the lower floors to hang out with Ness or Yantra or Lilin instead of them coming up here. Ifrit took up space in the room the way the furniture never could, and for some reason, Kirin's chest felt vaguely warm.

"Well, some of this should help with that." Ifrit set the bag down and nudged it toward Kirin with his foot. The bag tipped over and hit the short table Kirin liked to use to do homework, the edge of one of the posters sticking out, the side of Force's face just visible. Kirin sat on the ground with a sigh, pulling his notes over from where they were scattered across the table. Ifrit picked a loose page up out of the pile and raised an eyebrow.

"These are shockingly legible." He sat down cautiously, taking great care to make sure he didn't move anything.

"Those are notes from the textbook, not class. I have trouble writing and listening at the same time, so I usually just listen to the lecture and take notes from the textbook."

Ifrit didn't say anything but nodded, pulling his own note-book out from beneath the textbook. Kirin hazarded a peek inside when he flipped it open, and was unsurprised to see perfect, precise lines of notes, almost like it'd been printed rather than written. He found his mouth pricking up into a smile; somehow that was *so* Ifrit.

"How far did you make it into the textbook?"

"Chapter twelve, I think."

"That's fucking easy then, there's only one more, the one on era two mien-users."

"Yeah, but test's tomorrow, isn't it?"

"The main issue is just the fucking font size, yeah?"

Kirin nodded his agreement.

"I'll read through the chapter, then, and just scan in my notes for you to use and you can fuck with the text size that way. It seems like you learn best working with rather than against the format. If it's auditory you just want to fucking listen, reading you want to take notes." Ifrit spun his pen idly between his fingers. "For the final, we'll come up with a better solution to the fucking book issue, but reading out loud can be a stopgap for now. I can pause whenever you have a question, too."

Ifrit noticed Kirin gaping at him.

"The fuck's wrong with you?"

"I don't know man, you're just... better at this than I expect-ed."

"Shut the fuck up."

"Can I ask a question?"

"I just said you could."

"Not about that." Kirin saw the other man swallow, looking nervous again. "About you."

"One."

"What?"

"You can ask one question. Then we're studying."

"Why are you here?"

The question seemed to freeze Ifrit; his hands paused in the process of turning a page.

"You clearly know a lot about the school, more than anyone else, and you seem to hate it. Don't get me wrong, I think you'll make a great hero, but it almost feels like you don't *want* to be here."

Ifrit put the book down slowly, and Kirin wondered if he was about to get hit.

"If that's too personal, you don't have to answer—"

"They're fucking wrong about me."

Kirin shut up.

"The heroes, the people who stare at me in the street, even our fucking classmates. Everyone thinks I'm just an accident waiting to happen, one angry outburst away from destruction. That someone like me could only ever cause pain, and never be the one to help with it."

Kirin wanted to reach out, to take Ifrit's hand and pry it out of a fist.

"Even when I was a kid, they'd fawn over my mien, say how impressive it was, but even then, they'd look at me with this... *fear*. A curiosity now, a danger later. After... after Satol that only got worse. People would whisper in the street, and I could just *feel* it, them waiting. Watching.

"But I'm so fucking good at dealing with this. They can stare all they want, they can tell me I'm the villain all they want, but they're going to eat their fucking words once I have my license. Yeah, this stupid fucking system doesn't work, and it's easy as shit to buy a pass in, but this world hasn't seen a real goddamn hero in years, and it isn't someone who smiles and plays nice for the camera, it's someone who fights for the *right* thing.

"It's going to take years to get there, but so what? They're not going to stop hating me, and people are still going to die if no one does anything about it. So, until someone can fix this fucking thing, I'll work with it, because then none of them can touch me." Ifrit gave Kirin a crooked grin, the firelight reflecting in his eyes. "And if it makes them sick to their stomachs to see me on TV, well, that's just fucking desserts, isn't it?"

9

Closer

"After analyzing the newest sample you gave us, we can conclude a few things. Firstly, you're not turning into a diamond-like substance but are indeed changing parts of your body to pure, perfect, un-occluded diamond. However, the impact tests, as you are obviously aware of, proved that not only is your body sharp enough to cut through a bullet, but strong enough not to shatter on impact. It seems that's because of the way your skin cells fit together, each layer serving to reinforce the next. If you had enough control to harden only a single layer of skin, perhaps it wouldn't be enough, but the current method you use ensures that the force it would require to puncture through your mien is several orders of magnitude higher than that of a gunshot, or even a collapsing building!"

If Nwabudike noticed Kirin flinch, he didn't pause to acknowledge it.

"What this tells us is that your primary weakness is simply the need for carbon. Analyzing your breath samples, you do exhale primarily carbon dioxide regularly, but when using your mien, you exhale primarily oxygen, which is interesting. We'll still give you the oxygen charges, but even if they fail, you'd be able to purify the air simply by standing in it!

"Finally, the bloodwork did come back as we'd hoped. You can metabolize carbon monoxide just as you do carbon *dioxide*, without any ill effect. That's honestly what I'm most excited about, as it has such potential for allowing you to work in environments that other heroes or even trained rescue squads might struggle with." Nwabudike looked up at him with a smile. He was always so excited to get on with things that Kirin rarely got a word in edgewise. "Of course, it's just impressive to have one fewer thing to worry about killing you out there."

"I'm sure they'll find other ways that you and I haven't thought of yet." Kirin was looking over the sketch that Nwabudike had handed him, his first real look at what was going to become his hero costume. He'd gotten some sample fabrics, a few tests of similar styles, but this drawing wasn't something that'd just been lying around, no— it was just for him. He was proud of himself for not breaking down into tears right then and there.

"They can try, but I doubt they'll find a way." He did sound very convinced, which made Kirin look up. Nwabudike was still looking at him, his eyes shining with pride. Kirin's stomach lurched, the youthful faith all too familiar. "I've been watching the training practices to get ideas of how your suit would need to function in a fight. I've studied heroes for years and yet, I don't think I've ever seen anything half as crazy as you letting that explosion guy blast you through a row of buildings and walking away without a scratch."

"I'm good with blunt force trauma, but that's not all there is to fight out there." Kirin forced himself to hand the sketch back, standing up as he did. "This looks perfect, thank you."

Nwabudike broke into a blinding smile, immediately hustling back to his workstation, Kirin forgotten in an instant. Maybe he should've been offended by that, but over the weeks he'd grown to appreciate being ignored, and it was hard to dislike

Nwabudike with his earnest nature.

He slid out of the lab and walked down the hall, feeling a bit lighter than he had coming in. Everyone else had finalized their costume designs a few weeks before, only him and Ifrit still fighting with details. For him, Nwabudike hadn't wanted to settle on a design without fully knowing what he was working with, for Ifrit…

The doors in the tech buildings were all automated, so they didn't slam, but Ifrit made up for that by stomping his way down the corridor.

"Still not budging?" Kirin already knew the answer, but he'd learned that unless someone prodded Ifrit open, he'd just bottle everything up until an unsuspecting victim would receive the inevitable explosion.

"No. She's insistent that I pick a different primary color, but I already fucking *agreed* to having a second color on there. I'm not giving up the main one."

"I'm impressed the school hasn't forced you to choose by now." Kirin leaned back in the elevator, idly watching the floors slip by as they headed down. Pressure was waiting on the first floor, as she always did, though today she looked almost fully asleep.

"This is the *one* fucking thing we're allowed input on; they better not try to pull shit to make me agree."

"I think you can wear them down; they did say we need to have costumes finished before next semester starts." Kirin clapped Ifrit on the back as the elevator opened, the smaller man only grunting in response. Pressure yawned as she saw them, getting up from her seat.

"Come on, come on problem children. Today was supposed to be my day off. You've only got two weeks until the end of the semester, and everyone is up *my* ass to get this done."

"We're trying, promise." Kirin held up his hands in surrender, making Pressure snort. "We're not happy to be here either; even though we've done the finals for the gen ed courses, I'm still worried about the practicals."

"At least one of you is responsible." Pressure sighed, leaving them with a wave once they were outside the building.

"The fuck is that supposed to mean?" Ifrit watched Pressure's retreating back with a frown.

"Well, she's certainly aware that Phoenix is attempting to throw a party in our dorm tonight."

"...*what*?"

"And I know for a fact that he invited her."

"That fucking idiot invited our goddamn *teacher*?"

"He said she was cool."

"She's fucking *forty*."

"Hey, I don't think she's that old."

"I can't believe that absolute shithead."

Ifrit stewed in silence until they got back to their dorm, though his irritation only grew from there. Phoenix was commandeering the common space, already in his element, directing their classmates around to make the space "party ready," whatever that meant. Ifrit snuck off the moment they arrived, leaving Kirin to talk to Phoenix alone.

"You're getting him to come." Phoenix didn't even look away from Wyrm and Adlivun— who were setting up some kind of game board— while he spoke, fingers tapping on his arm.

"Phoenix, we've been over this. He just doesn't like big social gatherings."

"Neither does Kuafu! And neither do you, for that matter, but you're going to be there." When Kirin was quiet, Phoenix turned to face him. "Right, Kirin?"

"Yeah, I'll be there."

"Perfect. And if you're coming, he'll probably come anyway, but you're still responsible for making sure he's there."

Phoenix's attention was already wandering, his eyes following Dulu and Aïcha, who were laughing in the kitchen.

"Why do you think he'd come if I'm there?" Kirin was genuinely confused, though the look Phoenix gave him made him feel like he'd asked the stupidest question.

"You two are basically joined at the hip. Ever since midterms you have done *everything* together."

"Not everything—"

"You go for a run together in the morning, and then we all eat breakfast together upstairs, and then you have class together all day, and you hole up in your room at night." Phoenix counted off the list on his fingers. "And I'm not even counting whatever it is you two disappear into the bathroom to do together every couple weeks."

Kirin felt his face heat up and he opened and closed his mouth several times trying to think of what to say. He really didn't think Ifrit would appreciate him sharing the knowledge that his hair was in fact dyed— not that anyone other than Ness had been present for his initial... reaction— but the way that Phoenix said it made it sound like they were doing something else.

"Our schedules just line up really well." Kirin finally protested, ignoring the last sentence altogether.

"Whatever the reason, he goes where you go, and we never get the whole class together except for lunch, really. I think tonight'll be good for us, particularly with our rescue licenses being approved soon."

"That's only if we pass our finals. And, in case you've forgotten, we still have to take all the physical exams for our *actual* hero classes, not just the written ones for lecture courses."

"Come on, you of all people have nothing to worry about. You're indestructible and charismatic; if anything, you need to be concerned about how many random citizens will be swooning over you when you come in all rugged-like to save them."

"Very funny Phoenix, but I do mean it. We only have a week left to prep—"

"And exercising yourself to death is the worst way to do that. Now shoo; I need your social battery fully charged for tonight. Medusa made visinada, and I fully intend to spike it."

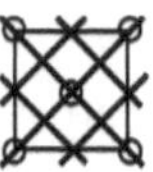

Phoenix did spike it, not that there was a lack of other alcohol present. The door was locked, the shades were pulled down, and their entire class was sprawled out on the couches. Everyone had calmed down and were now listening to the drunken wisdom of Dulu, who was the only person still standing, waving his arms around for emphasis.

"But if it *wasn't* related to AI, why did it crop up at the same time? Evolution takes *thousands* of years, and the emergence of miens just HAPPENS to coincide with another incredible world event? Like we know that the world would've become too hot to be habitable if almost all technology hadn't been shut down for several years, but most of the first miens weren't even helpful in that regard; none of them could do shit to deal with climate change! Even if we're to believe the argument that this was the 'next step of human evolution,' it's so strange that they appeared throughout the world at the same time, and during the same period the AI did."

"Do you think it was the AI that did it?" Adlivun was leaning against Phoenix, whose eyes were almost entirely shut. When she spoke, it jarred him, but she patted the side of his head, and he settled back down.

"No, no that's ridiculous. I think—"

"I swear Dulu, if you say you think it was the government—"

"But it makes sense, Ness!"

"Alright, I could buy that they were maybe looking into it, but miens appeared *after* the AI collapse. They wouldn't have *had* the research anymore when everything went offline." Kirin chimed in. He was almost entirely sober, since he'd been nursing the same drink for the past three hours. Heads turned to see him, as he and Ifrit were sitting behind the couch, in the corner of the room next to the kitchen. Ifrit was rather subdued after having several cups of the visinada, which had made Medusa smile widely, especially when he begrudgingly asked her how to make it.

"Okay, okay, but that actually *helps* the theory. It's a volatile time, why throw another unknown into the mix, right? Except I would guess that it wasn't intentional at all, but instead almost a containment breach due to the fact that all the labs working on it would have been shut down." It was lucky that Dulu's cup was almost empty, otherwise he would've been splashing people as he gestured with it. As it was, he kept waking up those who'd managed to fall asleep on the floor, his wings smacking them in the face as he paced.

"And the fact that it appeared in disparate locations?" Yantra prompted. She was smiling broadly, clearly not buying a word he said.

"It's like the space race, right? They were all trying to be the first to create genetically altered humans, and maybe they'd actually done it, and hadn't perfected it yet, and that's why so many miens have physical drawbacks. But, either way, if one company was researching it, you can bet everything that others were too."

The room was quiet as everyone considered (or fell back asleep).

"I don't know. It still seems like a reach when you think about the restrictions on human testing we have *today*, even with miens being a hot ticket item to debate, you know? Arguably, there's more a reason to look at people now than ever, and yet dozens of countries have signed on to state they won't do any human experimentation themselves and will attack any countries that do." Wyrm was frowning over his drink, swirling the liquid in the bottle.

"Again, it's a *conspiracy*." Goldhorn subtly took the cup out of Dulu's hand, and he continued speaking like he hadn't noticed at all. "They're in on it! Maybe consensual testing would be a good thing, would help us know more about why everything does what it does and how best to work with it. We've done a bunch of body scans with the tech department now to best see how to fit us; what's the difference? The only reason they don't want us to be looked at by scientists is because it'll lead the trail straight back to them."

"The difference is being treated like a guinea pig or not." Yantra spoke quietly, but the wind immediately went out of Dulu. When she saw everyone looking at her, she shrugged, uncomfortable, and continued. "We're all here voluntarily. We all want to learn more, not about everyone, just about ourselves. Some people don't want to."

"I did say consensual." Dulu sunk back into his seat, Naddāha giving him a pat on the head to soothe him.

"Does it matter?" Ness spoke up in the silence, materializing on the couch.

"What?"

"Does it matter where our abilities originated from? Some think it's from gods, some think devils, some from a lab, some from nature. There are as many theories on this as there are people, but I don't terribly care where it came from. It's here and that's that. I think that's why they don't bother to look into it."

"They don't look into it because they don't want any fucking more of us." There was nothing visually different about Ifrit's posture than usual, but something in his tone made Kirin tense. "They figure out where it comes from, and it's something replicable? Boom, every fucking asshole with money gets to be a *hero*."

"Maybe, but in the same vein, if they could figure out where it comes from, they could potentially figure out how to stop it." Enenra rarely spoke, and when she did, it was always softly. She was also sober, Kirin was pretty sure, since she'd had one drink and smoke had started curling off her fingers.

"I think it's probably always been around." Yantra was flipping an empty cup repeatedly, the rhythmic clatter of it against the wood of the table so loud in the room now that the music had been turned off.

"The stories of gods and heroes?" *And demons*. Kirin left out the last part with a glance at Ifrit.

"Exactly. Humans aren't exactly original, everything comes from somewhere, from some unexplained thing that we've seen, or a puzzle we're trying to solve. Maybe it was just far less common, and maybe we lost the thread for a while, but then it came snapping back, more than ever, and this time it stuck."

"That's getting dangerously close to saying we *are* gods." Kuafu's eyes were bright.

"Maybe we are. Not in the sense of all powerful, almighty, but in the sense of the old gods, the ones that people claimed came down to Earth and interacted with people. I don't think *that's* so far-fetched—"

"That's a dangerous line of thought to go down. We're people, nothing more, and we should not be conflated with gods, false or otherwise." Kuafu was on the edge of his seat now, ready to make Yantra stop, even if it had to be by force.

"What is your *deal* with that?" Phoenix whined. He was suddenly awake, though he didn't move at all from his perch on

Adlivun. "People talk about it all the time. We're inevitably going to be compared. Hell, I think Majesty's class is all *named* after deities. Look at fucking Bia!"

"That doesn't make it right."

"It's just words! And like Yantra said, it could honestly be true—"

"Words matter!" Kuafu was on his feet, the air in front of his hands shimmering though the light hadn't fully ignited.

"Of course they do." Lilin was in suddenly front of him, though Kirin wasn't sure how she'd gotten up from the floor so quickly. "No one's saying they don't."

"But you don't know the half of it." Kuafu was still breathing heavily, but the heat coming off him had lessened.

"You sure you want to go there?" Ifrit was the one who asked, and Kirin looked toward him with a raised eyebrow, but the red-eyed man was staring at Kuafu.

"If none of them understand—"

"You can't take it back once you do."

"I know what the fuck I'm doing!"

"You're drunk, dumbass."

"Then maybe I should talk about you instead, if you're so concerned about reputation."

Ifrit had vaulted over the couch and was in Kuafu's face before Kirin managed to stand up. Lilin had been shoved back, but Kirin couldn't tell which one of them had done it. She fell back into Clidna, who'd been struggling to her feet, the pair of them landing in a pile.

"You got something you want to say?" Ifrit was a good ten centimeters taller than Kuafu, but the shorter man didn't look intimidated at all.

"You tell me."

Suddenly, both their faces went slack, as if all the anger had been drained away. Ifrit's eyes went wide and his head turned rigidly to look at Naddāha.

"Stop it." Without any heat behind his words, he just sounded frightened.

"Not until you back up a few steps." She was standing now too, eyes flickering between the two men.

"Stop it *now*." Ifrit started to advance on her, but Kirin managed to intercept him first.

"Hey, hey, it's alright." Kirin put his hands on Ifrit's shoulders and was shocked to feel that the other man was *shaking*.

As if sensing Kirin's thoughts, Ifrit shoved his hands off, and quickly turned around and marched to the stairs, starting to run up before the door even closed behind him. The sound of the door slamming did little to fill the emptiness that his abrupt departure left. Kirin took a single step to follow him, but then he registered Ifrit's last expression, aimed not at Naddāha, but at Kirin.

Disgust.

"Well, he lasted longer than I thought he would." Phoenix said dryly.

"Not funny." Kirin tried to banish the memory of Ifrit's face by turning to Kuafu who still looked dazed. After a sharp glance at Naddāha, Kuafu's usual intensity returned, and Kirin felt some of the tightness in his chest loosen. "Are you alright?"

Kuafu's dark eyes flickered to Kirin, anger filling them again. The anger didn't seem directed at Kirin, nor Naddāha who'd just used her mien on him. Instead, he focused on Phoenix.

"Is everything a joke to you?" The question was asked softly, yet it fell like a stone, silence reigning as Phoenix stared back up at Kuafu. He finally stood from his position on the floor, wobbling slightly, but brushing off Adlivun's hand. Kirin took advantage of the distraction to slip back to his now solitary corner.

"Everyone out there's laughing at us." The words came out

quietly at first, strengthening into a bitter hardness as Phoenix went on. "They see us trying, trying to fit in, trying to prove we're not monsters, and they just *laugh*. I used to think that there was just some secret joke that I wasn't getting, but that wasn't it. The joke is thinking that they'd ever accept us, and that we should even fucking want them to. So now I laugh, at them, and at you, and at anyone who wants me to be something I'm not."

"That's a pretty sentiment, but not all of us get to." Kuafu was eyeing Phoenix though, like he'd just discovered something he hadn't expected.

"You're on probation too, then?" Naddāha stepped between the pair, the slight disturbance enough to cause Phoenix to fall back down to his pile of cushions on the ground. He didn't attempt to get back up, and while Naddāha was drawing the attention of most of their classmates, Kirin frowned as he watched an almost pained expression flicker across Phoenix's face.

"Not entirely." Phoenix muttered.

"Too?" Medusa cocked her head.

"Don't play coy; I know you are as well." Naddāha placed a bottle in Medusa's outstretched hand.

"Naturally." Medusa accepted the drink with a smile.

"No, what, not naturally." Aïcha shot upright from where she was lounging. "What do you mean?"

"At least a few of the people in our class are suspected— or confirmed— to have committed the crime of using their miens illegally." Yantra rolled her head back as she spoke, staring up at the ceiling like she hadn't said anything important.

"Criminals, huh?" Clidna was playing with the rim of her drink, her finger lazily tracing circles. "Good for you guys."

"Good for us?" Kuafu nearly spluttered.

"I can venture a guess as to what Naddāha did, but I'm not so sure about the rest." Medusa nodded to herself.

"We *are* glossing over this way too fast." Ness interjected. "I know what *I* did; what did Mr. Rules here do?"

She was pointing her thumb at Kuafu, who had gone rigid.

"I don't know if he's quite ready to talk about that, Ness." Adlivun said gently.

"Do you know what happens to people like us who think they're gods?"

Adlivun's eyes looked sad as Kuafu continued to speak.

"They're killed. There's no mercy, no chance to just put your hands up when the heroes come in. If you're a kid, they might spare you, if you can convince them that you didn't understand what was going on, that you didn't realize people were getting hurt. And maybe that's true, maybe you didn't know at the beginning, and having people tell you that you were special was just... nice. But then you grow up. And it's all you've ever known. People trying to please you, trying to ask you for advice and help, and you think that that's correct, that it makes sense."

Kuafu seemed oblivious to the horrified silence.

"Then, even when you start to see things that tell you no, it's just something that many people can do, you just think the world should listen to them too. That people like you *are* special, are *godly*, that they know more than everyone else in the world. You think that what you're doing is right. You feel it with all your being because everyone standing beside you, the people who raised you, tell you that it's true. You have purpose and meaning, and you are *good*.

"And then the heroes come, because in *your* name atrocities have been committed. In *your* name people have been killed for daring to question why a thirteen-year-old kid should be listened to. In *your* name towns have been burned. Your family, your friends, will look at you, begging you to do something, but in the end, you are not a god. You're a child, and all you can do is watch."

Phoenix looked like he was going to say something, but Kuafu cut him off.

"You then have to spend the next several years questioning everything that you thought you knew, everything that you believed. And people tell you to just listen to your heart, but that's no fucking good because last time you listened, a town was wiped off the map. So you stick to the rules. You try your hardest to follow the path that's been laid out before you, and you do not question it because it can't be any worse than thinking you're something you're not."

As the words sunk through the room, it felt like no one dared move, or even breathe. Kuafu had sounded like he should have been crying, but his face didn't betray an inch of grief, only intense desperation, hoping his words got through.

"Was it... was it Satol?" Ness asked quietly. "I know they said it was mien cultists, but I never really believed there *was* such a thing."

"No." Kuafu cut her off sharply. "That wasn't my group, but it could have been."

"And it's much closer than you think." Phoenix actually looked contrite, lines around his mouth tightening. "I mentioned to a few of you that I got dragged to one of those mien assessment groups, yeah? Basically the same shit. They decided that being demeaning to people with abilities was *rude*, so they swung the other way. I just had to sit there and listen to them venerate heroes, talking about how they *clearly* were inspired by something greater than mere mortals, that there *must* be a reason why they had abilities and others didn't, and that they only needed to listen to every damn thing people with powers had to say, and they'd be rewarded in the next life too."

"If you want to know more about Satol you should talk to Pressure." Yantra was looking at Ness, but her eyes weren't terribly focused.

"Pressure?"

"She was the first hero on the scene, after all."

Heads turned toward Yantra, who didn't notice anyone at all but Ness.

"I followed every scrap of news on that for years, and I never heard that." Kirin was proud that he managed to keep his voice from trembling. Already, he could feel the prickling heat just at the base of his neck.

"Haven't any of you wondered why you've never heard of a hero named Pressure?" Yantra shook her head. "It's cause back then she was still Force."

The name rang in Kirin's ears, a bright blue filling his vision, the poster in his room, steely eyes peering down from a billboard.

"How do you know that was her? The costume covered almost her whole face." Goldhorn leaned forward quickly, Dulu tilting out of the way and almost falling on Naddāha in his attempt to not get gored.

"I know a lot of things I'm not supposed to."

"She's right, though."

Phoenix turned and pointed an accusatory finger in Adlivun's face.

"*You* also know far more than you should, and I would certainly like to know how. You can't keep avoiding the question forever."

"It's all in the name." Adlivun's curt tone blocked any further questions.

"It's not shocking that you wouldn't know; though she was and still is one of the most prominent heroes— hell the whole city's covered in photos of her— she was also one of the most private. More's known about her partner, Valor, though he's faded into near oblivion in the past few years." Yantra continued, ignoring the interruption.

"How's she here, though? She's still active." Kirin had been about to voice the same concern when Aïcha beat him to it.

"Oh, there are *so* many theories about that." Yantra's eyes gleamed in a way that promised this wasn't going to be a short explanation. "Yes, she's still very much active, but though her mien is great for combat, post Satol, she hasn't been seen in combat calls at *all*. Obviously, now we know it's just that she's here teaching, but there were all kinds of ideas going around, like she'd adopted the kid who did it, or lost her license, somehow, or even some thought that maybe she'd *lost* her mien. I used to scroll through those for *hours*, just trying to see if any of them had any evidence. None of them did, sadly."

"But how do you know that Pressure is *her*? Surely someone would have figured it out by now. It's been almost a decade." Kapre was one of the most sober, but they were looking a little out of it, though that might simply be because of how late it'd gotten.

"You don't want to know how I know that, unless you want to be accessory to a crime."

"Pressure, Force, I suppose it's roughly the same name." Aïcha tapped her fingers along her lips, deep in thought. "But I don't know, her... well, her whole image seems different than what I'd expect Force's to be, you know?"

"I trust that Yantra wouldn't say that without proof, but I do agree with you." Enenra had to be considering it deeply, since she was fully back together. "Force pulled out the kid who did it. Found him next to another kid who was half dead. People used that photo for *years*, her carrying the boy, both covered in blood. She gained this aura of protectiveness, of justice. Pressure, well, she really doesn't have that."

"And why bother trying to hide who she is from us? I mean, it's unlikely we'd figure it out, but what's the point?" Dulu, previous king of conspiracy theories, seemed to be drawing a blank for this one.

"I imagine it's just a hero worship thing. I can't think of a single other hero who has such international recognition like Force does. I know both Aïcha *and* Ness have posters of her in their rooms, and I bet a whole lot more of you do too." Yantra pointed a finger around, accusing them all. "Or maybe it's even as simple as they don't want to remind us of Satol itself. I know it traumatized me enough as a kid."

"Isn't that just part and parcel with our jobs, though? We'll likely see things just as bad in the future." Antaeus didn't look happy at that prospect.

"Yeah, but that kid was only ten years old. I can't imagine anything worse than that."

"I still can't believe that they were able to use such a little kid as a weapon." Ness shook her head, more transparent than usual. Kirin thought he could see the grain of the couch cushions through her. "You'd think it would have made people realize that for some of us, our miens aren't controllable, not at that age, not ever, but somehow it just made them convinced we all had the power to level a city."

"The legislation is more likely to reflect that before the people do." Dulu dismissed his wings and then re-summoned them, thunder rumbling across the sky just a moment after. "If I don't release my wings at least once a day, it hurts *so much*. My... before I came here, I could afford it. So it wasn't that big a deal, but what if there are people like me out there, who are hurting themselves because they don't have access to a gym? Because they don't own their own homes? What do they do other than become criminals?"

"I know some people are still a little tipsy, so I'm going to remind everyone to watch what they say in here. You never know who might be listening." Clidna had been idly twisting a strand of ginger hair around her finger; now she was gripping it tightly in a way that had to hurt.

"There were bugs, but I dealt with them the first day we got here." Yantra shrugged when people looked at her.

"Good to know, that." Naddāha snorted.

"They gave us new phones and laptops— did any of us really think they *weren't* listening in?"

"I just don't get why they need to watch us so much. We had to pass background checks to get here, and if all the so-called issues some of us had are like his—" Aïcha waved a hand vaguely in Kuafu's direction— "it sounds like they were ages ago and not even your fault! If they really didn't trust us that much, why are we here?"

"They trust us individually, but I think they worry about things like what we're doing right now." Adlivun looked up to find every eye on her. "We're not supposed to talk about our lives before not just to protect our families if someone gets captured, but also because we're not supposed to interact with them. But they leave a mark on all of us, one way or another."

Her hands absently strayed to the scar around her throat.

"Dulu, you're sympathetic to people who use their abilities illegally *because* your mien causes you pain if you don't use it. Kuafu, you'll be more lenient with kids found in cults or other abusive situations because you know firsthand how overwhelming and all-consuming their rhetoric is. Alone, that's one weakness. But together? Together we're pulling at the threads of every lie woven together to stop people like us from questioning why things are the way they are."

Kirin felt the muscles in his back tighten as glances went around the room, not casual or friendly looks, but curious ones, each pair of eyes holding a single question. What did you do, they asked, to land yourself here, in this room? Not many fell on him, except one. When he dared look up, Adlivun was looking straight into his eyes.

"You think Majesty's class has the same problem?" Kapre asked.

The tension snapped as immediately Phoenix, Dulu, and Yantra collapsed laughing, the rest of the class following not long after.

"Shit, could you imagine any of them even *thinking* about the wider implications of hero society?" Yantra could barely get the words out, laughing so hard she could hardly breathe.

"Hello, my name is Bia, I think the best way to get someone's help is to attack them. Shall we debate the morality of heroism?" Naddāha managed to keep a straight face up until the last few words, leaving Phoenix howling.

"Guys, guys, come on, be nice." Lilin's mouth was twitching with a suppressed smile even as she tried to calm them down. "That was a horrible impression Naddāha; I don't think she knows how to ask a question instead of demanding."

"Oh, you're *so* right."

Conversation resumed around the room; discomfort shattered in the face of laughter. Kirin managed to make himself smile as he was pulled into some sort of game by Ness, but his heart felt like lead in his chest. While they might all have secrets, while they might all have been allowed in, it still meant that if any of them stepped out of line, there was a free pass for the school to send them away. Not even just back to their old lives, but *away*, for the rest of their days.

And Kirin wasn't sure how small of an infraction it would take for them to use that excuse.

10

Testing

"Stop shaking your fucking leg. You're vibrating the entire counter."

"Sorry, I'm just anxious." Kirin made a conscious effort to stop his leg from bouncing, but it barely changed anything. He'd felt wired since they'd woken up, unsure how prepared he was for the practical exam they had that very morning. It didn't help that this was the first time Ifrit had come to breakfast since the party the week before, and though they'd still been studying as usual, Kirin couldn't help but feel like he'd offended the man somehow.

Ifrit frowned, though it might have been because he almost messed up the omelet he was flipping.

"You'll be fine, dumbass."

"I know, but is fine enough? We get our rescue licenses if we pass, so it's got to be hard, right? And I know that I'm good in some situations, but not all. My mobility isn't great since I can only run and—"

"If we need to fly anywhere, I'll just carry you. And you're one of the fucking best in class, so shut up about 'some situations.' It's pissing me off." Ifrit pushed a bowl of rice with a rolled omelet to Kirin, who accepted it gratefully. He'd been making breakfast for their floor the past few days, and if Ifrit hadn't been cooking this morning he likely would have skipped breakfast altogether.

"Can you really carry me though? I'm not exactly light." Kirin thought out loud.

"If it doesn't come up today, you'll find out tomorrow. That's one of the main things I've been fucking working on, carrying other things and people when I'm in the air." Ifrit was surprisingly calm today, looking almost contemplative as he ate his own food. Maybe he'd just needed a few days by himself.

"Did you manage to carry two hundred kilos?"

"Fuck, you're really that dense?"

Kirin shrugged.

"But yes, I did, if you're really that fucking worried."

Kirin looked at the other man's relatively lithe frame, considering.

"You're really amazing, you know?"

Phoenix opened her door as Ifrit started to splutter.

"Damn, you guys are awake already? Where's the fairness in that?" She whined.

"Breakfast. Now." Ifrit shoved a bowl across the counter, and Phoenix's face lit up with a smile. She was certainly not a morning person, and if neither of them made her food in the morning, she'd constantly forget to eat. It'd silently become a habit, one of the boys making breakfast for the whole floor in the morning.

"We've got time though, don't we?" Phoenix asked, looking between the two of them. It was true that the class had been pushed back two hours to make sure everyone was well-rested, but Kirin had too much energy to sit still.

"I was going to go for a jog to warm up before the exam, and Ifrit said he'd join after he finished the dishes." Kirin finished his bowl and stood up to wash it, but it was wrenched unceremoniously out of his hands. Ifrit already had the water running, steam pouring off it as he scrubbed the dish like it'd personally offended him. Kirin bit back a laugh; Ifrit *was* nervous then, at least a little.

"You two are monsters. I'm sure we're going to be exhausted after the practical, and you're both willingly adding more exercise into the day? Madness." Phoenix did eat quickly, however, handing Ifrit her bowl before he'd finished washing their rice cooker. "If I join you, I'd die, right?"

"Maybe grab Kapre if you're lookin' for someone to keep pace with." Kirin gave Phoenix a squeeze on the shoulder as he stood up, Ifrit already heading for the stairs.

"It's collaborative, so don't go too hard!" Phoenix yelled after them.

"I'm not going to ask how you know that." Kirin called back.

When they arrived at the Disaster Simulator, the interior was much like the first time they'd seen it. Rows of houses and false streets stretched out as far as the eye could see. Nothing seemed out of place yet, but they'd once had to deal with a simulated sinkhole, so Kirin had no doubt that the landscape would change rapidly once the exam began.

Most of their class was in costume, their hero designs having already come in. Only Kirin and Ifrit were still left in plain exercise clothes. Even though it was just an exam, Kirin felt his heart swell gazing at his friends who already looked like heroes. Medusa was the most changed, in both appearance and posture. Instead of her usual blindfold, she wore a pair of goggles with retractable lenses. Apparently, there were screens inside that showed her the world outside, her cane nowhere to be seen. The first time she'd put them on, she'd nearly cried, looking at all of them in turn.

For a moment, doubt filled him. He and Ifrit stood out, not only for the lack of specialized equipment, but also two black stones in a sea of bright color. Everyone around them *looked* the part; would he ever? Ifrit didn't seem to share his doubts, instead standing with his head held high. This was what he wanted, Kirin realized. He wanted to be apart from it, just as much as he wanted to be a part of it.

"Alright kids, big day today." Pressure clapped her hands in front of them. It was the first time they'd all seen her in person since the party the week before, and Kirin looked at her more closely than usual. But nothing appeared out of place, nothing seemed to say that yes, this was one of the greatest heroes ever known. She just seemed like... Pressure.

"You may have noticed that we've got a set up like the very first lesson you had in here, and that's by design. Over the past several months, you've practiced getting people out of these types of situations, but notably you've been missing one big thing: a villain.

"After the semester is over, you'll receive your temporary rescue licenses. The hardest part of the next few months won't be rescuing people, it'll be avoiding a fight. Natural disasters are common, even post climate change, but the majority of calls you will be responding to will involve other mien users. You'll be licensed to *rescue*, but not to *fight*. Not even to defend yourself. This makes the job doubly difficult, but it does have a practical purpose. When you're in an active situation, your priority should always be to rescue as many people as possible."

Phantasm cocked her head at Pressure but didn't interrupt.

"Further down the line, when you can confront villains directly, there's always the temptation to go after those responsible. You'll see things that are horrific, things that fill you with rage. That we're able to act on that rage is both a blessing and a curse. I know in my career, there're times when I chased someone down instead of saving those who were in front of me, and I have to live with that. Always. Use this time to focus on prioritizing those in need above wanting to attack those who caused it."

It was hard to tell, but there was something brittle about Pressure's expression. She looked so small for a moment, her eyes deeply haunted. Then the moment passed, and it was smoothed away under her usual casual confidence.

"To simulate this as best we can, this will be like a normal day of training for you. Phantasm will conjure a number of 'civilians' for you to find and rescue, but there will be an active villain situation nearby. In order to pass, you must evacuate *all* civilians to a marked safe zone, and none of you may engage the villain in a fight. You'll have to assess the field situation, find all your civilians, *and* keep an evacuation path clear. The exam will run for six hours, or until all civilians are evacuated, or if one of you attacks the villain."

"Question!"

"Yes, Phoenix?" Pressure used the world-weary tone that she reserved for their energetic classmate.

"Can we defend the civilians? Like if the villain would be doing something that would hit them, can we step in the way?"

"Clarify."

"Can we use our abilities to defend? Like could Kirin stand between the villain and the civilians and block whatever attack, or would that count as engaging?"

Pressure and Phantasm looked at each other and considered it for a moment.

"In the field, situations like that would be subject to review by the Hero Commission on a case-by-case basis. They usually don't look kindly on anything outside of the exact scope of the licenses, so it would be best to avoid situations like that as much as possible." Phantasm replied.

"Thanks, Teach!"

Pressure rolled her eyes.

"I have a question as well." Kuafu spoke up, looking unlike himself dressed in such a bright shade of yellow. His costume was well designed, with fitted pants and a tight top to give him a good range of movement, but Kirin had never seen him wear anything lighter than a dark gray, so he felt that perhaps Kuafu's armorer had missed the mark slightly.

"Ask away."

"Who will be the villain in this situation?"

Pressure smiled.

Turning her back to the class, she raised her hand toward the town. A wave of force rippled outwards and buildings practically exploded from the pressure, chunks of concrete flying as a straight line was gouged through the town, breaking water mains and causing electricity to spark. There was a dull thud, and a slash was driven deep into the exterior wall of the building, hundreds of meters from where they stood. Any doubt Kirin had about Yantra's claim faded away. Pressure turned back to face them.

"Me, of course. Any more questions?"

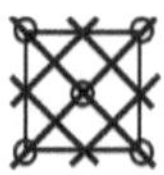

A chunk of rock hit Kirin in the face, breaking his concentration. The wall sagged for just a moment until he found his footing again.

"Are you alright? We can pause." Enenra was immediately at his side, her round face streaked with dirt and concern.

"Yeah, sorry, I'm fine." He readjusted his grip and lifted the wall a little higher, his face screwed up in concentration. They'd barely gotten there in time, the corner of the building just starting to go, but he'd managed to push his tired legs to run faster, shoving his whole body into the opening and crystalliz-ing before it fell.

"It'll only be a few more minutes; Kapre's found the rest of the civilians in this section. Ifrit's team seems to be doing well, or at least they were when he last checked in." Enenra had been vaporizing to wiggle into the buildings to check for obstructions whenever their group of three broke away from Kapre's, and it seemed that every time she came back it was harder. Now, the edges of her shaved head looked fuzzy, and her fingers passed through his shoulder once before she managed to give him an encouraging pat.

"Take your time." Kirin wished he meant it, but he was run-ning on fumes. They were five hours in, now, and every muscle burned. He hadn't been running this low on carbon since he'd arrived at the school, and part of him was beginning to think that he'd soon be useless.

"Civilian secured, we're good to move out." Medusa ap-peared, carrying a phantom over her shoulder. As time wore on, they were finding more and more "injured" civilians than before, leading them to have to carry their rescues all the way to the safe zone. If there was one thing that Kirin could be thankful for, it was that Ifrit had insisted they start their sweep from the furthest section and then move closer to their base; if it'd been the other way around, his legs surely would've given out by now.

The women exited the building, Enenra staying just outside as Medusa struck off toward the safe zone. She signaled to Kirin that Medusa was clear of the building and then headed off herself, Kirin starting his thirty second countdown.

As he counted, he could feel the sweat rolling down his

face, all that on his back and hands frozen in diamond for the moment, at least. But he made himself wait every single second, before shoving the building off himself and sprinting away.

He'd realized that crystallizing his ears deadened the sound, but with how low his reserves were, he'd let go of that luxury. The sound of the brick falling was now routine from the months spent in the simulator, so his steps didn't falter for a moment. A few seconds later he caught up to Medusa, lifting the phantom off her shoulder and onto his own.

"Was that the last one for this area?" He focused on putting one foot in front of the other.

"Yes, or at least the last that Kapre told us to get. We'll rendezvous with the others at the safe zone and if Yantra, Kapre, or Goldhorn are there, we can double check." Medusa seemed just as tired as everyone, yet the set of her jaw was determined. It was good that the goggles weren't meant to be seen through, because they were entirely covered in dust.

Enenra stumbled behind Kirin for a moment, her entire leg fuzzing to smoke before reforming. Kirin grabbed her around the waist and tucked her under his arm without breaking step. She gave two brief taps on his hand as a thank you, becoming more solid as they continued on.

"Where's Pressure now? I haven't seen any new destruction." He didn't have the energy to waste on looking around himself, still focusing on walking evenly despite the rubble. Enenra's face swung in and out of view with each step, the color slowly seeping back into her cheeks, the focus returning to her dark, almond-shaped eyes.

"Kapre's team went to the area closest to her, since they're the best equipped to avoid any potential blasts that might come their way." Enenra was sounding much steadier now, but she hadn't given the signal that meant she was ready to be put down. Her new suit had helped tremendously; she'd only begun to struggle with corporeality in the last hour or so. It was hard to see the faint lines of energy that slid up and down the gray jumpsuit usually, but now they were pulsing with light as she struggled to stay in one piece.

"That's good at least. Medusa, you doing okay?"

"It's better today. Still a little sick to my stomach, but nothing I need to stop for." Medusa gave him a wide smile, almost glowing. It'd taken her a few weeks to get used to her goggles, especially since she wasn't used to running and having her vision bounce around. Apparently, the small, light brown hairs that slipped out of her bun were the worst for her motion sickness; more than once she'd considered shaving it all off, joking that the snakes were driving her crazy.

"And the safe zone is coming into sight, so we're just about done." With the goal just a few dozen meters away, Kirin felt his back straighten and a wave of energy came over him. He could see Phoenix already there, tallying the teams who were dropping off shades and healing any of their classmates who were looking particularly ragged.

Enenra tapped his arm again and he let her down, walking farther into the cleared area to put the phantom down with the rest of the "injured" civilians. They'd been told to behave as if this were a real emergency, so Phoenix had established a "sick bay" area of the safe zone and was busy cataloguing the injuries that the shades would describe when prompted.

"Last one for your section?" She asked as he set his cargo down.

"As far as we know. Has Kapre checked in recently? Or Yantra? I want to make sure we're done before I get my hopes up."

"Not recently; they got back just after you dropped off your last couple civilians and left again, but Goldhorn is here. They're checking for any missed people now." Phoenix shooed Kirin away with a wave of her hand, holo screen pulled up from her phone with a running tally of injuries sustained.

Goldhorn was sitting on the entire other side of the safe zone, eyes closed and plants writhing underneath them. It was alarming to see that they were freely bleeding, but it must've not been bothering them since Phoenix hadn't taken care of it.

"Ifrit's group is on their way back with the last of the civilians in the west quadrant, Kapre and Yantra are just about finished with each of their confirmation sweeps to make sure we didn't miss anyone in the other three." They didn't look his way, but clearly noticed his approach.

"Do we think they've got the last few?" Dulu was sitting down, his wings folded neatly behind himself, his group scattered throughout the safe area.

"I couldn't tell you, but their pace is slow, so they're not rushing." Goldhorn looked striking in their costume, all gold and green, their white-blond hair reflecting the gold of their horns, but they were marred with dirt and grime which sullied the effect.

"And Pressure? Do we know where she is?" Kirin uncapped the water bottle that Aïcha unceremoniously shoved in his hands.

"It's hard to say. She doesn't stay on the ground for long."

"I haven't noticed any new attacks in a while, do we think that means we did it?"

"I hope so." Antaeus took the water bottle he was offered, sighing as he did. "My arms have been shaking for the last hour, I think."

Whatever Kirin was going to say was interrupted by a horrible screeching sound. Every hair on his body stood up and he watched as a line appeared just outside of the safe zone. Buildings, streetlights, cars— everything in the path of an invisible force was flattened to the ground, a chunk of the building across the street removed entirely. The sound of tearing metal echoed in his ears for a moment, but then everything was silent, still.

A breeze came from the force of it, bringing the smell of dust. And slowly, ever so slowly, the building began to tilt toward them.

"Goldhorn, Antaeus— stabilize the base as much as you can, but once it begins to tilt faster, just get out of the way. Everyone else! Clear the civilians as best you can, up into the watch deck if you need to. Start centered on the building and then move outwards in terms of priority. Those who are well enough to walk should, but we'll take care of the injured." Kirin could hardly believe it was his own voice he was hearing, because part of him felt like he hadn't even processed what just happened. This wasn't going to happen again; he wasn't going to be helpless *again*.

His classmates exploded into action, scrambling to move people out of the way. Goldhorn and Antaeus rushed forwards, Antaeus pulling a number of small items from the large pockets of his suit. The plants that had surrounded Goldhorn ripped through the ground after them, growing in size and thickness as they went. Kirin turned away from the building and grabbed as many people as he could, running as fast as his legs would let him, all tiredness forgotten. Antaeus and Goldhorn seemed to be holding the building for now, as the tilt had decreased, but the creaking noise was still filling the air, and even as he dropped off his civilians and turned back, he could see the pair struggling.

They held out for another five minutes before things got worse.

The moment the building had started to go, all thoughts of this being an exercise had left Kirin's head. There was only the pounding of his feet as he ran as fast as he could back and forth to clear the impact area, the burning of his lungs as he struggled to breathe, and the ache in his limbs as he hoisted another group of "civilians" over his shoulder. He'd fallen into a routine almost, and it gave his stressed mind just enough time to wander that he caught the flicker of brown hair that was visible just beyond Antaeus.

In a split second he was changing direction and running at the smaller man, who was still trying to move rubble into the opening to brace the building as best he could, Goldhorn's face similarly screwed up in concentration. The pair saw him only a moment before he crashed into them both, tucking and rolling away seconds before another wave of force passed just over his head. With no time to crystalize, Kirin felt the pressure ripple over his back, tearing open his shirt and spilling blood.

The horrible screech of metal filled the air again as Goldhorn's bracing fell away, the building above them newly unbalanced and crashing down rapidly. Kirin felt his strength fading as he got to his knees, Goldhorn and Antaeus still dazed under him.

"COVER YOUR HEADS!" He hoped the pair understood as he threw them to the side as hard as he could.

Goldhorn reacted for the both of them, covering Antaeus with their own body and then covering the back of their own head with one arm as they crashed to the ground beyond the edge of the building. Kirin went to take a step after them, but his legs gave out and he fell to the ground, vision swimming.

The sounds of bricks falling off the façade was distant now, as was Goldhorn's voice, and he looked up to see the building coming toward him with such sincere finality that part of him just couldn't look away. The wetness on his back made him feel cold, his eyes seeing a different building, nursing a different pain, but feeling just as weak.

He turned to the side to see Goldhorn yelling something he couldn't hear, their vines reaching out toward him but still so far away, Antaeus swaying on his feet but standing. Kirin could have smiled if his brain was working right— they were out of the path, at least.

Of course you couldn't save everyone.

As if the thought tricked his brain into coherence, Kirin summoned every last bit of strength that he had; unable to move he turned to his mien, crystallizing as much of his body as he could: his head, his neck, his chest. It felt weak and flimsy, like it did back then, but it was something, even if he couldn't bring himself to look away.

And suddenly his vision was filled with light as Ifrit appeared, wreathed in flame as he shot toward Kirin. The shine hit his skin and the space once filled with shadow was now illuminated by shimmering, glittering light, as Ifrit reached his hands out, and in a single shot, blasted away the building that would have crushed them.

The last of Kirin's carbon ran out and he fell to the side, too weak to hold up his body. He felt hands on him, horns peeking into his vision— Goldhorn, then— words being said to him that he didn't manage to process. All he could see was Ifrit there, silhouetted in a halo of fire against a clear sky.

One last line flitted through his head before he lost consciousness.

Wow, he thought, *so that's what a hero looks like.*

11

Assignment

Kirin couldn't speak for a moment as he caught his reflection in the polished white surface of Nwabudike's desk.

"It fits perfectly." His words sounded distant to his own ears, still staring at what he couldn't believe was *himself*. The man in the reflection was tall, his height accentuated rather than hidden by the close fitted top. The shine in his hair seemed less like an oil slick and more like obsidian, matching the black pants. The top was so light it was nearly white, but gold swirled across his chest and up his throat, matching the faintly shimmering outline around the pants pockets. With his hair pulled back and up he almost looked austere, intimidating.

"It's not chafing against your bandages at all?" Nwabudike spoke up again and Kirin wrenched his eyes away from his reflection.

"No, but hopefully I shouldn't have to worry about that in the future." He offered Nwabudike a genuine smile, realizing he'd been so surprised it must've come across as dissatisfaction. The younger man gave him a smile in return, his posture finally relaxing and his excited energy returning.

"Certainly not with this! The mask has a charge in it to filter for carbon monoxide and dioxide, and I have several extra charges tucked away in the *left* side pockets, but since you asked, I also have oxygen ones in the *right* side pockets. Do your best to not get those switched up." Now relieved, Nwabudike resumed his usual fussing.

"Now, the material of the shirt we did test several times, but obviously testing is never a match for the real thing so if you could just crystalize a patch for me to confirm it won't rip, I would be most grateful."

"Anywhere?"

"Somewhere it's tightest would probably be best, but yes, anywhere is fine."

The shirt hugged his shoulders and chest firmly, but the final had left his torso wrapped in bandages. The sleeves were form fitting too, however— to make it easy to slide on the leather gloves he'd asked for— and so he crystallized a patch of his forearm instead.

Part of him expected the edges of his skin to rip straight through, despite the extensive testing Nwabudike had done, but to his shock and delight, it held entirely.

"Oh, that's better than I could have hoped for!" Nwabudike clapped his hands and nearly fell as his protheses seized in his excitement. "Try moving around with it, try moving around!"

Kirin grinned and windmilled his arms, trying to cut through the shirt without success. The extra padding at the elbows wasn't noticeable at all; Nwabudike had even thought to add padding to the chest too, so if he needed to conserve carbon and stay fully hardened, he could still hold people without fear of cutting them.

"It seems perfect man, thank you." Tears very nearly threatened to prick Kirin's eyes, but he held them back as best he could. When he got back to the dorm he could cry, probably with Lilin if she put on another one of her dramas to give him an excuse. To hide his misty eyes, he moved to take the suit off and put his civilian clothes back on.

"I wish I could've had it up for the final so you wouldn't have to deal with the healing and all, but from what I hear you still did really well without it!" Nwabudike's eyes were shining when Kirin turned back around, and he scooted forward in his chair eagerly, pen in hand.

"Are you asking me for details? Because I don't think I'm allowed to give you any, firstly, and secondly, I had a building almost fall on me and had to get rescued, which isn't the most heroic way to end the first final."

"But you rescued several of your classmates, no? *And* rescued the second highest number of civilians?"

"Why are you asking me for details if you know all that?"

"Because I want to imagine what it was *like*. I don't get to watch you in action anymore until you start going out there and getting on TV; can you blame me for wanting to imagine what it'll be like with you out there with my design? Sure, I know roughly what happened, but only the pieces." Nwabudike moved his chair even closer, craning his neck to look at Kirin's face. "You're a *hero* already and I want to imagine it fully."

Something about his expectant gaze made Kirin flinch, the awe on Nwabudike's face unabashed.

"Soon, I promise. But right now, I'm in a bit of a hurry; Pressure's waiting." He tried to brush off the feeling of shame at seeing Nwabudike's expression fall, but a larger part of him just wanted to run away.

"Alright, but next meeting, you're giving me *all* the details, okay?"

"Of course, and thanks again man." Kirin gave him another smile as he paused at the door to put on his mask, though Nwabudike already had his head down as his hand darted across a page adding to his notes.

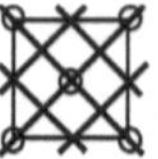

Ifrit had apparently finished before him as he was already on the ground floor when Kirin got out of the elevator, Pressure nowhere to be seen.

"She said to grab you and head to her office, she's rounding up the rest of the fucking idiots." Ifrit apparently had won his fight with his armorer, since he seemed to be in an uncommonly good mood. He looked dangerously close to smiling, even, as they headed out of the building.

"What for?" Kirin's back itched as the bandages pulled from his tensing muscles.

"Since it's been a few days I expect that we'll fucking *finally* be getting our test results and with them, our licenses." Ifrit had his head held high today; triumph clear in his eyes. Kirin felt almost exactly the opposite.

"Well, that's supposing we passed."

Ifrit shot him a look.

"Of course we fucking passed."

"I did almost let a building fall on me." It was the conversation with Nwabudike all over again.

"And you saved two of our classmates before you got there. Not to mention it was the end of a six hour exam and you threw two people almost thirty fucking meters! I'm beginning to think that those muscles aren't just for show." Ifrit snorted. "Do you think Shrink and Horns are going to fail?"

"Well, no—"

"Then why do you think you are?" Ifrit stopped walking and turned to face him. The morning sun seemed pale in comparison to the flame that danced around his throat, to the fire in his red eyes.

"I don't know. I should be able to take care of myself, right? The whole point of training is that we're supposed to be the ones helping people, and not the other way around. If I'm just dead weight out there, I shouldn't be out there, end of story."

"You did the best you fucking could while being *exhausted*, dipshit. It's fine that you needed help because in the real world, we all fucking do at some point. And also, I don't think most people's reaction to seeing a falling building would be to run at it to help someone else, regardless of who they were. You could've decided that this was just training, or that someone else was going to save them, but instead you decided to run, just in case something went wrong." Ifrit took a breath and turned away. "And for what it's worth, you looked like a real fucking hero to me."

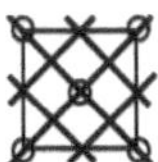

"Kirin, come in." Pressure was standing in the doorway, the framing familiar from the final interview all those months ago. At the time, he'd thought he could never be more nervous in his life, but he continued to find new depths of anxiety.

Ifrit had been the first to be called and had come back out looking pleased. He hadn't bothered sharing anything about how it went, only grabbed his bag and headed out. Kirin had wanted to get his attention, but talking into the silence felt unbearable, as he and the rest of the class sat waiting to find out if they'd passed.

He stood up slowly, almost trying to stretch out the seconds between getting up and going in, but she waved him forward impatiently, so he hurried his pace, and she shut the door behind him.

"How're you healing up?"

This office was rather different than Reader's had been, filled with dozens of photos of Pressure— or rather, Force— posing around the world. Her mask covered the upper half of her face in bright blue, but her smile seemed younger, more carefree. If he didn't know better, he'd think she was just a big fan, maybe because their powers were so similar. It was still hard, sometimes, to associate the powerful, aloof Force with their incredibly casual professor.

"I'm itchy, but that's the worst of it." Kirin took a seat where she pointed, though he would've rather remained standing. At least the chair in this office was not so plush as the ones in Reader's had been. Not that there would've been much room for such unwieldy furniture. It was shockingly small in there, just a simple wooden desk with a rolling chair for Pressure and one metal chair for a guest.

"That's good to hear. We didn't want Phoenix to heal that for you, as it's important to gauge how long it'll take for you to heal from deeper wounds. There may be points when you find yourself alone in the field, and knowing your limits is impor-tant." Pressure took a seat behind the desk, her tone suddenly businesslike. She tapped on the desk's interface, bringing up a holo screen. "Your performance for the majority of the exam was exemplary. You did a good job supporting the team you were working with, showed very impressive endurance for the duration of the test, and when it came down to it, where able to think quickly in an emergency situation when your safe area was compromised. There is, however, one point of weakness that I want to address."

She pressed play on the screen, and he was greeted with his own face, staring up at the building frozen. The crystallization took over a moment later, the blood underneath his skin puls-ing as he watched. The building didn't get as close to him as he thought before Ifrit appeared on screen, the video freezing as flames erupted.

Kirin found himself staring at his own face in diamond, almost unrecognizable from the fire reflected across it. Silence stretched for a few moments before she spoke again.

"Why didn't you try to run?" Pressure was watching him closely, her expression guarded.

"I couldn't. My legs were too weak."

"You didn't try to get up."

"I didn't think I could."

"But you didn't *try*."

"The others were clear, and I didn't think I could."

"If there was someone else down there with you, do you think you could've found that last little reserve of energy to get them safe too?"

Kirin frowned and thought about it.

"Maybe, I'd definitely try."

"Then why didn't you try for yourself?"

Her voice was soft, and not accusing, but Kirin felt the words like a knife.

"I... I don't know."

"That's okay." Pressure reached over the desk and patted his shoulder, the screen dismissing itself. "But that's what I want you to work on most. You're a great team player, and you have wonderful instincts when it comes to responding to crises. When you told Goldhorn and Antaeus to stabilize the building, you also told them to run the moment they thought they couldn't hold it anymore. I need you to apply that logic to yourself, too. You're just as valuable as everyone else."

Kirin didn't know how to respond, and after a moment of silence, Pressure continued.

"You were a toss-up vote on admissions, you know? Some of the members weren't so sure, even though you met and exceeded all the mien and physical requirements for entry. I, however, insisted on you being admitted. Do you know why?"

Kirin shook his head.

"One line that you said to me, just one. You said that you believed everyone deserves a chance to reach for their dreams, and everyone includes you, too. If you want to save everyone, that same rule applies. At the end of the day, you can always save at least one person. You can always save yourself.

"Now, I'm not saying to avoid danger entirely. It wouldn't even be possible since danger's a prominent part of our job. But I don't want you to be quite as reckless as you were in the exam. You train with your classmates, and in all likelihood when you're a professional, you'll likely end up working with some of them. However, you cannot rely on someone knowing that you're about to leap into danger and covering your back. Make sure you have a way out when you're trying something that risky, or at least make sure you have enough energy left to protect yourself when you do."

Kirin nodded quickly, still not quite trusting himself to speak.

"Considering all of the above, I'm not docking you as many points as I normally would, which means that overall in the class, you've placed second."

"Second?"

"Don't interrupt me."

"Sorry ma'am."

"Yes, second." She looked at him for a moment as if expecting him to interrupt again. "You had the most rescues with your team, were one of the most versatile players on the field, and were able to either lead or listen to the directions of someone more suitable. You supported your teammates when necessary and communicated well. All in all, the only mark against you was the fact that you put yourself in danger needlessly when you could've alerted the others instead."

"Don't I get marks off for engaging?"

"You didn't engage, unless I'm misremembering." Pressure said dryly. "Getting hit is not the same as fighting. With miens like mine, which have a wide ranging attack, it's common, if not expected, that someone will need to negate the effects somehow, though hopefully in a more effective manner than putting your body in front of it."

Kirin laughed nervously.

"Normally, this would be the part where I tell you that your high placement means you'll be one of the leaders in the class, meaning that you'd get to pick two of your classmates to form a squadron and when rescue calls come in, you'd be sent out together."

"Normally?"

"You have a choice, instead. When I told this to Ifrit, he immediately asked for you."

"He did?"

"Are you going make me repeat myself? I have sixteen other reviews to go through today."

"Sorry."

"You can either form your own squadron or be part of his. As part of his, he'll get final say on all calls, and you'd be expected to defer to him until the next final, when squads may switch depending on performance, or maybe even sooner if your group is struggling in the field."

"Who else did Ifrit pick?"

"No one else yet. He's got the form to officially request class-mates, and he's guaranteed to get whoever he asks for. You'd be given one with extra spaces, to add other options in case he's already chosen the people you would want."

"Did he... did he say what he'd do if I said no?"

Pressure smiled.

"I did ask him that. And I think he's finally starting to mature a bit, even if he's still a stubborn little shit."

"Why's that?"

"Because he said if you didn't want to be under his command, he'd just be under yours."

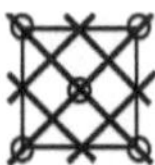

Ifrit ambushed him as he walked back into the dorm.

"Well?"

"Well, what?"

"Did Pressure not talk to you?" Ifrit looked irritated for the first time that day, or rather, disappointed. It was kind of cute.

"Oh, yeah, she did."

"And?"

"Guess you're stuck with me." Kirin smiled. Ifrit's face went from upset to beet red in a heartbeat and he shoved a paper in Kirin's face before heading toward the stairs. When Kirin pulled it away to read, he noticed it was the form that Pressure had mentioned for the squadron members. Kirin's own name was in the number one spot, the other left blank.

"I think you're supposed to fill this out dude, not me." Kirin followed Ifrit as he stomped up the stairs, almost laughing to himself at how Ifrit could make even walking seem aggressive.

"I don't fucking know who else would be a good fit, so I'm leaving it to you."

"I don't believe that. I know you like to pretend you don't like the rest of them, but at the very least you pay attention during training enough to know all their miens."

"They've got to be compatible, or whatever the fuck though." Ifrit's ears were slightly red.

"Are you worried that they won't like you?" Kirin asked.

"What the fuck? No." Ifrit whirled around. "I'm worried they won't trust me."

That gave Kirin pause for a second, which gave Ifrit enough time to spin back around and continue marching.

"I don't think anyone had strong enough opinions to actively distrust you, but I understand that you're worried about it. Is there any you think would be okay?"

They'd reached the fifth floor and Ifrit was already trying to slouch off to his room, halfway through the doorway. Kirin took a big breath and put his arm in the door before it fully closed, letting himself in. Ifrit raised his eyebrows, but didn't seem angry. Well. Angrier.

"Any thoughts?" Kirin prompted. He was heavily resisting the temptation to look around at Ifrit's room, instead forcing himself to sit down on the floor, feigning a relaxed mood he didn't feel, expecting to be kicked out at any moment.

"Blindfold bitch could be good." Ifrit finally grumbled. "Or maybe the one who turns to smoke? I can do info gathering and you've pretty much got everything covered on the ground, so someone with psychic abilities or stealth could do well."

Kirin pulled out a notebook and nodded as Ifrit talked, scribbling down Medusa and Enenra's names.

"If we're looking for stealth, Ness is the obvious option there. To round us out I don't think we need someone super physical so Wyrm, Goldhorn, and Dulu are probably out." Kirin tapped his chin with his pen. "Maybe Naddāha? I don't know much about her mien, but it seems to be something to do with emotions? That could be helpful with stealth."

"Not her." Ifrit growled. Kirin could have smacked himself as he remembered the party.

"Not Naddāha, got it." He looked at his list. "Ness and Enenra for stealth then, and Medusa if we're looking for someone with a physiological mien. Anything else you think we're weak on?"

"Between you and me, we've got up close covered, but we're both fucking physical fighters. If there's someone who can stay far away that could be an issue. I can aim fucking fine at point blank, but if they're far, or we're outside, that shit gets hard to control." Ifrit looked over Kirin's shoulder from his perch on the bed. "Your handwriting is ass."

"Thank you. Any ideas of who in our group can do long range with accuracy?"

Ifrit frowned, evidently thinking.

"Shadow bitch?"

"Lilin?"

"Probably."

"Do you genuinely not know any of our classmates' names?" The thought had never crossed his mind before. He'd meant it as a joke, but Ifrit suddenly looked guilty. "Ifrit, tell me that's not true."

Ifrit pointedly focused on the paper.

"Seriously dude? What's my name?" Kirin genuinely hadn't realized the other man had never said his name until just then.

"I know your name." Ifrit said, looking sullen.

"Okay, what is it?"

Ifrit paused.

"K...Kiri?" He sounded so hopeful, the usual pride with which he spoke gone entirely. Kirin was going to correct him, when he saw a flicker of worry pass over Ifrit's face. Something kept the truth from exiting his mouth.

"Um, yup, that's right." Kirin cleared his throat and looked back at his notes. "And Lilin is the one who controls shadows, or I guess darkness is more accurate. But if you were thinking of the person who controls shadow *people*, that's Adlivun."

"What's her range with the shadow people?"

Kirin shifted uncomfortably.

"I... don't know." He said slowly, thought the next words came out in a rush. "But she's likely going to be one of the squad heads so we probably shouldn't go for her anyways."

"She is pretty good." Ifrit mumbled under his breath, seemingly to himself. "Wait, what about the red head?"

"Clidna?" Ifrit gave him a look. "The one who screams?"

"Yeah, her."

"From what I've seen she is primarily long range, but I don't know if she can pinpoint any better than you can. The damage if she hits more people is less though, I'd imagine."

"She'll do."

"Shouldn't we ask her first? It might be worth it to see who else is a squad leader and then we can make sure everyone's teams are balanced too."

"You can chat with everyone. I'm good up here." Ifrit pushed himself farther back on the bed, trying to appear casual, but Kirin noticed how white his knuckles were. "But whoever you think is good from that list, I'm fucking fine with."

Ifrit thought for a moment.

"But don't write it down on the form, they won't be able to read it at all."

"Again, we're going to work on how you talk to people. But no worries, I think you have to fill it out anyways." Kirin took the cue to leave, standing and stretching, freely using the excuse to look around. Ifrit's room was more personalized than he might have expected. There were a few posters hanging on the walls, mostly for classic movies and a few bands that Kirin was surprised to recognize, but there was one that stood out. An early poster showing Force, her hands out in front of her, a knowing smile on her face. She stood watch over a relatively impressive collection of books, and a few small plants decorating the top of his desk.

Kirin realized Ifrit was waiting for him to leave, so he cleared his throat and headed for the door.

"I'll scout out the troops for you, boss, and make sure we get the best recruit." He mock-saluted, halfway in the hall.

"Don't call me boss. We're in this together, now." From someone else it might have sounded like a joke, but Ifrit's tone was serious.

"Alright then... partner." Kirin gave him a smile as he closed the door.

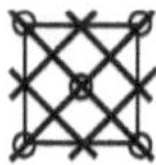

When Kirin got out of the elevator on the first floor, he was ambushed by Phoenix.

"How *dare* you put me in this position?" He put a hand to his head and swooned into Kirin's arms dramatically. "Because you decided to play second fiddle, now *I* have to lead."

"I'll go back and tell Pressure she made a mistake." Kirin deadpanned, dropping Phoenix to the floor. The rest of the class was gathered behind him— seated in chairs, on couches, or even on the table— roughly organized around Yantra.

"Has Ifrit picked your third then?" Yantra had found a very old whiteboard from somewhere and was drawing up the teams, crossing out the names of the people who'd already been picked. So far, it looked like it was only him.

"He sent me down here to do that."

"Already delegating... he's truly the master." Phoenix nodded sagely. "I want Kuafu!"

Kuafu looked up, startled underneath the dark hair that fell across his face.

"Is that really a good idea?" Lilin asked. As always, she was a contrast to Kuafu, her curly hair pulled up and out of the way.

"An apology, of sorts." Phoenix shrugged. "I want you to know you can depend on me."

"And I will do just that." Kuafu agreed. "I look forward to working with you and having more cordial conversations in the future."

Phoenix smiled in return as Yantra marked Kuafu's name off.

"Who are our leaders?" Kirin asked.

"Well, Ifrit and Phoenix, obviously, but we also have Gold-horn, Adlivun, Kapre, and Aïcha." Yantra tapped on the names as she went down the side of her grid. Kirin crossed Adlivun off of his own list.

"Good work guys." Kirin sent a smile to the others who were scattered across the room. "You picked out any of your groups yet?"

"If possible, I'd like to work with Lilin and Medusa." Adlivun was standing, leaning against the table Lilin was sitting on.

"Rats, I wanted Medusa." Phoenix sighed.

"I would like Wyrm." Kapre chimed up. "I need someone who can cover me while I'm incapacitated."

"Aaaaalright folks, that leaves a good portion of the class still up for grabs, who will be taken next?" Yantra was using her marker as a fake microphone.

"I'd like Dulu." Goldhorn was on the couch, and Dulu shot them a brilliant smile from across the room.

"And I want Antaeus!" Aïcha crushed the small man in a hug as she spoke.

"Is that just because you like squishing his cheeks?" Yantra asked as she marked him down.

"Probably." Antaeus sighed.

"Not at all! He's very multifaceted, and we work well togeth-er."

"You should take Yantra then, Aïcha." Kirin spoke up. "You and Antaeus don't necessarily have an easy way to gather intel on your own. Dulu, Yantra, Kapre, Ifrit, Goldhorn, and Adlivun are all good for that."

"I'd say Enenra is too." Ness spoke up from next to Kirin's elbow, but he'd gotten used to hearing her well before he saw her, so he just smiled and put an arm around her shoulders.

"That's true. So, should Phoenix take her?" Yantra asked.

"I'd be fine with that." Enenra spoke up. "Phoenix, we'll have to train together a little so you can know my limits, but I think it'll be fine."

"Agreed!" Phoenix reached across the table and shook Enenra's hand vigorously.

"That just leaves me, Clidna, and Naddāha." Ness said.

"I think I'd work better with Kapre's team, but I'm happy to go anywhere." Naddāha was looking directly at Kirin, a little too knowingly.

"I don't particularly care either way." Clidna considered the list of teams. "I feel like I've worked less with Ifrit though, and I want to make sure I can work with everyone if possible. And, if I'm honest, I want to make sure I can't hurt my teammates. Ifrit can turn off his hearing aids, and Kirin can turn off his *ears*."

"Ness, thoughts?" Kirin nudged her side.

"I think either team works for me, since all four of you are more close-range physical fighters." Ness shrugged. "If Clidna wants to deal with our lovely headache, I'm happy to pass off that role."

The rest of the class laughed, not meanly, but hearing it made Kirin's heart sink. Ifrit was abrasive, certainly, and definitely avoiding hanging out with the group, but he *was* working on being nicer, in his own way. As the conversation turned to what rescue missions the class was likely to face, Kirin realized that he was probably worrying too much. They'd be going out in the field shortly, so if anyone in the class didn't trust Ifrit yet, they'd have to, and soon.

12

Exposure

HE HADN'T QUITE REALIZED how soon "soon" would be.

The second semester started much as the first had, and the schedule was blessedly similar. Lectures on Monday and Thursday, with Rescue Training Tuesday and Friday, and Mien Development taking up their Wednesdays. While the lecture and lab classes were different, the two practicals felt like little more than a continuation, and it was easy to fool himself into thinking they wouldn't have to be out in the public eye just yet. But apparently being a member of the top scoring team meant they also would be the first in the field.

It was the third week of the semester, and Kirin awoke to an emergency signal blaring on his phone. His feet hit the ground before his eyes had fully opened, already pulling on clothes though he'd only need them to run through campus. By the time he was out the door, Ifrit was already waiting by the stairs, and they headed down without a word passing between them. Clidna was ready and waiting by the front door when they arrived; the trio jogged all the way to the roof of the Disaster Simulator, where a jet was parked.

Pressure met them at the back, the gate open and ramp down. Kirin felt like it started closing the moment they set foot through the door, the jet rising into the air not a second after the cabin sealed.

"Good hustle guys. We'll be getting there with the local heroes, I assume." Pressure gestured to duffle bags that were thrown farther in. "Get changed, and I'll tell you the mission when you're done."

Kirin's back stiffened, as there wasn't anything dividing the space, but he bit down his anxiety and changed his shirt first, sure that the other two would be too busy with their own costumes to worry about him. He still wasn't fully used to putting it on, but after a few tries got the mask hooked up correctly, feeling his carbon stores soar as he breathed in. It clung to his face like a second skin, much less bulky than he would have thought. The gold stripes blended the black mask into the light top, but he wouldn't be able to see the full effect until he managed to find a mirror.

"What's the situation?" Ifrit had finished changing before him and was standing by the back with Pressure.

"Wait for your teammates; I'm not going to say it twice." She waved a hand as if to brush off the question, but it was only a few moments more before Kirin and Clidna joined them. "This is a great first call for you all because it's one of the least dangerous and most common calls we get: mien appearance."

"We're dealing with a kid?" Ifrit's usual confidence disappeared in a blink.

"Most likely, though sometimes they're older. The older they are, the more dangerous the situation, typically. Kids might have little to no control over their abilities, but they also usually are just distressed or scared. If they're older... they're usually angry."

Clidna shot Ifrit a look, her eyes questioning.

"Generally, in these cases, your job will be to help maintain a perimeter around the affected area, and make sure no one gets too close." Pressure hadn't seemed to notice Clidna's glance, but she paused now. "If I'm being honest with you guys, the hardest part of this won't be dealing with our mien user, it'll be dealing with the public."

"Why's that?" Just as Clidna asked, the door opened again, blasting them with cold air. They certainly weren't in East City anymore, and wherever they were, it wasn't the northern hemisphere either.

"Go on then! I'll be back to pick you up later." Pressure nudged them forward and Kirin felt a small spark of fear. He'd thought that she'd at least stay with them during the mission, so they weren't completely on their own. But before he could protest, they were being handed off to a hero in yellow. "Take care of my kids, okay? No using them as meat shields."

The hero cracked a smile at that, and then waved the three of them down to the rooftop she was standing on. Kirin took a deep breath and followed Ifrit out, fighting the urge to curl in on himself. Most heroes operated in the area where they lived, so the arrival of the jet told the media that these were new, untested heroes. The mission Kirin had a decent amount of confidence in. Dealing with the swarming cameras... that he felt less sure about.

Sure enough, as they descended the ramp, a dozen flashes went off, journalists in hover cars just off to the side of the building. Clidna's hair was lifted and blown all about as the jet took off, leaving them with no safe sides, blinding lights surrounding them entirely. The flashes lightened the gray of her suit to near white, the orange panels seeming to turn neon.

"We tried to keep the rendezvous location as quiet as possible, but I swear they have me tagged by now." The hero had to shout to be heard over the wind and offered her hand to Ifrit. "Name's Lark, glad to have you folks joining. We'll head down through the building to give you a break from the cameras, and then I'm afraid they're only going to get more up close and personal once I send you out."

"Appreciated." Ifrit didn't pay any mind to the people crowding the edges of the roof, keeping his attention on Lark only. Clidna and Kirin fell into step together behind the pair. Clidna seemed to share Kirin's discomfort with the scrutiny, though she hid it well. It was only from the crease between her eyes that Kirin could tell at all. The number of photos increased tenfold as they reached the door, leaving Kirin blinking in the sudden dimness after it closed.

"I'm expecting big things since you're the first group out! I was last in my class, so I bet y'all are better than me already." Lark gave them a big smile, only the top of her face covered by her mask, though it wrapped around the sides as well. She was taller than Clidna, but there was a sort of friendly roundness to her that took away some of the intensity of her frame. The costume she wore was all grays and yellows, comfortable looking baggy clothing.

Ifrit, standing next to her, looked the very image of dangerous. Kirin hadn't taken a good look on the ride over, but this was first time he'd seen the other man's costume at all, since he'd only just gotten the final design before the semester began. It was black, like he wanted, with red detailing that served to emphasize his physique. Panels were cut out of the tight-fitting clothing, at his shoulders, his collarbone, his hips, even down his legs. The mask that covered the bottom half of his face was less decorative than functional, likely to deal with the smoke from his own fire. It was bulkier than Kirin's, with vents in the side, but it still seemed to highlight the sharp shape of Ifrit's face, with crimson lines delicately tracing his jaw and cheekbones. The detailing drew more attention to his eyes, the color of which put the other red to shame.

"...what we can." Ifrit was saying something, but Kirin had

missed the beginning of the sentence. They'd left the stairwell and were taking the elevator, though Kirin wished they could've run the whole way down the building. Now that they were *here*, he was burning up with anxious energy; it was taking all his willpower not to bounce on the balls of his feet.

"The situation is pretty standard and pretty simple. We got a report about half an hour ago of unregistered mien usage and looked at some cameras from the neighboring area. Looks to be a kid of about ten years old, maybe more, haven't found his parents yet. Every time someone tries to get near him, he freaks out, and the ground beneath them turns to quicksand, effectively. We don't know the full range of his ability, but we've seen him do that to someone about a hundred meters away that he couldn't even see, so we're puling people back pretty far." Lark explained as they exited the elevator, now in a parking garage. "You should expect there to be some protestors at your locations who'll want to get closer and yell at the poor kid, so your job is to keep everyone away from him, just as much as it is to keep everyone safe from him. Got it?"

The group murmured their agreement as they headed up a short flight of stairs to the door, where even more people were waiting with cameras at the ready.

"I assume you have someone who can fly?" Ifrit asked. The change in his personality was enough that Clidna's eyebrow raised, but to Kirin, it almost seemed natural. He'd *felt* the mask settle into place as they descended the plane, Ifrit's back straightening, his eyebrows pressing together. Without the bottom half of his face, he looked austerely serious, instead of pissed off.

"Unfortunately, no. It's made this situation string out for longer than it might have otherwise, since we haven't found a way to get close."

"You don't have any hover packs then, either?" Clidna made

a fair point. They weren't favored by many heroes, a new development in the last few years, but their seminar on hero tech had just covered them.

"We do, but none of us are trained to use them. A large part of the job, you'll learn very quickly, is to not look like you don't know what you're doing out there. We're the first and only line of defense against villains. We cannot afford to make fools out of ourselves."

The three students looked at each other, feeling the weight of the words.

"One of you can fly though, correct? I believe I read that in the rough mien summaries while I was waiting for you to arrive."

"I can." Ifrit looked uncomfortable.

"If all else fails, we'll call you in then."

"I think Kiri would be a better fit. He's been training with the hover pack and is at least competent with them." Ifrit gestured to Kirin as he spoke.

"Competent isn't enough, but hopefully, it won't come to it either way." Lark paused before she opened the door to the outside, giving the three of them a moment to contemplate the mob just on the other side. The glass must have been tinted, since none of the reporters directly in front of them noticed them at all. Kirin found his eyes drifting to Ifrit, who eyed the eagerly waiting faces the same he might a shark in blood-filled waters. "Chin up kids, you'll do great."

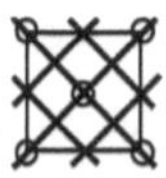

Kirin couldn't stop staring at the screen in front of him, briefly distracted from his task. It was just so strange seeing the man who lived down the hall from him projected larger than life onto the side of a building.

"This is... weird." Clidna muttered through their private line. The headsets they'd been given had been preprogrammed with direct lines to each of their teammates, one to Lark, and one general.

"You're seeing that too, then?" His words came out in a puff, his breath still struggling. He'd been running back and forth for the better part of an hour, freeing the civilians that were at the very edge of the kid's area of effect. Lark had given him very specific instructions to avoid the main street, and he'd lost track of where Clidna and Ifrit were. Last he'd heard, they were manning the barricades that kept the general public away from the scene. Or, the ones who weren't already stuck in it, at least.

"I'm fucking dying here, hurry up!" A voice from Kirin's left screamed. He hadn't noticed the man before, distracted by the feed. "I swear you're all in league with each other, fuck what the government says!"

"Apologies, sir, let me get you out of there." Kirin hurried over, dropping to his knees to get a better view of the man. He wasn't the worst that Kirin had found, only sunk up to his mid chest, but his arms were trapped down by his sides, which likely wasn't helping him stay calm. He seemed to think that it was worse than it was, tilting his head fully up, like he expected the ground to swallow him up to his neck at any moment.

"Finally! It's been hours!"

Kirin bit back a response, knowing it had been an hour and a half, at most. Many of the people on the outer edges had been stuck for even less time than that, the authorities having misunderstood the range of the effect and letting civilians back in too soon.

"This is the second time this has happened this month alone!" The man was still complaining.

"You may feel some additional pressure as I pull you out, but it won't hurt you. I'm going to grab you just under your armpits and then pull. If you're not feeling well enough to walk, I can carry you to the medical tent, or simply escort you there."

"Stop with the lip service and just get me out of here!"

Kirin sighed and reached down, feeling the now familiar resistance for a moment before the man shot out with a pop. He immediately brushed off Kirin's hands, taking a few steps backwards to put some space between them. While doing so he nearly fell, but he shot Kirin a disgusted look when offered a hand. Kirin just shook his head and started walking in the direction of medical.

"Yeah, that's Ifrit alright." Clidna's voice was a welcome distraction. "It's just odd to see him so..."

"Heroic?" Kirin spoke quietly, though his charge seemed perfectly content to ignore him anyways.

"I was going to say large." Clidna laughed, though it sounded a little strained. "But yeah, he does look impressive, I'll give him that."

It seemed that it had in fact come to the last resort, as the live feed beaming down from the side of several buildings showed Ifrit striding forward, flames under his feet keeping him just above the ground. The black of his costume reflected the fire around him, making him look more like a creature of flame than a physical body. At first glance, he looked confident— casual, even— as he strode toward the boy curled on the ground, but on a screen so large Kirin could see the furrow in his brow that revealed his anxiety. It was eerie, too, seeing just him and the child alone on such a large street.

His irritated cargo dropped off with the medical crew, Kirin was left alone as he wandered back out, free to gawk at the screens where no one could see.

"He's nervous, huh?" Clidna's voice infiltrated his thoughts. She spoke quietly too, not wanting to be overheard by whoever was around her.

"I didn't think it was that obvious."

"He's fiddling with his hands a lot."

Now that she said it, Kirin was able to tear his eyes away from Ifrit's face, and saw that she was right, he was fidgeting with his fingers, but it wasn't just a nervous tic. He was fingerspelling something to himself. R-I-K-I-R-I-K-I—

"I need to switch channels for a bit Clidna, sorry." Kirin changed to Ifrit's channel before she had a chance to respond. "You okay?"

On screen, a flicker of irritation passed across Ifrit's face, only visible by the way one of his eyebrows twitched.

"Sorry, dumb question. What'd you need from me?"

There was a pause and static filled the line, Ifrit nearly to the boy now. The kid's mien must have overwhelmed him, since he was still hunched over, hands over his ears, completely oblivious to Ifrit's presence.

"...what do I say to him?" He spoke so quietly Kirin almost missed it, Ifrit's mask hiding his words from being caught on screen. There were only a few seconds left until Ifrit was right upon the boy, and he didn't know what to say.

"Try to get a name. We don't know who he is." Kirin racked his brain for what the right thing to do was; their psychology class was really a de-escalation class, but they'd only had five or six classes so far, which wasn't giving him much to go on. "There might be a parent or guardian we could get to help him calm down. Maybe find out if there's something that happened to trigger this episode so we can help him avoid more in the future."

"But *how*?" Ifrit's voice was still quiet, but desperation and anxiety were still leeching in. Then— "It should be you doing this."

"Start by asking him if he's okay. If he's hurt anywhere. Tell him you're a friend and that you just want to get him home safe. He might not believe you at first, so try doing something to show him that you're there to help— or do something silly to cheer him up." Kirin saw Ifrit nod, almost imperceptibly, their conversation over now that he was standing just next to the boy. "And hey, you've got this. I'm not the right person to do this, you are."

Ifrit seemed to steady himself from that, and after a moment's consideration, he settled down into a cross-legged seat, still hovering just above the ground. He never cut the line, so Kirin left it open too.

The boy still seemed completely unaware of Ifrit's presence; his face buried between his arms as he desperately clutched at his ears. Next to Ifrit, he looked so small, so fragile, like one wrong move and he'd break. Ifrit considered something for a moment, took a breath, and then made his presence known.

Instead of speaking, tiny flames began to radiate off Ifrit, detaching and forming together into the outline of a bee, several more appearing and gently flying around the boy's face, finally getting him to look up. Kirin felt himself cringe from how *young* the kid looked, younger than Kirin's own siblings, tear tracks carving through the dirt on his face. For a moment though, all the grief was gone from his face and replaced with wonder as he watched the tiny fire creatures fly off and circle Ifrit's head, vanishing into the flames around his neck. The kid's eyes widened at seeing someone sitting so close.

"Can you hear me?" Ifrit spoke gently, signing as he did as well. The boy's gaze jumped to the movement of Ifrit's hands, his own still firmly clasped over his ears. After a moment, he shook his head.

Are your ears bothering you? Ifrit switched completely to sign, though he was doing so slowly, as if to avoid making any sudden movements. This time, a nod yes.

FUTURUS
LIVE

Could you hear anything before today?

The kid shook his head, his hands pressing against his skull tighter, Ifrit's own head swiveling to look at something off screen. He looked angry, his brows drawn together, but a moment later the expression relaxed, and looked back toward his mission.

Can you tell me your name? I can cover your ear so you can have a free hand.

The boy looked hesitant for a moment, considering Ifrit's outstretched arm. A second later he shakily removed one of his hands, Ifrit filling in smoothly, and began to spell out his name. Ifrit's arm hid it from view, hands over the ears being replaced the moment he finished.

Thank you for telling me, Caleb.

A beep in Kirin's ear alerted him that someone else was trying to talk to him.

"I don't want to startle you; I need to answer someone else and then I'll be right back on this line." Kirin spoke quietly yet he still saw the figure on screen jump. He switched channels, and Lark's voice filled his ear.

"I'm guessing you know sign? What are they saying?"

"The kid was deaf before today, and his name is Caleb. Don't have a last name yet."

Lark swore loudly in his ear.

"What's wrong?"

"Only one potential Caleb on the list. Foster kid, that's unlucky. No parents coming in to calm him down, then."

Can you tell me what happened? The more Ifrit got the kid to focus on him, the less pained he looked. Slowly, the hands came down from his ears.

It got loud.

Do you remember when?

I don't know. I was walking back to the house, and then it was so loud *and my head hurt, and then people were yelling at me and—*

Breathe. You just got scared. Can you tell me what you heard?

I don't know.

But it hurts a lot?

Yes. The boy looked like he might cry again.

Where does it hurt? Your ears only?

My whole head.

Does it hurt more when there are people around you?

When they're walking.

What does it feel like?

Like... like they're walking on *my head.* In *my head.*

And you wanted them to stop?

Yes.

You should be a hero.

That got the kid's attention like nothing else.

You've got a good mien that lets you feel the people around you and can even change the ground beneath them. With practice, you'd be a strong hero one day.

You think so? For the first time a smile pulled at the corner of the boy's mouth, his back straightening.

Yes. Ifrit stood up, still careful not to put his feet on the ground. *And being a hero starts by letting these people out.*

He reached a hand out to Caleb, who took it wordlessly, his eyes never leaving Ifrit's face. Ifrit picked the kid up, and the moment his feet left the ground, the people still stuck in the pavement were practically shot out, many gasping for breath and falling to their knees. Lark appeared on screen quickly, calling orders that Kirin could hear since he'd been so enamored with the video he'd forgotten to switch back to Ifrit's channel.

"Let child services know we'll need a hover pack for the kid. In the meantime, I'm checking on everyone who was in the ground right now. It looks like we have a few injuries, seems like it was mostly from flailing around themselves rather than anything our boy did. Hold the barriers until we've got the kid clear out of here and then let everyone get back to their business." Lark held her arms out, but Caleb clung to Ifrit, looking scared again. "Kirin, get over here so I can talk to the boy."

"Should I wait for someone to take over my position?" As he spoke, a hero in red appeared, waving a hand. "Never mind, I see her, heading to you now."

It wasn't far to where they were gathered, just one block over and a few up, but Kirin took it at a run, wanting to get the boy out in case anyone managed to break through the line.

Hi Caleb! He signed as he slowed to a walk. *It's nice to meet you.*

Caleb looked between Ifrit and Kirin, as if waiting for Ifrit to say it was okay to talk. Ifrit gave him a nod.

Hello.

I see you've made friends with my buddy there! But we're not from around here, so Lark is going to help you get somewhere safe, okay? She's very nice.

Caleb didn't look convinced.

And, I bet if you're a little bit lucky, she'll let you pet one of her bird friends.

He looked marginally more interested; the statement helped by a gray-winged bird landing on Lark's shoulder at precisely that moment.

Am I in trouble? Caleb looked sad more than worried.

No, not at all. You didn't know what you were doing, but we're going to get you help to make sure that you can control your mien, and then I expect I'll see you on TV saving the world pretty soon after.

I don't know if I want to save the world. Do I have to?

Not at all! But like Ifrit said, you've got a pretty strong power there, so if you ever think that you want to, I bet you could do it no problem. Kirin offered his hand to the boy for a high five. Caleb reached out hesitantly but gave his palm a good slap. *There you go! Let's get you inside and cleaned up though, okay?*

This time, when Lark reached out to him, he went willingly. He seemed enchanted by a new bird that landed— white and pink this time— though he didn't try to touch it just yet.

"Can you let him know that we're going to put him in a car to the station, and then he'll be met with an interpreter there? After that, we'll worry about what to do with him." Lark seemed relieved, her shoulders sagging now that the kid was in her arms.

"What do you mean what to do with him?" Ifrit asked stiffly as Kirin signed the message.

"He's a foster kid. Lots of families send kids back into the system if they present with a mien." She glanced down at Caleb. "Particularly one that received a lot of publicity."

Before Ifrit could say anything else, the car arrived, and Lark passed Caleb off to a plain clothed officer who got in with him, Caleb looking worriedly out the window.

It's going to be okay. Kirin tried for a smile, but all that served to do was wiggle his mask, the bottom half of his face firmly covered. *You're in good hands.*

Caleb wasn't really looking at Kirin though, his frantic eyes locked on Ifrit.

Be brave. Ifrit looked like he didn't want to let the car go. *It might be hard for a while, but it'll turn out okay if you just keep your head high.*

Promise?

Ifrit hesitated.

Promise.

And then the car was off, Caleb's face fading into the distance. Lark gave Ifrit a pat on the shoulder, already moving on to call attention to the civilians who needed medical help the most. For a moment, they were alone in the sea of motion.

"I hate that." Ifrit muttered, still watching the car drive off.

"What?" Kirin had a feeling he knew.

"Making promises I don't know if I can keep."

13

Disaster

It seemed like the dam had been broken after that first mission. Every single session of Rescue Operations, at least one of the squads was heading out, sometimes two or three at a time if there was a large enough rescue in place. Phantasm started leaving the holo screen on during regular practice, so they could see the incoming calls in real time, though she would sharply reprimand them if they let their performance falter by gawking.

The seminar stopped being about discussing the practice sessions, and instead, they watched the news feeds for the missions their classmates had been sent on, discussing how well their group performed during the rescue and which squadron would have been best equipped to handle it. It was easy enough to do, as the coverage of rescues was, if anything, skewed *towards* them, as they were the shiny new recruits on the field. That was the hardest part for Kirin; he still wasn't used to seeing the faces of his friends on TV, let alone his own.

He felt lucky that the first mission he'd been sent on had kept the press relatively far away, since he hadn't realized how many countries let journalists get far too up close and personal with the heroes as they tried to work. It was a radical shift from the general public, who in large part were determined to stay out of the way. Kirin had nearly botched a civilian rescue one time because he'd turned a corner and a great flash went off in his eyes, and he wasn't the only one with a similar story.

Ifrit seemed to get the worst of it. Maybe it was because he'd been the first of the class to be largely featured on the news, or maybe it was because he had arguably the flashiest power, but for whatever reason, the press could not get enough. And it was starting to wear on him.

Clidna was the best in their squad at deflecting attention, and they'd fallen into a routine of trying to supplant Ifrit with her any time they were asked to give a statement. Kirin would too, if he was really forced to, but standing in front of the press still made his mouth dry and his knees weak. Clidna dealt with the press, Kirin dealt with everyone else, and Ifrit dealt with himself.

It'd been working for them so far. After the first mission, they were largely relegated to the rescues like the ones they'd been trained for: destroyed towns, heavy flooding and evacuations, even a large wildfire once. Kirin still was in awe of that one, the image of Ifrit singlehandedly redirecting the flames away from houses burned into his mind.

Ifrit had been right, too, that having a more precise ranged attack would be helpful, and Clidna's shriek could shatter a boulder from a hundred meters away without hitting anything else. After a bit of coaxing, Kirin had convinced Ifrit to start teaching her sign as well, so she didn't have to type out anything she wanted to say once she lost her voice from overuse. It was only once she started getting good enough to talk to them casually in sign, and half the words in her sentences were curses, that Kirin wondered if having Ifrit be the one to teach her had been a good idea.

The one consistency in their missions was that they were all off the island. Each began with a short jet ride— not that any would be long traveling at supersonic speed— where Pressure would brief them on the situation and then they would be turned over to the local heroes to get more details. Perhaps it was technically more dangerous than putting out a house fire, but so far, Kirin was surprised to find that it felt all too similar to his old volunteer position. It was almost... familiar.

That changed abruptly.

They were awoken by a siren going off. Part of Kirin's half-asleep brain decided that it was simply his early morning alarm for a rescue mission, and he got dressed and was out the door before he could think about it, bumping into Phoenix who was in a similar state of confusion. Ifrit grabbed the pair of them and hauled them down the stairs, all of them fully awake by the time they broke out into the common room, most of the class already assembled. Pressure was just inside the door, looking grim.

"There's been a villain attack in the city." She said. "All licensed students are to change and report to the front gate."

It was only then that Kirin processed that she was wearing Force's iconic blue costume. But before he could ask for any more information, she turned on her heel and walked away.

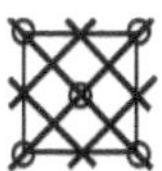

"We have reason to believe this is just a robbery gone wrong, but there is a significant amount of destruction within the city. None of the critical infrastructure underneath appears to have been damaged, yet you must proceed with caution. If you notice any significant dips in the landscape report them immediately." Majesty was briefing the first-year class, Shifter visible in the distance addressing the second years. Beyond the park, Kirin could see smoke rising. "You will all be on rescue crew and are *not* to engage, under any circumstances. There are still active villains fleeing the scene and if spotted you are to report their location to the professors on the designated channel and then clear the area. Retrieve any and all civilians you find and bring them to the safe zones you will find marked on your maps. And I will repeat again, if you come across any of the villains, *do not engage*. Am I clear?"

A clear shout of "yes ma'am" arose from the gathered crowd. Kirin could see Bia out of the corner of his eye, an excited smile on her face already. Despite the horrible circumstances, Majesty's whole class exuded eagerness, and the sight of their detachment made Kirin's stomach churn. It was with some effort that he made himself focus back on Majesty.

"Do the school proud and show the world that even the least experienced of our students are future heroes they can depend on." She surveyed the group a moment longer. "Dismissed."

Majesty's class started out immediately, but Pressure's gathered together.

"It looks like all the sections we're assigned to are adjacent." Goldhorn was holding out their phone, comparing the map on it with those of the other squad leaders'. "There's even some overlap."

They were right about that, and when Ifrit finally added his phone to the mix, their sections overlapped perfectly with Adlivun's.

"Alright then, we'll support each other as best we can." Kirin nodded and caught Adlivun's eye. She gave him a small smile, and he nodded again, not willing to hold her gaze for long. While they'd been friendly, there was still something about her that unsettled him.

"It'll be just like the final." Kapre seemed like they were trying to reassure themself as much as anyone else.

"Exactly." Lilin patted them on the arm. "We'll all be okay."

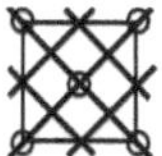

He'd been living on the island for months, but Kirin still forgot sometimes that it was entirely man-made. With a giant hole blown in the city, it was hard to forget.

The information spoken in his ear cut in and out, heroes learning more of what had happened and passing it along. A group, not just one villain. They had been attempting to break into one of the four backup power stations. Arrived in a large truck, seemingly with the intent to cart something out. Instead, they'd accidentally ignited the carbon monoxide tanks and created an explosion large enough to fully take out the blocks surrounding the plant and damaging dozens of others.

The power station was gone entirely, leaving the metal sub-structure of the island exposed, a gaping hole twelve meters deep. The fully licensed professionals had swarmed there, looking to close the gap before anyone could do anything ne-farious with access to the systems that kept the island alive. None of the students had been allowed near it, even the sec-ond years forced to stay several blocks away.

With most of the other rescue missions, they'd arrived at the scene close to half an hour after the situations had begun, meaning that some amount of clean-up had already occurred. But for this, they truly were the first line.

Adlivun and Kirin's costumes were looking more red than white now, Ifrit's insistence on black suddenly having a far more practical appeal. They'd moved hundreds of civilians, but there were still more that needed help.

"Drink it all. Then, we move." Lilin pressed a water bottle into

Kirin's hands, moving down the line of their group, insisting on the same for all of them. "We're no good to anyone if we drop from dehydration."

Behind Ifrit, she was fairing the best in terms of apparent cleanliness. Her suit was a deep blue that was verging on black, but the speckled stars she so complained about were red now, too, instead of bright white.

"There are a few more in zone fifteen, but we're not going to reach them all before they die." Adlivun was doing all their reconnaissance, although Ifrit had offered to do some too. She had the benefit— and curse, Kirin thought— of knowing when the next target to be rescued was beyond help now.

"Just crushing?" Clidna asked softly. Her voice was going, though with everyone combined, they'd managed to keep her from straining it too much.

"Mm."

There was silence except for the sounds of them finishing off their waters.

"We'll do what we can." Ifrit spoke up, looking almost shocked himself that he was the one giving the pep talk. "That's all we fucking can do."

The group stood, Adlivun wobbling slightly, but waving off Lilin's concern.

"Which way?" Ifrit seemed to be demanding information from Adlivun, though Kirin noticed him putting a snack bar into her hands. She was looking pale and growing paler every time she used her mien. A shadow of a smile crossed her face as she looked at the gift, starting to chew as they moved away from the safe zone and farther into the destruction.

To build skyscrapers on a moving island had taken some incredible feats of engineering, but the biggest shift was designing structures in such a way that they could account for a constantly shifting base. Even during a great storm, the city sat relatively stable on the sea, but there was an ever present, almost imperceptible sway to the ground— not enough to give Kirin sea legs once he was back on real land— that had thwarted early attempts to design the towering structures that littered East City. It'd taken an entirely new alloy of metal to make something flexible enough to stand, but that flexibility came at the cost of strength, which was being paid for now.

Though the explosion itself had been localized to an area of only a few blocks, debris thrown from the blast had created a domino effect, rending holes in swathes of high rises that created ominously tilting top levels. Had the structures been built with typical steel the destruction would not have been so widespread, but many buildings had bent too far with the impact and snapped.

Their group moved in relative silence, Adlivun leading the way, winding them deeper into the maze of rubble and shattered glass. Sometimes, passing through the intersections, Kirin would glimpse another crew hard at work, trying to pull someone out of the street or hurrying along. Though they never exchanged words, Kirin could see the same exhaustion and horror etched into their faces, even from so far away.

"Here." Adlivun finally stopped at the corner of one building, bringing their jog to a halt. The entrance was blocked by chunks of concrete, fitting together so firmly from the force of the fall that Kirin didn't think there was room for him to put a single finger between. He suspected moving any of it would jeopardize the barely stable building further. Clidna was already pressing her hand against it and opening her mouth to see if there was a way through, but then shook her head.

We'll have to go up and in. Ifrit, there's a clear window on the fourth floor that you can enter through. Check there first; if it seems stable, we can all head up. Clidna signed. The orange in her costume and even her hair was dulled by the dust that covered them all.

"Fourth floor. Got it." Ifrit would have shot off right then if Adlivun hadn't stopped him.

"There'll be a person in the hall on that floor. If you can get to them immediately, bring them down before anything else and we can send Medusa with them to go get medical help." Adlivun's eyes were pained, her face beading with sweat. "They need it."

Ifrit nodded once before taking off, the fire from his neck traveling down to his feet to propel him upwards. He seemed to locate the entrance that Clidna mentioned easily, though he took care to break off some remaining glass from the frame before going in through the window. Kirin felt his fingers tapping nervously as they all stared up, waiting to see any sign that the building was going to come down.

Tense seconds later, Ifrit reappeared, now carrying an older woman who was bleeding from her head and crying softly. The injury didn't look too bad, but if Adlivun said she needed medical help immediately, it was.

Medusa took the woman and put her in a hovering stretcher, clipping the lead line to her belt. She turned, her back now to the group, before a hand went up to open her goggles. The crying cut off abruptly, and Medusa started out at a slow walk.

"It looks fairly stable, but I don't know how much weight the flooring can fucking take." Ifrit ran a hand through his hair, slightly mussing up his curls. He looked so tired, Kirin just wanted to reach out and fix it for him. "I think bringing you two—" he gestured at Clidna and Lilin— "is fine, maybe one more if I stay off the floor."

"I'm too dense, I know." Kirin tried to lighten the mood, but his stomach clenched at the thought of being helpless on the ground. "Ad, are there other places that you and I could go while they're up there?"

"There're another few civilians trapped around the corner, on the first floor. We can take those." She nodded to Ifrit. "You're looking for three more scattered throughout that level and the one below."

He didn't bother to respond to that, gripping Lilin and Clidna around their waists and pulling them up with him. Kirin watched until they disappeared again. Adlivun had to tug on his arm to get him to start moving.

"They'll be fine, but our targets won't be if we wait much longer." She urged quietly. Kirin nodded and followed her around the bend.

Their new destination wasn't that badly damaged, but it sat on a corner and all the windows wrapping the first-floor shop had been shattered from the force of the explosion. Even from a distance, two people were visible, collapsed within the aisles of the store, shards of glass buried in their flesh. Neither moved, but the sluggish drip from their wounds was encouraging that it wasn't too late.

They headed into the building, the glass crunching underfoot. Whatever the design for their costumes, all their shoes had thick soles for precisely that reason. Glass was the symbol of the modern age, which meant it was a common hazard during rescues.

Kirin reached his target, a teenager who was only out to get some snacks, judging from the contents of the toppled shopping basket next to her. Her chest moved up and down shallowly, a bruise forming on her forehead promising it was the impact, and not the blood loss, that left her unconscious.

He reached first for the scissors in one of the pockets of his pants, cutting off the denim jacket she wore. The thick material— too thick for the season— had protected her somewhat, a good number of smaller chunks coming off with the clothing. A quick glance told him all the larger pieces missed her spine, good, and none seemed deep enough to hit an organ, but he didn't trust that enough to try to pull them out.

He gently rolled her onto her side and cursed quietly when he saw that there were several shards embedded in her chest and stomach too. These bled slightly quicker and had been pushed deeper by how she'd fallen.

"Ad, when you've secured your civilian, can you help me over here?" Kirin picked up the girl and put her on the stretcher, making sure to keep her on her side. "I think we're going to have to brace her like this."

Adlivun was there almost immediately, her eyes bright. They worked in silence, adding straps and inflating cushions to keep the girl propped up. She groaned softly once or twice, Adlivun's eyebrows knitting closer together every time she did.

"Do we need to get these two straight to medical, or should we meet back up with the others?" Kirin checked the bag he had slung over his shoulder once the girl was secure. "I have two more stretchers here, though Ifrit has the rope to lower them."

"They'll be alright for a short while; both just need some stitches and rest." Adlivun was looking in his direction, but not looking *at* him, her eyes unfocused and glazed white. "There's one more still living in the building they're in, but the injuries are minor. I don't know if I trust the place to stay standing should there be any additional damage, or even in its current state for the thirty minutes it'll take us to get to medical and back."

"You think there's a chance there'll be another attack?" Kirin moved the stretchers into the street, eyes instinctively scanning the scene. It seemed like it was just the two of them alone in the sea of concrete.

"We don't know where the villains went, but there's no way they got off the island. Since they're still here somewhere, I'm hesitant to say the danger's passed." She shrugged. "Two have been sighted, but I believe they suspected it was at least four."

"Then we better keep moving." Kirin offered a hand to help her step over the window curb, and then they were walking over the asphalt once again. The trams weren't running, and the sidewalks were covered in glass, so they walked in the center of the road, the stretchers out in front of them. Clidna and Lilin were already in front of the building by the time they arrived, Ifrit bringing the last stretcher down as they approached.

"We got all three you said before, but I think I heard crying from the floor above." He looked to Adlivun for confirmation, who nodded.

"Some of those you have already rescued need medical attention, the sooner the better." Adlivun urged.

"And those above? Will they make it?" Ifrit asked.

"Hard to say."

Kirin had learned that meant no.

"Why don't you three take these folks and head back, Ifrit and I will get the last person here and then join you." Kirin suggested. Adlivun hesitated a moment and then nodded.

"One more, and then you follow."

"I promise." Kirin gave her a thumbs up in lieu of a smile. She still seemed apprehensive but took the line from Kirin and clipped it on her belt, the three women heading away. Kirin handed Ifrit one of the remaining stretchers from his bag and the man shot off, moving back through the same window, leaving Kirin alone in the street.

His shoulders sagged, the exhaustion settling in. They'd been woken just at dawn, and it was far past noon now, the sun looking dangerously close to the horizon. They'd hardly eaten at all, only a rush meal as they were forced to take a break before getting right back up and out, but the carnage had driven the desire for food far from Kirin's mind. He'd done his best to keep the others' spirits up, yet it was getting harder as Adlivun more and more quietly said that the person they were trying to reach was already gone.

"Coming down." Ifrit's voice called and Kirin took a few steps back, making sure Ifrit had enough room to land. The smaller man did so a little harder than usual, the stretcher wobbling in his arms as the hover jet kicked in.

"Let me take it. You've been working yourself ragged." Kirin took it from Ifrit's hands, not failing to notice the slight shake in them. Maybe he should've eaten the protein bar himself instead of giving it away.

"I'm fucking fine. You look worse than I do." Ifrit sounded tired, not angry, however.

"Hey, that's just because I let them pick the color for me. None of this is mine."

Ifrit was about to say something when the hair on the back of Kirin's neck stood up. His back and chest were crystallizing before he realized what he was doing, and then he was slamming into the wall.

Ifrit's eyes were wide, his mask shifting as he yelled something, but whatever words were coming out were dulled by the fact that Kirin had managed to harden his whole head and chest in the span of time from the hit until he impacted the wall. The whole building above shook, and Kirin was back on his feet to move the stretcher. Some instinct had kicked in, and he'd sliced the line before the woman was thrown with him, but that now meant he had to pull it away by hand.

Ifrit was blazing from everywhere, the halo of fire a warning as he kept an eye out for Kirin's attacker, Kirin moving the civilian under the minimal cover of a subway entrance. The building stabilized itself, the rumbling dying away, and all was still.

"Villain attack at the corner of Fifth Avenue and Twenty-Second Street." Ifrit had his hand to his ear, his voice seeming to echo as Kirin heard it over his headset just a moment later. "Hero students Kirin and Ifrit in proximity with one injured civilian—"

It was so fast that Kirin didn't even see the connection, but Ifrit was hurtling back toward the building, his eyes widening, the fire around him blazing hotter, and then he was gone from view. A smooth edge surrounded the hole in the wall where he'd smashed his way through, the fire melting the edges as he went. The building shook as the villain leapt after him, Kirin racing behind as he saw the cracks appear around the new weak point. He just needed to leave a way out, he just had to give Ifrit a path out, just needed to get an arm through—

The whole building groaned as the opening collapsed, fractures spreading outward as Kirin's body slammed against the now impenetrable wall.

The world seemed to freeze.

You will be licensed to rescue, but not *to fight. Not even to defend yourself.*

Pressure's words roared in his ears. When did he last see another team that wasn't made of students? How close were they? Ifrit wasn't making any noise on the lines, hadn't since he'd vanished through. How long had it been? Was the villain attacking him or just running away? If Ifrit tried to use his mien in such an enclosed space, he'd likely hit the woman too; there was no way to create an explosion large enough and control the blast in every direction, and if he did that, *he'd* be the one losing his license, his chance to prove everyone wrong about him.

But what could Kirin do? He had the same restrictions, the same problem. What if he made it worse? There was a civilian on a stretcher that needed help too but—

His eyes.

When Ifrit had made eye contact, just as he vanished from sight, Kirin had seen. He was afraid.

Kirin made his choice.

"Villain attack at the corner of Fifth Avenue and Twenty-Second Street." His breath was ragged as he hardened his hands and drove them into the concrete to climb. "Hero student Ifrit attacked and trapped within a building with the villain. Female, with apparent super speed. Only entrance to building on fourth floor."

Static filled the line and then Majesty was in his ear.

"Standby, we will get heroes to your location. Do not engage."

"There is an injured civilian under the subway entrance." Kirin heaved himself through the fourth-floor window, the glass that remained on the sill pricking his legs as he swung them through.

"Do not engage, trainee." Majesty's voice was a low growl.

"I'm not going to." Kirin jumped on the floor, which was already groaning under the added weight. "I'm going to make him another way out."

The floor collapsed beneath him as he jumped again, dropping down one, two stories. Most of this floor was broken apart, chunks of concrete sticking up from the level below. Kirin ran in, knowing the area immediately beneath where he'd landed was entirely filled with debris. The floor here was more stable than he'd expected, not sagging at all. He didn't hear any sounds from the level below, which concerned him far more.

"Ifrit? Ifrit, can you hear me?" He switched channels to the direct line between the two of them. Only static answered him. "Ifrit, can you hear me?"

He reached the elevator shaft, throwing a meter wide piece of concrete out of the way. He pried the doors open, kicking one and denting it so it couldn't close again. As quickly as he could, he reached down and found the ladder, swinging himself into the shaft. He slid down until he reached the ground floor, crystallizing his palms to not slice them on the rusty edge.

The elevator itself was a crumpled bit of metal at the very bottom, so he had to brace himself on the thin ledge inside the doors, one foot still on the ladder as he forced the doors to open again.

Luckily, no great pieces of concrete blocked the shaft on this level, so he entered the hallway easily, trying to figure out where to go.

"Ifrit?" He whispered, the air feeling unnaturally still around him.

The entrance that Ifrit had been blown through was to his right, but the doorway had collapsed, another concrete wall blocking him. He stuck his head into the room on the other side of the hall— a store of some kind— but no Ifrit to be seen, no human shaped hole in the wall. Kirin turned back to the concrete slab and hardened his fists, finding his carbon stores hardly depleted at all.

"If you can hear me, stay away from the far wall." Kirin took a breath and punched.

He broke through with one hit, pressing his eye to the opening hurriedly, and only focusing on one thing. Ifrit, on the ground, unmoving. He took a few steps back, took a deep breath and *ran,* the entire side of his body becoming a saw blade that easily cut through the wall between them. He stumbled in, dust covering him, his pants ripped open from where his thigh and calf had pressed against the fabric, but he didn't stop moving, only dropped the crystallization, falling to his knees and gathering Ifrit's head on his lap.

The impact from the wall had broken Ifrit's mask, and Kirin took it off gently, making sure the edges of the plastic didn't cut his face. Kirin took off his own mask, switching the charge from carbon to oxygen and securing it over the other man's mouth, feeling the carbon in the air even through his own cloth mask. Ifrit slowly began to move as Kirin stroked his hair, fixing the crumpled curl from earlier. It was only then that Kirin noticed the villain in the corner of the room, collapsed. Her neck was at an odd angle, and with the dust in the air, Kirin couldn't tell if her chest was moving at all.

Ifrit opened his eyes and sat up quickly, nearly hitting Kirin in the face.

"Hey, hey, you're okay." Kirin got to his feet to help Ifrit up slowly. "Take it easy, I think you hit your head."

Ifrit's eyes still looked confused, but they were both distracted by the sound of someone drilling, and a circular section of the ceiling in the middle of the hall dropped down, Majesty with it. Her eyes flicked over the scene, Kirin standing there, covered in dust from when he'd come through the wall, Ifrit, looking completely unharmed, and the villain, unconscious and unmoving.

"What," she said through gritted teeth, "did you do?"

14

Belief

"It's been five days since the horrific attack on East City, and finally we have more information on the potential motivations behind such a senseless act of violence."

"Finally? We had an idea of what they were doing the same day!"

"Phoenix, shut it."

"In a shocking video posted online, which has been removed by authorities, but already copied to thousands of sites, a villain— or rather a villain organization— has taken credit for masterminding the assault on one of the city's backup power stations. Thankfully, all main power generators remain online, and the streets have been repaired; there has been no lasting damage to the city as a whole."

"No lasting damage? Thousands of people *died*."

"Sh!"

"The group, which has announced itself as Aether, has declared that the destruction of the power plant was only the beginning, and that this is their first foray into the light, promising to plunge the world into an age where only the strongest survive. Rest assured, the real heroes will be working around the clock to protect us and ensure that these criminals are found, and their reign of terror

stopped before it has truly begun."

The closing theme of the news broadcast began to play, and Kirin frowned.

"That's it? That's all they're going to say, really?" Ness spoke up from next to him, Dulu on her other side starting. "Yantra, were you able to find the video?"

"Who do you take me for?" Yantra extricated herself from the pile of all eighteen of them, crawling to the holo screen to plug her phone in. "Of course I did."

Kuafu frowned at that, but Lilin tugged on his arm, and he didn't protest. They were all sprawled out in between the couches, cushions thrown off the furniture, mattresses dragged out from the dorm rooms, and blankets piled high until they all had comfortable places to rest. Ifrit was wedged between Phoenix and Kirin, his jaw tense, but submitting to the forced socialization.

"I haven't watched it yet, but from the comments it's... something." Yantra paused as the screen flickered, a simple video screen and comment box filling the room. Comments were still pouring in, faster than Kirin could read them. "I don't think there's anything graphic, but..."

Her words trailed off, her eyes sad.

"I think we all want to know how they're excusing this." Kapre spoke up, softly as they always did, but their hair wasn't pulled up for once, instead draped over their face like a shroud. They'd had one of the hardest times with the rescue, second only to Adlivun in truly grasping the magnitude of death that had surrounded them as they tried futilely to fight it off.

"Alright." Yantra pressed play and hurriedly rejoined the group, Naddāha lifting her arm to let the other woman rest her head against her shoulder.

"If it's too much for anyone, just let me know." Naddāha added just before the video began to play.

"Hello, everyone." The speaker was a woman in a flat white mask, no expression or mark on it at all. It shone like pristine porcelain, so far from the blood and grime that had supposedly been her doing. *"I am sure you are angry; you are upset. I assure you that I am too. This is not how I wanted to greet you, but perhaps it is fitting."*

The video on the screen flickered, no longer showing the upper half of a woman with a nondescript background, but instead the interior of what seemed to be a factory. A power-plant.

"Get back freaks!" Someone was yelling, evidently a man in a suit, cowering behind a security guard. There were several of these men, all surrounded by guards in bullet-proof vests. *"Where the fuck is security? How did they get in?"*

Someone called back but their voice was lost over the sound of banging, of fighting off camera.

"Well, destroy the tank then!"

"But sir, if that causes a chain reaction, it could destroy the whole plant, or even worse, the neighboring buildings!" The speaker was not one of the guards, nor any of the men in suits, but instead a worker who had darted out from cover to protest.

"I don't give a damn! Get us to the bunker and then kill those bastards! It's worth it to lose a few lives if it means fewer monsters like them in the world!"

The video froze, the man pointing, his face contorted in anger, practically looming over the worker who had tried to stop him.

"I'll spare you the rest, as I suspect you know what comes next." The woman was back, her mask seeming to regard the camera though there was no way to see her expression. *"We only came to procure some items, robbery, yes, but no one was meant to get hurt. If any other camera footage survived, I could show you that*

in our approach, none of the guards were killed or even injured, but this is all that remains.

"I would have simply let my associates testify to what happened, but I fully understand that there will be a disinclination to trust us, for a time. Not only has the media spun this to be an intentional attack, but we have not given any reason for you to believe in us. Even the simple fact that our operatives were able to leave unscathed, while many others have perished due to the cowardly actions of one, makes it seem as though this was a planned outcome. It was not; it was the strength and might of our members that allowed them to pass unmolested while those who wished them dead perished.

"The world is changing, as we all have seen, but some, like our friend in the footage, are slow to change with it. They call us freaks. They call us monsters. They wish that we disappear from the Earth, but we are the true inheritors. Our motives are pure, our message simple: the world belongs to those who would take it.

"This is why I say that it is fitting our greeting is spurred by such an event. I will not let us stand accused of things we have not done and will show you plainly what we are. We are the Aether, the primal force in the world, perfect and transparent, bringing clarity and light. There is but one true rule that should be followed, and that is those with power can take what they wish." She sat up in her chair. *"For too long, men with puffed up egos have dictated what we do with our natural gifts, things passed down the generations into the hands of the worthy. You worship heroes as gods, and this is correct. Power is the one true god, the only thing deserving of praise. Might is life.*

"Why wait years for a chance at your full potential? Why struggle for the freedom to be who you are? Only a percent of a percent of those born with a touch of divinity may ever use it freely. The rest of us are told to be lucky we are allowed to use it at all. But, I ask, can they stop us all?"

Kuafu jerked forward, reaching for Naddāha. She took his hand, and the shaking of his shoulders eased. Outside, the rain fell harder.

"They seek to divide us. Just look at the way they portray us. Either the righteous hero or the evil villain. The words they cast us with tell you all you need to know. Obey, to the point of death, or become one of the hated. What better population control than turning us against one another, using us as weapons against one another? Cast aside the colors they paint us in, ignore the platitudes they fill your news with, and truly look at what us irredeemable criminals do, and see if a death sentence is fitting for the crime.

"Our world is built on the idea that you need to be given the right to be free, like the so-called normal people are free. Should they want to build what little power they have, they are permitted to, honing their natural bodies with no barriers, free to do so in public, whenever they so please. Why can we not? They fear us, as they should. We are gods among men, the inheritors of a legacy millennia in the making. Heroes were dead, they thought, and yet here we rise."

The woman tilted her chin.

"They want to fear us as monsters? So be it. Let them fear. But your power is within your reach, and should you want to take it, we are waiting."

The screen froze, the mask staring at them without eyes, without expression, but somehow challenging. Somehow *knowing.*

"We're going to be busy, then." Wyrm let out a breath.

"Not yet." Kuafu was still holding onto Naddāha, Lilin clasping his other hand. He looked calmer, but sadder. "People won't feel confident joining until they've proved they can back up their words. So far, they've botched a robbery and claimed to have survived. That won't be enough."

"They'll be trying something more, then?" Ness hadn't looked away from the screen, her eyes almost white from the reflected light.

"Certainly." Kuafu looked grim.

There were a few moments when no one said anything, the dark pronouncement filling the space in place of words. But then—

"I'm going to be honest guys, when we said 'feel better party,' I thought for certain that meant anything *but* watching the news." Phoenix had gotten up without Kirin noticing. "I'm putting on a movie, and you all have thirty seconds to tell me what, or I *will* put on another rom-com and none of you have the power to stop me."

The room erupted into arguments as Yantra tried (and failed) to snatch the remote from Phoenix, everyone fully aware of just how terrible their taste in movies was. Kirin and Ifrit were the only people who didn't join in, sitting at the back of the pile. They were up against the rear couch, the cushions cast off the top and instead providing back support, Ifrit hogging an entire blanket to himself. Phoenix had been prepared to take his door off its hinges to make him come down, but he'd been surprisingly pliable and agreed to it with minimal coercing.

It was the first time they'd seen him since the attack, since he'd supposedly been kept in medical observation during the week. No one said it aloud, but they all knew it was closer to interrogation than observation, if Kirin's own experience had been anything to go by.

He hadn't fared as poorly and had only been questioned for a day. The villain— whose name he still hadn't been told— was recovering, but she'd suffered severe brain damage, and had yet to wake up, if she ever would again. That was all he'd managed to find out from his questioners, officers whose faces remained in shadows as he was spoken to through a window in a wall. Ifrit, on the other hand, they'd kept longer, and no matter how many times Kirin had gone back, had been told nothing about where Ifrit was being kept.

And maybe that was why Ifrit was down with them. He'd looked surprised when he was invited, several of their classmates at his door insisting that he come. They all knew, after all, *why* he was being treated like a criminal.

But now he looked close to peaceful, head leaning back against the couch, his eyes closed. He did have dark circles under his eyes, and looked a bit pale, so maybe there was some truth to him needing medical attention, even if that wasn't the primary reason for his detainment. He only opened them again when the movie started to play, one of the animated ones Kapre had been pushing for. And still he sat quietly and didn't complain.

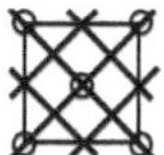

The movie was halfway over when Kirin felt Ifrit's head fall onto his shoulder. He felt himself freeze, hardly daring to breathe in fear of disturbing the other man, thinking he'd fallen asleep. But when Kirin snuck a glance down, he found Ifrit's eyes open, still looking at the screen. He pulled his own gaze back up, warmth bubbling in his chest.

"Thanks." It was so quiet that he almost missed it.

"Mm?" Kirin spoke quietly too, though Ness was the closest person to his left and she'd fully fallen asleep on Dulu by that point.

"For coming in after me."

Kirin opened his mouth to say it was nothing, but Ifrit wasn't done.

"And for talking to the police for me. And for... not thinking I did anything."

"You don't have to thank me for that." Kirin said gently. "You're my friend."

Ifrit looked up at him then, and Kirin forced himself to keep his face neutral. Because he hadn't realized that Ifrit was crying.

"I do, though." Ifrit pulled his eyes away. "I could, uh, hear you fucking yelling through the wall."

"They wouldn't tell me if you were okay." Kirin shrugged without thinking, wincing as he jostled Ifrit's head slightly. Ifrit started to sit up, but Kirin wrapped his arm around the smaller man's shoulders, and after a moment, he settled back down. "I was a little annoyed about it."

"A little?" There was an attempt at a scoff, but it got caught in the back of his throat. "Remind me to never piss you off then."

"You don't have to worry about it, you know." Kirin leaned his cheek against Ifrit's hair, noting idly that it was softer than he'd expected.

"Worry about what?" There was an attempt at his usual angry bluster, but a hint of anxiety dulled the edge.

"None of them think you did anything either. When I got back, and you weren't with me, Phoenix was about to march themself down to the police station. Clidna too. They almost did; Pressure had to come and talk them out of it."

"How'd she know to come?" Ifrit sounded doubtful.

"Uh, that may have been my fault." Kirin shifted and cleared his throat. "I *may* have had to be dragged back to campus, and she *might* have been making sure I wasn't trying to sneak back out immediately."

He felt dampness on his shoulder.

"You're a fucking dumbass." Ifrit's voice was thick, and from how he wasn't looking at Kirin, Kirin tactfully pretended not to notice anything.

"It's not right that they treat you like that. And we're all here to stand up for you if they do. *I'm* here for you, if you ever need me."

Ifrit didn't respond, just buried his face in Kirin's shoulder, and silently cried.

After the weekend, classes resumed.

There was shockingly little change in the atmosphere, like they hadn't all just witnessed something momentous, something horrific. Classes continued as normal, with the only mention of the events of the prior week being professors bemoaning the loss of class time. They made up for it with back work, telling their students it was necessary in order to catch back up with the almighty lesson plan.

Yet, slowly but surely, Kirin noticed a shift.

The tech students usually gave the hero classes a relatively wide berth, never aiming to sit close or talk to the hero students, but Kirin noticed that the seats around him and Ifrit were never filled by anyone other than their own classmates, regardless of the class. If they arrived late and grabbed the seats closest to the door, students who'd been sitting nearby would shift, leaving a gap. In the hallways, there was always plenty of room as people parted to let them through, and getting food from the cafeteria ceased to be a chore as the line would disappear at whichever station Ifrit chose. Worse, some students had begun to openly sneer at Ifrit, getting close only to mutter something unsavory under their breath or to glare.

He never complained about it, but there was just the slightest raising of the shoulders, the smallest deepening in the crease in his forehead, the tiniest widening in his necklace of fire. And Kirin wasn't the only one to notice.

"So, boss, what do you think of the new hero movie coming out?" Clidna stepped between Ifrit and a tech student who was making a beeline toward him. "I know, I know, you 'don't watch movies,' but Kirin's ratted you out and I know you have at least four movie posters up in your dorm."

Ifrit's gaze was redirected from the incoming man to her, and she chatted away as they headed off to class.

Another day, they were all headed to the cafeteria, and someone opened their mouth, eyes latched on Ifrit, a nasty expression on their face, when Goldhorn abruptly caused a giant corpse flower to bloom just off to the side of the walkway, almost perfectly in front of the offending party.

"The stench is said to be very close to that of a rotting corpse." They said calmly, ignoring the woman who was now on the ground coughing her lungs out. "It's very rare to get to see one bloom, so many consider themselves lucky to experience the smell."

"It's fucking rancid." Ifrit said, but even through his mask, it was clear that he said it with a smile.

The whole class seemed to have unanimously come to the agreement that Ifrit was only allowed to go out if he had a buddy, and while he grumbled about never getting private time, and tended to retreat to his dorm room even more than before, he never really tried to get them to stop.

It wasn't until Ifrit and Kirin were called back to the police station that the full magnitude of the situation hit.

"Thank you for your prompt arrival; we'll have you brought down, and you can do what you wish before we begin." The officer escorting them was very brusque and hadn't given them a moment to question what exactly was going on. She'd turned on her heel as soon as they'd entered the building and was maintaining a good three-meter separation as they marched on. Ifrit, for once, didn't seem to have much more information than Kirin, the pair of them sharing more than one confused look as they went deeper and deeper into the ground.

It wasn't until Kirin realized that they were going to the bottom level of the station that he figured out where they were going.

"The mien user holding cells." He said aloud, more to himself than the group, but fear flickered in Ifrit's eyes for a moment as they continued.

"She's finally awake." The officer opened the door to the cell block, the door made of steel nearly ten centimeters thick. "Close it behind you and stay a meter away from the cell bars and you'll be fine."

"Why're we here?" Kirin asked, feeling incredibly hesitant about that door shutting behind them.

"She's awake." The officer said, like it should answer his question, but as Kirin continued to stare at her, she seemed to understand that he needed more information. "Arresting heroes have first interrogation rights."

That dimly rang a bell in Kirin's head from their Hero Law class, though he hardly considered what they'd done arresting. Yet the officer was shooing him and Ifrit inside, and closing the door before he could fully process what that meant.

The cells were eerie, the ambiance likely created by virtue of their function, but certainly not helped by the bars giving off a chilly blueish glow. The power that burst off them had the hairs on Kirin's neck standing up, and he had to resist the urge to use his mien to keep them down.

"Oh, how lovely, some wonderful *heroes* have come to talk to little old me." The villain wasn't visible yet, but she at least, unlike them, knew the drill. "Come to convince me to see the error of my ways? To bruise me up just a little? To gloat?"

"None of the above." Neither him nor Ifrit were in uniform,

but Ifrit straightened his posture and adjusted his mask, striding forward toward the last cell in the row, where the voice seemed to have come from. "We're here to find out everything you know."

Kirin followed Ifrit, his footsteps loud in the echoing space. There were no overhead lights here, no openings for prisoners to potentially exploit, just the light from the bars and the little that spilled in from the door at the end of the hall, so as he walked forward it grew darker and colder. The empty cells he passed seemed like holes, a grim, hopeless place with no way out. Ifrit stood out like a star, his light warm where the other was harsh and clinical.

"And what makes you think I'll share?" They finally saw her, curled up and huddled against a wall, dark circles under her eyes sunken like bruises. His heart clenched, and for a moment it wasn't a stranger in that cell, it was one of his siblings. She looked to be the same age as the oldest of them, maybe even younger. An adult, but just barely.

"Because it would exonerate your organization." Kirin spoke up, her eyes darting away from Ifrit, looking shocked that there was someone else there.

"What do you mean?" Her eyes darted between them.

"Your boss is telling the whole world that you didn't mean to blow a fucking hole in the city. Awfully nice story when the only bastards who could confirm it are very dead."

"It's kill or be killed out there." Part of Kirin's heart went out to her, down here, in the dark for how many days now, only a thin t-shirt and pants against the chill.

"That's not what a lot of people outside think." Kirin eyed the line on the ground and stepped up to it, the electricity making the whisps of hair that fell out of his bun float now too. No wonder she was staying in the back. "Why don't you tell us what happened in there? I can't promise anything, but we can see about a reduced sentence for cooperation—"

He was interrupted as she burst out laughing, so hard that she struggled to breathe afterward, clutching her sides like she was in pain.

"Reduced sentence? Are you fucking shitting me? We all know the sentence for unlicensed mien usage is life, no matter how petty the crime."

"Usually. But this isn't a typical case. And helping take down a terrorist organization—"

She was up against the barrier in an instant, Kirin not even seeing her move. The current made her hair rise, forming a halo around her, black as night.

"We are *not* terrorists." She hissed.

"Then what are you?" Ifrit stepped up to the line as well, his eyes challenging. "It's fucking lovely to wax poetic about power, but it doesn't sound like a peaceful message."

"There's a space between peace and terror that can be worked within." The words came so quickly they felt memorized. "Just because we don't want to be slaves to archaic and discriminatory rules doesn't mean we want to hurt people."

"Claiming that power is the most important thing in life doesn't seem like a message of utopia either." Kirin spoke softly.

She was quiet, her dark eyes darting between the pair.

"It's a means to an end."

"That's one hell of a means."

"They won't *listen* to anything else!" The woman stalked away, back into the shadows of her cell. "How many years have people lobbied for even something as basic as allowing mien use in rental properties? How many years have students been denied entrance to schools because the boards were concerned about *property damage*? How many years have people begged for a special use license to make their lives just a little more livable, only to be denied if they were ever granted a fucking hearing in the first place?"

She paused in her pacing and shot a glare toward the pair of them, her eyes dark pools.

"How many of us have been killed by heroes for daring to appear different and that was deemed damage enough?"

"What's the end goal then? Because what you're talking about is not what we heard from your leader's mouth. You speak of equality; she spoke of a new world order with those weaker crushed underfoot." Kirin took a risk and took a small step closer. "You could've killed us, me at least for certain, but you didn't. I want to believe what you're saying, but you need to give us some confirmation of what really happened at that power plant."

She walked up to the bars, slowly this time.

"I won't kill my kin like you will." There was a raw edge to her voice.

"But you will kill others."

"I *get* to be angry about how we're treated!"

"You do. We all do." Kirin glanced sideways at Ifrit, whose expression was unreadable. "But you're hurting the people like you, too. The numbers for the new generation, *our* generation, it's not even one in ten anymore, it's one in *five*. Four thousand three hundred and twelve people are confirmed dead in that explosion and the damage caused afterwards. If we just use the old number, that's four hundred mien users dead. I have classmates who are amazing, but their miens don't give them strength or power in the way that mine does, and I want them just as safe as I want myself, and you. How can you get people to your side if you're killing us, too?"

"If she's put out her statement, she'll have found the footage from the plant." The woman finally showed a trace of remorse now. "We didn't do it, the bigots touring did."

"There's footage, but it cuts out before anything happens. She also said that you all got out alive and they didn't. Seems odd that could happen if they're the ones who set it off."

"I'm very fast." She said dryly. "Their own normalcy doomed them in the end."

"Three of the maintenance crew for that plant had miens that were registered." Kirin pulled up his phone. "One had reported that he could hear bees talking to each other, another that he could change his hair length and color at will. The third could just hold their breath for a very long time. None of those help with escaping an explosion."

"Why do you have that information?"

"Every number, every name, there's a person behind it. Maybe it's the naivety talking, but I don't want to see the data and forget that it stands for people, real people, with real lives. And so I can remind people that every time you think you're striking at a faceless enemy, there are real people who get caught in between."

"We weren't the monsters there."

"Then what *were* you doing?"

She hesitated. But at least it wasn't an outright refusal.

"We were just gathering supplies."

"For?"

She sent him a withering look.

"There wasn't even supposed to be maintenance that day. It was simple, get in, get out, no one gets hurt. But one of the councilmen for the city, he wanted a tour, for some reason, and so they were fully staffed instead of just a handful of guards." Her hands found her elbows and she squeezed.

"We managed to get into the building just fine, no one seriously hurt but knocked out, and then suddenly there was gunfire and blood and... and..." She took a shuddering breath. "There were all these men, with fancy suits and expensive weapons just standing in a line with no expressions like killing us was just as inconsequential as killing a fly. I knew when I signed up for this that people would want to kill me, would *try* to kill me, but I didn't realize how little they would care when they did it."

Out of the corner of his eye, Kirin saw Ifrit's hands tighten at his sides.

"I froze. One of my companions shoved me out of the way, and we were already *leaving* when they set off the explosion. They didn't care that we weren't trying to fight. They just wanted us dead."

"If you weren't trying to fight, why did you come and attack us? We weren't close to the power plant, and we were rescuing people when you found us."

"You were covered in blood! I couldn't reach any of my teammates and... and... I thought maybe you had..." She looked away, visibly shaking now. "I was scared. There were heroes. Figured I'd take you out before you took me down."

Kirin glanced at Ifrit, something about her last statement not ringing quite true. But from the stiffness in her posture, and the way that she wouldn't look at either of them, Kirin decided they'd gotten all the information out of her that they were going to get.

"Thank you for talking to us." He felt his heart clench slightly, knowing that the information she'd given was useless in the eyes of the police. "I'll see if we can't get you warmer clothes, or at least a blanket."

She didn't respond, heading to curl up in the back corner of her cell, looking so small compared to the size of the room. Ifrit had already started to walk back, but Kirin hesitated.

"What's your name?"

She did look back up at that.

"I'm not looking to find your family or anything, just a first name would be fine. I just want to know what to call you."

Again, she hesitated, weighing the words, seeing if she could sense a trap within them. It seemed like she decided nothing could go more wrong than it already had and sighed.

"It's Cara."

"I'm Kirin." He wasn't sure why he was still talking, Ifrit watching him with his head cocked. "I wish we could've met under different circumstances."

Cara didn't look away this time, her eyes following both of them as they vanished from sight. Kirin felt the weight of that gaze long after they came out of the hallway, long after they exited the police station, long after he'd lain down to sleep that night. Even when dreams came, they were filled with eyes that watched him, sad and accusing.

15

Remembrance

Kirin, quite frankly, could not catch a break.

He'd thought that the practical finals being called off due to the "more than satisfactory" performance in the field would mean that their break could start early, that he could start on the mound of laundry that had been building in the last weeks of the semester, or even that he could just sleep in. But he was quickly discovering that a good portion of being a hero was simply the art of keeping up appearances. So instead, he and the rest of his classmates had been piled onto a jet at three in the morning and were now cruising lazily over the ocean.

With his head pressed against the side, he took in the sight of the water. Since this wasn't an emergency call, they were packed into a commercial jet, not one of the supersonic ones that were little more than metal boxes. So, for the first time, he was able to enjoy the view.

East City was nearly to the Americas now, so they'd flown over the First Nations rather than back across the Pacific. He'd been asleep for most of the flight over the country, but he'd awoken for the very last of it, and now was watching the vast stretch of ocean that lay beneath them.

Europe was coming into view, the land seeming to appear on

the horizon out of nowhere, and though they were faint, Kirin could make out the tiny shapes of other aircrafts converging in the same direction. The early morning and the view had done wonders to distract him from his nervousness, but the reminder of other visitors set it creeping back in. He felt his hands tense on the armrests and heard a quiet but ominous crack.

"Kirin, you're breaking the plastic." Ness whispered to him, as so many of their classmates were still asleep. In fact, only Ifrit was awake, sitting directly in front of Kirin and facing the window, his face visible in profile. Kirin had watched him for a while, unsure if he wasn't sleeping with his eyes open, since he was so very still.

"Sorry." He forced his hands to let go, but the damage was done, the cover falling off. Ness sighed, picking up the offending piece and tucking it into the seat in front of her. It was strange to see her in her costume in such a casual space, but they all were, an almost comical sight. Hers at least wasn't terribly gaudy, a dark mix of colors that almost looked like camouflage. It looked to him more like early twenty-first century tactical gear than a hero costume, building up her small frame with plenty of padding and protection. Her mask blended with her hair, lenses covering her eyes too. Without his usual focal point of her eyes, Kirin felt like she flickered, like a candle in the wind.

Pressure's class was packed into the first six rows of seats, Pressure herself dozing in the front row next to Ifrit. A class overseen by a hero in bright yellow— Pollen— was immediately behind them, some of the students familiar from Ethics and now Tech Advances, and then there were three other hero classes between Pollen's and Majesty's. They'd already been boarded and seated when Kirin and his classmates arrived, and Kirin had felt their stares as he, or more likely, Ifrit, sat down.

They would make an easy target, he thought idly, having several hero classes contained on one flight. But they'd only found out the night before, and the time of departure had been announced by Pressure walking around and banging on their doors. It wasn't even until Kirin had woken up on the plane that he realized his hero costume was new. Almost everyone in the class who'd been assigned lighter colors had needed their costumes entirely replaced, the blood from the rescue staining too deeply. His mask and pants would have been fine if they hadn't been damaged, but he'd needed a new shirt since even the gold lines had started to look more like bronze.

"Kirin?" Ness nudged him. "You doing okay?"

He wrenched his thoughts back to the present and tried to focus on Ness. He found it easier now than it had been when he'd first met her, but sometimes it was hard to even focus on her words. Though he suspected right now it had less to do with her mien and more to do with his own distraction.

"Just tired." As he said it, he noticed that Ness herself had dark circles under her eyes. It was hard to tell through her mask, but with the light backdrop of the plane seat, he could just about see the difference. "Are you?"

Her eyes flickered to Ifrit, but he showed no signs of having heard them.

"It's just been a lot, yeah?" She sighed and leaned against him, Kirin picking up his arm to let her rest her head against his chest. "Just when it felt like we were starting to get the hang of rescues, we get tossed into a full emergency, and suddenly I realized just how easy the assignments they were giving us before were. And now we're going to put on a show to talk about how these sorts of disasters can never happen again, but the police are no closer to catching the people who organized the attack at the plant, and it all feels... slimy."

As she spoke, her image seemed to solidify slightly, and Kirin was forced to remember just how small she was. He'd never asked any of his classmates their ages, knowing they all had to be above eighteen to be considered for admission, but in that moment, she looked far younger.

"It does feel shitty, huh?" That startled a laugh out of her, a real smile pricking at her lips. "I knew this was a part of the job that I wasn't going to like, but I can understand the benefit of it."

"Yantra nearly made me watch a PowerPoint on the benefits of these sorts of appearances for public morale. It was *forty* slides." Ness's smile grew soft.

"Life is scary— always is— but when you have a thing to point at and it's all the news talks about, it becomes even scarier. While I agree it feels like it'd be better for us to be *doing* rather than just *speaking*, often the *doing* isn't visible to everyone. Reassurances can go far, especially when the world feels hopeless." Green was beginning to appear beneath them as the edge of Europe began to pass by.

"That's very mature of you."

"I have my moments, I'll have you know."

"I prefer when you act like an idiot."

"I'll make sure to slip on a banana peel or something while we get off."

"Please do."

They were quiet for a minute, the sound of the engine filling the space.

"Ness, are you alright though?" Kirin felt like he had to ask.

"I feel like there's an obvious answer to that."

"It feels like you're... disappointed about something." He wasn't sure if that was the right emotion, but it was the closest word he could find. It was at least somewhat accurate, as she pursed her lips. While there were soft sounds of others waking, the group around them was still sleeping soundly. Even so,

Ness seemed to be debating saying anything more.

"It's not what I expected." She finally said.

"The program? Or the school as a whole?"

"Both, I suppose." She sat up and he removed his arm, knowing she didn't like to be touched while she thought. "I had all these dreams, you know, about coming here and it being... different."

He didn't comment, letting her find her words.

"I thought maybe having a visible mien wasn't going to be a big deal, that I'd get here and magically feel *normal* or maybe feel *right* is a better way to put it. Or even... I guess when I thought I'd get to use my mien more, I could figure out how to turn it off fully someday." She held out her hand, looking at the fuzzy edge. "But if anything, it's getting worse."

"Your armorer couldn't get you anything like Enenra has?"

"I did ask. But I guess I'm not that... simple? It sounds mean to say, but I don't know how else to put it. My armorer said that it wouldn't make sense to have it on my costume because my mien is so 'ideal' for hiding my identity, and when I asked if I could have something like that for my own time she laughed, saying the school wouldn't want to pay for that."

"I mean, they give us a stipend, maybe you could pay for it yourself? It's not like we have any expenses to worry about right now."

"Maybe." She didn't sound convinced. "And it's just... I should be grateful to be here at all, right? I don't look the traditional hero role, and my mien is useful but not the *most* useful. When I used to think about coming here, the only person I told insisted that I wouldn't be able to get in because I simply wasn't memorable. They're right, scientifically speaking, but it still hurt."

She looked like she had more to say and was hesitating, so Kirin nudged her knee with his. She looked up from the ground at him, her bottom lip trembling slightly.

"Coming out, doing press, it feels so frustrating because I *know* that creating hope and trust in the hero system is what we need while there is the first ever active villain organization out there, but I just can't stop thinking about how I used to be on the other side of the screen, watching the new heroes walk around like they had all the power in the world, and thinking that if I could just get myself here, I wouldn't have to feel like this anymore." Her voice cracked on the last word, and she looked down at her hands.

"I don't think you should be grateful."

She looked up at him.

"That implies they did you a favor. You earned your position here, and you more than deserve it. Grateful implies you didn't deserve your chance, but Ness, you've got an incredible mien, even if it might work against you sometimes. Majesty's class isn't grateful to be here; they think it's their right to. I want you to feel like that, to know that you're worth it and your place here isn't some fluke, isn't some first attempt at inclusivity but rather a testament to how powerful you are. You are so unique that they don't even know how to deal with you yet, and you're breaking barriers for everyone behind you.

"Should you have to? Absolutely not. But you don't need to feel like you're lying to anyone because the fact that you're here means you get to tear up the way things have been done and build something new." Kirin's eyes found Ifrit, who was still looking out the window. "We all do."

"Do you really think they'll let us?"

"I don't really care if they will or won't. Because we *will* change things." More people were waking now, so Kirin spoke even quieter. "No matter what, we're going to start making this right."

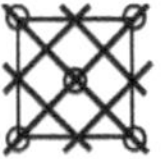

He'd spoken big words on the plane, but stepping out into the light, Kirin felt a lot of that confidence shrivel up and run away, the cameras flashing in his face too much, the shining city behind them too bright. He froze for a moment at the top of the stairs, eyes fixed to an unfamiliar skyline.

"Come on." Naddāha took his elbow and nudged him forward, some of the panic fading as she did.

"You don't have to do that."

"It's what I'm good at." She gave him a quick smile, her mask only covering the upper portion of her face.

"We're not on campus." Kirin's eyes were roving over the reporters now, wondering if any of them noticed anything. The cameras hovered near their heads like buzzards, the flashes hiding the faces of those who controlled them.

"The convenient thing about no one knowing how miens work," Naddāha muttered out of the corner of her mouth, "is that unless I admit to something, they can't prove a damn thing."

She leveled a knowing look at him as they walked on.

Satol was a city made new. Many of the buildings shone with screens, skyscrapers looking impossibly thin as they vanished into the clouds, the steel holding up the corners reflecting green from the newest heat-resistant alloys. The world had flocked here to hide the evidence of disaster, and a decade since that day, the city was flourishing more than ever.

They were shuttled into cars, Kirin separated from most of the class and left with Aïcha, Dulu, and Goldhorn. The other three were quiet as they passed through the outskirts of the city, no one saying a word until the car jumped to a track twenty stories in the air.

"I thought East City was new." Goldhorn's eyes followed a few pedestrians as they walked on a floating park, the trees merging with the metal. "This is..."

"Incredible." Dulu too had his head pressed against the window, a wondering grin spreading across his face. "I wish Yantra were here; I'm sure she could tell us all about the technology used to create these parks, even the electric roads."

"I'm sure we'll all be treated to a presentation about it when we get back." Aïcha said fondly, the only one of them who wasn't gawking openly. Instead, her gaze was locked forward, her sharp eyes noting every turn they took. If she was remembering them all, Kirin was immensely impressed, since the city was a veritable maze of buildings and greenery and cars. There were more cars here than Kirin could ever remember seeing, but the trains that connected so much of the rest of the world no longer had lines within the city.

It was shocking how much had changed in ten years. Though, having a solid layer of metal separating a city from the ground would force some radical changes. Where once there was a hodge-podge collection of buildings from different periods, now there were clean skyscrapers that could have been de-signed by the same person, so similar were they in style and materials. Cone shaped, they were ringed with fabricated pan-els that drew in sunlight to power the systems within, Kirin able to see people moving about inside through the few glazing panels that weren't tinted for privacy. Cars sped by both above and below, sunlight glinting off the metal siding, the slight blue tinge in the air showing the nearly invisible electric rails they followed.

The greenery was what drew Kirin most; story upon story of it, stacked, tucked neatly between buildings, *inside* buildings. There was one tower they passed that must have been closing in on a hundred stories tall that seemed to have an impossibly large *tree* at its center, the figures inside looking tiny by comparison.

The Cardinal Islands were a man-made wonder at the time of their creation, but they had been built in a rush, a concerted effort to lock everything relating to miens to neutral territory. While East City was still impressive, it looked positively antiquated compared to the clean white lines and floating greenery.

Their car started to dip down, signaling that they were arriving, and Kirin felt another ball of anxiety curling in the bottom of his stomach. The buildings that had moments before looked so serene now felt like a forest one strong gust of wind away from toppling over, part of him thinking he could see the distant tops swaying as he watched.

"Kirin, come on." Dulu was leaning back through the open door, looking at him curiously. He hadn't even noticed his classmates exiting, but Aïcha and Goldhorn were already outside, the flash of cameras turning them into little more than silhouettes. Kirin swallowed down his fear and stepped out, letting the blinding light wash over him as well.

Out of the corner of his eye, he saw another car pull up, but even that couldn't shield them from the barrage of photos and the shouted questions that threatened to overwhelm everything else. He focused on the carpet rolled out beneath his feet and walked forward, glad that at least for the moment, his feet weren't touching metal.

The car had dropped them at the entrance to a sunken amphitheater, but the line of entry stretched out a few dozen paces, some of the people in line recognizable. Phoenix was at the very end waving to them, Antaeus, Wyrm, and Ifrit with her.

"I'm still upset they don't give us fancy versions of our hero suits for these types of occasions." Phoenix sighed. Though a large portion of the crowd was costumed heroes, there were various diplomats present as well, the latter wearing elegant dresses and suits more fit for a movie premier than a memorial.

"This isn't a nice thing." Ifrit matched Kirin's thoughts, practically biting out the words. Usually, he was far more in control of his temper in front of a crowd, but he seemed incredibly on edge, the flame around his throat flickering ominously.

"I know." Phoenix actually looked remorseful, a sad smile appearing on her face. "That was stupid, sorry."

Dulu and Goldhorn looked at each other, at the same time that Wyrm and Antaeus did too. Kirin, for his part, also struggled to keep the shock from his face. He was fairly certain that was the first time Phoenix had ever *actually* apologized to anyone, and so quickly too.

"It's fucking whatever." Ifrit grumbled, but the flames died down.

"This is a whole lot of fanciness for a funeral." Yantra's car had appeared without anyone noticing, and Kirin saw Ifrit flinch as she spoke up.

"Yeah, we were just talking about that." Goldhorn kept talking, expertly steering the conversation to a slightly less sensitive topic. Kirin had stopped listening the moment the immediate danger passed, instead doing his best to sidle up to Ifrit discreetly.

"Do you want me to grab Naddāha?" Kirin leaned forward slightly over Ifrit's head as he spoke, pretending to be trying to catch a glimpse of the stadium ahead. They were still thirty or so people from the entrance, though Kirin could see security doing a thorough search of each person before they entered. It could've been a typical precaution, but the rigor with which each search was being conducted made Kirin think that Aether's appearance had left whoever was in charge of planning a little on edge.

"If she tries to use her mien on me ever again, I'm going to throw her into a fucking wall."

"Hey, my idea. She won't do anything unless you ask her to."

"Or unless she thinks I need it." Ifrit shot him a look. "Like if I'm taking a little too long to get off a fucking plane."

"That was helpful for me, I did appreciate it."

"But you didn't ask." Ifrit turned away from Kirin, resolutely facing the entrance, arms crossed over his chest.

"Let me rephrase. She won't do anything to *you* unless you ask."

Ifrit didn't even spare him a glance, his back ramrod straight. Kirin let it drop, his attention instead taken by the stadium that they were about to enter.

The stadium that seemed to have been made with molten metal.

Kirin's stomach lurched now that they were close enough to see the seats they'd be expected to sit in for the next several hours. It looked as though the seating had been carved directly into the ten meters of melted steel that now comprised the ground of Satol. It looked beautifully made, the entire structure an architectural wonder, according to the woman standing just in front of them in line, but the thought of cold metal against his skin made him feel like he was going to throw up.

Naddāha was suddenly at his side, her eyes wide and concerned. She reached out to touch him, but Ifrit grabbed her wrist.

"Don't."

"You know I don't need to touch him, right?" She said softly, and Kirin was sure it hadn't been intended as a threat, but Ifrit's eyes narrowed.

"You're just going to make it worse." There was such confidence behind those words that some more rational part of Kirin's brain wondered how he knew.

"I can—"

"Take away emotions, I fucking know." Ifrit let her hand drop, his eyes darting to where a camera was lazily floating toward them. "But you can't take away the effects."

She didn't look convinced, but Kirin just shook his head, the shame of his friends arguing for his sake overpowering the nausea for a moment.

"It's okay. I'm good now." On instinct he smiled, the nose piece of his mask hitting the bridge of his nose from the movement. She seemed to understand and slid away smoothly, leaving Ifrit and Kirin outside of the bubble of their classmates.

"Look at me." Ifrit's voice took on the same tone he used when he was explaining their homework to Kirin for the fifth time. "We're going to do some fucking breathing exercises or whatever, okay?"

Kirin just nodded, feeling confused. The line moved a little farther forward, causing his eyes to jump back to the stadium, but Ifrit punched him in the gut.

"Eyes on me. Breathe in for four." As Ifrit breathed in, the flames around his neck shrunk, the points dropping to half the size they normally were. "Okay, now hold for four. And out for four."

He led Kirin through several rounds, but Kirin stopped paying attention to the words so much and instead watched the flames shrink, hold, and then grow. It really was pretty, he decided, especially the lazy curls that snuck out and licked Ifrit's jawbone.

"Do I need to make some goddamn bees for you too?" Ifrit noticed Kirin wasn't paying attention to what he was saying anymore, snapping his fingers in Kirin's face to get his attention again.

"I wouldn't mind it?"

Ifrit rolled his eyes and looked like he was going to turn away when he paused. A crease appeared between his eyebrows and a few seconds trickled by with nothing happening. Kirin was about to open his mouth and say something when a tiny bee made of flame crawled out from the ring of fire around Ifrit's neck.

It flew around Kirin's face, the wings only moving jerkily if at all, spinning in lazy circles until Kirin put his finger out for it to land on. Just before it did, it collapsed into a puff of smoke, vanishing before his eyes.

"Rude, I wanted to hold it." He looked to Ifrit, whose red eyes were watching Kirin intently.

"Dumbass, it's still fire." Ifrit made another anyway, this time having it land on his own hand. Ifrit's costume had no gloves so it just sat in his palm innocently the light reflecting across all the creases. "I won't burn, but you fucking will."

"But I've got fireproof gloves!" Kirin held up his hands and wiggled his fingers, which got the barest chuckle out of Ifrit.

"You really are an idiot."

"HOW LONG HAVE YOU BEEN ABLE TO DO THAT?" Phoenix's eyes were suddenly level with Ifrit's palm. He startled and the bee vanished. "Aw, I wanted to hold it."

"That's what I said!"

"And you're even fucking dumber because at least *he* has some resistance to heat. *You* can't even heal yourself." Ifrit looked grumpier than usual, the crease between his brows remaining even though the creature was gone. "I've been working on it since last semester."

"That's still pretty fast, no?" Goldhorn apparently had been paying attention too, standing next to Dulu, both of them just behind Phoenix.

"Pressure wanted me to work on fine control, so I did."

"Dude, you're so cool." Dulu managed to make it sound like a complaint.

Before Ifrit could snap back, they were suddenly at the front of the line.

"That'll have to be turned off."

"He needs it on." Kirin put himself in front of Ifrit. "And he's got a license for it."

"If he's got a license, that means it turns off. And it'll have to. No open flames." The security guard was shockingly close in height to Kirin, fully comfortable with getting up in his face. "Or else no entry."

"It's fine." Ifrit pulled Kirin back, his face impassive. A second later the fire around his throat disappeared, his neck looking so vulnerable without it. "We good?"

The security guard pulled him off to the side, away from the group, Kirin fighting the urge to follow them. He was distracted shortly by another agent, who ushered him off to the side just far enough that he was out of sight of the cameras.

"Remove your mask, please."

He did so without complaint, though it felt so strange to be barefaced out in public. He pulled down the cloth mask under his respirator too, the guard pulling out a scanner to get his biometrics. A few seconds later, it flashed green and the guard nodded, Kirin quickly resetting his mask.

"You all are getting bigger every year, huh?" The man said in a friendly tone, but Kirin felt the weight of it like an itch between his shoulder blades.

"Well, so do they." Kirin replied softly.

"That's true." The guard handed him a wristband that fastened itself and blinked to life, a tiny green dot pulsing on the outside. "But I've seen you on TV, you know, and I feel like we're in good hands for whatever they want to try next!"

With a clap on the back, Kirin was sent back into line, this time meeting up with his friends inside the stadium.

There were fewer cameras here, only the main news feeds allowed in, tens of thousands of people slowly filling the seating. Some of his anxiety came back as they walked in, but as if the thought had summoned him, Ifrit brusquely pushed past someone to appear at Kirin's side.

"Big fucking deal they're making over something a decade old, huh?"

"It is a big deal." Kirin's eyes were drawn up to the skyscrapers that were visible even through the shielded opening in the roof. "They made something out of what was considered the greatest tragedy in our generation, and it worked."

Ifrit didn't seem to know what to say.

"But yeah, it's shitty that it's become a social event, almost. Yantra was right that this is, in some ways, a funeral."

"You know how many people died in this one?" There was an undercurrent in Ifrit's voice that Kirin couldn't place.

"No. I didn't want to look."

"Two-hundred-seventy-three-thousand-and-fifty, approximately." Ifrit looked up at the screen hovering above the stage, appearing younger without his flames. "They update it almost yearly, still, when families give up looking."

Before Kirin could figure out what to say to that, he was grabbed by Ness, and pulled down a row of seats.

"It's going to start soon. What took you guys so long?" She looked flustered herself, an unusually bright red visible on her cheeks.

"Security." Ifrit said it curtly enough that she didn't bother to ask anything further.

"Pressure's going to be speaking."

"What?" Ifrit, Kirin, and Phoenix all spoke up together. Adlivun, who was already sitting just beyond Ness, looked embarrassed.

"Apparently—"

The shield over the opening cut off the light from the city above, the amphitheater suddenly dark. Kirin hurriedly took a seat, trying not to think about it as he did, eyes focused on the stage.

"Honored guests, please take a seat. Our program will begin shortly." A voice filled the air, seeming to come from everywhere at once. "We ask that you please turn all cellular devices off, not just in silent mode."

Kirin reached for his, only to find that it was turned off already. He frowned slightly, realizing it had been turned off remotely.

"They don't even trust us to do that." Dulu's voice muttered from the row in front of them. He was hushed by Naddāha and Aïcha on either side. It seemed that the announcer had confused "shortly" with "imminently," as Kirin had just enough time to tuck his phone into his pocket before a spotlight turned on, illuminating the stage.

The sudden light hurt Kirin's eyes, the metal reflecting the spotlight right back in every direction, the crowd lit just as much as the figures on the stage. Among all the figures, he recognized one in particular, having seen her face on screens for his entire life. Pressure— no, Force.

She was among other costumed heroes, her hands clasped behind her back stiffly, her posture proud and stern. She looked so far from their laid-back professor that Kirin might have been convinced it wasn't her at all, if he didn't already have incontrovertible proof. Her hair was pulled back into her typical ponytail, but even that was more severe, every stray hair tamped down and forced into order.

"Citizens of the world, I welcome you to this, our tenth day of remembrance, with a heavy heart." The speaker was someone that Kirin vaguely recognized as well, though this figure he'd never seen in person before. It was the CEO of the foremost techware company, Futurus, a person by the name of Theus Moretti. "For the most part, we have had years of peace in the wake of the horrible events that occurred here, with the individuals responsible dealt with to the utmost limits of the law. Yet hardly a month ago, we saw a new threat emerge, claiming that they are not intending to do harm in the same breath that they destroyed thousands of lives.

"We are lucky, in some ways. With catastrophe comes aid, and when you look around this miraculous city today, you would not know of the tragedy that befell the people here. Even if you did, you would suspect such a thing must have happened in the distant vestiges of the past, and not just a single decade before. This is the legacy that we hope to leave; that even in the face of overwhelming odds, we can come together as the human race and say 'no, there *can* be good from this.' We have discovered new methods of transportation, revitalized lost space between buildings, and created a raised, walkable city that works not only in two dimensions, but the full three.

"Would we have arrived here without the entire city be-ing razed? Eventually, but we would not have such a thriving international community, nor would we have been forced to confront the challenges that we have overcome. An entire city, dozens of meters above the ground, no earth to be touched within the city limits." Moretti raised their arms. "We must never forget the lives that were lost here, but we must also never give in to terror and grief. Through the ashes, a phoenix rises."

A few platforms rose from the ground, the figures on them fitted with techware that looked even newer than what Majesty's class usually wore.

"The headquarters of our company have taken residence here, owing to the potential we saw in the people of Satol.

Many, many died during the attack ten years ago, but more survived, and we wanted to give back to those who still remained. After years of living in temporary shelters, we have seen every single person, every single family that stayed in the city limits housed in new, state of the art apartments." Several people in the crowd erupted into cheers or clapping at this statement, Moretti pausing to let them do so. "We funded mental health services, as even the strongest person needs support after such an event. And we asked the people what they needed.

"Unsurprisingly, many were concerned of what would happen should a similarly powerful mien user be found, if a similarly minded group settled in, now that this city stands as a beacon of resilience. So, we set to work."

The figures on the platforms suddenly lit up, energy running through channels on the edges of their bodies, almost turning them into stick figures made of light.

"This is the result of ten years of work, of ten years of asking ourselves, 'how do we give people their peace of mind back?' The answer, we found, was not in supplementing those who are already gifted, but instead focusing on the average person. While the international rate of mien births is one in five, in many countries, it is far lower. Here, that rate is closer to one in fifteen. While the cause and mechanisms behind miens are still unknown, we can find ways to supplement the typical human physique, and we have indeed done so."

On that cue, one of the heroes stepped forward, someone Kirin didn't recognize, who had a flat metal mask.

They raised their hands and a screech rent the air, making Kirin flinch. The metal that made the smooth stage ripped apart and formed a stout column in the center, just in front of where Moretti stood. They took a step back with the hero, and both waited. The crowd did as well, the assembled audience dead silent.

One of the people on the platform ran and jumped off the edge, falling a dozen meters. The metal crunched beneath their feet, but they walked forward, unharmed. Standing before the column, they looked small in comparison, even on the projected screen. The column was so thick that Kirin didn't think he could wrap his own arms all the way around, and the person on screen certainly couldn't. They sized it up for a moment, as if considering what to do. Then, faster than the camera could track, they kicked it.

Kirin heard the boom and felt the air from the blow before his brain processed what had just happened. The entire top portion of the column was gone, the interior showing it was completely solid. The top half was now embedded in the wall of the stage, some three dozen meters away.

"Strength augmentation, good enough to match a villain." Moretti stepped back to their position, a smile stretched across their face. "With this, we remove the immediate fear, and allow all to be equal in power. It took us ten years to get here, but they were ten years of comparative peace. Let us move forward into the next decade and ensure that all our citizens are safe."

There was a roar of applause from the crowd, but Kirin himself, and his classmates around him, were still.

"Protection from villains, huh?' Goldhorn said quietly from the row in front. "Funny how they'll be allowed to hit us, but it'll still be illegal for us to hit them."

Moretti had left the stage by the time the applause died down, the heroes still standing in their stiff line. It'd been hard to tell, but apart from the one who had assisted in the demonstration, none seemed particularly pleased with the show, or the reception of it. And into the spotlight stepped Pressure.

As she stepped forward, the ground before her rose, but without the horrible tearing sound from before. Whereas

Moretti had carried an air of triumph and hope, even in the proud set of her shoulders, Pressure was buried under the weight of despair. She waited until the very last sound had died off, and then she spoke.

"It has been ten years since I set foot in this city." Her voice was tighter than it usually was, her eyes shinier. "I have been asked every year to come and appear before the crowd that gathers to remember those who have been lost and to cele-brate what has come out of the darkness. And every year, I have refused.

"It is not heroic to admit that a decision was made in cow-ardice, but my absence was because of that, and that alone. I feel as though I failed this city, so how could I face you? It was one of your children who was used, one of your children who we heroes could not recover fast enough to stop from being turned into a human weapon. The official records of what happened ten years ago have been sealed and kept from the public, but in light of the recent attack on East City, I have spoken with the authorities in charge, and we have decided that the best way to avoid a similar tragedy from occurring again, is to set the record straight."

Kirin glanced at Adlivun, who was looking right back at him.

"The hardest thing I will have to tell you is that what hap-pened here was entirely preventable. There were many things that were handled poorly, from the initial reaction to the threat, to the orders we heroes were given. Mistakes cannot be learned from if they are not brought to light, and that is what I hope to do here today."

If it had been silent before, it was dead now. Kirin wasn't sure Ifrit was even breathing.

"The photo that every journalist uses when speaking of this calamity is a photo of myself, with a child covered in blood. The headlines have ranged from 'heartwarming: a hero saves the day' to 'are miens too dangerous? A child brings a city to its knees.' All are wrong.

"I did no saving that day. When I arrived on the scene, I found the boy in the photo hurt, crying, and terrified. All these things I expected, but what I did not in my wildest dreams ever believe I would see was a ten-year-old who was willing to kill themself instead of harming anyone else. I did not expect to find a child capable of holding up a collapsing building, and I did not expect to find all the villains disposed of upon arrival.

"The child in question, the one some tabloids have labelled a monster, had been held, kidnapped, by an extremist group for *three weeks*. At no point during those twenty-three days did his parents call the authorities. When interviewed and asked why they had not reported anything, his mother said simply it was incredibly convenient for them that he was gone. I personally spoke with his teachers and found that he was a model student, polite and gentle in class, incredibly conscious of how his mien could affect others. He had never gotten so much as a scolding during all his years of school and was so worried about hurting others that he wouldn't even report when other students were rude to him. So, I asked his parents again why they hadn't reported anything. And finally, I got the truth.

"His mother was embarrassed by him. She was embarrassed that her child was not quote unquote normal. No matter that her child was uncommonly gifted, was uncommonly good at controlling his ability at a young age, she was displeased by something that he could not control." Tears were shining in Pressure's eyes, a combination of rage and despair. "When her child suddenly vanished, she treated it as a solution to her *problem*."

She took a breath, collecting herself.

"Often the narrative of events will state that there was no warning for the attack, that the response was so delayed because the world had never considered such a thing could happen. But we were told. *Border control* was told. The people responsible for orchestrating the attack, most of them non-gifted individuals, traveled here, from across oceans and continents, and at every step of the way they reported their behavior. They sent a threat directly to the local authorities, to the border authorities, stating what they planned to do, *with detailed schematics for how they planned to do it*. In the document, they even named the child who they had kidnapped. The police did their due diligence and reached out to the child's mother. But since she denied that he was missing, they dismissed the veracity of the claim.

"The attack was not subtle. While many would not have sought out footage of the destruction, it does exist. Even in earlier videos and news articles, you can clearly see the beginning stages of their plan, the pipes running under the city being redirected, people falling ill from a mysterious cause. Yet it was not until the flames had *already begun* liquifying steel, that heroes were called in at all.

"For those of you who were there, you don't need to imagine it. But for those who were not, consider for a moment what it was like here ten years ago. The very ground was hot enough to melt metal, the entire sewage and power infrastructure compromised and set ablaze— where was there to go but up? Yet these buildings were collapsing, concrete passed over for cheaper steel in the majority of buildings. Once the ground was coated in liquid metal it only got hotter and hotter, and it was *loud*. Have you heard the sound of a skyscraper folding over itself and just falling? Once you have, you never forget it."

Kirin had gone rigid some time before, feeling his mien creep over his hands, his chest, as if it could shield him from the words.

"Do you know what this city was known for before? It was a

center for healthcare, one that people came to from all over the world. Of the over two hundred and fifty thousand souls that perished here, a quarter did not live within the city and were coming to seek medical treatment. The primary targets of the attack were medical centers, and that was not an accident.

"Today we face a new but similar threat. Might is power, they say, and power is all that matters. We heroes may seem to enforce that ideal. After all, our job is often violent in nature. But I would like to redress your— and once my own— misconceptions about what our place is here. We are not punitive; we are not almighty. At the core of it, we are public servants, looking to keep people safe. The taste of failure is a familiar one, for every single life lost means that in some way, we have failed in our duty. We are meant to stand here as the line between the common people and those who would cause grievous harm, but you will more often find us at the front lines of natural disasters, doing all we can to save those in need.

"The error lies with the way that we talk about heroes, how we laude the violence and not the rescuing. So much of the media coverage we receive is at that lowest, basest point. Fighting has always drawn more eyes than saving, and heroism has done little to change this. But most calls we address are not only calls to help those in need, but specifically to help children who are just like us, struggling with abilities that those around them too often do not understand.

"The real criminals we should be fighting are the injustice and inequity in our systems that do so little to support those with bodies that do not fit the supposed normal parameters of society." Pressure paused, seeming like she was bracing herself. Ifrit leaned forward, and he wasn't the only one. The whole crowd was sucked in, waiting with bated breath. "To begin to tackle this enormous challenge, myself along with a dozen of my colleagues are forming the first independent hero coalition. We will be working to create guidelines for countries, cities, and even schools to allow them to address the needs of this growing community of individuals with different bodies and abilities. We will start to create global support networks for those who find themselves with miens that have medical and financial repercussions, and fund workshops for the general public to better understand how miens work. The intent is non-violent; this will not be an independent justice organization, and most of us will remain active in our local jurisdictions.

"I started this speech discussing what we did wrong, and you might not understand why the conclusion is not another call to strengthen our heroes, to give them more funding and support. I have now been in this business for fifteen years, and time and time again, I see problems that could have been stopped at the root, but instead were tackled far too late. The rate of crime by individuals with miens has only increased, not decreased, despite the increase in heroes, and so something else *must* be tried. Heroes are the first to interview the captured villains, and I would always start my interrogations with one question: why? Why would these people, who come from disparate backgrounds, places all around the world, all turn to the same violent means? And it so often comes from desperation. I couldn't get a job. I was tired of people looking at me like I was already a criminal. I was so broken down, I thought it wouldn't matter anymore. No one in this world is inherently bad, but we can all be twisted should the right conditions exist."

Pressure looked up at the audience and hesitated.

"I want this world to be a better place, because I have a son who is growing up in it." The entire crowd seemed to draw in a breath. Never before had *any* hero admitted to having a family, never had they offered personal information that made them feel like a person instead of an image. "It's a selfish wish, I know, but the other thing that I want the world to understand is that everyone has someone to protect. Every life you see lost out there, every hero who falls, and every villain who dies too, that is a *person*, with all the messy background that entails. Perhaps the real lesson from what happened here ten years ago is that if we can change the path of one person, one *child*, we can save the world."

Pressure stepped back, silence filling the space as the crowd was too stunned to react. Then, the world exploded into sound.

16

Changes

Kirin turned up the volume on his headphones as he approached the entrance to campus. He'd already needed to go out to mail something anyway, so when Ifrit had exploded a spice container after finding out it was empty, he'd accepted his fate and headed out. After all, Ifrit dealing with the reporters camping outside the gate was *not* a good idea.

Campus security had started maintaining a cleared path for students to come in and out, but it didn't stop the reporters from yelling questions as he walked through, the walkway not so wide that the reporters up against the fence couldn't shove their arms in his face and try to get his attention as he passed. The music seemed to pulse in his ears from how loud it was, but at least it tuned out their voices.

He'd just made it inside the campus boundary when Ness was suddenly dragging him toward the dorms, forcefully enough that he almost dropped his groceries. It took him a good few seconds to stop the music, floundering off balance as Ness was nearly running.

"Words, Ness, use your *words*."

"No time, His Royal Edginess is having a moment and you're needed."

"Kuafu?"

"No, the other one."

Kirin thought for a moment.

"I'm lost."

She threw him an exasperated look.

"*Your* one."

"Ifrit?" She nodded in confirmation. "I, well, I mean I wouldn't say that he's *mine*, he's just my best friend and so we hang out a lot and—"

"He's going to blow up the entire first floor, so shut up and just walk faster, okay?"

Kirin quickly shut his mouth and started walking faster.

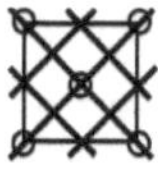

Kirin had hoped she'd been exaggerating the situation, but the entire first floor was covered in smoke when they got inside.

"He's in the training room." Ness relieved Kirin of the bags he was carrying and started off toward the stairs. "I'm going to go get Phoenix, just in case we find out you're not quite as bulletproof as expected."

And like that, she was gone, leaving Kirin alone to consider how to deal with the silhouette wreathed in flame.

Since the beginning of their third semester, they'd finally, officially been permitted to practice with each other, but none of them had quite found the time to do so. They were all too busy to get a good session going, and too tired from two practical courses on top of mien development. It seemed that the extra practice Ifrit had been putting in was paying off, as the enclosure couldn't contain the residue of his explosions anymore. Kirin sighed and pulled open the door.

Ifrit's head snapped to Kirin, though he surely couldn't see a thing through the smoke. Kirin could only follow the movement through the light outlining Ifrit's whole body. He pretended not to notice the other man's gaze as he went to the computer and tapped in a few commands.

"Get out." Ifrit hadn't sounded that pissed with him since they'd first met.

"You owe me a rematch." Kirin said simply. He didn't wait for Ifrit to respond, already settling into a fighting stance, the timer counting down the seconds reflecting in the gloom. Ifrit seemed about to argue more, but the countdown ended, and Kirin launched himself forward.

For how much Ifrit had seemed against it, he wasn't unprepared. As Kirin rushed forward, Ifrit shot himself to the side, landing in a crouch, his eyes glinting in the firelight. Not even a full second later, he was spinning out of the smoke, a kick propelled by an explosion aimed at Kirin's face. Kirin already had his arms up and took the hit with just one, hardening his shoulder and forearm against the force, grabbing Ifrit's other leg and throwing him backward.

Ifrit managed to angle a blast behind himself to keep from crashing into the wall, shooting back a moment later and grabbing Kirin around the middle. Kirin felt the air around him heat as the flames climbed down from Ifrit's neck and toward his hands, crystallizing his core before the flames could touch skin, his shirt burning away at contact.

Kirin clasped his hands and hammered down hard on Ifrit's back, but again the smaller man dodged just in time, shoving himself to one side. Kirin lost him in the smoke, crouching and preparing for wherever the next attack might come from.

He felt the slight change of air before anything else, sidestepping as Ifrit tried to come at him from behind. Ifrit's swing took him slightly off balance, allowing Kirin to land the first blow, on Ifrit's ribs.

"Come on now, don't tell me all that fire's just for show." Kirin felt a grin spreading across his face. Some of his own anxiety was bleeding out, lost in the pounding of his heart in his ears.

"You got a fucking death wish?" Ifrit was burning a clear space around himself, the heat radiating off the fire driving away the smoke for just a moment.

"I don't think you can even scratch me."

Ifrit's eyes narrowed, the challenge taken.

"I hope someone got Phoenix because you're a goddamn idiot who's about to eat his words."

Kirin didn't have time to answer, Ifrit's fire dying out in an instant, the room abruptly dark and his view of the other man gone. Kirin narrowed his eyes and waited, already digging his heels in trying to pinpoint where the attack would come from.

The blast was sudden, no warning change of air or tell-tale spark before everything around Kirin was fire. He hardened everything on instinct alone, closing his eyes to shield them best he could, the heat seeping into the crystal and threatening to char his flesh before he dropped it, rolling out of the way as Ifrit was suddenly there, punching down from the sky. Another blast, forcing Kirin left, another, back, another, left again.

Ifrit slammed both hands against the ground and fire bloomed outward, forming a carpet across the floor, the remnants of the soles of Kirin's shoes melting. Kirin crystallized the entirety of his feet and kicked the shredded fabric at Ifrit's face, buying him enough time to run and tackle the man before his skin started to burn. Ifrit lost control of the flames and they ceased, the pair rolling together until Kirin's back hit the exterior wall of the room. He heard laughing, and absently realized it was himself.

Ifrit was smiling too, even as he blasted Kirin up toward the sky, Kirin only just managing to avoid taking the hit without protection. He hit the ground on his shoulder, not even feeling it through the layer of diamond skin, flipping himself over with practiced ease. Ifrit was on him in a second, somehow managing to pick Kirin up and throw him over his head. It surprised Kirin so much that he forgot to harden at all and felt the shards of glass scratch his face as he was thrown fully through the wall separating the training room from the common area. Before Kirin could get back on his feet, Ifrit was there, sitting on his stomach, fist raised and ringed with fire.

"That's a scratch." Ifrit's other hand was wrapped in what remained of Kirin's shirt, pulling him up slightly. Kirin just stared dumbly, Ifrit looking like an avenging angel with the glass glittering in his hair, the fire flickering in those eyes. "That means I win."

Kirin couldn't find any words to respond with, hearing his heart pounding in his ears. Ifrit never looked this relaxed, a small smile playing on his lips and the crease between his eyebrows missing entirely. Without it, his whole face looked soft, and Kirin felt his fingers twitch as he was suddenly overcome with the desire to touch Ifrit's cheek.

"At this rate, I'm going to start hiring a babysitter for you two."

Kirin and Ifrit both flinched, turning guiltily to find Phoenix standing there with his arms crossed.

"Really? I was having a nice, relaxing afternoon with Ad and then it's 'Phoenix, come downstairs, your idiot floor mates are beating the shit out of each other!' If this is your idea of fun, don't expect me to keep helping you out." Phoenix reached a hand down and helped both of them up, Kirin feeling the minor cuts on his face closing as he did so.

"Sorry." Kirin couldn't keep the smile out of his voice, and Phoenix just raised an eyebrow before walking off.

"Don't apologize to me, you'll have to explain to Pressure how that wall got broken." Phoenix walked off, waving a hand behind him as he got into the elevator. "Even I can't heal you from death, remember."

The elevator doors closed behind him, and Kirin looked at Ifrit, relieved to find the other man still calmer than when Kirin had arrived.

"We should probably start cleaning this up." Kirin had to keep the soles of his feet hardened as he walked over the glass to the closet where they kept cleaning supplies. There was only one broom, but Ifrit took it out of his hands before he could do anything.

"Was my fault, I should have paid attention to where I was throwing you." Ifrit grumbled, already getting to work sweeping the glass into a pile.

"It was both our faults; I probably shouldn't have goaded you." Kirin's smile grew wider. "But dude, you threw me right over your head! That was *insane*!"

Ifrit didn't respond, but as the smoke had thinned, Kirin could see that the back of his neck was red.

"And that was reinforced glass you threw me through, the force you would need to shatter it is ridiculously high! Did you add a blast to that throw to make it stronger? I didn't notice anything."

"You were too busy gaping like a fucking goldfish."

A pause.

"But yeah, I did."

"You're so cool, dude." Kirin dramatically flopped back onto the couch. "How can I compete?"

Ifrit paused in his sweeping.

"You managed to give more than you got."

Kirin propped himself up on his elbows, but Ifrit's back was to him.

"Think you fractured one of my ribs with the hit you got in. And the first time I kicked you it cut up the back of my leg pretty bad." Kirin couldn't tell what expression Ifrit was making, but there was something different than normal about the tone of his voice.

"Oh, I'm sorry man, I—"

"Don't apologize, idiot." Ifrit sighed. "Thank you. It was... helpful."

Kirin had almost forgotten why he'd gone in there in the first place.

"You a little calmer now?"

"Mm."

"You want to talk about it?"

Ifrit turned around, his knuckles white from how tightly he was gripping the handle of the broom.

"Can we... not?" He sounded unsure of himself.

"If you don't want to, we don't have to talk about anything." Kirin got up and took the broom out of his hands before it was damaged beyond repair, taking over cleaning. Ifrit had managed to get most of the small pieces, and Kirin just pushed the pile into the dustpan with his hand, hardening it to avoid hurting himself. "But I'm here for you if you want to."

"I'll make food." Ifrit said abruptly, heading for the elevator. "Come up when you're done and... and put on a new fucking shirt."

He was gone suddenly, vanishing into the stairs instead, Kirin left alone with large chunks of broken glass. The words took a moment to sink in and he went pale, looking down at his midriff. The shirt had been burned up to the bottom of his ribcage, both front and back, but not more than that. He breathed a sigh of relief and hurriedly picked up the remainder of the mess, deciding that telling their professor could wait a day or two.

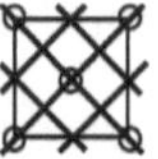

"I fucking hate the marketing professor." Ifrit's words startled Kirin since the pair had been sitting silently together for the first hour of the movie. Once Kirin had gotten upstairs and changed, Ifrit had shoved a bowl of food into his hands and dragged him into his room in such a violent manner that Kirin felt like they were hiding from someone. It may well have been that Ifrit was trying to dodge Phoenix, who had a nose like a hound for food, but he'd left a bowl out for their friend, so Kirin wasn't sure who they were avoiding.

"She is a bit old-fashioned, huh?" Kirin said carefully, not entirely sure where the conversation was going. It was a Sunday, after all, and they didn't have class until the next day.

"A little? Bastard is from the fucking stone age."

Kirin didn't say anything, knowing that if Ifrit stopped, it'd take him some time to get going again.

"I've been so fucking good about keeping a clean appearance out there, so fucking good about being *damn presentable* by their standards, and it's still not fucking enough! Asshole keeps saying that I'm too scary and that we can't have that, not now, not with Pressure." Ifrit snapped his jaw shut so sharply that Kirin was worried he might have broken a tooth. "All she fucking did was say that she wanted to *help* people and the whole world went batshit."

"We're still the big scary monsters out there, after all." Kirin looked at his own hands. "How dare we create our own spaces."

"And she's the fucking most perfect hero out there!" Ifrit nearly upset their bowl of popcorn, which Kirin clandestinely moved off to the side table instead of between them. "I've *scoured* the web for any single fucking time she might have gotten bad press and nothing! She switched to teaching at the height of her career, and *still* they think that she's 'up to something!' What the fuck do they want from us?"

"But this isn't about Pressure." Kirin said it as a statement, not a question, because he knew it was true.

"Might as well be, the way we're treated as a single entity." Ifrit settled down slightly, his shoulder brushing Kirin's.

"Are they making you change your costume?"

"I wouldn't fucking let them." Ifrit sighed and Kirin moved just the tiniest bit closer. "They're making me stop dyeing my hair."

"Oh."

"It was that, or the costume." Ifrit knocked his head against the wall, eyes shining.

"That's not too big a deal though, is it?" Kirin spoke slowly, trying to stifle his own disappointment. They'd taken to re-dyeing their hair together every few weeks, barricading the bathroom door so Phoenix couldn't bust in, and Kirin was only just then realizing how much he enjoyed it. "Your roots look pretty dark, so your natural hair color shouldn't be too far off."

"It's red."

"What?"

"My fucking hair." Ifrit turned to face Kirin, the fire reflected in his eyes. "It's red."

"Like… crimson or like—"

"Like bright fucking red!" Ifrit threw his hands up and Kirin mentally congratulated himself for having the forethought to move their snacks. "It's stupid, but I'd rather that than look like I'm in a damn clown suit."

"Huh." Kirin's brain was slightly failing him. That wasn't what he expected.

"It'll take forever to grow out too, and the roots are darker than the rest so it's gonna look like absolute shit for ages." Ifrit looked at Kirin like he was daring him to laugh. "They offered a fucking stylist or whatever to do it immediately, but I just... want to keep it a little longer."

"I think you'll look fine." Kirin rushed to find reassuring words. "I mean, you're attractive enough that it probably won't be as bad as you're thinking."

Ifrit raised an eyebrow at that.

"What?"

"You think I'm hot?"

Kirin had thought his brain couldn't short out anymore, but that sure got him.

"I, well, I mean, you are?"

"You're not sure?"

"I am sure, and you *are*, it's just—" Kirin noticed the grin that Ifrit was failing to hide as he spluttered. "You asshole, shut up!"

At that Ifrit laughed, loud and genuine, but the crease between his eyes didn't fully go away.

"You're really upset about this, huh?" Kirin said softly, once Ifrit had settled back into his spot, their arms pressed together from shoulder to elbow.

"It's whatever." Ifrit mumbled it, but he sunk down slightly, the ring of fire around his neck sputtering out on the side that faced Kirin, Ifrit's cheek now against Kirin's shoulder.

"It's not, especially not when you care about it."

Ifrit looked up at him for a moment.

"Why do you dye your hair?" He asked.

"Ah, I have to."

Ifrit sat back up at that.

"It was in my acceptance letter. I was too recognizable otherwise, so I needed to dye it."

"But it was dyed when you got here."

"Yes, freshly dyed in fact. I did it on the train." Kirin laughed slightly at the memory. "Not my brightest idea, but I figured it might give me a better shot at not getting noticed once I got to the station."

Ifrit snorted.

"Did you even fit in the bathroom?"

"If you ever get on a train and notice there's black marks on the ceiling, that was probably from me."

Ifrit smiled again, but it faded quickly.

"Why do you?"

"It's... habit at this point." Kirin looked over, but Ifrit was staring at his hands. "My parents had me start dyeing it when I was pretty fucking young, so people wouldn't notice that I was different."

There were quiet explosions from their movie, but Kirin didn't look at the screen at all.

"The area we lived in was more conservative than most, and while I think that there were some people who would've treated me differently, I think my parents were just ashamed." Ifrit narrated it idly, emotionlessly, as if he were talking about someone else. "You think it's impressive that I have a license? I got it when I was six, don't even fucking remember what I had to do to get it.

"I think they thought that black was less scary than red? Which is really fucking ironic now. Everyone around me just thought it was like smoke and never questioned a damn thing. At some point, it felt like the only thing I *could* control, so I owned it. Black was *my* color, and it wasn't just a villain's color. Colors don't mean shit, they're *colors*. And it's far more fucking practical when you're carrying bleeding people."

"Maybe if you told them that—"

"It's fine." When Kirin looked unconvinced, Ifrit rolled his eyes. "It was *my* choice. I'd rather the hair than the suit, so it's fucking fine. I don't have to be happy about looking like an idiot, but I'll do it."

"I don't think you're going to look like an idiot."
"Primary colors make stupid hair colors."
"Really? Blond is basically just yellow."
"Not unless you're in a shitty cartoon."
"I think blue hair could look nice."
"Dye your own hair blue then, see how it looks."
"Hm."
"Don't actually do that, dipshit!"

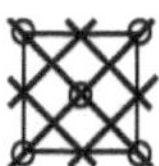

In Kirin's own meeting with their marketing professor, he was told in no uncertain terms that he was not allowed to dye his hair blue.

"The look we're going for with you is more classic hero, so blue isn't a great fit. It doesn't match your overall color scheme." She flicked through a folder of papers, jotting something down on a notepad on her desk. Her office was even smaller than Pressure's, Kirin's knees knocking against the desk every time he fidgeted.

"I'm okay with changing the colors of the costume, I don't have a preference there."

"No, the school decided that they wanted you in white and gold, real heroic colors." The marketing professor was old, potentially old enough to have been alive when miens first appeared, and maybe that was why they kept her on. "I don't disagree. You could be terrifying if we don't have you in something nice."

"I just think—"

"Your hair is not naturally black, correct?"

"Yes."

"Why black? And is the... sparkling from the dye?"

"It was the cheapest dye at the store, to be honest. And it's not from the dye, it's just always been like that."

"Hm."

"But as I was saying, I think blue might be a decent color for me, since it's soothing and has a lot of positive connotations with it and—"

"We'll go with gold."

"Gold?"

"For the hair. With the shine, it should look rather striking."

"Oh."

"That's settled then. We'll implement these changes and see how the public responds and then we can assess again. Your general numbers have been positive, but there is some thought that perhaps you should show some more skin."

Kirin blanched at that.

"I don't see how that would—"

"You're a bit on the larger side, so we need to deal with that frightening aspect somehow. Since you're young and fit, a good amount of skin could do well in keeping public opinions high. Everyone does love eye candy."

Kirin could just hear Phoenix laughing in his head.

"There are a lot of practical reasons that I need to be covered, though." He said hurriedly, before the professor could cut him off again. "My mien could hurt people I'm carrying if I don't have a barrier, and I do have some scars that wouldn't be particularly appealing for a hero."

"Scars?" She raised an eyebrow, looking back at his file. "The only ones I have listed are the ones on your chest, and those are hardly uncommon. I have the hand issue too, but that's all, and that's largely dealt with."

"Ah, yeah, I found out after admission that they hadn't made it onto my chart somehow. But um, they go from the base of my neck down my back to my shoulder blades."

"Hm." She tapped a finger against the pad in front of her. "And I assume these aren't the sort that a little surgery would hide?"

"No ma'am. And I discussed with my armorer about showing skin and how it might put me at a disadvantage with the villains, since they could easily infer what my mien does if they have a clear line of sight."

"Frankly, that is something that you should have been told to deal with instead of trying to cover up. The armorers worry mostly about the functionality, but now that you've been in the public eye for some time, it's my job to make sure that they do not see *you* as a threat. The court of public opinion rarely swings back around for those heroes who seem to be making the wrong kind of impression, and to have that stain on your image before you ever make it out of this school would be a mark of shame for us indeed." She put down the pad, steely blue eyes focusing on Kirin. "Do you know why that matters so much?"

Kirin shook his head.

"While more and more mien users are born every year, they are still greatly outnumbered. The heroes are the first line of defense against prejudice and fear. We cannot risk heroes looking like the bad guys, because then *all* mien users become bad guys. The more approachable you look, the more *attractive* you look, the more likely people are to view anyone with physical differences positively." She sighed. "I want to be happy that we're branching out and allowing more diverse body types into this school, but with the world the way it is, it's making us walk an ever narrowing path between what is and isn't acceptable in the eyes of the public. I've worked here since the conception of this program and have seen many young people pass through these halls. Every time I worry that what they face out there won't be angry villains, won't be dangerous natural disasters, but instead a raging public that forces them to fight back because they were confused with the enemy. My advice might seem harsh, but we haven't lost a hero like that yet, and I intend to keep it that way."

Kirin stayed silent, wanting to argue but not knowing how. She noticed, giving him a sympathetic look.

"We'll leave the high neck, for now. But I'll be recommending some added cut outs at the top of the chest and along the hips. Nowhere that a civilian would be carried against, but places that are visible."

"Thank you." Kirin found himself standing quickly, half afraid she would decide on something more drastic. "I'll go get some hair dye, then."

"No, we're going to have someone professionally do it this time." She leveled a stare at him that made him retake his seat in a hurry. "We have a hairdresser that we use for these things. You'll only have to sit with her once a semester, since she's gifted, and she can meet with you before you head off to go beat up your classmates. Just wait here a moment."

Part of Kirin wanted to help her stand up, since she did look so old, but she shot him a cool glance as she took her cane and slowly made her way to the door.

"Ma'am?" Kirin spoke up before she made it outside, earning an irritated look. "Why aren't we allowed to know your name?"

"Why would you need to?" She scoffed at the thought. "I'm no hero. I'm nobody."

The hair situation took even less time than he expected, allowing him to make it to the power gym before the rest of the class. Most of them were likely still in the dorm, since Marketing had been one on one meeting for that day. Ifrit, he'd found out, had been moved to a slot the day before, likely by someone who knew his temperament well enough to realize he'd need to cool off before he was allowed to be around anyone. After Marketing was Kirin's favorite class: Combat Training.

Pressure was the teacher for this class, but she almost always arrived late. Kirin and Ifrit were usually the first to appear, both eager to begin and Ifrit insisting on warming up properly before class. Until now, they hadn't been practicing on each other, only with Pressure. But today that was going to change.

Unsurprisingly, Ifrit was the first in the door, already changed into casual workout clothes and carrying a bag filled with electrolyte drinks and protein snacks. If there was one thing that Ifrit was as obsessed with as proper stretching routines, it was proper nutrition. Kirin was already on the ground, stretching his legs when Ifrit walked in.

"Hey!" Kirin practically glowed as he waved, fully expecting a string of curse words to find him when Ifrit realized. But when his friend met his eyes, he fully froze. "What? Yellow not my color?"

"What... what the *fuck*." Ifrit's hand was covering his mouth, but the sentence came out in a rush and without any vitriol.

"You said not to do blue; this isn't blue." Kirin rolled to his feet, bounding over to where Ifrit stood stock-still in the doorway.

"You fucking... you..." Ifrit's eyes were practically round, staring at Kirin with an expression he couldn't place. "Is that real?"

"Pretty sure."

"I just— when did you do this?" Ifrit's hand seemed to move on its own, lightly touching a strand of Kirin's hair, now shockingly golden, the light coming through the open door making it seem to glow.

"Ten minutes ago— OW!" Ifrit had changed from just touching his hair to pulling it. "What was that for?"

"It's real." Ifrit didn't seem to notice he was talking out loud. *"What the fuck."*

"I mean, you were worried about looking stupid— which you still won't, by the way— so I thought that if I *also* looked like a dumbass, you might be less upset about it." For the first time, Kirin felt doubt creep up. He'd expected at least a surprised laugh.

Ifrit's eyes flickered up to his own, but before the other man could say anything more, Aïcha walked in, chatting with Wyrm. The pair stopped when they saw Kirin, who gave a smile and an awkward wave.

"Kirin, that looks *so good!*" Aïcha immediately ran over, Ifrit detaching himself and stepping away as she ruffled Kirin's hair. "Seriously, you look like a hero from a storybook or something."

"Oh, uh, thanks! It was the marketing professor's idea."

"It does look really nice! And I always thought your hair was somewhat shimmery, but in this color, it almost looks like a halo." Wyrm was nodding too, showing his pointed teeth in a full smile.

"You really think so?" Kirin asked absently, trying to figure out where Ifrit had gone. More of their classmates were filtering in now, and he was practically swarmed, unable to pull himself away. It wasn't until Pressure arrived that he was granted a reprieve.

"Alright, alright, many of you'll be getting golden boy treatment too, soon. Leave him alone." She clapped her hands together and shooed them farther into the gym. They weren't alone in the big space, other hero classes filing in from different entrances, separated by faintly buzzing electric barriers. No sound flowed between the sections, the shields blurring the visuals too so they could only get a rough idea of what was happening on the other side. Sometimes Kirin watched, trying to see if they were all doing the same things, though today he was fully focused on their group. "Line up over there and warm up. I won't have you going into this cold."

Kirin sidled away, finally having located Ifrit, tucked off to the side where he'd have his own space to stretch. Kirin had fully expected to miss the entire sequence they usually did, but Ifrit seemed to have not even started, staring off into space, his face unusually flushed.

"You okay?" Kirin dropped to the floor to begin, eyes following Ifrit as he slowly did the same.

"Yeah." Ifrit only shot him a quick glance, clearly trying to focus on the exercise at hand. It seemed to work, or at least he didn't feel the need to say anything more, his usual intensity returning as they silently went through the motions. It wasn't long before Pressure was calling them back to the center of their space, her own eyes gleaming as if she were just as eager for the class as they all were.

Kirin offered a hand to Ifrit to help him up, and he took it, though hesitantly. Ifrit's hand caught his wrist as he moved to head over, causing Kirin to turn back to him and raise his eyebrows questioningly.

"...good." Ifrit mumbled something.

"What?"

"Your hair." Ifrit took a breath. "It looks good."

With that, he let go and walked to the group, Kirin left blinking at the wall.

17

Combat

"WE'RE GOING TO RUN this with random pairings of two at a time." Pressure had pulled up a holo screen behind herself, pacing in front of it. "Phoenix will be fighting last so she can heal anyone if there are any severe injuries. You might be inclined to hold back as these are your friends and classmates, but I'd strongly encourage you to fight as hard as you can. The other teachers would want to have you focus on fighting 'properly,' but I want to make sure that you can leave a fight alive. Up until now we've *only* worked on technique, and at this early stage I don't care about seeing you use what you've learned. Instead, I want to see how you fight *now* and how you try to deal with the miens of your classmates. For the purposes of this exercise, it'll be considered a win if someone is incapacitated or verbally concedes. Clear?"

The class nodded and she tapped a button on her watch, making the names on the holo screen spin. Even after they stopped, it took Kirin a moment to read the first pair.

"Goldhorn against Clidna." Pressure announced. Another few taps on her wrist and concrete seats rose from the ground. "Everyone else, take a seat and watch. We'll discuss how each match went once they're over."

Those not fighting clambered onto the benches, Kirin taking a spot in the back. He was starting to get anxious, almost wishing his name had come up first, but he was at least excited to see how Clidna would fare. She was always extremely competent on their missions and though he'd never admit to playing favorites, he was secretly rooting for her to win.

"Begin."

Ifrit's hands were on his hearing aids, turning them off in time. Clidna opened her mouth and let out a piercing shriek, chunks of the ground being torn up and flying toward Goldhorn, who didn't move a muscle. The concrete shattered around them, their body protected by a veritable net of vines, which had sprung from seeds just moments before.

No, not all the rubble had been smashed, some pieces had been *grabbed* by the plants, and were now being thrown back at Clidna, who shattered them in the air with sounds too high to hear. Goldhorn was advancing though, wrapping their head in green stalks to offer some protection from the noise.

They didn't make it within arm's reach before Clidna realized what they were doing and changed pitch; in a second, the vines exploded from the inside out, coating both Goldhorn and the rest of the class in chunks of greenery. Goldhorn was already creating new vines, but Clidna was taking her turn to advance, whistling just on the edge of Kirin's hearing range, making his head pound.

Goldhorn threw seedlings at Clidna, and they latched around her chest and arms, growing at an incredible rate as they reached for her mouth. Clidna only destroyed half of them with her voice, ripping through some with her arms, but not quickly enough. Goldhorn had held one vine back and now they brandished it like a whip, catching Clidna across the face and throwing her to the ground.

In that one heartbeat, it was all over. Goldhorn slapped a

hand over Clidna's mouth as more vines grew, tying her up from head to toe. Clidna continued to wriggle and fight until Pressure was leaning over her, tapping Goldhorn on the back.

"Goldhorn wins."

Clidna was released and offered a hand, but she stood on her own, looking somewhat disgruntled.

"Alright, comments?" Pressure turned to face the rest of the class.

"I don't think either one of them made anything we could really call a mistake, but I do think Clidna could've used stronger attacks to keep Goldhorn away." Yantra frowned slightly. "But now that I think about it, her bigger attacks are just that, bigger, and would have hit all of us over here too."

"I agree. I think Clidna *could* have been more aggressive, but not without hurting us as well." Ness materialized next to Yantra, but to Yantra's credit she didn't so much as flinch.

"Indeed." Pressure lightly touched Clidna's arm as she moved to sit down, Goldhorn already having made their way to the bleachers. "I'd agree that there were no mistakes. While this *is* training and the goal is to see how far you can go, we never have the freedom to work like that in a real emergency. You'd be right to be concerned about hitting others, particularly inside. You'll have to get used to fighting with one arm behind your back."

Clidna nodded, her shoulders marginally less tense. When Pressure removed her hand, the next names were already onscreen.

"Wyrm and Naddāha, you're up."

The next three matches passed rapidly, Naddāha beating Wyrm by making him collapse to his knees sobbing and then brutally kicking him until he passed out, Aïcha defeating Medusa through sheer speed and strength, and Dulu using his wings to blow Enenra to literal smoke. Kirin's leg was bouncing by the time Yantra managed to beat Kapre, earning a scowl from Ifrit.

Kirin only noticed Ifrit's fingers moving right before they stopped.

"Kuafu and Lilin." A small smile appeared on Pressure's face.

"Did you sign something?" Kirin whispered to Ifrit. But before he got an answer, the whole world was blanketed in darkness.

It was Lilin's power, he knew. There was a strange quality about the darkness that, happily, kept it from feeling like he'd just spontaneously gone blind. No, it felt almost as though it had weight, like a heavy blanket had been placed over everything, and it was simply time to sleep. Sight was reduced to nothing, and even sounds were dampened, even touch feeling hazy, like a dream.

There was a small noise that made its way to Kirin, and he strained to hear more, or even tell which way it came from. He was momentarily distracted by what felt like fingers brushing his knee, but then there was a flash of bright light and then he was blinking away stars. A smell— something acrid, something *burning*. Then a dull thump, a groan, and the darkness receded.

If Kirin didn't know any better, he'd think the person who fought with light had won, since Lilin was standing above Kuafu, dressed in a customary bright color (blue, today), Kuafu a huddled dark shape on the floor. But the singed edge of Lilin's hair gave away what he already knew as she helped Kuafu to his feet.

"Sixth match to Lilin." Pressure didn't look terribly surprised. "None of us could see what happened, so why don't you both explain your strategies instead?"

"I knew I would need to remember where she was, as her best play would be to blind me immediately. I roughly guessed the distance and headed that way once we began. From counting my steps, I knew she must have moved and shot light out ahead, behind, and to either side of me to see if I could spot her. I managed to catch the end of her hair, and moved in that direction, which I believe was my fatal flaw. When I spotted her, she also spotted me, allowing her to attack me from behind before I could retaliate." In typical Kuafu fashion, his report was given in terse bursts.

"I don't have much to add to that, other than the fact that I knew I needed to act quickly before he could figure out where I was. I planned to draw him to a specific spot and then ambush from behind, which is ultimately what happened." Lilin's voice was slightly lilting, as always.

"Did you plan to be seen to draw him to you?" Pressure was, Kirin noticed for the first time, taking notes. Maybe she had been during the other matches, and he'd been too distracted to see; he wasn't sure.

"No, my original plan was just to make a loud noise. I didn't actually know he could cut through the darkness like that." Lilin looked slightly in awe of Kuafu as she said it, and Kirin didn't fail to notice how the tips of Kuafu's ears reddened.

"Good adjustment then." Pressure looked behind herself to check who was up next. There were only five of them left to go, discounting Phoenix. But still his name was not there. "Ness and Antaeus."

The two of them stood, facing each other, Ness not at too much of a physical disadvantage since Antaeus wasn't much taller than her. She looked calm, while Antaeus was grim with determination. He must have felt like Kirin did, in that it wasn't a match that favored him. While he could shrink Ness, he'd have to get his hands on her first, and from what they knew of her mien, that was unlikely to happen.

"Begin."

Antaeus was standing alone, blinking in confusion. He was

supposed to be fighting someone, Kirin knew, but when he tried to remember *who* a splitting headache began to form. Surely it had to be someone in their class, yet how could it be? Kirin knew all of them. There was a shadow behind Antaeus and suddenly Ness burst into view and back into Kirin's memory. Antaeus whirled around faster than Kirin had thought he could, his hand shooting out and grabbing Ness by the wrist, but she was gone a moment later.

Antaeus stood alone, cradling a bleeding palm, eyes darting from side to side. Unlike before, he didn't look confused at all, which Kirin didn't understand since he couldn't see what had hurt the small man. Again, a burst of movement from the side and Ness reappeared, aiming to punch Antaeus in the head. The moment her hit made contact however, she began to shrink. The first touch had left her below Antaeus's shoulder, and now the top of her head was about level with his sternum before she vanished from sight. He was now bleeding from a spot on his face in addition to his hand, the skin having been ripped clean off. Despite the blood, he was smiling, hopeful, it seemed, as he gained confidence for the first time in the match.

That was short lived as he was hit in the face with a shoe.

Ness had materialized, somehow having removed one of her shoes in the short time since she had vanished, breathing heavily. Antaeus was distracted enough that she got in close without him noticing and kicked him hard in the side, aiming for a place where they were both covered by clothing. Antaeus stumbled to the side, coughing, and Ness followed it up with a roundhouse kick to the head which sent him to his knees.

Before he could move at all, Ness was on top of him, having retrieved her shoe and placing it under her elbow as a barrier between her skin and his as she pressed down on the back of his neck. His hand reached out and found the exposed skin between her sock and the bottom of her pants, and she began to shrink again before she grabbed him by the hair and smashed his face into the ground. His hand released, leaving a bloody handprint on her ankle.

Ness hesitated for only just a moment, probably expecting him to be dazed since blood was rushing out of his nose, but he rolled over with enough force to throw her off, both scrambling to get back to their feet. Antaeus used the same move Ness had, throwing her own shoe back in her face, giving him a second to get a solid grip on her wrist.

There was confusion for a moment as the class couldn't seem to decide if Antaeus had succeeded in shrinking her down or if she'd simply vanished again. It wasn't until Antaeus held his palm out for Pressure to see and she was greeted with a pouting Ness that they knew for certain.

"Antaeus wins." Pressure sounded pleased. Ness reappeared full size, and Antaeus pulled her into a side hug, though he was still bleeding freely. Ness flagged Phoenix to come over, though she was already on her way down.

"I wouldn't have guessed that if you'd asked me at the beginning." Phoenix admitted as she healed Antaeus. Despite the fact that Ness had lost, she didn't have a scratch, whereas he had angry patches of skin on his hands and face, as well as an almost certainly broken nose.

"Why?" Pressure seemed to disagree.

"I assumed Ness would just not touch him somehow. And her mien is really strong." Phoenix shrugged as she headed to sit back down. "And that was before knowing she could do *that*."

"That would've been the best strategy, wouldn't it? But similar to fighting an enemy you can't look at, like Medusa, how do you fight someone you can't *touch*? Especially if you don't have a long range mien."

"Get some tech to compensate?" Unsurprisingly, it was

Yantra who suggested it.

"That's one answer, certainly, but unfortunately not a viable one. People are very uncomfortable with the idea of heroes carrying weapons, so if you see a hero with one, they're almost always a healer who was only allowed one for protecting them-self."

"But she *could* touch him, so long as there was a physical barrier in the way." Aïcha was frowning. "I suppose it's easier said than done though, especially when he's trying to get her to attack those exposed areas."

"But at the beginning, wouldn't it count as a mistake that she went for his head?" Dulu protested.

"And who did that hurt more?"

There was a moment of silence as they all considered.

"It was a calculated risk." Kirin offered. "She knew that it'd allow him to use his mien, but whenever she vanished again, if his skin was in contact with her, she could hurt him too. If Antaeus had a lower pain tolerance, or if he couldn't react fast enough to activate his mien the second she made contact, she'd have had an advantage in the end."

Pressure looked to Ness.

"I didn't know if he could use his mien if the skin was injured, so I left myself open to try to take out a hand. Turns out that didn't work. When I aimed for his face, though, I was just taking an opening." She shrugged. "I bet wrong, and I underestimated the fact that he'd be willing to still use the same hand, even if it hurt."

"Fair enough. I don't think this pairing played to either of your strengths, but you did well regardless." Pressure stopped Antaeus to say something to him, but it was too quiet for Kirin to hear. Ifrit was watching them too, his eyes narrowed.

"What's his name?" It took Kirin a minute to realize Ifrit was talking to him.

"Hm? Oh, that's Antaeus." When Ifrit looked confused, Kirin finger spelled it as he said it slower. "An-tae-us."

Ifrit nodded slowly.

"Is it easier for you if new names are spelled out?" The thought came to Kirin suddenly, realizing that Ifrit had never been introduced to everyone one on one, only in a group, with everyone saying their names rapid fire. The names on each door had disappeared after the first day, either a programmed feature or the work of invisible cleaning staff Kirin didn't know, but it would make it difficult for Ifrit to figure out who everyone was. If they were talking alone it'd be fine, but even with a single other person sometimes Ifrit would struggle to follow along with conversations unless Kirin started repeating everyone's words in sign.

"If it's said slowly enough, it doesn't really fucking matter." Ifrit shrugged.

Kirin opened his mouth to scold Ifrit, to tell him that he should have let everyone know so they didn't think he was just being rude when he didn't remember their names, but Antaeus was sitting down and then the names were spinning again.

There were only three options left. Him, Ifrit, and Adlivun.

His name settled first, and in that moment, he realized how badly he wanted Ifrit's name to come up instead of Adlivun's. But of course, luck never cared about what he wanted.

"Kirin against Adlivun."

He stood up, rolling his shoulders to deal with some of the anxious energy, letting it flow down to his hands. Adlivun walked slowly up to him, a measure of concern written on her face. Maybe she was just nervous too. No, it wasn't worry. It was... regret.

"Begin." Kirin crystallized his torso and back, as well as the tops of his thighs. He didn't run forward, fully content to wait until Adlivun came to him. She seemed reluctant, however, not even calling up any of her shades, instead looking at something he couldn't see, a point just to his left.

"Adlivun." Pressure's voice came as a warning, as if she expected this. Kirin shot a glance to the sidelines and found he wasn't the only one confused.

And then Adlivun was running at him, alone. She threw a punch at his face, which he didn't bother to dodge, hardening his cheek right before she hit, leaving her with a bleeding fist.

"Adlivun."

Kirin sidestepped her next hit, feeling slightly disoriented by her method of attack. She wasn't a small woman by any means, second in height only to Kirin himself, but she almost never attacked on her own. There was something desperate about her gaze, like she was cornered.

Before Kirin could try and ask what was going on, or even just grab her, she suddenly collapsed, her dark skin going pale, a bubble of the same shadow substance that her creatures were made of appearing right where Kirin had been reaching. He took several steps back, unsure about what she was doing. She was struggling to her feet, Kirin seeing their classmates behind her.

"Don't... look." She panted it out as she stood unsteadily. "Kirin, I can't stop him—"

Whatever she was going to say next was lost to the blood rushing in Kirin's ears as the shadow in front of him formed into a familiar silhouette. Broad shoulders, tall and even in the strange, colorless visage, it was easy to see that the eyes were the exact shape as Kirin's own.

The mouth moved, but no sound came out. It didn't matter. Kirin knew the words, could hear the voice that once would have gone with them.

There you are, son.

18

Regret

He couldn't move. Couldn't breathe. The air suddenly felt hot, pressing in on him from all sides. His back felt cold, so cold. Behind the specter of his father, he saw Adlivun falling to her knees again, sweat beading on her far too pale face. He wanted to move, to see if she was alright, help her up, but he couldn't will his limbs to do his bidding, not when they were frozen in terror.

He was eleven again. The sounds of crashing almost overwhelmed his dad's voice, even though they were just an arm's length apart. And he couldn't move.

"Kirin." Ifrit was suddenly there, blocking the shade from sight, hands grasping his shoulders firmly. For a moment the rushing in Kirin's ears fell away, as he focused on Ifrit's eyes, on the pressure from his fingers, on the fire around his throat. And then Ifrit was thrown bodily to the side.

For the first time in a decade, Kirin was nose to nose with his father.

Or whatever shadow of him remained.

Kirin was now taller by a hand's span, but he felt so small as the judging gaze cut right into him. *Why are you here?* The eyes seemed to accuse. *I never wanted you to be here.*

That was enough to crack through Kirin's shock, to let him swing his arm out, connecting his fist directly into his father's face.

He hadn't quite thought about what punching a ghost might feel like, but he suspected that this was no mere shade, instead something closer to what Phantasm did, only with the additional horror of the faces of the dead. The shape seemed to bend slightly under his attack, before his father— no, he couldn't think about that, the ghost— was forced back. There was a flicker of shock, but that quickly turned to anger.

When the specter came to attack, Kirin was ready. He was not weak. He was not useless, and he was not going to lose. His father was a big man, and he never bothered to hide how he was about to attack, so when the swing came, Kirin caught it with his right hand, hardening his shoulder and elbow to not give a single inch. The second attempt was predictable, and Kirin caught it again, locking them eye to eye.

If this wasn't a true shade of a human, it was an incredible impersonation of one. His father's eyes darted to Kirin's left hand, a slight raise of the eyebrows indicating his surprise. Kirin used that opening to kick out, tearing through the bottom of his shoe to gouge a large gash across the specter's shin, wisps of black smoke rising from the wound. His father stumbled backward, face set in a familiar expression.

This is for your own good.

The ghost didn't seem to be able to speak, but Kirin could hear the words resonating in his head.

Maybe it wasn't just the desire to prove something, but some rage too that propelled him forward, not giving a moment's rest as he swung and swung and swung. Some part of him dimly realized that his fists might be visible to his classmates, that when he hardened his chest to stave off any blows his father *did* manage to land, he'd torn straight through his shirt, but he wouldn't show that he was still afraid of being seen. He wouldn't let his father think that he was still scared.

He'd pushed the ghost far enough back that they'd reached Adlivun, who looked a second away from fully passing out, and Kirin kicked as hard as he could to shove his dad away, scooping Adlivun up with one arm and tossing her over his shoulder as gently as he could.

"Sorry…" Her voice was so quiet. "I didn't know he would… force it."

And then the ghost was back in front of them, Kirin shifting his stance to keep Adlivun out of harm's way. He might not know exactly what was going on, but she'd clearly not intended this, and Kirin wouldn't see her hurt. He could do both. He could defend and attack.

He'd hardly had the thought when the specter was back on him. He was aiming not even for Kirin but for Adlivun, forcing Kirin to give ground. Kirin felt sweat trickle down his face as he dodged, narrowly avoiding a fist that swung just a hair's breadth away from his face. A second blow caught him on the opposite side of his head, and he couldn't do anything to stop his neck from snapping to the side without hurting Adlivun. He bit back a curse, only just blocking in time to stop a hit to the back of his knee from bringing him to the floor.

Unbidden, more words came back to him, just as clear as the day they'd been said.

You're too weak.

A hit to his stomach left him winded, only his mien keeping him standing upright instead of doubling over. Adlivun had gotten clipped on the side, coughing, *wheezing*, over his shoulder. His attention divided, he took another hit to the face.

There isn't anything you can do.

Kirin only had one arm to shield himself, the other supporting Adlivun, and there was no opening to strike back. He widened his stance and held, crystallizing every area he could without hurting Adlivun, weathering what felt like a storm of blows.

I won't let you hurt yourself when it won't help anything.

Seeing that hitting Kirin was having no effect, his father switched to *only* aiming for Adlivun, targeting her back, her legs. Kirin was forced to release his mien, blocking her body with his own, shifting back and forth to keep himself between the two. Despite his father's large size, he'd always been fast, and having a body that was only partially substantial had only made him faster. An ankle snuck out and suddenly Kirin was falling on his back, forced to shove Adlivun off to the side as he fell backward, feeling his head crack against the ground.

I won't see you die for a dream that could never have been real.

His father's face was looming over him, the coldness of the shade penetrating deep into his bones as an arm was pressed against his throat. He crystalized the skin, hissing black steam coming from the inflicted wounds, but the pressure didn't let up.

How could someone like you ever be a hero?

Kirin's mind cleared.

He reached for his father's chest and hardened his fingers, grabbing into the substance that made up his body. It felt cold and fluid, nothing like the warmth he'd had in life. And with all his strength, Kirin threw him to the side.

"Can he hear me?"

The words were directed at Adlivun, who was trying to crawl back toward him, arms shaking. Her eyes searched his for a moment before she answered.

"Yes."

Kirin got to his feet; the action mirrored by his father. They both shook out their hands, rolled their shoulders, and ran at each other.

He ducked, a swing whistling over his head as he grabbed the specter by the middle, hardening his shoulder and feeling the essence start to leak out. He followed the move through to the ground, but his father rolled them over and forced Kirin to kick him off, both on their feet and circling in an instant. Kirin made the next move, a feint to his head, a seemingly wide swing that would leave his own side open, but when his father moved to counter, Kirin grabbed the hand and held it, grabbing the other too when that blow came.

They remained locked in stasis for a single minute before Kirin started gaining the upper hand, his strength superior between them. He headbutted as hard as he could, his whole forehead turning to diamond as he slammed down. This gash seemed to pour unlike the slow leak of the others.

"You're wrong." Kirin spoke so quietly it was almost imperceptible, but it wasn't for fear that anyone else would hear. These words were for his father and his father alone. He needed to say this, had needed to for ten years now. "I could have saved you. I know you were scared; I know you thought it would happen again, but I *could* have. I did, once you went quiet. I got out, dad, and I could have taken you with me if you had just *trusted* me."

He could still hear it, the banging, the metal falling, and his father telling him to do *nothing*.

"I have had to live with that for *ten years* that you would have rather died, that you thought so little of me, that you were so convinced I couldn't do anything, that you *did* die instead of even letting me try."

His father wrenched free, slamming his fist against Kirin's face. But somehow the shade had lost substance, and it didn't make Kirin move at all. On the second attempt, Kirin caught the arm again.

"I was never weak; I was a kid, and all I ever needed was you to say it was okay to reach for what I wanted. I just wanted to make you proud."

Something softened in his dad's eyes, dead though they might be. That look was one he remembered, from the first time he'd told his dad he was a boy, from the day they got off the train for his first consultation. The day his father died.

"I know you were just trying to do what you thought was right, but I have always been able to protect myself, and I have always wanted to help others. Hiding from who I am never did any good, and I won't do it anymore. This is the last time I let your doubts, the fear you put in me, haunt me." Even as he said it, he hesitated. The look in his father's eyes was sad, but for once, there was no fear.

Maybe this wouldn't be the last time; maybe Adlivun could bring him back again, and this could happen with less terrible timing, but some part of him knew he wouldn't have had the courage to do it even if that were the case. Here, in front of everyone it was different; knowing they believed in him let Kirin believe in himself too.

"I'm going to see this through. I'm going to become a hero." Even since coming here, he'd never dared say it out loud. He knew how much his father wouldn't have wanted it; he knew how his dying breaths had been spent telling Kirin he was too powerless. And how those words had crushed Kirin. From the look on his father's face, the words Kirin was saying now were having the same effect but on *him*. So in case this was the last time, Kirin added the one thing he'd wished his father had told him as he destroyed his dreams.

"But I still love you, dad." And with that, he hardened his hand and cut right through.

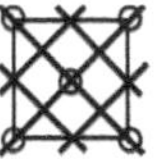

The rain was pouring down. Kirin rested his face against the window to let the coolness of it help him gather himself together, feeling like he'd been stretched thin and wrung out. Usually, he hated the two-hour lunch break in the middle of class, but today it felt like a gift.

Everyone else was downstairs in the common areas like usual, he suspected, but he'd retreated to his room, not feeling hungry or willing to participate in conversation. He hadn't even heard what everyone had said during his review, his ears ringing. Now that he was alone, he felt ready to snap.

Adlivun had tried to talk to him right afterward. However, it'd felt too raw, and some part of him felt ashamed to face her. She knew, had always known, that he was the biggest fraud of them all. What *hero* would care about the fucking law when their own father was dying in front of them?

A knock on the door startled him, and he highly considered ignoring it. It was stupid and childish to try and pretend that he could just hide from everything, and it wasn't fair to Adlivun either. She'd looked almost as wretched as he'd felt, her eyes pleading as he'd turned away. She had nothing to be sorry for; it'd been the right choice not to tell him. He didn't know how he would've reacted if she'd said something, didn't know what he would've done.

But it wasn't Adlivun waiting at the door, it was Ifrit, two bowls of rice steaming in his hands.

"You didn't eat." Ifrit hesitated in the doorway, his uncertainty present even in how his fire was lower than usual. Kirin just stared at him, slightly shocked by the turn of events. It'd been an hour since they got back to the dorms, and, typically, Ifrit ate quickly and headed straight back to the gym. The sight of a messy kitchen drew Kirin's eyes, and he realized that these weren't the leftovers from the weekend, but that Ifrit had been cooking since they'd gotten back. "Can I... come in?"

Kirin wordlessly stepped backward, letting Ifrit through, the other man shuffling in quickly like he thought Kirin would change his mind. He then turned around sharply and shoved the bowl at Kirin before taking a seat on the ground, cross-legged, his awkward posture bringing a small smile to Kirin's face.

"Thank you."

Ifrit grunted, his face in his own food, though he wasn't really eating much of it. Kirin slowly sat down next to him, not sure what to expect. They sometimes ate together now, when they were doing homework, but it was more usual for Ifrit to just leave it in front of Kirin's door, not seek him out. But there he was, on the floor, looking uncomfortable.

"Are you okay, by the way? I forgot you got thrown." Kirin started to eat and dimly registered it was familiar Korean flavors, instead of the heady spices Ifrit usually favored.

"It takes more than that to do anything to me." Ifrit said dismissively, making Kirin crack a smile at how he could say something so arrogant casually. "But fuck if I'm okay, are you?"

Kirin froze with his fork halfway to his mouth. He could usually count on Ifrit to *not* pry, but then he did always have the worst luck.

"I'm okay. It was just a long fight, you know? Sorry that I made you worry, I—"

"Kiri." His mouth snapped shut as Ifrit interrupted, looking frustrated. "You're not weak for being fucked up about this, okay?"

Kirin put down his bowl and sighed, leaning his head back against the bed.

I don't know if I'm okay. Kirin signed, finding it easier than saying it out loud. *How much did you all see?*

He turned his head to look at Ifrit, who was watching him closely.

I don't think everyone else saw much, but I saw you talk to it. And... Adlivun came looking for you.

She say anything?

Ifrit hesitated.

It's not your fault if she did.

Yeah. She said that you might need to talk. So here I am. From the tense set of his shoulders, Kirin suspected Ifrit knew more than he was letting on but wanted to give Kirin the chance to share instead.

She's right about it being all in the name. She can summon ghosts, it seems.

Ifrit didn't respond, though he slid just the smallest bit toward Kirin.

And she had one of mine. The weight of it fully hit Kirin, the shock, the terror, the grief. He struggled to keep back tears, not wanting to cry when they had to be back in class in so short a time. *I didn't realize how much I resented him until he was here.*

That's okay. People always fucking idolize the dead, but they're people, and people aren't saints.

He was right, that I couldn't do much when I was a kid. Who can? But I was always more than he gave me credit for, and since then, I have worked so fucking hard, but seeing him... I felt like none of that mattered. That to him, I'd always be a powerless child.

You're not.

I know that most days. But sometimes... sometimes the things he said get stuck in my head, you know? He couldn't even talk, but I could hear *what he would say. What he* did *say.*

Ifrit moved closer so their legs tangled, the movement tentative, but Kirin basked in the contact, focusing on it like a lifeline.

I want to move on, but every day it feels like I'm letting him down, because he wouldn't want me to be here. His dying fucking words were that I couldn't *be a hero. And now I find out he's been here the whole time, and clearly doesn't approve?* Kirin dropped his chin to his knees, wanting to be small and insignificant. *I just feel selfish.*

For what? Being your own fucking person? Ifrit looked livid. *You do know why he said that, right?*

Kirin shook his head, slightly mesmerized by how angry Ifrit had gotten for him.

He was dying. You were still going to be here, free from his influence. He wanted you to feel guilty. He wanted you to give up on something you wanted, and that was the only way to do it. But you don't owe anyone— living or dead— your life. It's not selfish. It was never his to decide what to do with in the first place.

And if he's right? If I'm not good enough?

Ifrit smashed his forehead against Kirin's, not allowing Kirin to look anywhere but at him.

"He's not right." Ifrit looked so convinced it tore at something in Kirin's chest. Though Ifrit released him and moved back, Kirin felt rooted to the spot. *You deserve to be here. You are strong and powerful and a fucking good fighter with barely any training. By this time next year, you'll be a better hero than we've ever seen before.*

Ifrit hesitated, and then moved closer again, pulling Kirin into his chest. Kirin was so surprised he forgot to wrap his arms back around Ifrit, instead finding his hands gripping Ifrit's shirt.

"Even heroes doubt themselves. We've all got insecurities. But these aren't your own. It doesn't matter what he wanted, or what anyone else wants, it's your life. You owe it to yourself to do what you believe in."

Wrapped up in his arms, the warmth from Ifrit's fire and chest bringing life back to his numb fingertips, Kirin gave in, and finally cried.

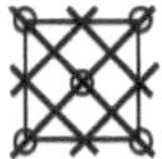

He felt Adlivun's eyes on him as he and Ifrit walked into the gym, but whatever she saw reassured her, and her shoulders fell just a fraction. Kirin tried for a smile, and found that it was easy, her face lighting up, though she still looked pale.

"Are you alright?" Kirin found himself sitting next to her as Ifrit and Phoenix took their positions. "You still look…"

"A little dead?" She offered a small smile. "There's a reason I don't pull shades that close to corporeality. I'll be alright, but I won't be able to bring any here for a little while."

That left Kirin with more questions, but before he could ask anything, Pressure called for the match to begin.

It seemed like an unfair fight, from Kirin's perspective at least. Even when Enenra was paired against Dulu, she'd had some way to fight back, or stop herself from getting hit. But Kirin had never seen Phoenix heal herself before, so she was essentially an un-powered person fighting the strongest in the class. She didn't look all that anxious, however.

Ifrit ignited, his flames spreading over his shoulders and down his sides, not approaching Phoenix but instead eyeing her warily. He noticed that she was far too relaxed, clearly wondering if she had something up her sleeve.

In the end, it was Phoenix who raced out to engage Ifrit, not the other way around. She didn't seem to care about the fire, getting in close quicker than Kirin would have expected. When they were told to run during conditioning she always complained and was at the back of the pack, but perhaps it was her endurance that was lacking, as her speed was obviously not the issue. Regardless, Ifrit was still faster, and he shot off to the side and landed a kick on her back. It connected solidly, but Phoenix hardly seemed to feel it.

They danced back and forth, Ifrit never extending himself too far, never going out to meet her and instead, letting her come to him. She hadn't managed to land a hit yet, but he still seemed concerned, as if he were waiting for something.

Phoenix used his own reticence against him, tripping him as he moved to back out of range after landing another hit. Kirin had thought at first that she must've been healing herself, since every attack failed to bother her in the slightest, but when Ifrit had to correct his balance, a smile split her face, and Kirin could see the blood flowing from her lip.

"Come on pretty boy, we don't have all day. Don't you have anything better than that?" Phoenix taunted, her eyes shining. Ifrit's brow knit, her words failing to get a rise out of him, and instead making him more cautious. His flames even flickered lower, as if worried she could use them against him somehow.

Maybe that was it, then. If Phoenix was a healer, could she maybe do the opposite as well? Kirin tried to wrack his brain for the last time that Ifrit had been injured, but he wasn't number one in their class for nothing. If she could call up old injuries, they would have to be very old indeed.

"All those pretty flames and you won't use them, what a shame." Phoenix drawled, spinning away from Ifrit and managing to get behind him and inside his guard. She might not have a mien to augment it, but she'd clearly been paying attention to the lessons they'd learned in class. "What, afraid we'll all see how little control you really have?"

That struck a nerve, as fire flared down Ifrit's back, nearly scorching her since she'd been standing so close. She still wasn't concerned, not even taking a single step back as her clothes caught on fire.

"Come on, this is all you've got, really? How can you expect to stay on top of the class when your abilities are cheap party tricks? I could get a flame thrower with more *force*."

Ifrit turned around, his movement sped by a blast, his metal rings striking together as he fired another explosion off, just small enough to force Phoenix away from him. It hit squarely, causing her to be thrown backward and knocked to the ground, but she was laughing.

"Come ON! You've got more than that!" The fire had burned a hole through her shirt, and Kirin could see the blackened skin underneath. It didn't appear to be healing, but Phoenix didn't seem to be in any pain either.

Ifrit had tempered his anger, however, the fire reduced to just the ring around his throat as he approached, the brief rage removed and instead a grim look of determination had replaced it. His approach was measured, and slow enough that Phoenix got back to her feet. She spat out blood to the side, a crazed grin spreading across her face.

"There he is." Her voice was singsong. "Come on scourge."

Ifrit's eyes widened at that, and he cut the fire entirely, instead opting to kick Phoenix in the face. Her head snapped back and when she lifted it again, blood was freely gushing from her nose, dripping into her mouth.

"Do you really think no one will ever know? Hm? It's not all that hard to figure out."

Ifrit punched again, this time with added firepower, using the explosion to get extra rotation into a kick that sent Phoenix back another few meters. She got up again, but her left leg struggled to hold her weight, leaving her to lean more heavily on her right. The smile was still there.

"Should I tell them?" Her voice had dropped to a mock-whisper, though it carried clearly. "No, should I tell *him*?"

Ifrit's movements were so fast they were hard to follow. He brought both hands together in front of him, a line of fire zipping away from where he stood, to a point a meter or so to the left of Phoenix. Kirin had seen him practicing this, a remote detonation for a much more powerful explosion. She saw it too, her head turning, looking like she was going to jump away from it, eyes widening in fear.

And then she smiled.

And jumped straight into the explosion as it went off.

19

Shaken

Ifrit stood there in horror. His eyes went wide, staring at the place where she'd stood, the smoke from the blast covering the scene. The rest of the class was silent too, the sound from the explosion still ringing in their ears, Phoenix's last smile burned into their eyes. Ifrit took a stumbling step forward, his face so pale that Kirin wasn't sure how he was still standing. Kirin was halfway to his feet when he heard footsteps.

They were coming from the cloud of smoke, and then Phoenix emerged, *chunks* of their body missing, but healing as the class watched, horrified. Bones re-knit, muscle appeared and wove itself together, smooth unblemished skin growing to cover the new flesh. Even Phoenix's nose, which had been broken before, was reset, now perfectly straight, only the blood crusted to their lip giving any indication that anything had been wrong.

"You can't shut me up. You can't make me stay down. So why don't you just give up when you're outclassed?"

It only took the slightest glance at Ifrit to know that was not going to happen.

The shock that had come over him was now wholly trans-formed to rage. The fire was cut, and he ran forward unassisted, murder in his eyes. Phoenix blocked his first swing, but the second caught them in the stomach, and that hit was followed by an elbow to the face which had them spitting out blood. Ifrit wasn't done either, landing a solid hit to Phoenix's jaw that resounded with a loud crack; Ifrit had broken a finger.

But that didn't slow him down at all. A kick to the knee sent Phoenix to the ground, a kick to the face following immediately. They still smiled through it all, even as Ifrit hit them again and again and again.

"Concede." Ifrit's words came out as a growl.

"You'll have to kill me first." Phoenix said in a singsong tone, but there was something sad in their eyes.

With one more hit, however, Phoenix's head snapped to the side, and they lay still, finally knocked out by the onslaught. Ifrit stood up abruptly, like he couldn't stand to be touching them, wiping at something on his face and leaving a smear of Phoenix's blood behind. In that moment, he really did look like a demon, his eyes cold and angry. Kirin wondered if his own face had looked the same as he'd torn his father to shreds.

A moment later, however, Ifrit sunk to the ground, looking sick.

All of a sudden, Pressure was there, though Kirin hadn't noticed her get up. She raised her hand over Phoenix, and a second later, Phoenix was healing, his skin visibly repairing where it was broken. He woke up, coming to sit with his legs crossed, looking casual as ever. When he reached over to help Ifrit with his hand, he was slapped away.

"We're going to end class here." Pressure said calmly, but there was an edge to her voice. "Everyone, please head back to the dorms and rest. We'll be skipping seminar for today."

The class rose to leave, Kirin forcing himself to walk around the wall to Ifrit instead of leaping clean over it, when Pressure spoke again.

"Ifrit, you stay."

Though Kirin dragged his feet the whole walk back, Ifrit had not appeared on the horizon before Kirin reached the dorm. It was cold, January, and he wasn't dressed to be outside, but part of him wanted to be waiting there, outside the doors, when Ifrit finally came home.

However, that was too dramatic he decided, after his fingers and toes started to go numb, and it was when he went inside that he ran into Phoenix.

He looked miserable, sitting just inside, his eyes lifting hopefully when he heard the door open, and then lowering again when he saw it was only Kirin. Despite having fully healed from the fight, he seemed on edge, jumpy. Kirin wasn't sure he could entirely bring himself to care.

"I thought it'd be fine, you know?" He whispered it so quietly, his voice sounding so unusual that Kirin almost missed it. "I'm not a natural fighter, so when Pressure was having me come up with combat strategies, this was her idea. To just... let them see that they couldn't win."

Despite the low-burning anger he felt toward Phoenix at the moment, Kirin found himself sitting on the ground slowly, not sure how to react.

"It's just practice, I know, so I just wanted to goad him into being a little reckless, a little too big. He's got such good control I wouldn't stand a chance otherwise; I had to get him to do something big enough to actually kill someone. And it worked! But then his face..." Phoenix broke off, his eyes wide and his face pale. "I was going to go back and talk to Pressure so she wouldn't yell at him for the way he reacted at the end, but

Adlivun said not to and I just..."

He buried his face in his hands and took a breath.

"I know you think I'm good at this Kirin, but I'm really, really not." He gave Kirin a wobbly smile as he pulled his hands away. "I think I know what to do, but I always mess it up. Ad says just to apologize and move on, but I just keep thinking about it all. Kuafu seems to be fine around me, but part of me thinks he still resents me, and while I do like to piss off Ifrit, I never wanted to hurt him."

"I don't think any of us thought that was your intention." Kirin spoke carefully, turning the words over in his head. He wasn't so sure he did believe that, but when he thought of how Phoenix had immediately walked back his comment at Satol, maybe he was trying, in his own way. "Because in your mind, we'd all see you were fine a moment later, and then it'd be okay, right?"

"That's how it's always been before, anyway." He picked at his sleeves, not appearing to realize he'd just said something deeply concerning.

"Phoenix," Kirin said as gently as he could, "how did you figure that out about your mien?"

He offered him a real smile that time, a glimmer of his old mischief in his face, though it was blotted out in a moment by sadness.

"How do you think?"

"Did you die or were you killed?"

"Does it matter?"

"It always matters."

He sighed and rubbed at his face, which did look suspiciously puffy now that Kirin had a clear view.

"Remember that mien assessment group I mentioned ages ago?"

Something dimly rang a bell from the party months ago, so

Kirin nodded.

"They basically wanted to make me into what Kuafu was."

"A figurehead?"

"A god." He said it without feeling. "My supposed friends brought me there, but I guess it was just a clout thing, who could find the most impressive mien. Since I could heal, they said I was a deity of Life, and I should make sure that none of them ever got sick. But back in the old days, I was pretty married to following the rules, if you can believe it. It didn't matter that *they* owned the property, the law said it had to be my *own* property. It didn't matter that they were consenting to my mien being used on them, the law said I couldn't use it on anyone. When my mien manifested, it was because I healed a cut on my brother. I had to sit at the police station for three days before they decided to let me go, and not before telling me to never, ever do it again."

Phoenix looked at his hands.

"One of the leaders of the group was sick, apparently. Cancer, something thoroughly curable, but they didn't support the procedure because it 'wasn't natural' or some bullshit. Which is where I came in."

Kirin moved to take his hands, so he'd stop pulling at his skin. They were ice cold.

"They wanted you to heal him." It wasn't a question.

"Oh boy, did they. And when I wouldn't?" He whistled through his teeth. "They were angry."

He put his head down.

"You know what sucks the most about not being able to die?"

"I'm going to venture a guess and say that I don't."

"No body, no crime." His head thunked against the side of the door. "Every single one of those fuckers walked free."

"Even with your testimony?"

"It was my word against theirs. What proof did I have? Every time I die, I heal perfectly, there's no evidence left except a little blood. Do you know how hard it is to convince someone you've been attacked without a shred of physical evidence? Bloody clothes? Easy to fake. A photo? Well, it's blurry and it could have been staged, and now you're trying to stir things up. And the more that you try and get help, the more people know what you can do, and the more they realize what they can do to you."

"You're not here because you just really wanted to be a hero, are you Phoenix?"

"No." He whispered it to his knees. "I'm here to hide."

They sat there in silence for a few minutes, neither really having anything to say. Then—

"It's okay if you're mad at me. I'm mad at me too." There wasn't a trace of sarcasm in his voice.

"I'm a little mad at myself, if I'm honest. I should've realized that you're just as terrible at all of this as the rest of us."

"All this?"

"The whole people thing."

"Ah, and here I thought trauma was the thing that made us all so good at communicating."

Kirin laughed at that, rubbing his own eyes. They'd been talking for a good long while, and Ifrit still wasn't back.

"Phoenix?" He cringed slightly at the name, realizing now just how cruel it was.

"Yeah?"

"You don't have to act so happy all the time if you're not."

He shrugged, a small smile playing on his face.

"I don't mind it. Sometimes I can convince myself I am."

"But when you really can't, don't try, okay?"

Phoenix punched his shoulder lightly, and pain he hadn't noticed in his lower back faded.

"I feel like I should be saying the same to you. If I actually had half a brain cell, I would've yelled at you for trying to comfort me when you looked like you were going to pass out earlier yourself."

Kirin had fully forgotten he'd seen his father's ghost just a few hours before, and the reminder made him flinch. He really did need to talk to Adlivun about that.

"It's a good thing you're quite empty up there, then." He flicked Phoenix in the forehead instead of addressing it, which drew a genuine smile out of him.

"I should give you space, right?" The smile faded. "I was thinking of buying more spices or something as an apology, but you just restocked us yesterday. And it doesn't really feel sincere anyways, since it's the university's money and not mine."

Kirin thought about it for a minute.

"Start with an apology. And even though it's not an excuse, explain to him why you did it. I think he'll appreciate the fact that you *didn't* think he'd do anything that could seriously hurt you unless you really pissed him off. And even then, you knew he wouldn't attack you directly."

"As much as he'd like to pretend otherwise, he really is a softie." Phoenix cast a glance at the still broken wall behind them. "Well, unless it's with you."

"I won't tell him you said that." Kirin stood up. "I'll go make us dinner. You wait till he gets back and talk to him immediately. He's probably going to be angry, but I think it'd be best to let him know you realize it was wrong *now*, and not later."

"Yeah." Phoenix pulled his knees into his chest again, looking out the window. "I'll talk to him."

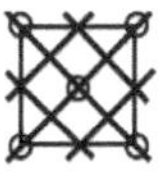

Kirin was surprised when they walked onto the floor together, Phoenix looking more upset than Ifrit. And since everything was upside down, apparently, Phoenix took his food and walked into his room silently, while Ifrit sat down at the counter.

"Okay, I'm getting freaked out, what's going on?" Kirin couldn't stand it any longer after Ifrit had been eating calmly for several minutes. "Did Naddāha get to you?"

At that, a dark look crossed Ifrit's face. Not Naddāha, then.

"No." At least Ifrit's way of speaking was the same, even if he seemed practically serene. "Resurrection Bitch and I talked, and it's fine."

"Just like that?" Kirin knew that he himself was still angry, and it hadn't even been directed at him, so he had an incredibly hard time imagining that Ifrit was okay.

"Just like fucking that." Ifrit made eye contact as he slurped his soup loudly.

"The fuck did Pressure say?" Kirin found himself walking to the door before he realized what was happening, about ready to curse their professor out for... what, exactly? Calming down his friend?

"Fuck, she just made me sit in her office and calm down." Ifrit was standing now, some of his temper coming back. "What's wrong with you?"

"Wrong with me?" Kirin found himself almost yelling and forced his volume down. "I've been worried *sick* and so has Phoenix and then you just waltz in here and announce everything's fine?"

"Isn't that a good thing?"

"Not when you're very much not!"

Ifrit suddenly had his hand in Kirin's shirt, pulling him down so they were nose to nose.

"What did he say?"

"What?"

"What did he tell you about me?"

"Just that he thought he really needed to piss you off to get you to do something drastic, and that he was thinking about buying more spices to apologize, but I'd just bought some—"

Ifrit released him suddenly, looking more upset than when he'd walked in. He looked... scared.

"I'll be right back."

And with that, he marched away, leaving Kirin blinking after him, alone on their floor with the food he'd cooked going cold.

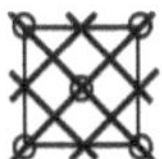

The exhaustion of the day had finally caught up to Kirin and he'd passed out on the couch, until Ifrit woke him up by sitting on his stomach.

"Wha—" He froze mid flail when he realized who the dark shape belonged to. "Oh."

"You're not going to ask where I went?"

"If you want me to know, you'll tell me." Kirin tried to shift to get comfortable, but Ifrit glared at him when he moved, so he fell still.

"Why're you so fucking nice?" The way Ifrit said it didn't make it sound like a compliment. "You *can* ask if you're curious, dumbass."

Kirin was quiet for a moment.

"Where'd you go?"

Ifrit stood up abruptly, and Kirin quickly swung his feet to the floor, expecting Ifrit to run off again, but he just sat down in the now vacant seat next to Kirin.

"I went to ask Adlivun what she knew."

Kirin blinked, not connecting the pieces to the conversation that they'd been having before Ifrit had left.

"I... I wasn't pissed at Phoenix, not really. It was a fucking good strategy, and honestly, I don't think he'd have tried that with anyone else. I think he assumed I'd get it, and I do. I'm not mad at him, not any more than you are at Adlivun. But he did know how to strike a fucking nerve." A muscle in Ifrit's jaw twitched. "I don't want you to hate me."

"Hey, I won't—" Kirin reached a hand out to touch Ifrit's shoulder, but pulled away at the irritated look Ifrit gave him.

"I don't..." Ifrit struggled to find the words he wanted, his hands balling into fists on his knees. "Every single fucking one of us has some messed up shit in our pasts. Most of us probably more than just one thing, if we're being fucking realistic. And what I keep telling myself, what Pressure keeps telling me, is that I don't judge you for your shit, and you won't judge me for mine. It's just..."

His eyes flickered over to Kirin, who gathered his courage to reach over again and take Ifrit's hand. Ifrit's knuckles were white, and Kirin gently started uncurling his fingers as he spoke.

"You're just scared that *your* past is the one that somehow everyone can't understand. That what *you* did is somehow just so much worse than everyone, and we'll all see you differently." Having worked Ifrit's hand open, Kirin started to massage Ifrit's palm, trying to make the tiny crescent shaped marks go away. The skin on his palms was rough, though the tips of his fingers, when they brushed against Kirin's own, were soft. "I felt the same way."

"But you're just so *good*." The tone of Ifrit's voice was so raw, and his utter conviction in the statement drew a chuckle out of Kirin.

"I assure you, I'm not." He gave Ifrit a smile, but Ifrit didn't reciprocate, his face crushed into a mixture of self-pity, anguish, and some other emotion that Kirin couldn't quite place.

"You are." Ifrit plowed on before Kirin could interrupt. "But that's not the fucking point. The point is… I was trying to be calm because I assumed everyone already knew. And as Pressure said, if you knew, there was nothing I could do about it so might as well just accept it. But then you didn't seem to know a damn thing and I realized that Phoenix wasn't just trying to make me feel better by saying he didn't know shit, so I went to Adlivun, and she confirmed that Phoenix doesn't know anything that he couldn't guess on his own."

Kirin didn't say anything, moving onto Ifrit's other hand.

"And now I'm stuck wondering if it's fair to you that I get to know all your shit without your consent because of some fucked up mien garbage without sharing any of mine." Ifrit's shoulders were tense, his jaw clamped shut but failing to hide the way his bottom lip trembled ever so slightly.

"I don't need to know anything about you that I don't already know." Kirin said calmly, not missing how Ifrit was shaking all the way down to his hands. "I appreciate that you want to say something, so it doesn't feel unequal, but I don't feel that way. And I'd hate for you to feel like you need to share things you're not ready to in an attempt to make me feel better."

"You're too fucking nice."

"And you're too mean to yourself. And to my taste in music, but that's beside the point." Kirin had finished stretching all the muscles in Ifrit's hands, the digs from his fingernails smoothed away, but he couldn't bring himself to let go for some reason. "I don't care about what's in your past. It's not my business. It's not who you are now, and that's who I care about. Everyone's done things that they regret, everyone has things that they don't want other people to know about. The beauty of a new life is those things can stay buried, right?"

"But what if you resent me when it comes out?" The question was barely said in a whisper, Ifrit desperately searching Kirin's face as if he expected to already see the beginnings of distrust waiting there.

"Well, I'm mad at Phoenix right now, I'll have you know." Kirin was glad he hadn't let go of Ifrit's hand since it was easy to now stroke along his knuckles to soothe him.

"Phoenix?"

"Was it a good strategy for trying to win a fight? Sure. But it was cruel and not something that I would've done during practice. Do I hate him right now though? No. Do I resent him? I wouldn't even go that far. People clash, people argue, it's just life. If it's something ridiculous, like you willingly went and killed a bunch of kids just to see if you could get away with it, or— I don't know— had been responsible for putting pineapple on pizza, maybe I'd judge you a bit, but even if it *is* something comically evil, you clearly feel bad about it now. And that says you've changed as a person and that counts for a lot."

Ifrit was quiet for a few seconds.

"You put having pineapple on pizza in the same category as infanticide?"

"Are you about to tell me that you like it? Because I *will* be judging you for that."

"I feel like you're fucking confusing magnitudes of things."

"There aren't many crimes in this world that are wholly un-forgivable, but that is one of them." Kirin, secretly, liked pineap-ple on pizza, but also did agree it was an affront against nature.

"You're such a dumbass." Ifrit leaned his head against Kirin's shoulder, the tension gone all at once.

"I'm beginning to suspect that I should be taking that as a compliment."

"You're a dumbass," Ifrit repeated, "but you're not a *jackass*."

A compliment indeed.

20

Interrogation

 leaving his room the next day.

Ifrit had assured him that no one else could have seen anything, and realistically, they wouldn't have known what they were seeing anyway, but some part of him was terrified to open his door. He hadn't slept well, the entire weight of the day before coming to rest on his mind as he lay there alone with his thoughts, and now the sleeplessness and paranoia were catching up to him.

He was standing right inside the door when someone knocked on it heavily. After the initial jump, his shoulders relaxed; it was probably just Ifrit, annoyed at being made to wait for their morning run.

"Kirin, could you please come with me to my office?" It wasn't Ifrit's voice that called; it was Pressure's.

The dread rose to a near flood, and Kirin slowly opened the door to greet her.

"Good, you're up." She looked like she'd been awake for a good long while already, despite the sun having just barely risen. "I have to apologize for the early call, but I needed to catch you before class."

Kirin nodded woodenly, following her as she walked away

without explanation. Ifrit was standing in the hall, his eyes flicking between them as the elevator doors shut. Part of Kirin wanted to say something, to ask what this was about, but the great majority of him was frozen solid. He doubted he could've opened his mouth, let alone formed words.

Pressure seemed content to let the silence grow, occasionally looking at her phone until they arrived at her office, which had more paperwork than Kirin remembered. They hadn't heard any additional information about the hero coalition that she was planning, but if the mounds of paper on the floor were anything to go by, at least something was getting done.

"I meant to speak with you yesterday, but unfortunately, there were other things to be dealt with." Other things being Ifrit, then. "I wanted to touch base about how you're doing."

Kirin blinked at her, thoroughly surprised.

"I'm... okay." Maybe if he said it enough it'd be true.

"Kirin." Her tone was stern, far more motherly than he would've expected her to be. She was though, wasn't she? "You've just been through a relatively traumatic shock. You might've been able to act well enough when you had other people's problems to focus on, but that's not a viable solution in the long run."

"If you think they're going to run out of problems, I assure you that you don't know my friends." The line slipped out without him thinking.

"Indeed," she said dryly, "I think you'll all keep me very busy in the coming year. But we're not talking about them, we're talking about you."

Kirin couldn't stand looking her in the eye anymore, and instead looked down at his hands.

"I don't know what there is to say." He answered honestly.

"Aren't you going to ask me why I didn't stop the fight?"

His head snapped up, and he realized that the smile Pressure was wearing was rather sad.

"Adlivun is a good kid, you know? She might be the youngest in the class, but she's really got a good head on her shoulders. When she realized who one of the spirits trying to work with her was, she immediately came to me and let me know. She didn't want to compromise your identity, though your father was clever enough to never give his name, and only stated that one of the students here was his son."

"You knew?" The question came out as a hoarse whisper.

"I know a lot of things, Kirin, but I won't say anything unless I need to." The words held more weight than just the context of this conversation. "Adlivun is the same. Because of the nature of her mien, she knows far more than she should, about you, your classmates, even about me. She's a valuable ally."

"If you're worried that I'm upset with her, I'm not."

"I know." Pressure gave him a reassuring smile. "Your behavior yesterday convinced me of that. I just wanted you to know that it was on my recommendation that she didn't say anything to you. I thought it might be detrimental to your success here, as well as to you, broadly."

"You might not read minds, but I guess someone in that interview really did."

"I didn't lie. Reader can't go through your brain and take whatever they want, but even if you think about something for a split second, they can go through and look at it in more detail. That piece of information I will ask that you keep between you and me, since it would greatly disturb a lot of people to know exactly how much of their souls they're baring to get here."

"You don't say."

"It's cruel, but it's necessary, and even with everything in your past, I still wanted you here." Pressure folded her hands in front of her. "I said that to you once before, and I meant it. I would be sad to see you go."

It took Kirin a moment to realize the question behind her statement.

"I'm not planning on leaving."

She let out a long breath, visibly relaxing and leaning back in her chair.

"That's good. I wouldn't have stopped you if you'd asked, but I'd greatly regret letting you go. You're an uncommon talent, kid, and I just want you to succeed."

"Then why didn't you stop the fight? Since you knew."

"There we go, asking questions. That's better. I think you and I know that you needed to deal with that portion of your past. It's not done and over with, unfortunately. It'll take time to process and accept what happened, but I don't want to see you held back by ghosts anymore, Kirin. You're free of that now, and I want you to start believing it too."

It seemed like that was all Pressure had to say, so Kirin got up to leave, but he hesitated at the door frame.

"How much does Adlivun know?"

"That seems like a question you should be asking her, not me."

"I don't know if I'll be able to face her for a while, knowing she's seen through me this whole time."

"She's known about your father since the first day you arrived, that's true. But you were okay with how she treated you before, so doesn't that mean your fears of people dismissing you out of hand were wrong?"

Kirin looked at Pressure, repeating that sentence over in his head.

"Was that the real reason you let it go on? So we could have this conversation?"

"There are easier ways to start a conversation than having you fight a literal ghost from your past, you know." Pressure shook her head. "No, you just remind me of someone else

I know very well, whose emotions are somehow intrinsically linked with his fists."

Walking into Rescue Operations wasn't as nerve wracking as opening his door had seemed, but it still felt harder than it needed to be. After his meeting with Pressure, he arrived late, the whole class assembled inside as he changed into his costume and went out to meet them. Happily, it would be some time before the new design changes were implemented, because he didn't think he could stomach the extra stress today.

When he walked into the room, he was immediately accosted by Aïcha.

"I don't think I could properly pull it off because the difference in our strength is too great, but can you try and explain that grounding technique you do sometime?" She looked bright-eyed that morning, like she'd gotten inspired during the night.

"Grounding technique?"

"When you were fighting, though Adlivun's shade seemed to match or even beat you in raw strength, there was a moment when you just seemed to take a position and refuse to move from it, and it was really badass." She nodded to herself at her own statement. "I'd absolutely like to know the method behind it, to see if I can replicate it even a little."

"It has a lot to do with my mien, so I don't know if I can really explain it well—"

He'd not even finished speaking when Dulu marched up to him.

"How the hell did you manage to cut that thing so easily man? Don't tell Pressure but I *may* have been practicing with Adlivun just a little bit, and nothing I seemed to do could hurt her weird ghost things, but you tore into it like it was just so easy!"

"I don't know that I was doing anything in particular; maybe you just need something really sharp?"

"Kirin!" Ness was at his elbow, tugging on his arm. "I also call sparring with you; I think I relied too heavily on my mien and not enough on my own physicality. I've been training with Aïcha, but I think I need something a little more overwhelming to force me to try different things instead of just relying on one strategy."

"Are you saying I'm not enough of a challenge?" Aïcha mocked offense.

"You're too fast; I can't land a single hit on you. He's big enough that I'll at least hit *something*." Ness responded in her own melodramatic fashion.

"None of you assholes are training with him if he doesn't do his fucking warm-ups." Ifrit was there, grabbing Kirin's arm and pulling him farther into the room. Phantasm wasn't there yet, although Kirin had been on the verge of being late.

"I don't know what that was about." Kirin laughed nervously, somehow feeling like Ifrit was angrier than usual. Well, that would make sense, wouldn't it? Given the day he'd had yesterday. "Weird, isn't it?"

Ifrit looked at him with a flat stare, irritation clearly mounting.

"You were fucking incredible yesterday, of course they're all over you." Ifrit nearly scoffed. "The fuck did Pressure want with you?"

"Pressure?"

"Yeah, our fucking teacher? The one who grabbed you at the ass crack of dawn?"

"Oh." Kirin suddenly felt the urge to look anywhere but at Ifrit. "She was just... checking in?"

While it was in fact the truth, Ifrit didn't look convinced.

"Checking in about *what*?"

Before Kirin could answer, Phantasm came bursting through the doors, eyes sweeping through them.

"Class is canceled for today. Yantra, come with me. Now."

Without waiting for a response, she left just as abruptly as she came, Yantra hurrying after her and shooting a confused look back to the rest of the class. The sound of the doors banging shut echoed through the room, feeling extra ominous in the large space.

"What do we think that was about?" Dulu was looking at the door, eyes narrowed. Ness appeared at his side, shaking her head.

"Whatever it was, I don't think it's good."

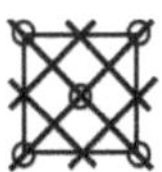

Ifrit and Kirin settled into their usual stances as the timer counted down, both tuning out the sounds of combat around them. Kirin was so focused on the blinking light of the timer that he started to move forward even as the program was abruptly shut off, straightening out and blinking slowly as he tried to figure out what had gone wrong. Clearly Ifrit hadn't canceled it, as he too was looking around, the crease between his eyes looking concerningly deep as he searched for the source of his irritation.

It turned out to be Pressure, standing directly next to the control panel of the room, looking faintly exasperated.

"We're in the right room, aren't we?" Kirin asked. She'd been surprisingly calm about the fact that they'd destroyed the training room in their dorm, the only penalty being that they were banned from using any practice rooms but those with walls made *entirely* out of concrete.

"I don't understand how you boys can still be so eager to fight. Was yesterday not dramatic enough for you?" She shook her head. "This is a fine room to use, but not right now. You're needed down at the police station."

"Is it the same thing that Tech needed to go for?" Ifrit was already grabbing his bag and sliding his mask on, his eyes flashing in a way that Kirin had come to understand meant he was excited.

"Yantra? No, I don't think so. Not that they told me much." Pressure threw an annoyed look over her shoulder at Kirin, who'd fallen in to step behind the pair since the hallways on this level of the power gym were oddly narrow. "You'd think I'd get a little more respect from those assholes, considering one of them asked for my autograph last time."

"They asked for us and didn't say why?" Kirin cut in.

"No. Just that they needed to see you immediately."

"And where did Tech get taken to?" Ifrit demanded.

"You've got some nerve kid, you know?" Pressure ruffled his hair, Kirin fighting back a laugh at how affronted Ifrit looked. "The station also. *That* I do know the reason for, but I don't think they'd call the pair of you in for a cyber-attack."

"Someone tried to hack the police station?" Kirin's eyebrows shot up.

"Last night, apparently."

"The fuck did they wait for? We've been woken up in the middle of the damn night before, but they waited till morning to go get the fucking local technopath?"

"Listen, I don't tell them how to do their jobs, and thankfully they don't say shit about how I do mine, so I can't explain that. However, I do know that they have no qualms about disturbing us at any time of day, so I'd guess they didn't realize it until this morning." Pressure walked through the gate with them, putting on her own mask. Kirin absently wondered how heroes ever kept their identities secret when her costume mask covered the top half of her face, but the surgical one she wore around campus only covered the bottom. "And I think you both know better than to mention that I told you any of this, correct?"

They both nodded, though Ifrit somewhat grudgingly.

"Is Yantra the only technopath around here?" Kirin didn't think to ask until they were in the car, Pressure apparently personally driving them. "I thought they were pretty common, as far as miens go."

"There are a few; I think this was an all hands on deck type of call. I wasn't the one who answered, Phantasm did. She'd be the one to ask if you need to know more, but I doubt she'd be willing to share much at all with you. Very strict with the rules, her."

"Are we not supposed to know about the calls that come in?" Kirin was glad that the drive was short, because Pressure's car was quite small, and his head was pressing against the roof.

"Technically, all our work is labeled confidential, and the details are only available for public view after the International Hero Council reviews them. The official reasoning is so that we can ensure none of the information in the cases can compromise or otherwise hinder hero operations. As students, you exist in a somewhat awkward space. You're allowed to go out into the field and perform some duties, but you don't have the clearance to know a lot of the behind-the-scenes things that a full hero would get access to. When a call comes in, we teachers decide what information is critical to the success of the mission and that's usually what gets relayed to you. Most professional heroes are fairly relaxed with the confidentiality around students, since it's easier on them the more you know, but Phantasm has always been one to tightly adhere to the law."

"No wonder she's Sunshine's favorite teacher." Ifrit mumbled from the front seat, making a corner of Kirin's mouth twitch.

"You've already experienced part of that awkwardness with the capture of that villain, no? That was a fun meeting to sit in on, them all debating who should be listed as the arresting hero." Pressure snorted. "Majesty really wanted her name to be attached to it, and she nearly threw a fit when Phantasm pointed out that there's precedent for hero students having arrests attributed to them."

"Is it really that big a deal? I would think that it's just a bookkeeping issue."

Ifrit was the one who answered, not even turning around.

"It's a fucking popularity thing. Once declassified, hero records are available to the public, and there are *hundreds* of shitty websites out there that track how well heroes are doing just by arrest numbers. The most fucked of them track that by *kill* totals."

"Oh."

"Majesty thinks she can break my record." Pressure said smugly, and Kirin could practically hear Ifrit rolling his eyes. "She's not even close."

"That's right, isn't it?" Kirin mused out loud to himself as they pulled up to the station. "You do have the most arrests of all time."

"And the most kills." Ifrit's voice had an edge to it that Kirin couldn't name, but Pressure didn't react at all, except faint lines appearing under her eyes that made her look far older.

"Never mind that. They'll bring you back to the school, so I need to head back. Be polite."

"We will be!" Kirin waved as Pressure started to pull away.

"That wasn't meant for you Kirin, and you know it!"

When they walked into the building, Yantra was immediately visible, sitting at a computer at the end of the room, entirely focused on what was in front of her. The rest of the technopaths that Pressure mentioned were around, but none of them were even bothering to touch the computer itself like she was, instead standing, usually with their eyes closed.

"This way." An officer guided Ifrit and Kirin away, Kirin sparing one last glance at her, her eyes reflecting the lines of code on the screen.

They were taken a similar way to how they'd headed for the mien user cell block, but their guide veered right instead of heading for the elevator. A few more confusing turns later and they were left alone in what clearly was an interrogation room masquerading as a sitting room.

"What the fuck do you think they're going to say we did now?" Ifrit looked tired, suddenly, sitting down on the far-too-comfortable-for-a-police-station chair that was in the corner of the room. Kirin took a seat next to him, fiddling with a stray thread on the upholstery.

"Maybe the school decided to press charges for that training room wall. Should've known we wouldn't get away so easily." Kirin faked a dramatic sigh. "I'm too young to go to jail."

"If they didn't want us to break it, they shouldn't have made it so breakable." Ifrit grumbled, but Kirin could see the beginnings of a smile in his eyes.

The door opened then, and they were greeted with a plain-clothed officer, who gave them a too-friendly smile and closed the door behind himself.

"Hello gentlemen, sorry to bother you. I'm Officer Scott." He seated himself in the chair across from Kirin's, looking entirely like a kindly neighborhood dad. Kirin felt his stomach sour. "It just came to our attention that the proper close out procedure was never followed for the arrest you folks made a few months ago. Just doing our due diligence and making sure the loose ends are tied up."

"Really?" Ifrit sounded skeptical, but he was doing a good job of at least keeping his expression forcibly neutral. "Seems like there are bigger problems than paperwork to be dealt with right now."

"Oh, that scene in the lobby is just about strengthening the cybersecurity of the force. We do it every so often." Kirin didn't like how easily the man lied. "And you've filled out all the paperwork already. This is just the verbal discussion of what you learned from the villain during your initial interview with her."

"Oh." Kirin had assumed they'd been watching the whole process over cameras and hadn't thought to question it when no one bothered to ask them what she'd said. "Well, it's been a minute now, but I can summarize, if that's alright."

"Please do." The officer pulled out a pen and pad, balancing it on his knee. Kirin had a brief flashback to his interview with Pressure, and how she'd seemed so disarming then too.

"Primarily she was discussing how people with miens are treated in society, as an explanation for why she did what she did. She knew the organization would have footage from before the explosion, so potentially, I think, they might have transmitted the footage out themselves to ensure that it both survived and that their comrades had access to it. She also said that they were there to gather supplies and hadn't realized that someone was going to be touring. That, to me, indicates it's more likely that they don't necessarily have inside information, but were just going off what they could gather through observing who went into and out of the power plant and when. She refused to give any information on what they were gathering or what they planned to do with it, though it does tell us that this was indeed a first strike instead of their ultimate goal." Kirin hesitated for a moment, eyes looking at Ifrit. "Is there anything I forgot?"

Ifrit made a big show of considering it for a minute.

"She seemed low level in the operation, if not the lowest level. The way she spoke sounded like she was re-iterating bullet points, and she seemed unaware of how bad things would be if she participated in an actual crime, instead of just discussing one. It's hard to say if the whole group was just as inexperienced— which would almost indicate that the explosion *was* somewhat planned since the whole group was expendable— but she wasn't a career criminal."

The officer nodded as he wrote down what they were saying, or at least pretended to. Kirin wasn't sure if it was possible to have handwriting that messy, or if the man was just scribbling on the paper to make it look like he was listening.

"That's about what we gathered from the following sessions, but it's good to hear that you felt the same as us. Often, we find that the villains either think the heroes will be more understanding of their plight— I can't remember the last time we had a villain come in who *didn't* talk about how unfair the world is for mien users the second a hero walked in— or they're angry enough that they slip up. Your case was a bit unusual, but at least you're getting good hands-on experience with the full legal process!" The officer gave them a big smile that made Kirin want to punch his teeth in. No wonder things weren't getting better when this man could sit there and attempt to *commiserate* over people rightfully pointing out the reasons they'd ended up where they were. To belittle their struggles as if they were whining, as if a full-blown villain organization hadn't sprung out of negligence like this. "Since it's been a moment, I do want to see if we can learn a little more if I jog your memory with some things that were said."

He gestured to Ifrit.

"You had asked why she attacked your compatriot here, and she responded that she attacked at random, because she thought you might have hurt her accomplices. When she said that, you looked at each other. Was there something off about that statement?"

Kirin thought about it, trying to call up the scene.

"She said she was trying to take us out before we could do the same to her. But she wouldn't look us in the eye when she spoke." Kirin heard how terse his words had become, but Officer Scott was apparently oblivious to tone.

"Mm." The officer took his notepad back out, and that time, Kirin was convinced that he'd just been scribbling before, since this new note was far closer to handwriting than the first. "Is there any reason for her to attack you, specifically?"

"Not apart from the obvious."

"She could have killed me." Ifrit said bluntly, his arms folded across his chest. "Could have killed either of us. She had a knife, I believe, but she didn't use it. Maybe the idea was to knock one of us out and try to set us up as a plant. I don't really think she was thinking all that much, when she did it."

"So you did notice that she was armed. When was that?" Officer Scott was laser focused on Ifrit now, all pretenses of being casual abandoned.

"After I woke up. I f— I remember because when I regained consciousness, I saw it strapped to her leg and wondered how I was alive, since she could have easily stabbed me before I saw her coming."

"I see." The officer didn't bother writing it down. "She also mentioned that when they were being shot at, one of her accomplices saved her. What do you make of that?"

"It says that at least those who were with her didn't consider her to be expendable, even to their own potential harm." Kirin was fighting not to cross his own arms, but he wanted some physical barrier between him and this man.

"Also says that at least one other person there believes the sh— stuff they're selling. Protecting each other, isn't, I assume, standard behavior for hardened criminals." Ifrit was struggling more than usual to keep his temper in check.

"We sometimes see comradery between longtime criminal partners, but it's true that these would be people who just started working together, which makes it somewhat unusual." The officer seemed intrigued by that line of thinking, like they hadn't considered it before. "Did it seem like she was telling the truth? That this was something that certainly happened?"

"I'd say so." Kirin looked to Ifrit for confirmation, who also nodded. "She seemed shocked by the whole situation, and when she recounted it, it felt very much like someone recounting a traumatic event, detached from the things she was saying, but horrified by them."

"That's a fair point." He was playing with his pen now, looking troubled. "We had assumed that it was just a pity play, but I think it does make more sense what you're saying. She wouldn't say a thing to us, but she did want to convince you of the goodness of Aether, so we assumed that was a lie to make it look better. But nothing in her behavior indicates she was being... insincere."

"If you need us to speak with her again, we could try that. Maybe pretend to be interested in the organization to see if she's willing to talk more about them, even in a positive light, to see if we can get her to slip up and reveal anything more that way?" Kirin suggested it half-heartedly, just wanting to check on her.

A flicker of something passed across the officer's face, but Kirin couldn't tell what it was.

"That's certainly an idea." He said slowly. "We'd need to make her feel like she couldn't be overheard, so she'd be open to having the discussion, thinking that you're genuinely considering it. Yes, that's a good idea."

Out of the corner of his eye, Kirin saw Ifrit's eyes narrow.

"Well, I think we've gotten everything we needed for today from you two, so I'll let you go." Officer Scott stood up, offering his hand out to shake, clearly trying for an impressive grip that failed to wow either of them. "We'll look into setting up that meeting in a safe and suitable manner and let you know if we can proceed with it."

"Glad to be of help." Kirin was resisting the urge to look at Ifrit to see what expression he was making, because now even Kirin could feel that something was off. It didn't feel like suspicion from the officer, but maybe... deceit?

When they were guided back to the lobby, Kirin making sure to take note of the path they took in detail, this time, Yantra was standing there waiting for them.

"I've finished here, do you want to walk back with me?" There was some kind of message that she was trying to send with how intensely she was staring at Kirin, but he wasn't sure he knew what it was.

"Uh... sure. We can walk back, it's not far."

"See? I won't be by myself, so it's really no worry." Yantra turned back to an officer who was small enough that they'd been completely hidden by her body.

"Are you three sure? Things are getting scarier out there these days, especially for kids with miens." This woman felt out of place, a round, friendly face and so short she only reached Yantra's elbow.

"We're not kids." Ifrit growled, at the same time as Kirin said, "what do you mean, scarier?"

"Just that we've been getting more calls to interrupt potential fights between adults and kids who are obviously... different. Those power suits, or whatever they want to call them, are making a lot of people comfortable harassing anyone who looks strange."

"I hadn't really heard about that being an issue." Kirin

frowned.

"The only people who can afford those damn things are the richest people here, and they can pay to keep their name out of the paper. Besides, these are poor kids we're talking about. Since when has the public ever cared about them?" She walked away, shaking her head. "It's a right shame what we're allowing to happen in this world. Hope we're not too late to stop it."

They were walking in silence, which Kirin appreciated. He was still mulling over the conversation with Officer Scott, not even touching the idea that kids were being attacked in East City, a place that supposedly had the best treatment of mien users anywhere in the world. Ifrit was in a worse mood than usual too, and not the kind that he could be talked down from, but one that just needed to smolder out on its own.

Yantra seemed jumpy, and Kirin thought it had little to do with what they'd just heard. He couldn't confirm, and would deny it if asked point blank, but some of the little skittering noises he heard between trees and in alleys sounded a tad too metallic to be real animals.

"Let's head this way." Yantra spoke up when they were nearing the park, pointing down the more circuitous route to the school. "Figure we could use the exercise since class got canceled."

Ifrit and Kirin looked at each other, and Kirin shrugged.

"Fucking whatever." Ifrit grumbled, plowing ahead into the tree line.

It was another few minutes before she said anything more.

"What did they want to talk to you about?" Her tone was casual, but the way that she was looking over her shoulder made it seem forced.

"They just needed us to review what we'd found out from the villain that we got credit for arresting."

"That was a while ago that you did the interview though, no?" Yantra's eyes were narrowed, her voice now icy.

"Yeah, that's what we fucking said." Ifrit hadn't missed the shift, and his temper was flaring, hands clenched at his sides.

"Apparently it just fell through the cracks, and they didn't get to it until now. But I think they're hiding something. When I asked if I could speak with her again, since the officer said she wouldn't talk to them, he got... weird about it."

"Weird how?"

"I'm not sure. Just... off."

"Well then, I have good news and bad news." Yantra seemed to have made a decision then and there, pulling the pair of them close to her and throwing her arms over their shoulders in a way that could *not* have been comfortable. It was, however, necessary, as her voice dropped to near imperceptible levels. "The good news is I know why they were being weird about it."

"And the bad?" Ifrit asked through gritted teeth.

"The villain. She's dead."

21

Worsening

"W‌HAT?"

"*How?*" Ifrit's tone made it less a question and more a demand.

"The attack on the police server. While the system didn't detect it until the morning, once it did, it set certain protocols into action."

"What protocols Yantra?"

"I'm not supposed to know this." She looked over her shoulder again, nearly smashing her nose against Ifrit's head with them all huddled so close. "They had us just trying to figure out *what* was accessed in the server. They seemed to care less about how they got in. But I started poking at the alarm system itself, to see what tipped off security and then trace backwards from there."

"What fucking protocol?"

"Whenever anyone hacks into the system and tries to access a file on a villain, it auto triggers a release of toxic gas into their cell."

"What?" Kirin said softly. In his mind, he only saw Cara, tiny in the dark room, shivering and scared. There were no windows there. One door, thick as his thigh.

"If I had to guess, the assumption is that anyone accessing the villain's records would be looking to break them out, so the reaction is to make sure they won't get out, ever."

"She didn't even have a fucking trial." Ifrit pulled away from Yantra, looking sick. "And she didn't really do any shit worth dying for."

"They were looking for information on her?" Kirin was trying to run through the questions that the officer asked, trying to work through what he'd been getting at. Maybe it was just to try and figure out if they'd missed anything of importance, now that they couldn't learn anything more from her.

"Kind of. The weird thing is, I think they knew." Yantra finally let go of Kirin, slowly rubbing her arms like she was cold.

"Explain."

"They were in there for *hours*. Looking for every backdoor, every way around touching the actual information regarding her. Instead of looking for her name directly, they seemed to be manually going through lists of arrests, as far as I can tell from the access log, and then manually going through the medical records—"

"Medical records?" Ifrit interrupted.

"Yeah, from right after the attack. It was downloading them which set off the program."

"Why did they want her medical records? The only reason I could think was to show abuse or say that something was wrong with her arrest. But we were told she had brain damage from hitting the wall, and that was the only reason she was out so long." Kirin's eyes were drawn to Ifrit, who was suddenly looking a little pale.

"Well, if there's anything odd about it, we'll know." Yantra said it a little uncertainly, eyes flickering between the two of them.

"You didn't."

"I don't like the feeling that they're hiding something. But what I don't like even more... is that I think whoever hacked in triggered the protocol intentionally once they had what they wanted."

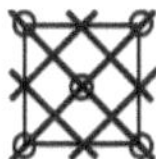

It wasn't until a week later when Yantra stopped by Kirin's room and knocked on the door that the records were mentioned again. Ifrit was already there, and so the three of them crowded around a computer that Yantra had brought, which certainly wasn't school-issued.

"I'm not going to ask where you got that." Kirin mumbled under his breath.

"Some places around here still take cash, you know. And I suspected that they weren't going to be searching us when we got here, so I had fully withdrawn my accounts before I left for school." She pulled a small chip out from one of her earrings, and Kirin stopped wondering how she'd snuck it out of the police station. "I don't steal when I don't need to."

"I don't know if this counts as stealing." Ifrit spoke up, rather subdued. He had been the whole week. "Considering it's all fucking supposed to be public record."

"I doubt either of you would be surprised how often that isn't true." Yantra hesitated before booting up the computer. "You guys don't have to see this, you know. I should've asked before I told you."

"Just open the damn thing. We're already in this." When Kirin shot him an irritated look, Ifrit rolled his eyes. "But we're fucking glad to know what actually happened, okay?"

Yantra looked between the pair of them, and a touch of a smile appeared before she sobered back up.

"All you two remember from the attack is that Ifrit was

thrown against the wall, and then she followed, and you suspect she hit her head?"

"That's about it." Kirin paused for a minute. "Actually, I think
when the building was damaged, one of the backup heating
lines must have been as well. There was a lot of carbon monoxide in the air when I got inside."

"Shouldn't have been, unless the failsafe didn't work." Yantra
looked puzzled.

"Failsafe?"

"When the power plant went down, it should've caused all
the lines to immediately seal off to avoid the risk of farther
explosions. And unless the line was in use, there shouldn't have
been anything there in the first place."

"Maybe the explosion was too big, then, even bigger than
the expected failure condition?" Kirin felt his lack of knowledge
keenly. He made a mental note to look into what protections
were put in place to prevent these things, preferably in a way
that wouldn't get him put on a watch list.

"Maybe." Yantra bit her lip and then turned her attention to
the screen. "We'll never know, really."

Despite the computer being on, she was hesitating, whether
out of fear that it might be traced somehow, or fear of what
they would find, Kirin didn't know. The moment stretched on,
the three of them staring at the screen, Yantra's hand hovering
above the slot for the chip.

"Just fucking do it." Ifrit's voice made her jump, and she
dropped it, but the magnetic grip pulled it right into position,
the file opening not a second later. Ifrit and Yantra leaned
forward, squinting at the dense report, Kirin taking one glance
at the font size and knowing he'd need to wait for one of them
to tell him what it said.

Whatever it was, it wasn't what they were expecting. Ifrit's
face was regaining color, his countenance darkening, even, the

more he read. Yantra's eyebrows kept climbing higher than he thought possible, her eyes zipping across the page. After a few minutes of watching them, he couldn't take it anymore.

"What?" They looked up at him, slightly dazed. "What is it?"

"They…" Yantra cleared her throat. "The Aether. They *chipped* her."

"What does that mean?" He looked between the two of them, as if he could find answers in their faces.

"Do you remember that lecture, from History of Heroics, about the ways that early mien users were experimented on?" Yantra said it slowly, as if the words were being forced out of her.

"Unfortunately not well." The desire to grab the computer and read the report for himself was growing, as if stalling for a little more time would make the reality any less unpleasant.

"There was a theory, very early on, that all miens could be identified by an extra area in the brain, and that monitoring that area could in turn lead to discoveries about how miens work and where they come from."

"Okay."

"Well, it's bullshit, obviously, but there were chips made that monitored brain activity, and before the ban on experimentation went into place, they were installed— unwillingly— into a number of people." Yantra's eyes were wide.

"And you're telling me that fifty years later, she has one?"

"Had." Ifrit said quietly.

"There's no mention of brain damage in here— well there *is*, but it's just a short mention that any further exposure to toxic air would've caused her to have some— and the majority of the report is on the chip. The reason she was unconscious for so long? They tried to remove it."

"*Why?*"

"It doesn't say. Concern for her well-being? So they could use whatever data might have been on there? So Aether couldn't get any more information? Worry that it was actually a planted virus that she could stick in the wall? This is just a medical report. It doesn't say *why* they did what they did, just what happened and the results."

"Did they get it out?"

"No. It seems like it was in there for a while and her brain had healed around it."

Ifrit and Kirin looked at each other.

"What?" Yantra noticed the glance.

"How long was it in there?"

"The report says that the scar tissue looks to have been several years old, and the development of her brain around it was lightly stunted, which gave them a good guess of about a decade ago."

Kirin found Ifrit's eyes again, the same thought mirrored there.

"Now you know something I don't. Spill."

"From the way she talked to us, I don't think she's been with them for very long. Maybe Aether has been around for a while, and we just never knew, but she didn't seem like she had been." Kirin bit his lip. "And I don't like what that implies."

"You think there's someone else going around sticking things in people's brains?" Yantra didn't look convinced or pleased about the idea.

"I don't really think anything at this point. I was fully willing to think it was Aether, trying to get her back..." His voice trailed off, eyes suddenly going to Ifrit. "They were asking about the other Aether members protecting her. They were trying to see if we thought they might come for her. If Aether was behind this attack or if there's someone else involved."

"Why wouldn't they just fucking *ask* that then?" Ifrit had stood up and started pacing, the fire around his throat flickering from the speed with which he changed direction.

"The fact that she's dead is going to come out eventually. I'm sure they'll play it off to the public by saying she hit her head before being taken in, and just never recovered. But you two know that's not the case, so they likely didn't want to tip you off."

"But we're going to be working closely with them in the future. We were going to find out *someday*." Kirin wished that Ifrit would stop moving around; it only made his own desire to run worse.

"Unlikely. While this protocol is in place, people rarely get in far enough to crack it. There's a whole division of cybersecurity people in that police department alone; they have an incredibly strong system to begin with. That's why they were freaked out that someone got in. Their team couldn't crack it, so finally they called the heroes."

"Could you tell how they did it?" The thought was strong enough that it stopped Ifrit in his tracks, his whole attention focused on Yantra.

"Yeah, I was able to backtrack everything they did. It was hard, I won't lie, but I'm pretty sure they weren't a technopath because of it."

"What do you mean?"

"There's a reason none of the others could figure out shit, and I could." She didn't sound haughty, just factual. "Most technopaths rely on the fact that they can just *understand* code, and float within it and bend it to do what they want. They were all spending time trying to *ask* a computer what happened, but all it can tell them is the commands that were input, or more accurately, what the output was. If that information has been purposely erased, there's nothing for them to access."

"But you don't do that." Ifrit had his eyes narrowed.

"Ever since I was little, I thought computers were basically magic. It made sense in theory, right, that it was just math and numbers and things that you could program to make it work, but it all seemed so... magical that it could just do these things. It was just as mystical as miens were, to me, and I was determined to speak the language as best I could. It only seemed natural then, when things turned out as they did, since people almost thought I was a technopath before I ever had a mien."

"Do you still think it was Aether if you think the hacker didn't have any abilities?"

"Firstly, just because they're not a technopath doesn't mean that they don't have a mien. Dulu's also slightly obsessed with computers and his mien has absolutely no overlap with technology. Secondly... it does feel weird though for a mien supremacy group to *not* be using a technopath for this if they have one at their disposal."

"It could be possible though. We really have no idea what their numbers are, who they might have..." Kirin's voice trailed off. "They really have gone quiet, haven't they?"

"Admittedly, I don't think they planned to come out in that way. I was talking about it with Kuafu— which he will categorically deny, and you never heard about— and he made a good point that this wasn't the type of clean-cut crime which he'd expect a group like this to announce themselves with."

"Is there such a thing as a clean crime?"

"No, but there are ones that make more sense. We know this was a botched robbery, and they made their statement to claim it simply because it made their point, perhaps in a better way than what they were planning would have. Or maybe the woman that you grabbed was important to their plans and they just needed to find a recruit to replace her. But whatever the reason, it wasn't a *great* introduction. Like 'hello, we fucked up! Please join us.' Isn't a great message."

"They're planning, then?"

"Presumably. They lost an operative, and now the world is looking. Hard to look for something when you have nothing more than a made-up name, but that still makes it difficult to move about freely, and certainly more difficult to grow the operation. Every person who comes looking now could potentially be a spy, every person who asks for their information could be trying to take them down." Yantra tapped absently on the edge of the computer, causing the screen to flicker. "I don't think they did this."

"Not that I disagree, but you seemed convinced it was them a few minutes ago."

"I just didn't think there might be an alternative, to be honest. You have someone attached to a theoretically large and definitely shady organization, and then something shady happens to her. Seems on par."

"You haven't explained that bit, by the way."

"Hm?"

"The fucking reason you think it *wasn't* an accident?" Ifrit cut in, clearly getting frustrated with the back and forth.

"Oh, right. Well, that's again just how they went about doing things. They were so careful combing through everything, and when they found this, they opened it first. They hid it well, but I was able to get a time stamp, and that was about three hundred, our time. The alarm was triggered at eight."

"It might take *me* that long to read something, but I'm going to guess that a hacker sophisticated enough to make it through their firewall wouldn't need the same length of time."

"Almost certainly not." Yantra agreed. "The one thing that's frustrating is that I can tell they were trying to alter something in the record, but I couldn't quite figure out what. I know it didn't work, and—"

Her eyes lit up and she looked back down to the computer,

suddenly tapping away at something. A moment later, the image flickered, and the photo in the file changed.

"That's it. That's why they downloaded it." She looked between Kirin and Ifrit, both looking confused. "They couldn't alter it while it was on the server, so they downloaded it. They're going to edit it and *re-upload* it."

"Wouldn't that set off alarms?"

"They didn't know someone had gotten into the server because there was some signal that was set off, they knew because she dropped dead in her cell. Whoever's on the other end is good, really good. The security protocols are more concerned about viruses, but a single PDF with no issues? It wouldn't really care about that. And now that she's dead, the protocol could be triggered without any ill effects anyways."

"And if we can figure out what they changed, we'll have a better idea of who's doing it."

Yantra nodded, eyes bright.

"All we need to do is wait for the new file to go online. And then we'll know exactly what they were trying to hide."

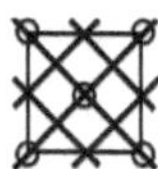

Kirin hated waiting.

He'd always been impatient, especially as a child, always bouncing on his heels and trying anything and everything to make the time go faster. Back then, his mother would laugh and say that she'd never met anyone so bad at waiting as him, but she'd never met Ifrit.

Ifrit never stopped moving these days. Kirin was woken earlier and earlier in the day, their morning runs getting ever longer. The fifth floor was filled with the smell of spices constantly; Phoenix had been able to win back some points by filling their pantry not once but *twice* in a single week from Ifrit's non-stop cooking. It had gotten so bad that the whole dorm was able to get a taste, something Ifrit had always opposed before.

Kirin's grades had also never been better. Ifrit made him sit down and do any and every assignment they received the moment class was over, going over it once, twice, three times until it was perfect. There were almost two months left in the semester, but Ifrit seemed determined to finish all their coursework with a month to spare.

Yantra was faring far better than either of them, often rolling her eyes when she was met with expectant gazes any time she walked into a room. But it was wearing on her, too, if the creases under her eyes were anything to go by.

It was on one of Kirin's particularly bad days that Aïcha decided to turn on the news.

Theus Moretti was on the screen, their teeth flashing in the light of the cameras. A smaller square off to the side showed images from their presentation at Satol, the kick that destroyed the pillar shown in slow motion. The screen turned to show various other scenes of Futurus, Moretti's company. They were propaganda shots really, of them handing out blankets, Moretti walking around the wreckage of the city with plans in hand, smiling faces as the new buildings were unveiled.

"Since the announcement of the new line of techware that mimics the incredible power of miens, Futurus has leapt to the forefront of public consciousness. Once firmly a tech developer like many others, some are now calling them the first hero company, since they have begun to level the playing field between those with miens, and those without them."

An avatar of Moretti appeared on screen, clearly a pre-recorded message.

"We thank all our heroes for their service, and it certainly seems rude to claim that this new and relatively untested technology

could ever do what they do every day to protect us." Moretti's smile was saccharine, their expression slightly too prideful to make the statement feel genuine. *"However, we are thrilled with the response that the public has had to our latest development. Futurus has always strived to be a company for all people, and with this we hope to bring enhancement of the human body to the next level. Super strength was only the first model, and you all shall have to wait and see what surprises the second might hold."*

"Aïcha, can you turn this off?" Kirin felt a sour taste rising in his mouth as the announcer continued on about the great demand for the new techware from all over the world.

"Sure, put on whatever you want." Aïcha tossed him the remote; it bounced off his chest as the doors burst open.

A cold wind blew in, the bright light from outside silhouetting Dulu in the doorway, who was visibly covered in blood.

"Where's Phoenix?" He barely paused for breath as he came in, kicking against Adlivun's door as he started to try to pry open the elevator doors, clearly planning to fly up the chute instead of waiting for the lift itself.

"Ad's—" Aïcha started, but Phoenix appeared in Adlivun's doorway, hair slightly mussed.

"What's going on?"

"Goldhorn." Dulu threw Phoenix over his shoulder without giving them time to react. "They need help."

"We were told to wait to go in, since someone was already there talking to the kid." Ness had been ambushed when she returned to the dorm, conspicuously without either of her teammates. She'd changed out of her costume, but Kirin could see the streaks of rust red on the edges of her hair. "The local heroes thought that maybe it was a parent, or someone trying to calm the kid down, and so they had us wait. Dulu was watching from the air, Goldhorn was in an alley with line of sight, and I was supposed to sneak closer so I could try and hear what was going on."

Yantra pulled them all away from the door, pushing Ness into a chair since she looked like she was about to fall over. The rest of the class had heard and come down to the first floor, Ifrit even making dinner in the kitchen.

"I... I noticed that whoever was speaking to the kid, they weren't standing on the ground. I reported that in and then Goldhorn was told to just try to grab the girl from the side, so we could get her away from the other person. But then... they didn't respond."

For a moment there was only the sound of Ifrit chopping something, and a quiet jingle for some restaurant from the TV.

"Dulu couldn't see them. So I went over to their location. And they were just..." Her voice cut off.

"Phoenix is there now." Lilin had come back, gently placing a cup of steaming cardamom tea in Ness's hands. "Goldhorn will be fine. We just need to relax and wait, and they might be able to tell us more."

Ness's posture relaxed for just a moment, when a familiar voice spoke up from the screen.

"*Hello again, world.*" Kirin's head snapped up and he was greeted with a flat, white mask. "*This was our intended first meeting, but now it is simply a reintroduction. I suppose that saves me some time, since I need not explain who we are and our purpose, and I can just immediately dive into our operations.*"

An image flashed into view, and Ness's cup dropped to the ground. A child, a girl, on the ground, the air around her thick like jelly, people frozen in place. A friendly figure leaned over her, unaffected by whatever had caught the rest. The audio was cut and so the words were silent, but Kirin could lip read well enough to guess what was being said.

You're safe. I won't hurt you.

"*We often hear how miens today present unpredictably, violently, and that this is evidence of the inherent deadly nature of these abilities. That this proves we must be regulated and controlled, and only a chosen few are worthy to use their natural gifts. But very rarely do we hear why these cases happen, and even rarer do the children involved make it out unscathed.*" The white mask filled the room again, a commanding presence. "*This lovely girl is Jaya, who was terrified and running from bullies at school. You see, everyone knew she was likely to have a mien, as both her parents do. The children around her would poke her, pinch her, even hit her, just to try and make her have a reaction. They were cruel, as children often are, when they are taught something is different and wrong.*

"*When asked what she was thinking when this started, Jaya let us know that she just wanted people to get away from her, so she could be alone. The news broadcasts will talk about how terribly this disrupted the workday, how horrible it was that a mere child could do this, but they will leave out the fact that she was being harassed, and her body reacted to keep her safe.*" The camera pulled back slightly, revealing white gloved hands resting on a table. Everything about this woman was white, pristine, crisp; everything except a silver pin with a stylized A that was pinned to her chest. "*What would have happened to this child, had she been apprehended by the heroes? Would she have been allowed to return home, to her parents, who were not even allowed to get close to try to talk to her? Would she have been marked for future torment by her peers, who had finally goaded her into a reaction? Would she live a good life, with the whole world knowing her face?*

"*We will not leave these things to chance. Our children deserve better; they should not be plastered on every screen for the cruel world to see, berated by adults online who would just as soon condemn a six-year-old to death for being scared. This brings me to our core tenet: we will protect our future."*

Slowly, almost shyly, the girl from the earlier video crept into view, hands mostly covering her face. When the woman in white reached out her hand, the little girl took it.

"With permission from her parents, she will be staying with us. We have the power to protect these precious children from harm, and they will be raised safely, without judgement, without fear, somewhere they will not be found." She gave the girl's hand a squeeze before she moved off camera, glancing over her shoulder once. *"We will not take any child who does not wish to be here, but any parents who are afraid for their children are free to seek us, to ask for safe harbor.*

"This will come as a shock to most of the world, but the quote unquote advancements that Futurus is proposing already threaten children who appear different. Even in the most pro-hero city in the world they have been targeted, attacked, and injured. It is always sorrow to part, but we will ensure that all these children have the right to be just that, children, without fear that one misstep will see them locked away forever."

The screen went dark then, the change so stark after all the bright white. A few moments later, the news started playing again, as if nothing had happened.

"That's their plan then." Yantra said, dazed, her hands gripping the back of the couch as if it was the only thing keeping her upright. "In order to boost their numbers... they're recruiting *children*."

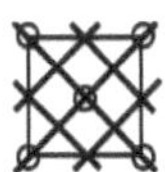

Phoenix arrived not long after the message had aired, Dulu

with them, but Goldhorn was still nowhere to be found.

"Goldhorn's stable." Phoenix said tersely before heading up to their room, Adlivun following them like a shadow. Dulu didn't offer anything more, his usual calm energy interrupted by the way his hands just couldn't seem to stay still. The common room slowly emptied as the hours ticked by, Naddāha being particularly vocal about everyone getting some rest.

"It won't help them for us all to be exhausted, so we should take care of ourselves to be ready for anything they might need once they get back." Kirin didn't fail to notice that she wasn't taking her own advice. He only allowed himself to be pushed out at midnight, when there was still no sign of Goldhorn on the horizon.

When the elevator dinged open on the fifth floor, he was surprised to see Ifrit still up, sitting with his head down and knee shaking. His head perked up immediately, and he was on his feet and approaching Kirin before the doors had fully shut.

"Do you know what fucking time it is? You're going to be a nightmare in the morning if you don't sleep and I don't want to deal with that shit." Ifrit's words were thoroughly undermined by the way that he was looking at Kirin's face, the worry poorly masked by false anger.

"Sorry, I wanted to be there when Goldhorn got back." Kirin gave a weak smile.

"Are they?"

"No. Naddāha insisted I head up anyway though."

"Did she?" There was an edge to Ifrit's voice.

"Yeah, her and Dulu are still down there though; I suppose that's enough of a welcome without making them feel mobbed." The words of the broadcast started to circle Kirin's head, which was exactly what he'd hoped to avoid by staying up so late. "I should get to bed, though; you're right, it's late."

"Don't do that." Kirin had made it past Ifrit and was about to close his door when the shorter man spoke up again. "Don't do that thing with me that you do with everyone else."

"What do you—"

"Cut the shit. You're not okay, are you?" Ifrit was staring into Kirin's face like there was a secret written there that he could unearth by looking hard enough. "Na... Nada... feelings bitch was staring at you after the broadcast stopped."

Kirin opened his mouth, the *yeah, I'm okay* ready on his tongue, but there was something desperate in Ifrit's expression that made him close it again. It was almost... fear.

"I might not..." Ifrit cleared his throat and stood up straighter, arms crossing over his chest almost petulantly as he went on. "I might be shit at the whole feelings thing, but you *can* talk to me. If you need to."

Kirin felt a warmth bloom in his chest, Ifrit in front of him with his face red, looking embarrassed but so determined at the same time. Kirin idly wondered for a moment what Ifrit would do if he asked him for a hug.

"You're right, I'm not great." Kirin sighed and leaned against the doorframe, feeling his muscles groan in protest against even that slight stretch. "But it *is* late. I'm not so upset that I won't be able to sleep, and if I'm a nightmare when I'm tired, you're a terror. You should get some sleep too."

Ifrit looked hesitant, like there was something more he wanted to say, and Kirin finally saw how his friend was behaving: fingers tapping along his arms, his eyes looking everywhere but Kirin, muscle tense in his jaw. Kirin didn't doubt that Ifrit wanted to check in on him, but maybe it was also Ifrit saying that he needed someone to talk to as well.

"I could use someone nearby, though, if that's good with you?" Kirin suggested it slowly, hoping he'd read the implication correctly.

Ifrit's eyes widened slightly, and though his blush spread to his ears, he shrugged as if it was a casual thing.

"Fucking whatever."

And so, Kirin found himself stretched out on Ifrit's floor at one in the morning.

Ifrit had fallen asleep almost immediately, leaving Kirin alone to stare at the ceiling. He was glad, in a way, that Ifrit insisted on keeping the window open even with the frigid temperature outside, because it gave him an excuse to wrap himself in thick blankets, pretending the cocooning was only from the cold, and not to fight against the building uneasiness in his chest. The open window even allowed him to hear Goldhorn's approach, and Dulu and Naddāha running out to meet them, though he pointedly tuned out the murmured conversation between the three.

Ifrit didn't snore, which surprised Kirin. He had such a presence when he was awake that Kirin would've expected that to continue even into his sleep, but Ifrit was peaceful, his brow smoothed of creases for once, the lack of fire making his whole countenance softer. He was almost leaning off the bed, face toward Kirin, mouth open slightly. He looked so warm, so comfortable, that Kirin found an ache in his chest, wishing he were up there next to him.

"I'm scared we're not on the right side, you know?" Kirin whispered the words, watching Ifrit's face for any sign that the other man was waking. "I don't believe for a second Aether's actually doing what they're claiming to, but if someone could create a safe place for people like us, wouldn't that be a good thing?"

He rolled over, eyes going back to the ceiling instead of his friend, Ifrit's quiet breathing feeling like encouragement to go on.

"And even if they have something else going on, if even the slightest bit of it is true, if they can create that image of security for those kids, isn't that good? I wanted to be a hero to help, and maybe someday to start changing the way we see people, to maybe make heroes be *real* heroes, to protect anyone who needs protecting and not just hurt those who need hurting. Will those kids hate us when we do? Will we be able to promise that they'll be safe from the rest of the world?"

"Of fuckin course we can." The words were slightly slurred, Ifrit's eyes not even open when Kirin looked back over at him, surprised. "You're gonna show them all, right?"

The confidence in Ifrit's voice made his breath catch, and he didn't say anything for a minute. His hesitation seemed to irritate Ifrit, as he opened his eyes just the tiniest amount to squint at Kirin, who suddenly felt like he didn't know how to breathe at all, anymore.

"Right?"

"Mm. Yeah." Kirin finally found the air to form words, and Ifrit, satisfied, rolled over to face the window, Kirin left blinking at the space where he'd just been. Maybe Medusa's power was transferable, Kirin thought, because he felt riveted in place by the memory of those crimson eyes creased into half-moons, staring at him like he could do nothing wrong.

22

Orders

Sometimes Kirin felt like TV shows were wildly different from real life. Other times, he thought they might have a point.

Despite being fully aware that he'd slept on the floor, and nothing at all untoward had happened, when he walked out of Ifrit's room in the morning and directly made eye contact with Adlivun, who was leaving Phoenix's, he immediately felt like he'd been caught doing something wrong. He stumbled mid-step under her watchful gaze, feeling like he needed to justify himself.

In his overly tired and largely surprised state, the only thing he could think to say was: "Coffee?"

Adlivun smiled slowly and shook her head.

"I didn't know you drank coffee, anyway." She said as she waited for the elevator.

"Ah, I don't really, but Ifrit does, and he's going to be extra tired today— wait." Kirin heard the words only after they left his mouth, but it was too late. Adlivun raised an eyebrow and walked into the elevator, the doors closing before Kirin could insist that was *not* what he meant to imply. He stared dumbly after her, before shaking himself and starting the coffee maker. Adlivun would know what he meant, after all, she was coming out of Phoenix's room with her hair all rumpled and clothes from the day before too— wait.

Kirin thought about it for a few seconds more, before deciding he was too tired for all of it. Coffee machine now bubbling away, he headed to his own room to change, pretending things would make more sense with a new shirt and some cold water.

He felt marginally more alive by the time they were all walking in a sleep-deprived crowd down to the power gym for Mien Training, the class absently forming a protective circle around Goldhorn, who looked to be the most rested out of the whole group. Phoenix had it worst, their eyes listless, Naddāha not so surreptitiously looking at them out of the corner of her eye.

Pressure was already waiting for them at the gym, looking just as haggard as the class felt. There was clearly a tiny bit of hope in some of the group, Antaeus in particular looking at her with bright eyes, that she might cancel class. But she quashed those hopes immediately.

"Sometimes calls come in back-to-back with no rest." Pressure called over their assembled group of the broken, the beaten, and the damned. "Go through your regular warm-ups and then meet in the center of the gym."

There was some light grumbling, but Kirin was feeling ready to lose himself in the rhythm of practice, his brain shutting up while his hands were moving. Ifrit was quiet that morning, almost pensive, and it was starting to freak Kirin out a little. Even after he'd woken up, he'd seemed peaceful, instead of his usual morning routine of appearing like he'd just crawled out of a particularly deep grave. Maybe it'd really been helpful to him to have someone sleeping nearby. Kirin was more than willing to sleep on his floor again, if it meant he could see the soft expression Ifrit got when he slept.

They did make it through their stretching routine with little fanfare, but when Kirin helped Ifrit to his feet at the end of the set, he noticed.

"I guess it really is red." Without thinking, he reached out to touch a lock of Ifrit's hair, where the roots had grown out enough to make the true color visible. It was only the length of his fingernail, really, but the bright scarlet was starting to show. It wasn't as bad as Ifrit had made it out to be, and against his skin it looked... well, in a word, it looked stunning. "That's gonna look so nice when it's grown out."

Ifrit was looking up at him, his eyes wide, and Kirin quickly dropped his hand and took a step back.

"Sorry—" His apology was cut off by Pressure.

"Come on, we're just waiting for you two, let's go." She clapped her hands and gestured for them to walk over. Kirin hazarded a glance over his shoulder, but Ifrit's expression was back to neutral, giving away nothing of his thoughts. "I'm aware that today is supposed to be Mien Training, but because of yesterday's events, I thought this would be a better fit.

"We'll be working on one of the other jobs heroes receive: guarding. It's a relatively rare assignment, but as a skill, it's useful. Many of you have miens that could easily be adapted to protecting one or multiple targets. You just need to know how to apply it. Wyrm?"

Wyrm slowly walked toward Pressure, who gave him an encouraging, if tight-lipped, smile.

"Range is something a number of you struggle with, and when you're trying to protect someone, keeping the enemy away from them is the best strategy to keep your charge safe. Aïcha, I'm afraid you'll be drawing the short straw today. I'll be standing behind Wyrm; he'll be guarding me. Aïcha, your job is to try and grab me, got it?"

They both nodded, Aïcha looking eager to prove herself, Wyrm standing to his full height, a slight crack heard as he rolled his shoulders.

"Alright, begin."

Both leapt into action quickly, Aïcha with her uncanny speed, heading straight for Pressure. Wyrm didn't move much at all, instead miming a throwing gesture with one of his hands, just in front of where Pressure stood. Aïcha was only centimeters away when she froze and fell to the floor with a crash, seemingly unable to move.

"Phoenix." Pressure said calmly, stepping away from where Aïcha lay on the ground unmoving, her eyes looking side to side in a panic. Wyrm moved her slightly, cleaning something that Kirin couldn't see off the floor. "There are more ways than one to protect a target. Standing directly next to them all the time isn't the best method, and oftentimes, it's impossible to do so anyway."

She looked over the class, the picture of sternness, but also a bit of sadness in her gaze.

"I suspect that in your future careers, protecting one another is going to become more of a necessity. But you can't be on top of each other all the time. That's simply not how active situations work. Today, then, we'll focus on how you can look after your colleagues, even from afar."

There was an undertone of why, exactly, they were doing this today, but it was a fun enough challenge that the class was able to get lost in their work. Goldhorn was banned from using their mien, owing to the need to rest up, which meant the class took turns protecting them, while one or two attacked. With the two-on-two challenge, it was plenty entertaining, particularly when those involved got competitive.

Some of his classmates who he might not have expected to really care were getting quite excited about the whole thing. Antaeus, Ness, and especially Aïcha were all bright-eyed and eager, Yantra quietly collecting bets before each match. Kirin was flattered to hear that whenever his name came up, the odds were expected to be highly in his favor.

Whatever else could be said about Pressure, she certainly knew how to handle them. As the class went on, the tension and frustration in all of them was fading, focused instead on something they could control, something they could work on.

For Kirin's part, it was also relaxing to watch his friends work, to see how far they'd come just in the short time he'd known them. Even if he failed, there would be someone to have his back and fix whatever mess he made, and he would do his best to be that support for them as well. Though some of them, he thought, wouldn't need it.

Adlivun was up this time, paired with Lilin, Goldhorn positioned between the two. Aïcha was attacking, Kapre with her, neither looking particularly concerned about the strong team they faced.

Pressure began the match with a nod, and Kirin focused his attention on Adlivun, this being the first time he'd seen her shades since his own fight. They appeared not around her, but around Goldhorn, the feeling of wrongness he ascribed to the figures now weaker. They appeared at first as amorphous, roughly humanoid in shape and size, but the edges weren't smooth, and they appeared to be made of almost liquid with how the substance within flowed. They surrounded Goldhorn, removing them from contact with the ground entirely, and just in time too, as a hole opened right where they had been standing.

That was curious, though, Kirin noted. In order to touch Goldhorn, the figures became more distinct. Not nearly as resolved as his father had been, no facial features or clear figure, but more rigid, the proportions settling into what they would be for a human, all four roughly Phoenix's height and build. When Kapre extended the hole to include where the shades stood, they began to fall slowly, as if sinking into mud instead of open air.

He glanced to the side as he wondered why Lilin hadn't hidden Goldhorn from Kapre's view but found that question easily answered by the fact that she was unconscious on the ground, Aïcha sprinting away from her and toward Adlivun. Sometimes Kirin wondered if she was an era-two mien user, having both super speed and her inhuman legs, but with the way she trained, her agility might have just been practice, rather than natural-born gifts.

Adlivun was expecting the attack, though with her attention split, she was struggling. The shades flickered as they became less substantial and then more, Goldhorn briefly falling before the ghosts had solid enough hands to catch them again. Aïcha pressed her advantage to the fullest, making the taller woman dodge and weave as Aïcha seemed to be everywhere at once.

Adlivun ultimately lost the battle, with Aïcha landing a firm kick to the head that sent Adlivun crumpling to the ground. Phoenix headed to revive her before Pressure even called the match over, heading straight for her instead of Lilin who'd been down for longer. Since Kirin had still been watching the spirits, he realized why.

The moment Adlivun lost consciousness, the shades didn't disappear, but instead did the exact opposite. They began to sink faster into the gaping ground beneath them, features that were vaguely familiar starting to appear just before Adlivun was back and dismissed them away. Her face looked pale, even after Phoenix moved away, and she seemed unsteady as she got to her feet.

The next group was just getting set up and ready to go— Enenra and Dulu versus Kuafu and Medusa— when Majesty burst into the room.

She was covered in blood, but the lack of damage to her otherwise pristine hero costume showed it wasn't her own.

"The healer. Where is she?" She snapped.

"You don't order around my students." Pressure was there in front of her, though Kirin could have sworn he never saw her move.

"Reader's orders." Majesty slapped a piece of paper against Pressure's chest and strode past her, looking between all their faces. "Healer? Which one of you is that?"

Phoenix glanced at Pressure and didn't step forward, Adlivun adjusting her posture so that they were more hidden behind her.

"It's alright, Phoenix." Pressure had finished reading whatever had been handed to her and her mouth was set in a thin line. "There's just someone who needs help right now."

"I'll go with them." Adlivun's tone was icy; she was not suggesting it.

"Please do. I'm sure there's no issue with that, right *Majesty*?" Though her face was kept perfectly impassive, the disdain in Pressure's voice was clear for all to hear.

"This shouldn't take more than a minute." Majesty didn't wait, simply turned on her heel and headed back the way she came, Phoenix and Adlivun following quietly behind. Pressure, however, grabbed Phoenix by the shoulder and whispered something in their ear, Phoenix not looking at her and nodding before following Adlivun out the door.

The class was quiet, suddenly, the brief sense of calm gone in the wake of the intrusion.

"Has one of the other classes been attacked too?" Goldhorn was the one who spoke, and if Kirin didn't know them as well as he did, he would've missed the way their chin trembled slightly.

"Indeed." Pressure rubbed her hand against her forehead, looking weary suddenly. "Keep going with this, but after lunch, we'll need to have a meeting with all of you."

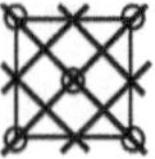

Phoenix and Adlivun came back during lunch, Phoenix immediately going to the kitchen to wash their hands. Adlivun was usually expressive, but just then, her face was shuttered, save for a crease between her eyes.

"Was it the same person, do you think?" Goldhorn wasn't eating much, just pushing around their food with their fork.

"It could be." Phoenix was doing the same, also looking ill. "The wounds were similar."

"Does it take a lot out of you to heal?" Antaeus apparently noticed the poor complexion as well, his eyes concerned as he studied Phoenix's face.

"It depends, but not in the way you might think." Phoenix put their utensils down, entirely abandoning the pretense of eating. "The severity of the wound honestly doesn't affect how hard it is to do."

"Should we be talking about this?" Kuafu muttered partially under his breath, but left it at that after Lilin gently patted him on the back.

"Instead, it depends on how well I know a person. If I know them well, it's easy to put them back to how they were, so to speak. I just reach out and they're... there. I don't know how to make it make more sense than that." Adlivun put a cup of water into Phoenix's hands, and they obediently took a few sips before continuing. "But if I don't know someone... I have to look. Really look for them. And sometimes, I don't like what I see."

The whole table was quiet for a moment, mulling over what Phoenix had said.

"Who was it?" Yantra had to lean forward to see Phoenix, Wyrm blocking her view otherwise.

"One of the four people who attacked us in the beginning of the year, if you can believe it. Well, I guess she was the one who *didn't* attack. Inanna, I think, is her name."

Ness flashed out of existence for a moment, her fork clattering to her plate.

"Love and fertility?" Yantra frowned. "I both do and don't want to know how that works."

"It's like a worse version of Naddāha's mien. She panicked when she woke up and used it on me."

"Ew." Naddāha visibly recoiled, and then blushed. "Sorry, ignore me."

"No, it did feel... gross. Like someone just *forced* you to like them. The only nice thing about it is that it feels so foreign that it was pretty easy to realize what was going on." Phoenix shrugged, but their movements were too stiff to be casual. "It was whatever."

Adlivun abruptly stood up and went to clear her dishes, the sudden departure leaving the table in silence once again. Phoenix took a moment to recompose themself and then went on.

"The wounds she had though... they *were* similar to what you had, Goldhorn. Like... like someone just shoved a hand through her stomach. She had some other gashes too, like she was stabbed."

"Maybe her mien convinced them to hold back for a minute or two." Goldhorn looked interested at that, almost hopeful.

"She didn't remember anything." Adlivun was back, sitting down smoothly as if nothing had happened. "If anything, her mien must have upset them."

"They took her statement right when she woke up? They made me go all the way to the local hero office to give mine." Goldhorn frowned.

"No."

"Ah, right." Goldhorn smiled slightly. "All in the name."

"Do you... do you mind if we ask you what happened?" Enenra spoke up quietly, not looking up from her now empty plate, her anxiety betrayed by the small wisps of smoke curling off her buzzed hair. "We're supposed to try to prepare to protect against these people, but we don't even know what they can do."

"That implies that I do, which I'm afraid I really don't. I never saw them coming, never heard anyone nearby. Only time I realized I wasn't alone was when they ripped a hole through my small intestine." Goldhorn was shockingly calm about the statement, even gaining some of their appetite back and taking a few bites of their food. "The police made me go over and over and over the scene, trying to see if there was any information that I could give, but there wasn't. It was like they just appeared."

"You don't think they can portal, do you?" Clidna asked, playing with a butter knife. "Would explain why the Aether agents on the island were never found."

"No one has ever been able to, that we know of, but we know so little about miens. Not reassuring, I know. However, just because something is *possible* doesn't mean that it's *likely*." Yantra was using her lecture tone, which was relaxing, somehow. Familiar. "It's more likely that they would have something like Ness's mien, that allows them to be undetectable until they want to be. It would still be problematic, yes, but we have plenty of invisible heroes to speak with who can give us an idea of what they can or can't do."

"I suppose it's too much to ask that they give us a list of what all their members can do, huh?" Ness shook her head. "Or at least let someone see them so we could prepare better."

"I think you, of all people, don't get to complain about that."

"If we're looking at the positives, it's good practice, you

know?" Goldhorn was leaning back in their chair, looking contemplative. "We're always going to have this disadvantage. Villains will always be unknown. They'll always be something we have to work around, and chances are we won't get an understanding of what they can do at all. But we, at least, have a trump card that they certainly don't."

When Kirin's eyes drifted to Phoenix, he wondered if they'd been lying about how much healing took out of them. If anything, the weight of expectation seemed to add to their exhaustion, their head bowing like the pressure was going to cause them to snap.

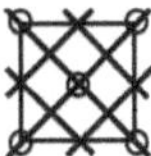

If Kirin ignored the fact that Pressure called them there expressly to discuss the situation, he could pretend this was just another debrief after Rescue Operations or Combat, since they were using one of the classrooms that were typically reserved for the seminars after their practicals. Pressure wasn't there when they filed in, and though Yantra and Ness— and oddly, Clidna— made a valiant effort to keep the energy at least somewhat positive, the atmosphere was rather gloomy.

Pressure herself didn't arrive until fifteen after two. Shifter followed her silently, and manually shut the door after himself.

"This is a long overdue meeting, but it works out for the best that it was delayed." Shifter was the one speaking, not Pressure. He looked even more sleep-deprived than usual. "Due to the recent targeting of our students, we'll be structuring the squads differently than we have previously."

A sigh of relief blew through the room; it was true that they'd never redistributed team members at the beginning of the semester, though they hadn't taken a final, technically. There was plenty of footage of their fieldwork, however, which Shifter *had* made them review. He'd been kinder with his feedback for that than he was for their typical rescue missions, but everyone had gotten some comments, Kirin's being to *think* a lot more before he acted.

"Unlike the first semester, these are assigned teams, and there will be no switching. These are designed to balance everyone's skills, and— most importantly— to ensure that you all make it back to campus safely." He flicked on the screen and immediately Kirin's eyebrows shot up. "As you can see, we're pairing you instead of forming usual groups of three, as Phoenix will be the third member of every group.

While Kirin might be a slow reader, he was rather good at math. There were eighteen students in their class, minus Phoenix that left seventeen. That meant one group would only have two, Phoenix to heal and one person to work, no one to watch their back. He didn't know who, exactly, he'd been expecting it to be, as he zeroed in on the only row that held a single name, but he didn't like the result regardless.

Since the person who was listed all alone was Ifrit.

23

Expendable

Kirin hated that it made sense. Ifrit was a strong, well-rounded hero, who could do delicate operations as well as large scale destruction, and on his own had no obvious weaknesses. But Kirin found himself really, really disliking it.

Shifter was still talking, but Kirin was busy skimming the chart for his name, and finally was able to get his brain to sift out the letters enough to read it, as well as the name next to his own. He stumbled over it twice, the double K confusing for a minute, but Kapre was to be his third. Again, it made sense. Kapre had a strong mien, but it came with a strong drawback. They needed someone like Kirin to watch over them while they couldn't protect themself.

"Pressure will fill you in on the rest." Shifter was apparently done, giving the class a curt nod before he was out the door, moving faster than Kirin had ever seen him before. Pressure was doing the opposite, dreading moving up to the position he just vacated, the first time the class had seen her look uneasy.

"I wasn't sure if I wanted you to know any more than this. It certainly would be reasonable that the groups needed reworking, given the present circumstances." She began slowly.

"Are two attacks really enough to warrant Phoenix having to

go on every single mission?" Yantra apparently couldn't hold in the question any longer. "That seems unfair to them, and overly strenuous."

"I agreed to it." Phoenix spoke up, but they didn't raise their gaze from their desk.

"Indeed. I was getting to that, Yantra." Pressure sighed. She seemed to be doing that a lot, lately. "On their own, it's true, this wouldn't have been near enough to call for it. Unfortunately, these are not isolated."

She pressed a button on her phone and the image on the screen changed to a list of masked faces and dates next to them. Kirin recognized some of the heroes from the news or ads, but many he found himself drawing a blank on.

"Whoever's attacking the students now has been very active since the first message Aether put out. A good two dozen heroes have been killed, and all had wounds identical to those Goldhorn and now Inanna suffered." The words left a chill over the room. "At first, it seemed like Aether was holding up their ideals, crooked as they may be, as all the heroes killed were actively engaging with other mien-users and had been given orders to kill. Goldhorn's mission was designated as purely non-combat, or a peace call, as all the missions we send you on are. This was the first time we saw this kind of wound on a peace call, as well as the first time anyone other than a full fledged hero was targeted.

"There was a lot of discussion why Goldhorn was attacked. We never suspected that it was because they are a student, and assumed it had more to do with them being assigned to remove the child from the situation, since it was almost imme-diately after that order that they were attacked. But Inanna was alone, away from the scene, finishing up her rounds when she was attacked. That, combined with the fact that she had ver-bally confirmed with a journalist that she was a student upon arriving on the scene, has made us change our assumption."

Pressure flashed an image on screen and the whole class recoiled. It wasn't either of the students shown, instead one of the earlier heroes, but the gaping hole through her chest was made no less horrifying by her unfamiliar face.

"Whoever this villain is, they *can* kill, but both Goldhorn and Inanna were dealt blows that pointedly were not immediately fatal. We don't know if this was intentional— and if it was, we don't know why— but we are hopeful it will continue if there are indeed future attacks. Regardless, Phoenix offered to be put into every lineup, so we decrease the chances of any… permanent damage."

"And?" Phoenix prompted Pressure to say something more, a stormy look on their face.

Pressure looked grim, her knuckles white as she continued.

"I'm also sure you've all noticed that your class is treated… differently than the other hero groups."

"No shit." Ifrit muttered, Kirin only hearing the words because he'd pulled his chair in so closely that their legs touched.

"For years, the Institute board has maintained that the world would not accept heroes who looked visibly different than a quote unquote normal person. There used to be both a minimum and maximum height requirement, and previously written into the mien examination guidelines was the stipulation that the mien could not express itself physically when not in use."

Kirin could see Wyrm shift uncomfortably out of the corner of his eye, Goldhorn absently touching one of their horns.

"While I announced the new hero coalition recently, it's been operational for some time. One of our top priorities was diversifying the makeup of heroes, since many people are most familiar with miens exclusively *through* heroes. Normalizing the appearance of, say, someone like Ness by having her here can encourage people out in the world to be more open about their own neighbors and colleagues too. Many of you are painfully aware that while miens are present in nearly one fifth of children these days, many miens are hidden or aren't expressed physically at all, and so most people are unaccustomed to seeing folks with anatomical differences and may react negatively, even aggressively.

"The idea we originally proposed was to start integrating more visible miens throughout the hero classes, but the board only agreed to have all those deemed 'risks' confined to one class, which, I'm sure none of you will be surprised to learn, is your own."

"And now, when things are getting scary, they can use us as cannon fodder." Clidna's voice was trembling with barely contained emotion.

"The university doesn't want to seem cowed by these recent attacks. They worry the public will lose faith in us, as an institution, and in heroes more broadly. But despite this, a good many students in the hero program are legacy students. A good, good many." Pressure's lip curled slightly in disgust. "Their parents are often *on* the boards that discuss these issues or are otherwise heroes who donate generously to the school year after year. We've already gotten many calls from heroes who are insistent that their child either be advanced and allowed to fight back, or not sent out into the field at all."

"If Phoenix wasn't here, would they just let us die?" Antaeus's voice was small.

"They might, but I wouldn't." Pressure said, firmly enough that Kirin believed it. "I was going to argue that you all be pulled from missions as well, and the board can make up whatever story they want to cover it. But then Phoenix suggested this instead, which means I can hold my favors until we really need them."

"Plus," Phoenix spoke up, a hint of their old mischief in their voice, "we'll get so much more practice over Majesty's bastards, we'll kick their asses once group combat begins."

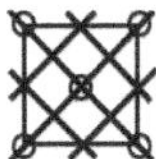

For the second day in a row, Kirin couldn't sleep. He was back in his own room, staring up at the ceiling, wondering how Ifrit might react if he asked to bring his mattress back in when there was a quiet knock on the door.

He'd hardly opened it when Yantra shoved her way in, pulling Ifrit behind her. He looked angry at the manhandling, but not as angry as Kirin would've expected if he'd just been forcibly woken up.

"It changed." Yantra practically tossed Ifrit into Kirin, dropping her laptop on his desk and shining a small flashlight around like crazy, at every crack and cranny in his room. It took Kirin's sleep deprived brain three tries to focus on what she was doing, instead of the fact that Ifrit's shampoo apparently smelled like apples. By the time he thought to question it, she was already done, opening her laptop and glaring at the pair of them. "What are you doing? Come over here and make sure to lock the door."

Kirin reached around Ifrit to shut and lock the door, and it was only then that he realized he wasn't wearing a shirt. But by then, it was too late.

"What... what happened to your back?" Yantra sounded aghast, and he quickly straightened and turned to face her, only to remember that Ifrit was standing directly next to him, and now had a clear view. He could already feel his skin starting to itch and his fingers going numb, not at all prepared for that conversation.

"He's got scars. So what?" Ifrit shoved his way past Kirin, a bundle of fabric slapped against Kirin's chest. "I've got fucking plenty too."

Yantra went wide-eyed, pressing her hands against her mouth, realizing how rude she'd been. Ifrit was bristling, the hand still against Kirin's chest suspiciously warm, and in the silence, Kirin realized that Ifrit was shoving a hoodie against him. He took it and put it on quickly, noting it had to be Ifrit's by how short it was on him.

"It's okay." Kirin tried for a smile, though his heart was still racing. "They're pretty bad looking, huh?"

"I just... was that metal?" Yantra's eyes flickered to Ifrit, but her curiosity seemed to overcome her fear of upsetting him, at least for the moment.

"I'm surprised that's what you were focused on." Kirin made himself settle on the ground, Ifrit doing the same after a second, though he still looked murderous. "Most people are obsessed with the, you know, diamond part."

"That's real diamond?" Yantra's eyes lit up. "Oh, Kirin, that's so *cool*."

He really didn't know how to respond to that.

"You said the fucking thing changed?" Ifrit had his arms crossed, but his expression had come down from "fire hazard" to "spit in your food," which was something, at least.

"Yes, it did." Yantra's gaze lingered on Kirin like she wanted to say more but thought better of it. "And it's not what I thought it'd be."

She picked up the laptop and joined them on the ground, the screen lighting up her face in the relative darkness. Ifrit leaned around to see the words better, but Kirin stayed where he was, picking at the sleeves of the sweatshirt.

As Ifrit read, his eyebrows sunk lower, his expression more troubled.

"Right? It's not what I would've expected." Yantra shook her head.

"What?" They both looked up at him suddenly, as if they'd forgotten he was even there.

"They changed two things." Yantra scooted over to show him the screen, Ifrit surreptitiously making the font larger. "Firstly, they edited the injuries she had when she was arrested, saying it was blunt force trauma instead of toxic gas inhalation, and they added a little line stating that the type of chip in her brain usually has a serial number."

"Really?"

Yantra nodded.

"A lot of medical implants do, but I have no idea why you'd want a serial number on something that's blatantly illegal."

"I doubt there's actually one fucking on there." Ifrit seemed to have seen everything he wanted to, as he was leaning back against Kirin's bed and looking pensively at the ceiling, only briefly making eye contact with Kirin before looking off again. "But whoever did this wants the police to look again."

"You don't think they triggered the security system just so the police would be able to get to the chip, do you?" The thought entered Kirin's brain and he couldn't shake it.

"They would certainly have known that the chip couldn't be taken out without killing her from the report." Yantra bit her nail, deep in thought. "This all feels weird though."

"What did you expect to change?"

"I fully thought they were going to make it look like she'd been brutalized, and then release the statement to the world, or hide the fact that she'd had this chip at all. I doubt people would be terribly concerned about a villain in prison being killed, but I *do* think at least some people would care that she was being mistreated. It would be easy to spin a compelling story about it anyways, since she was so young.

"As for the chip, clearly someone made it, and a while ago too, which means this illegal operation has gone unnoticed for years now. I thought it'd be *most* reasonable for whoever did it to kill her just to hide it, but it looks like it's the opposite. They were willing to kill her to make sure it came to light."

"Can you track where the changes came from?"

"No, unfortunately whoever's on the other side is very good. Maybe even better than me. I could only really see what they did and how they went about it, but no idea where they're accessing everything from." Yantra looked almost impressed. "I'll be very interested to see what the autopsy shows."

Silence settled around them once again, Kirin slowly reading through the report as Yantra retreated into her own thoughts and Ifrit's hands tapped out a staccato rhythm. He'd made it all the way to the end when Yantra seemed to come to some conclusion.

She slammed the laptop shut rather sharply, looking straight ahead at nothing in particular, though her gaze was focused.

"Aether's got to be behind this."

"What makes you think that?" Kirin asked.

"This is evidence of illegal experimentation on mien users. Whoever is doing it has some level of sway, some non-insignificant amount of power, so that they couldn't just come out in the open and say it. They're opportunists, that we know, and I don't think they really intended for her—"

"Cara."

"—Cara to get captured, but once she was, they were willing to make the most of it. Even if that meant killing her." Her voice trailed off slowly at the end. "That's... disappointing."

"That's one fucking way of putting it."

"No, I just mean like... they're awful, right? And fundamentally wrong, in a lot of ways. But they seemed so adamant about the whole 'not hurting others with miens' thing that I almost believed them. Sure, Pressure said they're attacking heroes, but heroes kill other mien-users. Is the grabbing children thing almost certainly their recruitment drive? Definitely. But those kids might *actually* grow up somewhere that their abilities aren't something to be scared of, where they would never have had the traumatic awakenings that they did. And yet, in the end, we're just as expendable to them as we are to this damn school."

Kirin didn't know what to say, so he laid a hand on her arm, and she gave him a weak smile.

"It's such a double-edged sword out there, you know? Wanting to be special, like any kid does, and maybe even believing that you are, before you have any proof of it. And then seeing how people that are called 'special' are also called 'demon' in the same breath, and you get scared that all that hatred will apply to you one day." She gripped the laptop with both hands, her knuckles going white. "If you don't have one, you're just no one, but if you do, they might want you dead."

"That's what we're fucking here for." Kirin and Yantra both looked over to Ifrit, who was pointedly looking the other way. "Shit sucks, but just thinking about how it sucks isn't going to change fucking anything. We're here, and that means we *can* do something, and that's why they're fucking scared."

He looked over at them, eyes flickering with fire.

"Because we're going to fucking change this."

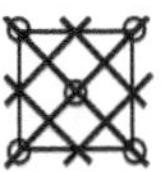

They stayed up for a while longer, Kirin putting on an old hero movie and the three of them climbing onto his bed. It wasn't until Yantra started nodding off that Kirin gently kicked her out, and she waved them bye with a yawn, eyes half shut as she got into the elevator.

"Wait." Kirin grabbed Ifrit by the hand as he moved to go back to his own room. "Uh... could we have a sleepover?"

Ifrit just stared at him, as if he didn't process the question.

"I just... I couldn't fall asleep earlier? Like before Yantra came in, I was having trouble and you seemed pretty awake too when you got here, so I thought maybe you had been struggling too, and I didn't know if... if maybe that would help." Kirin cleared his throat as Ifrit still failed to have a reaction of any kind, good or bad. "It's okay if you don't want to. I just thought that maybe, I mean, since you seemed to sleep so well last night— not that I was watching you!— it could perhaps be helpful to—"

His rambling was forcibly stopped by a hand to the face.

"Shut up. I'll grab my shit. Open the fucking window though."

Kirin moved to do as he was told, feeling like his brain was buzzing slightly, though he wasn't sure why. In his mental fog, it took him several tries to get the window open, and Ifrit was back with his blankets and multiple pillows before Kirin had finished cleaning off the floor. Wordlessly, Ifrit stooped down to help, uncharacteristically not commenting on how many pa-pers were on the ground. It wasn't his fault this time, honestly; when he'd opened the window a pile on his desk had been blown off.

The breeze was irritating, icy against the exposed skin along his hips, which reminded him a bit late that he was still wearing Ifrit's hoodie.

Ifrit usually felt hot to the touch, but even in the wan light of the moon, Kirin could see goosebumps on the other man's arms, and after a moment's hesitation, he took the sweatshirt off and handed it back.

"I don't fucking need it. You can wear it." As if to prove his point, Ifrit sat down resolutely on top of his blankets, instead of under them, though the effect was ruined by the almost imperceptible shiver that ran through him at the same time.

"It's okay, I'm pretty warm right now." Kirin offered it out again, and Ifrit took it slowly, as if waiting to see if Kirin would change his mind. Once it was in his hands, he just sat there, still staring. "You're too nice."

Ifrit narrowed his eyes, sensing that his own words were being used against him.

"You can ask, if you want to know."

"You never take off your shirt in front of people." It was a statement, not a question, but that seemed as good as Ifrit was going to manage.

"Well, you've already seen, so it's not like it'd do any good anymore." Kirin moved closer to his bed, forcing himself to turn and slide past Ifrit's pile on the floor, even though it exposed his back fully to his friend. He was proud of himself, honestly, for being so relaxed about the whole thing. If he ignored how tense his muscles were, how the tips of his fingers were starting to go numb, he could almost pretend he wasn't anxious at all.

"Is that why you wear those shirts all the time?" Though Kirin hadn't heard Ifrit stand up, his voice sounded close to Kirin's shoulder, close enough to make him flinch. He regretted it immediately, silently cursing himself. He was *fine*. It was just Ifrit, who wasn't going to judge him at all.

"Yeah, they go up my neck and over my shoulders a bit, so if I wear low cut shirts, they're pretty visible, or the bandages are since I usually keep them wrapped not to hurt anyone. If it's a bad day, I'll wear my hair down with a looser shirt, but those are pretty rare." He was stuck now, standing by the edge of the bed, facing away from Ifrit, trying to convince himself to just lie down, but his muscles wouldn't cooperate, keeping him frozen in place.

"It hurts?" The concern in Ifrit's voice broke the spell, letting him turn around to reassure his friend.

"Not really! Just sometimes my muscles get really tight, and it's hard to stretch properly because the scar tissue goes pretty deep in some areas; honestly, I think it itches more than anything else. So, some days, I don't like having anything tight against the skin because it just makes the itching that much worse." He was breathing shallowly, his heart racing, but he was doing great. He tried to focus on Ifrit's face, on Ifrit's eyes, which were roaming the crystal tendrils that crept over the ridge. Ifrit's hand was raised slightly, like he'd been about to touch Kirin.

A moment of silence stretched between them, and Ifrit did reach out.

His hand brushed gently up to the diamond skin that curled over Kirin's shoulder and kissed his collarbone. The crystal almost looked red from certain angles, but the pulsing of his veins was hidden from view, firstly by the facets of the diamond itself, and secondly from the jagged edge of metal that puckered his skin.

Ifrit's fingers came away a moment later, a thin strip of blood appearing on the pad of one.

"It's sharp." Kirin knew it was redundant, but he couldn't think of anything else to say. The fire around Ifrit's neck was getting caught by the crystal, sending a dusting of light back across his face and turning his eyes to liquid amber.

Ifrit made contact again, more cautiously this time. Kirin wanted to look down to see where he was tracing, since he couldn't feel a thing, not through any of the patches outlined in metal. But he couldn't tear his gaze away from Ifrit's, the way he was following a path on Kirin's skin like it was the most important thing in the world, every now and then his fingers grazing the unblemished skin off to the side. Kirin was careful not to flinch again, hardly breathing, afraid of scaring Ifrit off, but every time it felt like electricity running through him, rooting him to the spot.

His breath caught entirely as Ifrit's palm brushed the side of his neck, following one of the scars that trailed farther up. Ifrit was so focused, his lips parted slightly in concentration, head tilted slightly, though the usual furrow in his brow was absent. He looked... softer without it. Something stirred in Kirin's heart as he wished he could bottle that expression and tuck it away forever.

A finger reached the edge of the path but continued upward, until Ifrit hit the ridge of his jaw. From there he traced forward, the edge of his nail scraping ever so faintly along until he found the natural scar, brushing the shape of it with the pad of his thumb. Kirin couldn't contain the shiver it elicited, and Ifrit's eyes jumped to his, widening as if he hadn't realized what he was doing.

He pulled away abruptly, looking off to the side and clearing his throat. The sudden lack of contact made Kirin almost gasp, involuntarily taking a half step forward.

"Why do you hide that?" There was something off about Ifrit's voice, but Kirin felt like his head was full of cotton and he couldn't put his finger on what.

"What?"

Ifrit looked back at Kirin, his face flushed from the cold air streaming in through the window. The wind had picked up significantly, but Kirin felt overly hot, not cold.

"The scars. Why do you hide them?"

That left Kirin puzzled for a moment. Ifrit, of all people, *knew* how much appearance mattered for heroes, knew how they were expected to be beyond perfect, beyond human. And then it clicked; Ifrit wasn't asking him why he hid the scars from everyone, he was asking why Kirin hid them from *him.*

"I hate them." He was glad that Ifrit's eyes flickered in the firelight, because it made it so much easier to focus on them.

How could anyone think red was an ominous color when Ifrit made it feel so safe? "They remind me of things I don't like to think about. I can't even pretend they're not there because every time I move, I feel them, like constantly having a knife in your back."

"That's not how you usually scar." Ifrit took a tiny half step closer.

"Nah, thankfully." Kirin almost brought Ifrit's hand back up to the scar he'd been tracing on his jaw, but he lost the courage when their fingers came close. Instead, he pointed at it, the result of tripping and hitting his face against a stair as a kid. "If I'm using my mien on a part of my body and it gets cut off or... otherwise separated, it just stays like that."

"That's really metal in there?" Something flickered across Ifrit's face, almost like recognition. The crease between his brows was coming back and Kirin wanted to turn back time, to bring back that peaceful, open-mouthed wonder from just a few minutes before.

"All the way down." He responded to the question instead. "The doctor wondered if trying to remove the metal might help, to reconnect the tissue and see if I could change it back, but... trying to reconnect something hasn't worked in the past."

"*How?*" Ifrit was so close that if Kirin leaned forward even slightly, they'd be touching. But Ifrit's eyes were suspiciously bright.

"It was supposed to be a good day, you know?" Kirin found himself sitting on his bed, not trusting his legs to hold him. "Where I was born, they didn't have too many doctors, certainly not specialty doctors. Since I was getting older, closer to puberty, my parents got me an appointment with one of the foremost transition specialists in the world."

"In Satol." Ifrit sat on the very edge of the bed, their usual roles reversed as *he* seemed concerned about scaring *Kirin* away.

"That was my first big trip, too. My dad and I went alone, since my siblings had just been born. My mom was worried about us traveling so far by ourselves, but she said that since I was there, it'd be okay." Kirin allowed himself a sad smile. "My mien had presented itself by then, and she used to say that if I worked on it, I'd be invincible one day. That nothing could ever hurt me unless I wanted it to."

Instinctively, he clenched his left hand.

"We were on one of the lower floors in the building when it fell. We were more or less alone, actually, cut off from the other people by a lot of metal that was starting to melt. I was stuck under some, so I couldn't really see it, but he had... he had gotten impaled, basically, with some rebar. He knew he wasn't going to make it.

"It's frustrating too, because Yantra's right. They'd rather I was dead, because these scars show I did use my mien, illegally, to get out. I think he knew, somehow, that it was going to get stuck, and didn't want me to have to walk around with a visible mark that I'd broken the law, when there was never a chance that I could save him. And I couldn't even get myself to move while he was conscious, knowing just how badly he didn't want me to use it." Kirin couldn't look at Ifrit anymore, the shame flooding him as he lowered his watery gaze to his hands.

"I don't know if I can explain just how *hot* it was in there. Maybe if I'd waited a little longer, I would've just been able to walk out, since there was metal just *liquifying* everywhere. That saved me, apparently, because when it snuck in around what I was able to harden, it seared the flesh enough that I didn't bleed out." Kirin took a shaky breath, trying to ignore the way that his back felt like it was burning all over again, like the flames were just out of sight. "Kept me awake, too, which meant when the explosion went off, I had time to react, since it turns out we were right next to it."

Ifrit had been in the middle of moving subtly closer, but he froze, his eyes wide and horrified.

"Your dad died in the explosion?" He asked in a hushed voice.

"No, he died from blood loss alone." Kirin had been practically feral when he'd gotten free, clutching his dad's body like if he just waited long enough, if he yelled loud enough, the heartbeat would come back, his *life* would come back. When the explosion finally hit, Kirin had shielded the corpse, only thrown free at the very end. "We know that for sure. I got stuck, again, under part of the building, but I don't know how I got free of that. When I woke up, I was in the back of an ambulance, with Pressure, actually, if you can believe it.

"Apparently, I wasn't just close to where the big explosion went off, I was so close that the kid who did it got blown right next to me. I don't remember much about him, and I'd honestly hoped she'd forgotten I was there, but her speech says that she didn't. I'm half afraid that she knows it was me, but she's never said anything about it and I'm happy keeping it that way." Kirin lapsed into silence, not sure what else to say.

"There were blanket pardons for kids who used their miens there, since there were too many mien activations to properly track." Ifrit said slowly, like he was piecing together his own thoughts. "If you're worried that she's going to turn you in or something, she won't."

"I don't even know if it's that, it's more like... I don't want to be seen as that pathetic kid, you know? When I came to, I was freaking out, the only reason I calmed down at all was because there was someone else there too." Kirin frowned. "I never really bothered to think about it, but I guess I *do* remember the kid, since it must've been him. I wish I'd realized that then, and maybe I could've said something to, I don't know, make him feel better? Let him know it wasn't his fault?"

Still in his own thoughts, Kirin was caught entirely off guard when Ifrit grabbed him and practically slammed him into a hug. Kirin's instinct was to pull away, worried that Ifrit was going to cut his hands on Kirin's back, but one of Ifrit's hands was in his hair, the other resting on his waist; Kirin's face pressed against Ifrit's neck, which smelled faintly of ash from the newly extinguished flames.

"You're too fucking nice." Ifrit's voice was muffled, since one of Kirin's ears was pressed to Ifrit's throat, where he could more readily hear the man's heartbeat instead of his words. "She won't think you're weak. You were what, ten when it happened?"

"Eleven." Kirin protested weakly, but he didn't try to pull out of the hug.

"Whatever. It wasn't your shit to deal with, and fuck were you just traumatized. Stop only thinking about everyone else. Take care of yourself too." Ifrit's hand trembled slightly as he stroked Kirin's hair. "It seems like no one ever told you it wasn't *your* fault, either."

Kirin's hands were pressed against Ifrit's shirt, and he felt the fabric bunch underneath his fingers as they slowly curled into fists.

"I don't think you need to hide a damn thing." Ifrit's voice was firm, even if his hands were not. "You're a fucking hero and have been since you were just a *kid*. We're going to figure this shit out, Aether can fuck off, and you and me, we're going to make sure no more kids have scars, okay?"

His hand slid from Kirin's hair to his chin, tilting up Kirin's face to look at him. Without Ifrit's fire, the room was dark, only lit by the half moon outside.

"Okay." Kirin's voice was small, even to his own ears, so he gave a nod too, to make sure Ifrit understood.

Ifrit's hand let go of his chin, and Kirin braced himself for the rush of cold when Ifrit moved away entirely, but it never came. Instead, Ifrit shifted slightly, pulling Kirin's head back down to rest in the crook of his shoulder, his hand moving jerkily as he smoothed back Kirin's hair. The longer he did, the less awkward he got, Kirin feeling the tension slip from his body as he leaned back against the wall, Ifrit's cheek resting on Kirin's forehead.

Kirin felt strange again, like his heartbeat was racing, but also so much at peace. The angle should've been uncomfortable, yet the feeling of fingers in his hair was so *good* that he found himself starting to drift off.

"We should probably go to bed now, huh?" The words came out slightly slurred, his cheek pressed against Ifrit's chest.

"Mm, yeah." Ifrit cleared his throat and let go of Kirin, who blinked drowsily, confused as to why Ifrit had stopped. When Kirin sat up, Ifrit stood immediately, wiping his palms on his pants like they were sweaty. Kirin opened his mouth to protest, to try to walk back what he'd said, but Ifrit cut him off. "Marketing in the morning. Bitch'll be mad if we're late."

"Don't remind me." Kirin's head still felt muddled, but the cold air was finally starting to reach him. Ifrit too, it seemed, as he put the hoodie back on, and Kirin idly wondered if it smelled like his shampoo now, instead of Ifrit's. "And Ifrit?"

Ifrit looked back at him, the moonlight striking just right to make his eyes look like they were almost glowing.

"Thanks."

Ifrit just grunted in acknowledgement and rolled over, seeming to fall asleep instantly. Kirin pulled his legs into bed more slowly, a smile playing on his lips as he put his head on his pillow. The scent of apples and smoke lulled him into unconsciousness, his dreams filled with warm arms and gentle hands, and a gruff voice telling him that everything would be alright.

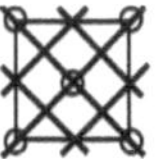

In the new group lineup, Adlivun and Aïcha were the first team to move out, Phoenix working on standby, waiting to be called in the moment either were injured. The whole class was tense; Pressure worked them extra hard in Combat Training to try to force them to focus. It wasn't until the three of them walked back in, however, that everyone relaxed, feeling that perhaps the trouble had been overstated after all.

Ness and Wyrm were the second to go, for a typical mien call, and they encountered resistance. The heroes on duty interceded almost immediately, but Wyrm still had a chunk practically scooped out from his side before Phoenix could get there, the villain disappearing before anyone could catch a glimpse.

"I was standing right next to him, too." Ness confided with the class, tucked against Yantra and wrapped in no fewer than three blankets. "I didn't even see a thing."

The weeks passed, and it happened again. And again. And again. Medusa nearly lost her arm, but felt something just in time and dodged, only getting stabbed in the hand before backup arrived. Antaeus was hurt severely, apparently a whole portion of his shoulder just *gone* briefly, until Phoenix got her hands on him. Lilin's hit was nearest to her heart, but she was taking it better than most, because she, at least, had gotten a glimpse.

"She was small, smaller than Ness, but I did notice that she had a similar kind of blurry quality." Lilin explained to them after giving her statement to Pressure and the other assembled heroes and officers. "It didn't seem as strong, I guess would be the way to phrase it, and once I caught sight of her, I only lost her again because I blacked out."

That, unfortunately, led to Ness being asked to spar with every single one of them, both in and out of class, which she did gladly, if not tiredly.

Each of their missions was, technically, confidential. But they'd begun texting the group chat to say when their missions were only rescues, and not mien appearances. It helped, that they didn't need to be on edge every time one of them got sent out— which was now every single day, since the school insisted on sending students at the same intervals as before, despite having one class instead of twenty— but on days that the assignment *was* reported to be a mien appearance, the tension in the air was palpable.

With a month left in the semester, a month left until they'd be allowed to fight back, only Kirin, Kapre, and Ifrit had never been assigned to a mien appearance mission. Ifrit only texted Kirin when he was sent out, and it was then on Kirin to relay it back to the rest of the class. Until the message came through, he felt like he was paralyzed, terrified that Ifrit would be out there alone with no one to watch his back.

It felt inevitable that one of them would face the same thing that all their classmates had, and that pushed them to practice harder, wake up earlier, and run themselves ragged. They started so early in the morning and ran so late into the night, Ifrit had taken to sleeping on Kirin's floor permanently, so they could wake each other up. Pressure nearly burst with pride during combat classes, watching how far they'd all come.

It was Monday, rather late in the day, when Ifrit and Phoenix were pulled out of class by Shifter, who now swapped in and out with Pressure to bring them to off campus missions. His face was grim, and Kirin couldn't tell if it was just his usual haggard appearance, or something more. Ifrit straightened up and walked out without a second thought, Phoenix following more slowly, constantly exhausted. She wasn't sleeping, Kirin knew, from the number of times he'd run into her making food late into the night.

Then came the waiting. With the supersonic jets the school used, it rarely took longer than an hour to arrive on site, usually closer to thirty minutes. But that hour ticked by without any word. Kirin began checking his phone every five minutes, every minute, every thirty seconds. The rest of the class grew fidgety too, even Pressure's mouth pressed into a fine line. An hour and a half. Two.

The first half of the class ended, but Pressure said to not bother coming back from the break. Instead of the usual rush to the dorm, they clumped together anxiously, waiting for news.

"Nothing from Phoenix?" Ness asked Adlivun hopefully, but the tall woman only shook her head.

When they made it to the dorm, Aïcha vaulted over the couch to turn on the news, while Yantra ran to grab her laptop, the rest of the class filing in and filling out the couches, all eyes plastered to the screen. The first broadcast wasn't showing anything of note, no great disasters or fights, so Aïcha switched to a different feed, which was showing something equally mundane as the first.

"Yantra?" Adlivun was the first person to ask, which felt wrong, since she usually knew so much.

Yantra looked up from her laptop with a frown.

"I don't know where they are." She admitted. "Usually, it's on at least one of the rising hero speculation pages, since they practically track our movements, but I can't find anything about where they might be, at least not from anywhere public."

"Can you check other perhaps not so public places?" Surprisingly, it was Kuafu who asked. He didn't look conflicted at all, either, his dark eyes flashing with determination.

Before Yantra could say anything, Kirin's phone buzzed.

He practically jumped out of his skin, and nearly dropped his phone, or worse, hardened his hand and destroyed it. Within seconds, the entire class was arrayed around him, peering at the message on the screen.

"'Just a glorified fucking publicity mission.'" Dulu read out loud. "'They made us parade around to get footage for fucking ages so couldn't message. Doing charity work for a bit and then coming back.'"

The whole class breathed a sigh of relief, and then almost at once dispersed, now that the anxiety had passed. It was fine. They'd be back soon, and while Ifrit might be annoyed about the boring mission, it wasn't a deadly one. Almost a waste to make Phoenix go too; she really needed some rest.

Kirin was about to go to his room, maybe just to take a nap, or at least do *something* to relax, when his phone went off again. Kapre, who had been settling into a chair on the other side of the room, their hair pulled up and legs swung over the side, had pulled theirs out too. His heart sank slightly, and he opened the message.

Mien appearance, East City. Hero students Kirin and Kapre to report to DS immediately.

24

Alone

PRESSURE WASN'T ALONE WHEN they got there, Majesty standing off to the side looking angry.

"You can say no." Pressure drew their attention immediately, though Majesty was pretending they weren't there. "Phoenix won't be able to get back for some time, so I am giving you full authority to turn down this mission."

Kirin and Kapre looked at one another, uncertain. Majesty, however, was apparently done with waiting.

"There is an active situation just outside the park, and I was told that one of you is invincible." She snapped. As always, she was already in her costume, which still bore bloodstains from when her own student had been injured.

"What's the situation?" Kirin crossed his arms and looked down at her.

"A mien appearance." She snapped her mouth shut after the last word, unwilling to give more information than that, so Kirin looked to Pressure, who, for once, seemed reluctant to share.

"A child of a known hero has suddenly and violently produced a mien." Pressure began slowly. "None of the local heroes are able to get close safely; Phoenix was the only person with a healing mien on the island, and most of those on the continents are unwilling to bring themselves here, considering the recent string of attacks."

"What's the kid's ability?"

"Think of it as a mix between ours." Pressure pointed to herself and Majesty, who threw her hands up and walked away to brood. "A type of visible, glowing force that, thus far, has been able to cut through anything and any*one* who has gotten close."

"How old is the kid?"

"Nine."

Kirin looked at Kapre, who was staring right back with sad eyes. He didn't need to ask.

"We'll do it." Majesty straightened up, her face briefly going slack with shock. "Give us a few minutes to change, and then bring us there."

"I can't sense anyone within a five-block radius." Kapre's voice came through Kirin's headset in a way that sounded slightly tinny, or perhaps it was because of his mien. "You're good to proceed."

Kirin nodded, though there was no one around to see him. Drones were surveying the scene from the air, but they were up high enough that he'd be surprised if they caught the movement. All around him was rubble, the child's power more developed than Kirin would've expected for someone so young. There was currently a one minute gap between blasts, and he'd only just gotten into position, at the edge of the range of their power.

The child was a speck a few streets away, but when the wave came, he could still hear them scream.

He was surprised by the force of it; the strength was like Bia's, if he remembered correctly from all those months ago when Majesty's class had attacked. His pants were immediately filled with tears, the extra oxygen charges for his mask falling away as the pocket was ripped clean through. He'd only crystallized the top layer of skin, as he usually did, but even at such a great distance, he felt the push, the slight give as it hit.

When the light faded, he unknit his joints and moved forward, breathing in deeply to replenish his stores and add another layer of protection, going deeper into his skin. This time, when the blast hit, he was only pushed back a centimeter, despite having made it past the first street.

"Visibility on child now." Kirin had to unharden his jaw to speak, which felt like such a waste of carbon, but it had to be done. "They look uninjured but distraught."

"That's to be expected." Pressure's voice came through, the sound just as distorted as it had been with Kapre. "A few people died when the first wave came."

Kirin crystallized his mouth again, not wanting to say something he might regret. How many times would this have to happen? How many kids would have to live knowing they'd damaged someone beyond repair?

He hadn't made it very far when the next eruption came, but somehow, he knew it was going to be stronger than the first two, and not only because of the now reduced distance between them. He had to dig his hands into the ground to keep from being pushed backward, and he heard the quiet sound of diamond hitting pavement, as some of his hair was chopped off. It was lucky that he had curled in on himself too, as the portions of his clothing not hidden by his arms and torso were shorn clean off. His shirt was faring better than his pants— he made a mental note to thank Nwabudike later for all his rigorous testing— though the sleeves were torn to pieces and the shoulders were starting to go. His arms, fully crystallized, were exposed to the world, and the realization locked him in place for a moment.

"Kirin, are you injured?" Pressure's voice came through, and he realized that the drone could see enough for her to tell he was still on the ground. Not wanting to drop the crystallization on his face, he stood rather than spoke, and could hear her breathe out sharply over the comm.

The child was now only a dozen meters away, and they heard him stand, or rather they heard the concrete crack as he pulled his hands and feet out of it. Their eyes widened, and he hardly had time to shield his heart and face when the next blast came, being pushed back a meter before it passed over him and into the remains of a nearby house.

"Go away!" The kid's voice was so high-pitched and desperate his heart broke from the sound. "You can't take me away!"

Kirin pulled his arm away from his face to show that he meant no harm, only for another blast to hit him square in the head and shatter his mask into pieces.

The cloth mask he always wore underneath was torn apart between his sharp skin and the force, but the cameras were too far away to see any detail, and with his face entirely crystallized he wasn't sure anyone would recognize him anyway. It did, however, make for a scary figure, and the child recoiled, looking terrified.

"It's alright." Kirin released his mien on his entire face, willing to take the risk if it helped the child calm down. "I'm not going to take you anywhere."

"Are you a hero or a villain?" The kid raised their hands, though they hardly seemed able to control when the waves shot off. They looked even younger than nine, with a shock of bright blue hair and matching eyes. Hair that was the same color as Majesty's.

"Right now, I'm just here to help you. Not a hero, not a villain, just a friend." Kirin was able to creep a few steps closer, hands held out to his sides. "Who are you afraid of taking you somewhere? The woman from the TV?"

The kid shook their head, and that was enough to trigger another wave, their whole body glowing from the inside before it shot off in every direction. The light had been enough warning for him to cover his face with his arms, only needing to stiffen his shoulders to take the force of it. His feet had already been dug in from the previous hit, so he didn't move at all, and when he put his arms back down, he found a pair of eyes looking at him almost hopefully.

"You know about her?" Though they were alone, the child whispered, swinging their head around to check for interlopers. The movement pulled their stained t-shirt away from their collarbone, revealing purple bruises that looked painfully fresh. "I'm not supposed to talk about her."

"We can talk about her, if you like." Kirin tentatively took a step forward, making sure to stab his feet into the ground.

"I was hoping you might be her." They admitted. "It was hard to tell from far away. But you *are* wearing white."

"Do you not feel safe here?" He resorted to sitting on the ground and scooching closer, only about five meters left between them. Though it kept him from moving backward, the next blast hit him just right, and he felt his earpiece snap. Kapre would have to follow his progress through the ground now.

"I don't want to be a hero." The kid said it guiltily, as if it was a confession.

"You don't have to be."

"My dad says I have to. Says I won't be anyone if I'm not. And now that everyone knows I'm not normal they'll hate me if I don't." They were so matter of fact about it. "The lady in white said that I could be safe there. That I could just grow up, like a normal person."

Yantra's words from a month before rung in Kirin's ears. A double-edged sword indeed.

"If we all went away, we'd have to stay away." Kirin barely braced in time, a small cut appearing on his cheek where he hadn't fully managed to crystallize. He ignored it, though he could see the blue eyes follow the red line with fear. "If we all hid, we'd have to stay in hiding, forever. It's not fair that you and I have to spend so much time convincing people that we're people too, and I wish I could promise you that no one will ever treat you poorly, but a good friend of mine doesn't make promises he can't keep, and I try not to either."

"She said it'd be safe." They repeated, more stubbornly.

"Maybe for a little bit." Kirin was only a meter away; he could practically lie down on his stomach and reach them. "But they've done some bad things, and the police are already looking for them, the heroes too."

"Then where is safe?" The tears had returned, and when the attack hit Kirin this time, he was flattened to the ground, feeling the rest of his shirt get torn free. In such bright light, the darkened patches on his back stood out, gray against brilliant white. And maybe that was a good thing.

"I wish I could point somewhere and say 'this is safe,' but I can't do that right now." Kirin was so close, using the act of sitting up to put him within arm's reach. "I'm not going to lie to you, so I'll tell you the truth. When I was your age, someone like me could *never* become a hero."

"Is it because you're scary looking?"

Kirin cracked a grin at that.

"Exactly. Weird looking too, huh? All big and shiny."

"I like the shiny part."

"Well, thank you." Kirin released his palm and pricked the center, focusing hard to do what he'd been practicing, stealing the idea from Ifrit. It seemed to work, or at least it was a diamond in a very rough dolphin shape. He put it on the ground and nudged it toward the kid, who was at least interested enough that when the next wave came, it only felt like being hit with a car, instead of a train. "But I never thought I'd be able to become a hero. I thought that they'd say I was *too* scary and just send me home. Imagine my surprise when instead, they told me that I got in."

The kid looked up from the little trinket with wide eyes.

"Right? Super surprising. I'll admit I was too scared to ask my teacher how I'd made it, but one day she told me why anyways. Do you know why?"

They shook their head.

"She said that they want to have people like me there. That maybe if we show people that even folks that seem pretty scary aren't, that maybe if everyone got used to us, people wouldn't be so afraid anymore. That's all it is. They're scared, because, well, we're a little scary."

"I'm not scary." They protested.

"You sure scared me." Kirin adopted a very serious tone, jutting out his bottom lip and nodding, earning the smallest of giggles. "I don't think you're really scary, though. I think you were just scared yourself."

At those words, their eyes got sad again, and two successive hits came, throwing Kirin back on the ground hard enough that it cracked underneath him. Before he could get up, a small face appeared in the corner of his vision, peering nervously at him. He released his mien on his head, having to drop even the crystallization of his hair so he could pry himself from the hole he'd made.

"I'm okay, don't you worry. It'll take more than that to put me out." He gave a smile, which seemed to reassure them some. "But do you want to tell me what happened to make you so upset?"

The kid looked around again, though no one could have snuck up without them noticing. Kirin felt a slight nudge underneath his finger, and saw a small bump in the pavement, one he was certain hadn't been there before. He tapped twice, letting Kapre know everything was okay.

"I don't know if I'm allowed." They finally whispered.

"I won't tell anyone, I promise." Kirin held a hand over his heart and raised the other. "Hero's honor."

After another furtive look around, they scooted closer, so they were right up against Kirin's side. He released his mien where they touched, cursing the loss of his shirt. He'd just have to move them if they showed signs of glowing again.

"My dad wants me to be a hero real bad." They focused on the little creature he'd given them, walking it across the ground. "He was mad that I hadn't shown a mien yet, so he kept saying I didn't want to be a hero bad enough. That I was being bad, by not wanting to."

"What do you want to be?"

"I wanna be a teacher." They frowned. "He said that's not allowed though."

"In some places. But if you work really hard, I think you can do it."

"Really?" This time, when they glowed, Kirin didn't think it was from their mien. "You really think so?"

"I know so." Kirin released his hand and ruffled their hair. "Even if it's hard right now, *I'm* gonna work my hardest so that you can take it easy, okay?"

"Okay." They agreed.

"Now what do you say we go meet some of my friends? Kapre's really cool. I think you'll like them a lot. Maybe if you're reeeally lucky, they'll even make you your own pond." Kirin stood up slowly, doing his best not to startle them as he towered over them. They looked at him with perhaps even more hopeful eyes as he reached out a hand. They took it, tiny diamond dolphin still firmly clutched in their other hand.

The ground suddenly rocked beneath them, and Kirin released his mien entirely, wrapping the child up with both arms as he shielded their body with his own. The vague gray shadow he'd seen out of the corner of his eye resolved itself into a person, smaller than Ness, her hand just missing where his back had been seconds before. There was no time to consider how on Earth she'd made it onto the island, as bright light suddenly made his own skin glow, his bones dark lines within the flesh. Kirin's momentum carried them both to the ground, and Kirin braced himself on his forearms, creating just enough space for him to crystallize his chest and neck without harming the child, before the force of their power almost threw him off.

"It's okay, there's just someone else here now." Kirin focused on keeping calm, ignoring the fact that he was now bleeding. He hadn't managed to fully use his mien, too scared to hurt the kid, and now deep cuts ran the length of his arms and the tops of his thighs. They hadn't seemed to notice, cowering within the shelter of his shadow, the gray figure just out of his vision. "This is going to seem scary for a second, but I'm just calling for help."

Kirin slammed his arm into the ground, trying to get Kapre's attention so they would send in help, when he was kicked hard in the face.

It wasn't the most forceful hit he'd ever taken, Ifrit's weakest punch far more damaging, but the edges of the stitching on her shoe scratched up his cheek before he ducked his head further, making sure the kid was covered from all sides. They were looking at him with terrified eyes, tears streaming again.

"I'm going to pick you up, and then we're going to run, okay?" He managed to keep his voice calm even as he felt a blade slash across his lower back. She couldn't do her more damaging attack multiple times in a row, then? "Don't look back at her, focus on me."

He waited until he received a nod and took a breath.

Quickly triggering and releasing his mien on his feet let him practically spring up from the ground and start sprinting, the kid hugged to his chest and the backs of his arms hardened to prevent any attack from hitting them, which surely the law would allow. The woman was hardly expecting him to move and lurched out of the way, fading to invisibility once he was up, but he didn't stop running for one block, two. Kapre and Pressure were ten blocks north. He just had to get this kid there. He wasn't bleeding as badly as he'd originally thought, and he could run for a good long time still.

And then a gunshot went off.

He stumbled but kept going, briefly afraid that it'd hit something vital because he didn't seem to be in any pain, only to realize what had happened. They'd hit one of his scars.

The second shot didn't find him so lucky, lodging just above his hip. They were no marksman, that was for sure, and the distance between them was growing, Kirin was certain, until she appeared directly in front of him.

Kirin made a choice.

There was a lush lawn right next to them, and his footsteps had been forceful enough that Kapre should have been able to track them, and what Kirin was doing. He couldn't stop before he ran headlong into her, her arm already a blur. Kirin threw the child to the side, the ground coming up to meet them, their eyes horrified. A moment later, they were swallowed, the ground smooth and level once again, the kid likely tucked into a hidden cave until the danger had passed.

In Kirin's eyes, the villain was running in slow motion, the distance between them shrunk down to heartbeats. Oddly, his shoulders loosened, the weight of a different choice falling away now that death finally seemed to have caught up with him again. His legs hadn't gotten the memo, still trying to push him backward, to make the space stop shrinking, but the law decreed he either die a hero right there, or live as a villain for saving himself. The ultimate test of loyalty for people the government could hardly stand to trust.

And yet.

An expression came to him out of a memory, of flickering light and open-mouthed wonder, of crimson eyes shining in the dark. Of scars that never healed.

He turned faster than she— or Kirin himself— rightly thought he could, his back to her as she reached out. She screamed, both in anger and pain it seemed, and he rolled away unscathed, her hand cut and bleeding as she found diamond and metal harder than smooth human flesh.

She plainly wasn't used to being injured, stumbling away and failing to fade into invisibility again, looking up at him with murderous intent. But before she could act on it, the ground opened and she was caught within, arms pinned down by her side as she writhed, trying to break free from a prison of concrete and stone.

"It's not mine!" She screamed as she flailed, nearly smashing her face on the rim of the pavement. She couldn't do much more than that, since everything below her neck was encased in earth. "Move— now! It wasn't mine!"

Kirin tensed, suddenly remembering that there had been someone shooting, fighting the urge to use his mien fully as he looked around. The only attack he was greeted with was a grip on his leg, but when he looked down, it was only the child from before, covered in dirt. Looking over to where they'd been interred, Kirin realized they'd used their mien to force their way out, soil splattered all over the street.

"It's okay. She's caught now." Kirin leaned down and patted their head, only now truly seeing the blood on his arms. It was sheeting down to his elbows, but a quick inspection showed it wasn't deep at all. Same with the cuts to his legs; the bullet wound in his back seemed to be the worst, lodged against his hip bone, though it only bled sluggishly, and didn't hurt so badly that he couldn't stand.

"But the man..." The child trailed off, looking behind Kirin and suddenly looking frightened again. Kirin turned around to find himself staring down the barrel of a gun.

"Afraid you're not the one that we're looking for today." The gun cocked.

And then the man's body exploded.

The kid had stepped out from behind Kirin without him knowing, and somehow, instinctively, only aimed the blast forward. Kirin stood in shock, blood and gore raining down around them as the weight of what just happened hit him.

"Look at me." He grabbed the kid by their shoulders and made them face him, his hands shaking. "Listen. This is very important."

They looked eerily calm, but their gaze met his.

"When the police, when the heroes, when your *father* asks, tell them that you didn't do that on purpose." He couldn't even look at where the man had been standing, was entirely ignoring the woman in the hole behind him. If Aether meant *any* of the shit they said, she'd keep her mouth shut. "You were scared. You didn't know what you were doing. It was an accident. Do you hear me?"

They nodded, fear and understanding setting in, but slowly, too slowly, when Kirin could see Majesty's bright hair only a few streets away. He shook them once, as if the motion could instill the proper sense of panic in them.

"Say you understand. Do not tell anyone, ever, that you did

that, okay? If you do, they will take you away, and I won't be able to help you then. I'll say it was an accident too. It'll be our little secret."

They nodded again, firmer this time. Kirin's heart was pounding in his chest, faster than it had been when he'd been getting shot at, faster than when the villain appeared in front of him. He was *not* going to let them kill this little kid. He was not.

When he picked the kid back up and straightened out, the woman in the hole was regarding him coolly, but with something like respect. He didn't have time to say anything to her—and what would he say? Threaten her? Beg her to keep quiet?—before Pressure and Majesty were there, Kapre running along behind them.

"Bán, come here." Majesty reached out and the kid shrunk away, looking up at Kirin. "It's okay baby, you can come with me today. It's okay."

Kirin felt Bán's grip on him tighten. Majesty, for once, looked human as hurt flickered across her face.

"I'm sorry sweetheart. I'm not mad at you." She took a step forward hesitantly, as if expecting to be cut down any minute. "Can you come with me, and we'll get you cleaned up? Kirin here needs to wash up too."

Bán looked at Kirin for a moment, who gave them a smile and gently put them down.

"Your mom'll take you from here, okay? If you get scared again, or need anything, she knows where to find me." Kirin ignored the screaming in his legs and kneeled to be more eye level with them. "If you ever need me, you can come find me."

When Bán didn't look convinced, Kirin leaned closer.

"And if you want me to go scare your dad a little, I can do that too."

That got a small giggle, and Bán took one last look at Kirin before stumbling back to Majesty, who wrapped them in her arms and pressed her cheek to their hair, inhaling sharply. After a few moments she picked them up, giving Kirin a curt nod, some semblance of her composure returning as she walked away. Bán's face watched Kirin over her shoulder with unblinking eyes until she turned a corner and they were lost to sight.

Once they were gone, Kirin sagged, the pain from his arms, his legs, his *back* coming in sharper than before. Kapre rushed forward, but he waved them off, struggling to his feet.

"I want to find out what she knows." He managed, turning to look back at the villain still trapped in the ground. Frustratingly, she seemed to have passed out from the pain, her head lolling behind her. He cursed softly, suddenly desperate to know who she'd been talking to.

Kapre crouched down, briefly slumping to one side before their eyes opened again.

"She's just unconscious." Kapre confirmed, slowly standing back up. "I can feel her heartbeat, it's steady."

"Kirin, sit down until medical arrives." Pressure had one hand to her headset, looking worried again. "How much of that blood is yours?"

He realized that he was covered in a fine mist of blood spatter from head to toe, the only thing discerning that he was injured at all was the density of blood, not the presence of it.

"Not that much." His back twinged in protestation against the sentence. "Bán freaked out and had another episode when the man arrived, and he got hit close range."

"It's a good thing you're relatively indestructible then." Pressure nudged the largest remaining piece of the man, his foot, with her own. "Still, you must have reacted incredibly fast. Good job."

"There was always a light that came beforehand." His mouth felt dry. The scars on his back hopefully were enough to confuse any camera that might have been watching, the shine coming from Bán distorting the image anyway. It was plausible. It was. It was why he in particular had been called to this mission.

Pressure didn't question him further, stepping back to let medical through, who promptly began fussing over Kirin, and their captured villain. Kapre had to go back on the ground to release her from her prison, revealing the full extent of the injury to her arm.

It looked like it had been crushed and finely shredded at the same time, the skin punctured all over and the forearm altogether too flat. Kirin shuddered slightly, thinking that it was true that some miens just did not pair well against each other.

"Who..." Kirin suddenly found himself short of breath, feeling dizzy. One of the paramedics came over to him and caught his head, just as everything went black.

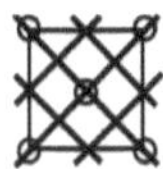

When he woke up, he was in a hospital bed, but clearly back on campus, if the view from the window was correct. The sun was low on the horizon, and though he felt like a steaming pile of garbage, he didn't also feel like a *dry* pile of garbage, so he guessed that he'd only been out for a few hours at most. That must mean that Ifrit was back too, probably irritated after spending so long filming. Maybe Kirin could convince him to watch one of the cheesy movies that Ifrit always grumbled about, but Kirin loved, on account of his injuries.

There were fresh bandages on his arms and legs; when he wiggled slightly in the bed, he could feel some against his back too. It stung more than properly hurt, and he found himself smiling, fingers and toes all still moving and without pain.

The door slid open, and he looked up to see Ness, who looked back at him with wide eyes.

"You're awake!" She shoved the juice she was carrying into his hands, sitting down in a nearby chair and scooting closer. "How do you feel?"

"Fine!" Kirin responded cheerily, which was honestly the truth. He'd expected to come off much worse, and if it wasn't for the lingering discomfort, he would've suspected that Phoenix had been by, so minor were the injuries now. But maybe she had been by and was just too tired to heal him fully. He really needed to make sure she was sleeping more; he should talk to her about that later. "What time is it?"

"Just about seventeen hundred." Ness said slowly. "You've only been out for a couple hours; they were able to stitch everything together and expect with some medication, you'll be healed within the week. The bullet was stopped by your bones, which are, kind of unsurprisingly, ridiculously tough, so it wasn't much worse than the knife wound."

There was something in the way she was hesitating, the way that she was chewing her lip that made him put the drink down without taking a sip.

"We giving Phoenix a break from healing finally?" He said, trying for a light-hearted tone, but feeling that something was very, very wrong.

"I should text everyone to let them know you're awake." Ness pulled out her phone. "They've been worried sick."

"Ness." Kirin caught her arm, and she flickered closer to the colors of the wall, like she was trying to hide. "What aren't you telling me?"

He knew it wasn't going to be good, but what he hadn't expected was for tears to well up in her eyes so suddenly, or the way that she looked at him, almost pleading.

"You should rest more."

"That's not an answer." His heartrate started to increase, dutifully noted by the faster beeping on the monitor.

"I should let Pressure know you're awake too—"

"Ness." Her eyes jumped to his and then back away. "What is it?"

"Ifrit and Phoenix." She took a breath. "They're gone."

25

Gone

"You need to be lying down!" Ness frantically pushed against Kirin's chest, trying to get him to go back, to rest, but he plowed on ahead, ignoring her as he stormed across campus to Pressure's office. "There's nothing we can do right now, you need to—"

"I need to know what happened." Something in his voice got her to stop pushing, and she had to hurry after him as he kept walking. "Gone where? They're not dead, I *know* he's not dead."

"We don't know." Ness's voice was small.

"Pressure will know." Kirin was trying to convince himself more than her. "She'll know *something*."

Ness didn't try to stop him again, instead following him quietly, the second blurry shadow behind him that day.

When they got to Pressure's office, they weren't alone.

Adlivun was pacing by the door, biting one of her knuckles so hard she was bleeding. She looked up at their arrival and opened her mouth to say something, but Kirin ignored her and barged right in without knocking at all.

He hadn't quite made a plan for what to do or say when he got there, and perhaps that was for the best, considering he hadn't expected Pressure to be crying at her desk. Ness and Adlivun crowded in after him and both came up short, all standing there awkwardly, unsure how to proceed.

"What can I do for you?" Pressure's voice was icy as she looked up from her computer, tears still rolling down her cheeks. She wasn't sobbing, or collapsing in on herself, a quiet fury radiating from her, the twin tracks— if anything— making her look terrifying instead of weak.

"What..." Kirin's throat was dry again, and he briefly wished he'd drank the juice Ness had offered him. "What happened?"

"That's what I'm trying to figure out." Pressure looked back at the screens hovering around her, the light casting her in an oppressive blue.

"Ness said they're... they're gone." He couldn't let himself consider what that meant.

"Taken is perhaps a better term."

"Taken where?"

"If I knew that, do you think I would be sitting here?" She hissed, half rising from her chair, the anger flashing through her eyes now directed purely at Kirin. "That's my—"

She stopped herself, forcefully. Smoothed back her hair, collected herself.

"We don't know. Shortly after you lost consciousness, I received word that Shifter was in critical condition. Until he wakes up, I'm looking through every piece of camera footage in that city to find out anything I can." She sat back down and returned to looking at the screens, but a touch of her anger had fled, and she instead seemed so worn.

"The local heroes don't know anything?" Adlivun spoke up timidly.

"The three of them had already left to come back here, and no one bothered to escort them. It wasn't until someone reached out to the pilot to ask why they hadn't taken off yet that anyone realized they'd never made it to the plane at all."

"What's wrong with Shifter?" Ness asked.

"Multiple gunshot wounds, and some burns." Her mouth tightened.

"Why are you looking into this and not the police?" Kirin felt there was something more to her anger, something that wasn't just explained by her being upset at two of her students being taken.

"Because of the nature of Shifter's injuries, and the presence of Phoenix's, but not Ifrit's blood, as well as the prior… infringements, the official stance the police are taking is that this is a case of a student gone rogue." Her hands faltered on the keyboard, and she folded them, looking up at the three. "They've declared Ifrit to be a villain."

Kirin usually liked spending time alone. Some days coming back to the fifth floor and finding Phoenix sitting on the couch and chatting his ear off felt like it would drive him crazy, but when the elevator opened and Ifrit wasn't in the kitchen, Phoenix not laughing about some joke they'd just made, the whole space seemed desolate. The lights turned on as he walked in, but it still felt dark, dreary.

He'd hardly eaten anything at all that day, and not a thing since breakfast, but he couldn't get himself to open the fridge. If he did and saw the angry notes that Ifrit had left there months before warning Phoenix away from eating the freshest stuff first, it would all feel too real. If he ate any of it, he'd be too worried that the space in the fridge would never be filled up again.

Even going to his own room felt hard. When he opened the door, everything was still pushed to the corners of the room,

Ifrit's mattress still on the floor with blankets rumpled since they'd both woken up late that morning. The small depression in the fabric that showed where Ifrit had slept felt like a gaping hole, an open wound that needed sutures. Kirin could barely stand to be in there long enough to change his clothes, and then he found his feet taking him back out to the common area, pretending that they were both still there, just asleep.

The night was fast approaching, but he had no desire to lay down, even less to stay awake. One of Phoenix's sweatshirts was tossed over the end of the couch, and he numbly thought that maybe he could go give it to Adlivun, that maybe it would be nice for her to have until they got them back. They were going to come back.

The thought spurred him on to some level of action, and he was crossing the room and in front of Ifrit's door before he fully realized what he was doing. He hesitated at the threshold, wondering if Ifrit would mind, but he shook his head, and, with a mental apology, walked inside.

He just wanted to grab a hoodie for himself, maybe even the one Ifrit had shoved against him weeks before, but the whole space was so *Ifrit* that Kirin almost started crying right then and there. His notebooks were lined up neatly on his desk, one of the textbooks open with a bookmark holding the spot in case a breeze from the open window blew it shut. The posters on the walls were of movies that Kirin had now seen, knowing which parts were Ifrit's favorites, which lines he'd mouth to himself like a mantra no matter how many times they watched it. He hurriedly rummaged through the dresser and found the sweatshirt he was looking for, before leaving the room quickly, fighting against the burning in his eyes.

No sooner had the door closed behind him than the elevator chimed softly and opened. Despite himself, his head whipped up hopefully, only for the weight of everything to settle back

A HARRIS
DYLAN BYRON
AST TR
FROM EAST

down as the rest of the class piled out.

They were loaded with pillows and blankets and food, Adlivun first among them to get off. Her eyes were red, and she looked just as wretched as Kirin felt.

"We thought maybe you wouldn't want to be alone, at least for tonight." Ness was at his elbow, giving him a small smile. "We brought snacks; Dulu cooked."

He couldn't bring himself to speak, but Clidna was there, so he quietly signed a *thank you* and let himself be led to a chair, while his friends busied themselves with moving things around to make a space big enough for sixteen people to sleep. A warm drink was pressed into his hands by Aïcha, Dulu already in the kitchen and setting down large containers of food. Goldhorn had turned on some music as he started pulling out pots and pans, as if knowing Kirin couldn't stand hearing someone moving around in there, knowing it wasn't who it should be.

"Come on." Naddāha was there, coaxing him out of the chair and into the cocoon of blankets they'd made on the ground. "You've got to help us pick which movie to put on."

Kirin looked at her then, and his heart broke all over again. If he was right about her mien, if she could feel the emotions of others instead of just taking them away, how hard was this for her? How could she stand the weight of it, of everyone's sorrow, and still be standing? He only had his own to contend with and already he felt like he was one stiff breeze away from shattering into a million pieces.

"Enough of that, too." She said quietly and gave him a kiss on the forehead before stepping back, heading toward Dulu to help with serving the food. "Don't you start feeling guilty for being a human."

Clidna had taken up residency on his right-hand side, asking him questions in sign so he didn't have to speak. *Do you want to be touched right now or should we give you physical space? Do you want a movie or a show?* He wished he could show her more gratitude, but she seemed to understand without words and was content to stay there all night.

Adlivun was on his left, and she spoke almost as little as he did. He'd handed Phoenix's hoodie to her wordlessly and didn't miss the way her eyes misted as she took it. She had her head on his shoulder and was hugging the fabric tightly against her chest, the weight comforting. The image of her coming out of Phoenix's room that one morning made Kirin feel as though she, at least, was feeling the same stone of grief that he was, no special powers required.

The food Dulu had made was good, richly spiced but so different in flavor from what Ifrit made that Kirin could get himself to eat it without crying. Adlivun ate too, but it did take some quiet prodding from Medusa to get her to start. For a time, the room was filled only with the low murmur of people talking onscreen and the sounds of utensils scraping along plates.

Once they'd all eaten, it was late indeed, and Kirin nearly lost control of himself again when he realized that they were really staying, that he wasn't going to be alone on that empty floor. One by one, people began drifting off to sleep, until he suspected he was one of very few who were still awake.

"Kirin?" A quiet whisper came out of the dark, and from behind the couch he caught the glint of light on metal. It was Yantra, who had snuck away from her position next to Ness. She climbed over the back of the couch and sat on it, which couldn't have been comfortable considering all the pillows had been pilfered and redistributed among their friends on the floor. "I just wanted to let you know that I'm looking." He sat up at that, cautiously optimistic. Somewhere deep in the pile of bodies, he heard someone shift.

"I don't want to get your hopes up, since I haven't found anything, but I'm scouring every site out there, and whenever there's news about them, we'll know." She bit her lips. "Do you know what the police are saying?"

He nodded.

"I don't think it's true at all, but I'm monitoring their stipend accounts, just in case they manage to escape and use it to buy anything. I think the school froze the accounts anyway— not that there was enough in there to vanish entirely to begin with— but any attempts to use them will still show up." That detail hadn't even occurred to him; if they *did* escape, would they have the funds to get back? Would they know how to reach anyone here if their phones had been taken? A new depth of worry squirmed in Kirin's stomach. "But, um, a large reason that the police think he did this is because of his past."

Kirin was suddenly back in time, seeing Ifrit's face pinched in worry thinking about whatever happened to him, or whatever he himself had done.

"I don't want to know." His voice came out croaky, after having not been used for hours. "He didn't want to tell me, so I don't want to know."

Yantra's eyes looked sad.

"I think we might be able to figure out where he is though; it all seems connected, somehow. Maybe if we just talked it through—"

"*Yantra*." She stopped. "He'll tell me himself. When he gets back. He can tell me then."

She nodded slowly.

"Who he was doesn't matter, because we're not looking for that person, we're looking for him *now*. We'll find him. Together." Before he could see her response, he stood up, not sure where he was going, but he couldn't stop the tears now, and he didn't want her to think it was her fault.

As he did, he realized that the light glancing off her earrings was coming from under Phoenix's door. One look around and he realized who else was missing. While Yantra slipped back off to join the sleeping group, Kirin found himself sliding into the one bedroom on the fifth floor he'd never been in before.

Adlivun was inside, on the ground and wrapped in a blanket presumably pulled from Phoenix's bed. He'd expected boisterous colors, piles of clothes on the floor, but Phoenix's room was surprisingly subdued and organized. There was a simple corkboard on the wall, detailing due dates and self-imposed progress charts. On their desk were little plastic bins filled with index cards, meticulously labelled by month and year. The whole space felt... controlled.

Except Adlivun.

There were signs of her infiltrating the space, a few pieces of her clothes tucked on the desk chair, a beanbag chair in the corner with a small pile of Adlivun's books stacked next to it, stacked retro CDs with little sticky notes telling Phoenix what order to listen to them in. These things felt living, comfortable, whereas the rest of Phoenix's room felt dead.

Adlivun hadn't looked surprised when Kirin walked in, instead just offering a sad smile.

"Someone tattle on me?" He asked, trying to be lighthearted despite the tears on his face. He sat down next to her, and she offered part of the blanket to him, the pair of them not quite fitting underneath.

"Phoenix did." She said softly.

And it clicked. Adlivun worked with the dead. While Phoenix never *stayed* dead, they certainly did die. At least two times, that he'd witnessed, and they'd confirmed many, many more.

"They're still here?" Kirin asked. Adlivun didn't respond, a shade materializing in front of them. As the color drained out of Adlivun's face, Phoenix's became more solid. They were still noticeably a ghost, made out of shades of gray, but the way they smiled and fluidly sat down seemed so much like the real them that Kirin felt he could be convinced that he'd somehow gone colorblind instead.

"Hey there." Phoenix's ghost said. "And I didn't *tattle*, I just gave her some warning. There is such a thing as privacy, you know."

"I wouldn't know, actually, as I suspect I haven't had it since coming here." Kirin leaned his head against Adlivun's. "Can you tell us where you are?"

"It doesn't work like that." Adlivun mumbled, at the same time that Phoenix began to talk again.

"I only know what I knew when I died, which was... I want to say four months ago? I don't have a magical mind link with the current version, you know?"

"Current version?"

"No one ever asks questions; this is the problem." Phoenix sighed. "But I'm going to go, before Ad passes out."

And without appearing to fade at all, they just vanished into thin air.

Kirin felt himself looking around for a moment, trying to see where they'd gone off to, which earned a sad chuckle from Adlivun.

"They're still there, in the same spot even." Her eyes focused on where he'd last seen Phoenix, though it was just open air to him. "They're just too worried about me using all my energy."

He watched Adlivun's eyes follow something invisible to the balcony door, her lips tightening as she seemed to lose sight of them.

"And now they're being altogether too nice and leaving us alone, so you don't need to feel watched." She buried her face in her hands. "I wish I could turn it off."

Kirin didn't say anything.

"I know they're gone, right? They're not here. I can't touch them; I can't feel their warmth." She pulled the blanket around her tighter. "But they're *there*, just on the edge of my sight. I can talk to them, I can laugh with them, but it's just... a ghost."

Kirin put his arm around her, giving her a squeeze.

"I'm so sorry."

"You're not allowed to be sorry for me. You're already too miserable." She wiped her nose with the back of her hand and sniffed loudly. "And I at least get how much this hurts."

Her eyes weren't pitying, only understanding, and somehow that was worse. He looked away and instead pulled at the hem of the too short sweatshirt he was wearing.

"I should've offered to double up." He finally said. "I should've insisted that I be added to their team, that they weren't left a person short. I should never have let them go out alone, not once, not ever."

"Or I should've offered. Or anyone else." Adlivun shrugged. "Are you saying you're mad at all of us then for not offering?"

"No! But it's different, right? You're not... you're not..." Kirin didn't know what he was trying to say. He knew that everyone else in their class cared about Ifrit. The first time he'd been accused of wrongdoing proved that. But it wasn't the same. Deep down, he knew that the way they all cared for Ifrit and the way that he did wasn't the same at all.

"No, I'm not." Adlivun caught his meaning without him saying anything further, which was lucky as he hadn't quite figured out what he meant in the first place. "Not for him. But I am for Phoenix."

The confession wasn't startling; he'd known it the moment he realized where Adlivun was, but he still felt that it was sad.

"I didn't mean that—"

"Kirin. You don't need to apologize. And I thought the same thing. Why didn't I say something right at the beginning? They said no arguments, but maybe if I'd said I didn't want to change, but instead double up, maybe they would've allowed it?" She sniffed again. "Of course, Phoenix scolded me for that. It's so weird being sad that someone's gone and having them comfort you, you know?"

"I wouldn't, no." They both laughed, though it was choked by tears.

"It used to be harder, dealing with my mien." Her hand absently went to the scar around her neck. "When the dead realize you can see them, hear them, sometimes they think that you owe them your ear. Even worse when you don't realize what they are, and you don't know how to show them to anyone else."

She shook her head as if banishing a particularly foul-tasting memory.

"Everyone carries ghosts with them, some more than others. You had a big one, but just one. Ifrit has hundreds. But Phoenix... Phoenix has thousands."

"All of themself?"

Adlivun nodded.

"I don't control the dead. I ask them if they want to work with me, while they're still here. Most fade after a few months. Only if they're particularly angry or determined do they usually stick around. Or if they're stuck in that place between life and death.

"And Phoenix dies. But they're not dead. Every time they've been killed, they get a new shade. I didn't know what to make of them, at first. They came to me, offering a deal. Said they'd keep the annoying ghosts off my back, spy on anyone or anything I wanted, and all they wanted in return was that I keep them company."

She looked wistfully back out the window, maybe seeing someone there, maybe just wishing she did.

"I thought that meant talk to the shades, keep them occupied, but they didn't care about that. They wanted me to find the real Phoenix, the living Phoenix, and keep *them* company. I almost never accept requests about the living from the dead, but Phoenix is... different."

"Just in how many ghosts they have?"

"No. Everything about them is strange, unexpected. The shade that spoke to you? They shouldn't be able to do that. Their ghosts take so much less energy than others do; you saw what happened when your father just assumed his own face, but Phoenix can have a conversation with you for a few minutes before I start getting anywhere close to passing out. It felt like I befriended them under false pretenses, yet I couldn't help it."

"So is Phoenix just... around?"

"Many of them run around freely, but a good number stick by me, as if they don't know where else to go. I send them off to watch certain spots that might be important, and honestly, I wasn't half as strong as everyone thinks I am before I met them. With all the ghosts they carry, I have eyes and ears everywhere, and somehow, they have such a knack for knowing what is and isn't important. Day three of being here, I knew the ins and outs of campus, half of the secrets people were hiding, and where they like to watch us from."

"But at least on day two you started listening in on Pressure's conversations."

"Oh, that was the first thing I did, after the weird interview stuff." Adlivun allowed herself a small, self-satisfied smile. "I wasn't sure at first, but she's a good person, or at least is trying to be."

"She cares, at least."

"More than you know." Adlivun leaned into his shoulder more, as if she'd suddenly gotten cold. "She's going to find them, right?"

"If she won't, Yantra will. And the moment either of them know, you will." Kirin felt himself looking out the window now too. There was no moonlight that night, but the moon always came back. "We're going to get them back. But in order to do that, we need sleep."

Adlivun nodded, sitting up and drying her face off.

"We should be ready." She seemed to be thinking out loud. "Maybe we'll even know more by morning."

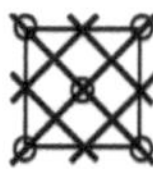

When the sun rose, there was no news to be had. Yantra had stayed up the whole night, but she had come up blank to her own frustration and everyone else's sadness.

"There's no footage, no claims that anyone has them, *nothing*." Kirin didn't know if it was from the late night, or from the knowledge that her friends were still out there, but she was starting to tear up. "No one seems to know anything at all, and the police aren't fucking looking and—"

She broke off as Ness put a hand on her shoulder, and in the gloomy silence, they all got up and started getting ready for the day.

It was a Friday, and they should have Rescue Operations, with one of their groups being sent off into the field, but with Shifter still hospitalized and Phantasm covering his classes, there was nothing for them to do but sit around the whole day, forced to acknowledge why they had so much free time.

The weekend felt even longer. Yantra was struggling, never parted with her computer for long, Ness having to bring her food and water or else she'd forget she needed it at all. They began rotating through who sat with her, since it strung out their nerves every time she seemed to have a lead only for it to fade into nothingness. She was so focused that she never seemed to notice when the person sitting with her swapped out.

It was late Sunday night when Kirin relieved Dulu, who patted him on the back and headed up to the fifth floor. They'd been rotating who slept up there, too, never fewer than four people crashing on the makeshift beds in the common area. Adlivun had taken to sleeping in Phoenix's room, but Kirin couldn't get himself to sleep in either his own or Ifrit's, choosing the couch every night.

The TV was on when he stepped inside, the news playing in the background as always. He wasn't sure if she paid it any attention at all, but the one time he'd tried to turn it off, she'd glared at him, so on it stayed. It was something to look at, which he appreciated, since his focus wasn't strong enough to read or even aimlessly scroll the web, but most often, he just stared at the ceiling, waiting for his timer to go off so he could remind her to rest.

The news was infiltrating his thoughts today, talking once again about Futurus. They'd just revealed the latest in their techware line it seemed, and the reporters could not stop fawning over it.

"To think you could reach the speed of a car!" One of them was saying. *"This is a game changer for certain, especially for those who live in areas with high concentrations of mien-driven crime. It could provide a quick and safe route out of danger for those who need it most."*

He was distracted by a bright flash of light from Yantra's computer, which she frowned at, her fingers briefly freezing on the keys.

"What is it?" Kirin sat up, not really expecting her to respond.

"It's the autopsy." She hesitated, finger hovering over the blinking icon. After a moment, she closed it and went back to her main screen, looking even more downtrodden.

"For Cara?"

"I'd set a program to watch for new uploads to her file, and it was just triggered." Her eyes flickered to Kirin's face and back. "It's not important now, though."

"Maybe it is." He got up and walked around her, looking at the screen. "I think if you're getting nowhere in the present, maybe the past *can* hold something."

She looked at him for a moment and then nodded, bringing up another browser and typing in something so quickly that he couldn't make it out. A few moments later, a report appeared, and she duplicated it, pushing one version to the screen closest to Kirin and enlarging it, and reading the second one on her own.

He read through it quickly— the font not being terrible for once— and felt his heart sink. It might be a momentary distraction, but it wasn't going to be anything that would be of real use to them. The report largely focused on the chip itself, which was unsurprising, but there was no serial number on it, nothing that would indicate the location of the manufacturer. Except, in the very last paragraph—

"They recovered the data from it." Yantra breathed out the words and then suddenly her hands were flying over the keyboard again. "I need to find that report."

"Won't they notice you in there?"

She paused long enough to shoot him a dirty look.

"They gave me complete access to their servers. I made sure to leave myself a back way in."

"I guess I can tell what suspected crime landed you in our class, then."

"You'd be surprised." She said dryly. "Go get us some food and by the time you're back, I should have it."

She found what she was looking for before he'd finished

heating up their food, and when he came back, she was already reading, her eyes wide. She looked up as he entered, motioning for him to close the door.

"It wasn't trying to figure out how to *create* her mien, it was looking at how her brain responded to it, what areas were activated and if there were any specific neurotransmitters that were released during use. In particular, it was noted that the dorsolateral prefrontal right cortex responded differently, so I *think* what it's saying is that her perception of time was different when she used her mien, which makes sense because moving that quickly without being able to react to your surroundings would be deadly. That's just an interesting side note, but that's not why I'm excited."

"Why's that then?" Kirin sat down, expecting her to start lecturing him, but instead she just turned up the volume of the TV.

"...as you can see, our tests show that this is safer than driving a car, and it really allows people the freedom of movement that those naturally born with this type of mien would have." Moretti was on screen, some graphs showing behind them. *"We've done so much research into this particular techware, as it was the most requested power subtype by our clientele, specifically because it would make it so much easier to get away from dangerous situations. Satol, even the recent attack on East City, saw a death toll much higher than they might have, if we'd had this technology in hand."*

The interview continued, but the volume was turned down as Yantra looked at Kirin with bright eyes.

"You don't think?" He said, hushed, as if someone might be listening in.

"It's too great a coincidence. Let's say for a minute that I believe their full techware line isn't based on illegal research into miens— which I would like to clarify that I absolutely do *not*—

but if I did, it still wouldn't be enough. How does someone who has never had superspeed react quickly enough to stop from slamming into a wall? How does someone with brand-new superstrength know how to turn it on and off? These are the kind of logistical questions you have to ask when you're giving people powers."

"I agree with you, but the fact that a brain monitoring chip found on someone with the same ability as the new techware they're releasing doesn't prove anything." Gears in Kirin's brain started turning.

"No, but it certainly would get people looking." Yantra stood up quickly and nearly fell over, so long had she been sitting down, but she waved off his concern and began pacing. "It's not a terribly long and complicated process at all to request— or I suppose in this case subpoena— records, and the timing is just *too* coincidental for me. Someone wanted this to come to light and they wanted it to happen *now*, when Futurus was announcing the new line, so that maybe someone would put two and two together."

"Are you saying they *wanted* Cara to get captured?" Kirin thought back to when he spoke with her, the only thing that had seemed off was *why* she had attacked them. Had she been told to? Or had she been intending to get captured the entire time?

"I think so. I don't know if she knew that was the plan. I don't know how it was going to work if things hadn't gone up in smoke, literally, but I think that this has all been planned for a very, very long time."

"Smoke." Kirin repeated the word, something else tickling the back of his brain. "What would they need Ifrit and Phoenix for though? I assume it's still Aether who took them. I don't know why Futurus would want them. Sure, they both have really incredible miens, but it's a huge leap to go from augmenting already existing abilities to creating new ones."

"That's the only thing I'm unsure of right now. Maybe… maybe they thought they could convince them to join? I know—" She held up her hands to stop him from protesting "—I know they would never, but Aether wouldn't. It seems unlikely, even without knowing them, so I suspect that there's got to be a better reason than that. Or maybe the pair of them were attacked and got away and are in hiding because they were nearly killed. We don't know. I can't say much more than that. But if we're right, if Futurus is Aether's main target right now, we still have a pulse on where Aether might be headed."

"Satol." Kirin's heart was racing.

"I think so. They want to gain public support; they *want* to recruit, so when they attack, they need to make it at least understandable. Whether people are afraid of being experimented on or just scared that miens will be *recreated*, human experimentation is still reviled. Having proof that Futurus has been testing on people— on *kids*— for years means they're easy to attack and not upset the public. And Satol is their pride and joy, the so-called proof that things can be rebuilt better."

"They said the chip was put in Cara's brain about ten years ago." There was a larger picture, but all he could see for the moment was that cold, dark cell. "They used the anti-mien sentiment in the city to get away with this."

"I know. I know." Yantra put a hand on him. "But we need to go talk to Pressure right now. It's a stretch, but maybe, just maybe, Ifrit and Phoenix are going to be at the center of this. I can't say for sure. I wish I could, but it's better than anything we've gotten yet. We know they're not dead yet. We just need to get to them before anyone else does."

"How are we going to explain this to her? Are you planning on admitting that you hacked into the police server because you found information the last time you hacked in, when you were allowed access, and that we've been going through police records for months now?"

Yantra opened her mouth and closed it, looking embarrassed.

"And if she says that it's not enough of a lead to act on, we've just told her where we're headed, and she can try to stop us. I think you're right. I think that this all has to be connected, but we're not going to find out anything here." Kirin's heart was practically beating out of his chest, all the energy from the past several days finally, *finally* having a direction. "You don't have to come, but I'm getting myself to Futurus's headquarters— tonight."

"Of fucking course I'm coming." She looked offended that he would even suggest such a thing. "But we're on the other side of the world, on an island that has no airport. How do you plan on getting there?"

"What are the chances you know how to fly a jet?"

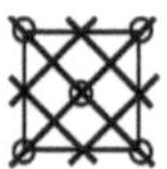

It was a dumb plan. He knew that. It was a catastrophically idiotic plan with a high chance of failure. It'd seemed like a stupid idea even when he'd thought it up, felt worse when he and Yantra snuck by their classmates who were still awake, and was absolutely confirmed as reckless when they nearly got caught by patrolling campus security. But neither of them stopped.

They darted from shadow to shadow, hiding behind the dorms as they worked their way to the barrier gate. Once they reached it, Yantra's hands flew over the keypad as Kirin kept an anxious watch. It felt so exposed here, likely intentionally so, Kirin hunching over in a pathetic attempt to be less obvious.

He had to literally bite his tongue to keep from asking Yantra if she could go any faster, knowing that she was no less worried about it than he was.

When he felt like he was going to have to say something, the barrier cleared, the way into the hero section open, about to lock behind them and let no one else follow till morning. It hadn't even fully reset before they had sprinted all the way across the moonlit path and into the shadows of the nearest building. Kirin's head whipped to the side, thinking he'd seen someone else moving about, but when he looked closer, he could see that they were totally alone.

"You didn't see anyone in here on the security cameras, right?" Kirin whispered, though it still felt far too loud in the quiet air.

"I didn't. No one's supposed to be in here after classes end, which is why the usual code wouldn't work. I can't check again though, unless you want me to bring all the cameras back online." She hissed back. A sheen of sweat covered her face, making her shroud of hair stick to her cheeks and forehead.

"No, keep them down. We'll just have to be careful." Kirin peered around the corner toward the Disaster Simulator. The jet was still parked on top, having remained there ever since the last ill-fated mission. Taking a breath, Kirin took off toward it.

They made it to the base of the building, but once there, they paused.

"Should we just... go in?" Yantra asked uncertainly. "I'm fairly sure that there's a scanner right by the door that tags everyone who comes in, so I don't know how we'll get around it. *That* will set off some alarms even if me opening the main door doesn't, and I don't think either of us want to find out the school's emergency protocols."

"Could you turn it off when you do the door?"

Yantra shook her head.

"This whole building is on a different system than the rest of the school. It's self-contained; we'd have to be inside it to turn it off. Probably like that so no one can access the scanner data without physically being here."

"That's fine." Kirin looked up the sheer concrete face. "We'll just go up the outside."

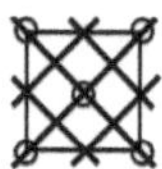

His forearms screamed as he dug his fingers into the wall, Yantra clinging onto his back so tightly he worried she'd be stabbed through his shirt. Around the side, tucked into the shadow of the wall, they were almost hidden, and their own dark clothes helped with blending into the background. Even so, Kirin suddenly wished they'd grabbed Lilin, who would've made the secrecy of it all so much easier.

But as they made it onto the roof, he discarded the thought. The jet loomed before them, and he knew that they weren't going to come out of this unscathed. Good intentions or not, they were still about to steal a billion-dollar jet and run off campus; no one else needed to be involved.

Yantra had hurried to the side panel, gesturing for him to follow. She pointed, and he ripped the thin metal cover straight off, giving her direct access to the computer. Yantra's hands were a blur as she poked and prodded until the back opened to allow them to board.

They were in, the door still gaping behind them.

"Yantra?" Kirin asked nervously, feeling too exposed again.

"I need to get to the front to close it." Yantra's face was pale, the first real touch of fear in her eyes. "It should've closed once we were on—"

As if prompted by the words, it began to seal, the emergency lights flickering on and bathing them in red. They looked at each other, anxiety not quite worn away yet.

"I'll figure out how to get us airborne." Yantra ran to the front, Kirin following, his doubt growing as he saw the cockpit for the first time. It wasn't nearly as straightforward as he'd hoped, and if he wasn't mistaken, Yantra seemed to have instructions open on her phone. "You start charting a course for Satol; don't use your phone. My laptop is in my bag. Use that instead."

Kirin silently did as he was bid, pulling the computer out and turning the screen on quickly.

"I suppose just find the shortest route?" He was so focused on pulling up maps of passenger flights that it took him a second to realize that she was being awfully quiet. "Yantra?"

When he looked up, she was slumped over the controls, unconscious. He was on his feet immediately, crystallizing his whole body and looking for her attacker, as much as he could without being able to turn to his head. Cursing silently, he dropped enough of his protection to move, wanting to make sure that she was at least breathing, since he couldn't see what was wrong.

But no sooner had he begun to move when he felt a sharp prick on the inside of his elbow, looked down to find a syringe protruding from his arm, and then suddenly he saw no more.

26

Action

He awoke to water being splashed in his face.

He'd expected that. In the few moments between feeling the prick of the needle and the blackness, he knew that whatever awaited him wouldn't be good. He'd expected handcuffs and bright lights, looming faces and angry words. So it was rather jarring to instead find Pressure standing over him in her pajamas.

"Now I'm going to give you exactly five seconds to explain what the fuck you two were doing." She said it with the icy tone that anyone with a mother knew. "One."

"It was my fault!" Both Kirin and Yantra spoke up at the same time, looking at each other in shock. Kirin hadn't even gathered his wits enough to look around, but when he did, he thought he'd lost them entirely. Because he wasn't in a police station. He wasn't even on campus, as far as he could tell. Instead, he was sitting in a comfortable living room, on the floor.

"I don't give a damn *whose* fault it was. What were you doing?"

"We were just—"

"It's a long story—"

"They were trying to get to Satol." A voice chimed up from the corner of the room. Kirin's eyes widened as he realized it was Shifter. Shifter, who certainly didn't look like someone recently in critical condition.

"Satol?" Pressure looked confused.

"Well, you see—"

Whatever Yantra was about to say was cut off abruptly by a simple wave of Pressure's hand. Pressure pinched the bridge of her nose.

"Do not try to lie to me right now. Do you know how lucky you are that Shifter found you instead of one of the actual campus guards? If it had been anyone else, you would be arrested, if you were lucky, or far more likely dead, and I cannot take—" Her voice broke. Kirin felt horrified, seeing how upset she was, and in that silence, she collected herself. "What were you doing?"

"How's he not dead?" Yantra nodded to Shifter, though she could have pointed. Neither of them were bound, simply on the ground. Kirin had been lying down when he was woken, but the shock of it had pulled him upright.

"I don't think you're in a position to demand answers right now." Shifter's face was forcibly neutral, but Pressure's eye twitched.

"No, I am. You want to know what we were doing, but how can we trust you?" Yantra's voice was suddenly angry. "The very first thing this school ever did was lie to us about who you are, and now you want us to just... explain ourselves to you? When you've lied to us *again*, saying there's no information about where our friends are because the only witness is comatose when he's apparently good enough to be up and drugging people? No, fuck that. Take us to the police. At least they're upfront about how they don't trust us at all."

Pressure's eye twitched again.

"I'm going to ask one more time—"

"It's because the police don't trust us that you were told I was critically injured." Shifter stepped farther into the room, though he was still far from close to any of them. "My mien has been greatly downplayed to the police, and the world as a whole, and strictly speaking only the people in this room know that I can reknit organs and skin."

"So you could've gone after them?" Kirin's sense of reason was lost behind rage now too, coming to his feet. He was moving forward before he knew what he was doing, and it was a blast from Pressure that stopped his advance, the force of it rattling the windows.

"No. I went down, and very much was in danger of dying. Once I stabilized at the hospital and woke up, only then could I repair the damage." Shifter didn't seem to be phased by Kirin's anger, not having moved a single step backward. "The injuries I sustained should've left me bedridden for months, if I couldn't get to a healer, but that allowed us to move in secret."

Before either of them could ask why they'd need to do such a thing, there was a knock on the door.

The room silenced. It was far too late to be a casual call. Pressure's eyes drilled them in place as she walked back to the door, Shifter entirely out of sight when Kirin looked back his way.

The door opened.

It was, shockingly, more of their classmates. Adlivun stood at the forefront of the group, eyes wide and haunted, looking half a moment away from passing out.

"What is it?" Pressure looked concerned, not surprised, searching specifically Adlivun's face for an answer.

"Can we come in?" Naddāha gave her best smile, cheeks beautifully flushed from the chill. "It's cold outside."

Pressure moved aside without a word, letting them in just as the rain began to fall. Lilin was also with them, as well as Dulu and Ness, both of whom looked at Kirin and Yantra with wide eyes when their presence was noted. Yantra gave a weak smile and half a wave, slowly getting to her feet.

Pressure disappeared into a room at the back and then reappeared with Shifter, both carrying steaming mugs of tea. The cups were forced into all of their hands, Adlivun alone refusing, pacing in front of the TV, and then they were seated awkwardly around the couches before Pressure seemed ready to hear a word of anything.

"Out with it, then." Shifter was the one to speak up, drawing eyes to him. Pressure was looking pale now, and Kirin wasn't surprised that she seemed unable to speak.

"If you have any idea where they might be, we need to go— now." Adlivun was focused on Pressure and missed the look that Kirin and Yantra shared. "Can you get access to the school's jets?"

"Maybe. But I'd need a good reason to." Pressure's color returned, and Kirin realized she'd been expecting Adlivun to tell them all that it was too late. If they had to go, that meant there was hope.

"There's no *time.*"

"Adlivun, I trust your judgement immensely, but this is not something I can do lightly—"

Adlivun let out a sound halfway between a cry and a scream and suddenly the room was filled with people, so many that they were practically packed on top of one another and though there had to be nearly a hundred specters that Kirin could see, they all had faces that were clear as day. And they were all Phoenix.

Except one.

Standing just to Kirin's left, so close that they almost touched, was a shade that was fuzzy around the edges, like it wasn't fully there yet. While the rest of the ghosts were looking at Adlivun, this one was only looking at Kirin with a set of familiar eyes, now drained of their startling color.

"No." Kirin whispered and reached out, only for the shades to vanish as Adlivun fell to her knees.

"Phoenix is *dying* every second, and they can't tell me why." Adlivun's voice brought him back. "Ifrit is alive, but barely. It's like he's been kept from death by something. Or some*one*."

"Can Phoenix give you any information about their location?" Shifter was taking over now, standing in front of Pressure, who looked shell-shocked.

"Only that it's dark, and that it's just the two of them." Adlivun looked ashamed, as if somehow, it was her fault they only knew that. "They were knocked out when they were attacked... when *you* were attacked."

Kirin watched the rest of his classmates size up Shifter and come to the same realization that Yantra had.

"Indeed." He was, at least, consistent in not wanting anyone to know. "What can they tell us?"

Phoenix materialized next to Adlivun, eyes angry. Then, in a strange parallel to how Shifter was speaking for Pressure, Phoenix responded in place of Adlivun.

"We were attacked from behind." Their voice was echoey, like they were at the bottom of a deep well. "*You* were guarding the rear, so they took you out before we even knew anything was wrong. Didn't even hear you fall. Then they hit Ifrit, stabbed him, but since he was right next to me, I was able to heal him before they even finished pulling the knife out. Someone then said to grab me too, and that's all I remember."

"How are you dying, Phoenix?" Shifter asked. The phrase sounded so cold.

"I don't know. We're alone, in a dark room. Ifrit's chained to a chair, and I'm handcuffed to him."

"Are there any windows?"

"I don't know; it's dark."

"Define dark."

"I can't see anything." Phoenix's voice faltered. *"Couldn't* see anything."

"When you were attacked, did they say anything, anything at all?"

"Someone said 'she said it wasn't hers, so it must be ours.' That was it."

It's not mine! The words echoed in his head. *Move— now!* Kirin felt a sharp pain in his hand and realized that he'd crystallized his fingers without meaning to, stabbing himself in the palm.

"It's definitely Aether." Kirin spoke up. "That woman we captured, that's who 'she' was."

Understanding flickered on Pressure's face.

"And we might have a lead on where they're going." Yantra said softly.

"Let the rest of your class know to meet us at the Disaster Simulator," Pressure finally found her voice, drawing herself up to her full height, "and everyone needs to go change into their costumes."

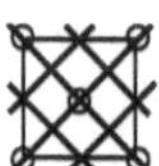

"How sure are you?" Pressure had Yantra and Kirin with her in the cockpit, eyes sweeping the ground as it sped by. Her despair was gone entirely, replaced instead by simmering rage, which was boiling up to a fever pitch. Shifter was piloting, which was for the best, since Pressure couldn't seem to sit down.

"Fairly. The death of Cara, the release of the new techware by Futurus, it's all too coincidental. Futurus is based in Satol; it just makes sense." Yantra usually stood up taller in her suit of gray and purple, but now she was cringing back, afraid that

Pressure's anger would be turned back to her. "The autopsy revealed her full name, too, and when I looked into it more, she was from the area around Satol. Her parents reported her missing when she was just seven, and from what the police were able to gather, she was never seen again. There was a note in the case file that her parents suspected one of their neighbors might have done something after the rise in anti-mien sentiment, since she wasn't the first— or the last— child to disappear."

"Start combing maps of the city. Look for any excavated areas deep below the surface, starting at the heart of the city and working outward. They also might be directly underneath Futurus's base." Pressure's grip was tight on her forearms. "Adlivun."

The tall woman had been lurking in the doorway, and she came forward without a hint of shame.

"However far your shades can reach, have them start scouting as well. Once we touch the ground, I'll have Kapre do the same."

Adlivun nodded once before heading back to the main cabin with the rest of the class. Her spot was quickly filled by Dulu.

"If there's a spare computer, I can help Yantra with searching the city maps too." His usual affable temperament was overridden by sadness, his blue eyes faintly red and his dark skin ashy. Pressure tossed a bag at him without looking, and then he was gone as well.

"Yantra, leave us. I need to have a word with Kirin."

Yantra, despite still looking afraid of Pressure, glanced at Kirin for approval. He nodded, and then and only then did she leave. The moment the door closed Pressure's posture sank. Shifter glanced at her out of the side of his eye, and Kirin felt distinctly awkward. This was a side of Pressure he'd never seen, even when she'd been crying, she'd still felt... powerful. But now she looked too frail, too human.

"How much do you know?"

"What?"

"I know Adlivun knows, and I wouldn't be shocked if Yantra did too. But how much do *you* know?" Her eyes were searching, intensely watching his expression, some of her usual confident air filling back in.

"Know about what?"

That seemed answer enough, and the corners of her mouth turned down, her expression sad.

"Do you have the extra cartridges for your mask?"

"No, they shattered when I was helping Bán." Kirin was lucky he had anything to wear at all after that mission. The new prototype for his costume had only been finished earlier in the week, but since there'd been no updates to the mask, a new one hadn't been made. Only a cloth mask covered his face, not even of the special material that protected his chest.

"Right." Pressure pinched the bridge of her nose. "I suspect you'll have to go in alone."

Part of Kirin didn't care at all if he had to run through a rain of bullets without his mien if it meant he could reach Ifrit.

"Maybe Ness, *maybe*. And that would be pushing it." She sighed and switched to rubbing at the sides of her head. "How are you doing on carbon stores?"

"I'm perfectly fine." That was a lie, but there was no way that she could know that. He hadn't been recovering carbon as quickly as he usually did, now that he thought about it.

"Well even if you weren't, you're about to be." The plane was starting to tilt downward, and when he looked through the window, Satol was gleaming white right in front of them. "I need you to listen to me, okay?"

Kirin tore his gaze away from the looming city and to her face. Her expression had changed again, this time desperate.

"If anything happens, I'm trusting you to get everyone back safely. You're a good person Kirin, and I need you to hold onto that, more than I want you to be a good hero." She reached up and put a hand on his shoulder, and for a brief moment he was eleven again, looking into the face of Force, the best hero the world had ever known. But then they were back, and he was looking at Pressure, a woman who was stumbling under too much weight. "You only have two tasks for this mission: get them back, and don't die yourself."

When they disembarked, a group of local heroes were already there and waiting.

"I knew the school's response times were quick, but this was so rapid it felt like you knew before we even called." A man in yellow clasped Pressure's hand, and though his costume looked distinctly sunny, his face— or what was visible of it behind his mask and bushy black beard— was grim. "Name's Mesmer. We haven't approached yet, since we don't know the whole situation. But we'll be grateful for whatever help you can provide."

Pressure's face displayed no hint of surprise as she fell into step with Mesmer, the rest of the class following close behind. Yantra had been instructed to stay in the jet with Shifter, but a small metal mouse ran out before the gate closed again.

"Why don't you give the students a brief rundown of the situation?" Pressure said smoothly, as they came to a halt at the end of the landing pad. They were at the top of a midsize building, not the airfield at the edge of the city that they'd arrived at last time. A lift the size of a full room was climbing up the stories to come fetch them, Kirin fighting the urge to run for the stairs instead.

If Mesmer thought it was odd they didn't know the mission, he didn't show it, taking it in stride. The only betrayal of his nervousness was the way he flattened down his mustache before he spoke.

"The extremist group Aether has infiltrated and is holding the entire research center of Futurus hostage. There are an unknown number of civilians in the building, as any attempt to enter or scan the tower has failed. While there has been some movement on the roof, for the most part Aether has been quiet, though the occupation is very new."

"I can get inside." Ness startled Mesmer, and even Kirin, as she appeared at the front of their group. "I can get through."

"We are holding on infiltrating the building until we find out what they want. They expended many lives to erect a broadcasting tower on the roof, so we suspect a message from them is imminent."

Despite this assertion, they were moving slowly down the building, leaving Kirin to fight the urge to punch through the window and just jump the rest of the way to the ground. He could sense the whole class behind him practically vibrating; Kapre, in particular, wasn't faring well, as they couldn't sense a thing until they were touching the ground. Of their class, only Adlivun was even remotely calm, her eyes flickering over the city as she stared out the glass sides of the elevator, undoubtedly watching her shades spread out below.

Reaching the surface level presented no immediate relief as they were forced to walk to the active line, since vehicles and trams were cordoned off from the area entirely. Wyrm and Dulu were surreptitiously holding up Kapre as they sent their consciousness into the ground.

While the cordon was successful in keeping cars out, it had failed to keep out all the people. Civilians, police, and even some bold or maybe just opportunistic journalists littered the sidewalk, staring up at the multitude of screens that covered the façade, all now showing a silver stylized A. Preventing anyone from entering was a line of concerned-looking heroes, who sagged with relief at backup being brought in.

Their class joined the line, connecting electric barriers to widen the perimeter around the building. It was horrible to have his back turned to the screens that might give him the slightest clue as to where his friends were being kept, but Pressure silenced everyone's complaints with a hard look, and so Kirin joined the rest in turning to check every few seconds. Pressure was doing much of the same, but until they knew more, she had a point in making sure they were keeping up appearances.

In a small mercy, they were all right next to each other, which meant Kirin heard when Adlivun rushed over to tell Pressure she'd found the first trace.

"One of his shades, it's definitely here." Adlivun's eyes were shining. "They're *here*, somewhere."

Kirin looked to Pressure hopefully, and found she was looking back at him.

"Not yet," Pressure said quietly, eyes still locked on Kirin, "we don't move until you have an exact location."

Adlivun nodded and stepped back in line, hope etched into her face for the first time in days.

As the minutes ticked by, Kirin wished he felt the same. They were *there*, somewhere, but Aether was too. And they were planning something, clearly, or else why announce their presence? His fingers were just about shaking from the building adrenaline, when the screens behind them flickered to life.

"*Hello world*." The white mask was back, and though it was the same as ever, it seemed to be mocking them. "*For those of you who are not just outside, I am speaking to you live from the*

Futurus research center in Satol, and it is for a terrible purpose that we have chosen this site."

"Yantra, anything?" Kirin couldn't take it anymore and paged her.

"Not yet." Her reply came back terse.

"Futurus has been promising a lot of big things lately, and I will admit that they have absolutely delivered upon them. For so long a time, techware has been the realm of the hero, as it only accentuates pre-existing abilities and does not have the power to bestow the incredible gifts some of us are blessed with. And now, only a decade after the city they took up residency in was razed, they have come out with something that most people would consider unthinkable. How is that, one wonders?"

"Call came, you're going in." Mesmer was down the line talking to Ness, who didn't need to be told twice. She jumped over the curb and ran straight at the wall, blinking out of existence just before she crashed into it. A moment later and her report began in Kirin's ear.

"First floor appears clear. Several dead security guards."

"As a whole, worldwide society holds that it is not acceptable to perform human experimentation, to use unwilling subjects in any level of observation. This, happily, has extended to the study of miens and how they work. But in the wake of such a tragedy as what happened here ten years ago, Futurus saw an opportunity."

"Second floor has three people roaming. All are armed; they're wearing the new techware suits. Can't tell if they're Aether or Futurus."

"Received. Do not attempt to contact." A voice Kirin didn't recognize spoke on the line. "Please proceed to the next level."

"The funny thing about our society is that as much as we love to digitize files, we can easily tell when someone is hiding something because they refuse to. Futurus, a company that looks to the future even in its name, has hundreds of boxes, in this building alone, of

records that do not exist in its servers. It's very convenient this way too; these files are up to a decade old now, after all. People can easily claim that they never saw them, that they had no idea. Who, then, has been running the experiments that are still ongoing?"

"Taking some time to get to the third floor. They're guarding the stairwells."

"I find, sometimes, that it is best to read things as they were written, but there is unfortunately a mountain of words to get through here." She held up a thick stack of papers with one hand, the mask briefly blurring as the camera focused on the sheaf. It was dropped a moment later, some of the top papers lazily flying off and flashes of words tantalizing the audience. *"My summary will have to do for the time being, but fret not. All of these documents have been scanned and are available for your viewing pleasure on Futurus's main website. They've spent an awful lot of money on the security for this building, and far too little on their cybersecurity."*

"On the third floor. It's... empty."

"In summary: shortly after the attack on Satol, Futurus began paying families, neighbors, and anyone who was willing to kidnap children with miens. These children were then kept by the company, and all received implants to monitor their brain activity, looking to find out the secret behind how their miens worked. They used children, children taken from their families unwillingly, children who were then stripped of their autonomy and experimented on, poked and prodded, until Futurus had what they wanted."

"Fourth floor, empty."

"I'll spare you all the gory details, but rest assured, it is far worse than you might imagine. And if you are inclined to believe the best in people, to believe that this is all in some long-forgotten past, I find it critical to tell you more about how the Aether came to be."

"Fifth floor, empty."

"Ness, get out of there— now." Pressure switched all their

headsets to the line reserved for their class, her voice suddenly urgent. Ness, however, ignored her.

"Aether is founded from these children, from these now adults who were the lucky ones, those who escaped the laboratories in this very building. This organization would not have existed, had Futurus not decided to pilfer our youth, our future, for profit. It is their wanton cruelty toward a group already demonized for even the slightest infraction, that has made this not only inevitable but necessary. While those born with gifts are made to be monsters, this company— which has employed such monstrous means— has been internationally lauded for such wondrous ends.*"*

"Sixth floor, empty."

"Ness, come back here— right now."

"This began with the abduction of a child that was ignored. We gave the police a chance, the same chance they had before. We made a scene, a mess for them to find. This time, they knew within *hours that something was wrong, and yet, once again, they assumed the worst. Someone who has never done anything wrong except exist, and the police condemned him to death."*

Kirin's mouth felt dry.

"Yantra?" The word came out as a whine, but he received no response.

"The mighty hero Force revealed to us the events that happened here ten years ago, but she cunningly left out one small detail. Some of you may remember the heyday of Force and Valor, but for those too young, let me set the record straight: she was not the hero you have seen, not the hero everyone worships today. The woman tenderly holding a child and carrying him out of the flames was a change in attitude, a welcome one, but not what she was made for."

"Seventh floor... there's no one here."

"Ness, I said get out!" Pressure sounded near tears.

"Force was sent to Satol to do what she did best: eliminate the

threat. Her orders that day were to kill."

"I'm going to the top."

"Heroes are meant to be used as a weapon against us, against their own community. Force might see the error of her ways now, but how many lives did she take before she started to feel guilt? How many did she send to a life of imprisonment and enslavement before she considered what her actions were doing? Heroes, the police, these disgusting Futurus lackies, they do not care about us, they do not care about justice, they care about oppression. They care about keeping us from our true potential.

"They have made incredible profit off the pain of our people, and who out there can stop them? Look at this empire they have created; this city built on lies and deceit. They have made metal that can no longer be melted, a city that cannot be burned. They feared the child who was used before might be used yet again. They built this city as a monument to the supremacy of technology over natural power. This is a city of fear and hatred, pointed square in the face of someone who should have borne none of the blame. Tell me, people of Satol, do you think you've done enough? Do you think the heat-proof metal and the weight of concrete is enough to protect you?

"You have time to find out, listeners, but not much at all. This is just a taste." The mask was lifted slightly, just enough to reveal a smile underneath, and skin almost as white as snow. *"Tell me if you still feel confident. If not, I suggest that you run."*

The screen shut off; the afterimage of that smile burned onto the black. There was silence for a moment.

Then they all watched the tower explode.

27

Hero

Dulu grabbed Clidna around the waist and shot into the air, the sky giving a sharp crack as lightning flashed in his wake. Clidna shattered a window and Dulu wrapped his wings around them as they crashed through. Goldhorn began sprouting seeds along the ground; great trees erupted and began racing skyward, catching the top of the building as it began to tilt dangerously over the city. The crowd around them screamed and fled as the tower groaned, glass splintering from the deadly force.

Dulu emerged from the building, someone else dangling from Clidna's hand, but suddenly he wasn't the only person silhouetted against the sky.

From the surrounding buildings, dozens— *hundreds*— of people were appearing, some flying naturally, others using hover packs to stay afloat. They weren't heading for the fleeing civilians, but instead gunning for the knot of heroes at the base of the tower.

Three detached from the main host and headed straight for Dulu. Clidna's scream could be heard from the ground as they were surrounded by a bubble of pure sound, the attackers rebuffed for the moment. Dulu's wings folded, and they plunged toward the ground rapidly, Clidna's scream no longer holding any power, only fear. Only five meters from the ground, Dulu snapped his wings open again, but the moment he did, gunshots went off, blasting holes in the white, feathers ripped off in a spray of scarlet. He careened to the side, and he, along with Clidna and Ness, were lost to view as the rain started to fall.

There was a cracking sound from overhead, and they looked up to see the trees Goldhorn had created snapping under the weight of the steel, the tower tipping once more. Kirin was torn between trying to help support the building or running to where Dulu had seemed to fall, but then Pressure spoke up.

"Kirin, take Kapre and Medusa. Adlivun, go with Wyrm and Naddāha. Keep searching; if we find them, we stop this before it gets worse. Everyone else, clear the area. Goldhorn, I want you to start making a web to contain the debris on my mark."

Goldhorn didn't have to ask when that would be, as Pressure lifted off from the ground.

She shot into the air, a blast shattering the entire top of the structure into millions of tiny pieces, Goldhorn weaving with branches and leaves to contain the fragments of glass and metal. The attacking villains zeroed in on Pressure and headed straight for her, guns blasting away. But every single bullet, metal or glass, froze a meter away from her, creating a shell of violence that soon hid her whole frame from view. When the villains were only an arm's length away, all the projectiles were thrown back at twice the speed they'd first possessed, screams filling the sky as bodies began to drop. Kirin found himself staring as even the rain failed to wash away so much blood.

"Come on, we need to go." Medusa grabbed Kirin's arm and suddenly Kapre was there too, only to collapse once more as their consciousness was thrown into the ground.

"Which way?" Kirin asked, trying to shake himself out of his daze. He didn't even know where to begin; Pressure had given them no further instructions and was already fading from view as the vines formed a solid roof overhead.

"Head farther into the city, toward the second research building!" Yantra's voice was suddenly in his ear, hopeful, so hopeful.

Kirin didn't hesitate a moment longer, throwing Kapre over one shoulder and Medusa over the other as he began to run. They shot out from underneath Goldhorn's tree cover, and he heard yells from behind them, showing that their departure hadn't gone unnoticed.

"We'll draw some our way." Adlivun's voice was calm in his ear, and he caught a glimpse of her group running parallel a few streets away. She gave him a nod, and then they peeled off, heading to the right, shades appearing in her wake.

Some of their pursuers broke away, but the majority stayed hard on Kirin's heels, gunshots hitting the pavement uncomfortably close. Kirin pulled Medusa and Kapre in front of his chest, shielding them as best he could with his body. One shot grazed the top of his shoulder, a red line appearing against the white.

He ignored it, focusing all his attention on the green Futurus logo that glowed through the rain like a beacon. It was only a few blocks away, so tantalizingly close, but they were being gained on far too quickly.

"Kirin, put me back over your shoulder." Medusa's voice was calm, even though Kirin's own heart was pounding wildly.

"There are too many!" His breath came out in ragged bursts as he heard another shot hit one of his scars, a narrow miss of his spine.

"Kirin, I'll take care of them." He could hardly spare a glance at her face, but out of the corner of his eye, he saw a faint wobble in her chin. She knew as well as he did what would happen if she did as she was planning. But she was willing, if that was what it took.

"Go down!" Yantra yelled in his ear so loudly and suddenly that Kirin tripped, sending the three of them to the ground. It should've been a fatal mistake, but the moment Kapre's skin brushed the too-level pavement, the road beneath them vanished.

It was a long fall, the moments stretching as they descended, Medusa screaming from the shock. Kirin redoubled his grip on them both, resolving himself to shelter them from the impact when it inevitably came, hardening as much as he could without harming either of them. Kapre was clinging to him, their long hair blowing into his face, their tears flying up toward the shrinking sky.

He landed on his back, mercifully, but even with the protection he'd given himself the wind was knocked out of him. Medusa's shout was cut off too, but both his companions got to their feet, unharmed except for confusion as they looked around.

They were in an old subway tunnel, evidently far, far beneath the new surface of the city. Distantly, he could hear the villains calling for backup, some specks hovering in the opening as if they were afraid to follow. Kapre was touching the dirt around the metal tracks, slumped forward as their mind raced through the ground.

"That way!" They leapt to their feet and started forward, but after only a few steps, they started to wobble. Kirin finally caught his breath, and as he did, his eyes widened, and he threw Kapre back.

"You two need to go back above ground— now." He breathed in deeply, feeling the carbon in the back of his throat. The air felt heavy, dense, but he knew neither of them could feel the change.

"We can't just leave you here alone!" Medusa went to approach him, but she was stopped by Kapre falling to the ground. With Kirin several steps away, Medusa draped one of Kapre's arms over her shoulders, mouth set in a worried line.

"Get back to Pressure. Tell her we found them." A tunnel opened to their left, Kapre listening in. Even if they didn't fully understand what was happening, they had felt the effects of the poisoned air and were making a way out. Medusa was pushed toward it as the ground started to move under her feet.

"They're going to come in here!" Medusa grabbed onto the edge of the wall, preventing herself from disappearing entirely. "They'll catch up to you, and what'll you do then?"

"I'm going to get our friends back." Kirin crystallized his whole face, the cloth mask shredding from the sudden sharpness. Medusa looked at the sky above, a distant glow, and understood. She was losing her battle against Kapre but held on for just a moment longer.

"Kirin, don't get caught."

Then he was alone.

"Yantra, which way do I go?" Only static answered him, and looking up through the hole Kapre had made, he knew why. The metal between him and the surface was thick, the chute they'd come through wide as he was tall and still looking tiny in comparison with the depth of the metal. Even as he stood there, tiny figures were growing larger, finally heading down into the tunnel with him.

He turned and started running the way Kapre had gone, the only light coming from the hole above his head. The air was filled with carbon monoxide, so much so that his skin felt like it would burst. He hardened, let it go to move a leg, an arm, re-crystallized, did it again and again, and he never ran out.

The villains were reaching the bottom now, having descended slowly. The tunnel was growing dimmer, but far in the distance, he could see a red light. It was a straight line, no turns, no offshoots, and the moment they saw him, shouts filled the air, though they sounded oddly muffled.

There was a grinding noise as a chunk of the floor lifted itself up behind him, the old subway track torn apart, and something crashed into it with an almighty boom that shook the very ground. The light from the outside had been cut off, leaving Kirin in only red, but the barrier was torn through seconds later, chunks of rock hitting his back even as he ran. A moment later, someone grabbed the back of his neck.

He was thrown to the side, but not without pain on their behalf as their hand was sliced open. Kirin released the crystallization on his back to peel himself from the corridor wall and kicked his attacker in the stomach with an un-hardened shin. They reeled back and Kirin turned and fled, his mien taking over his back as he did. The footsteps of his attacker, and several others it sounded like, were growing steadily closer. They must've had to abandon their hover packs, for fear of igniting the very air around them.

Kirin ducked, some instinct feeling the change in the air, and it proved to be the right decision, as a fist passed just overhead. He was under them now, releasing his mien and punching up, hitting them squarely in the metal mask they wore. It cracked and their eyes widened in horror before they dropped to the floor.

He stared at the prone body for a moment and then it clicked. The masks. They couldn't breathe down here. So far from daylight, he knew he couldn't be seen using his mien, but someone would have to recover these bodies, someone would see the marks he left and know. Unless he didn't need to use his mien to take them down at all.

The rest of the group was almost upon him, guns at their

sides, undrawn. Using primitive combustion propulsion would mean certain death for them all right now, so instead they would have to fight him up close. He turned to face them, his smile frozen in diamond.

The first tried to aim for his stomach, but all she got for her trouble was a kick to the head that shattered the mask and sent her flying into the wall. The second was wiser and slowed down to wait for a third, but even two on one they proved to be little trouble when Kirin was used to fighting someone almost too fast to see. One aimed for his ankle and the other his shoulder; the high kick he intercepted by grabbing their ankle and swinging them into each other, both crashing to the ground. Before they could get up again, Kirin was there, smashing their faces together and they were down for good.

Five more were coming down the tunnel, but Kirin would take them once they arrived. Kirin broke into a sprint, aiming for the red light illuminating the only door in the corridor, and with every step the carbon in the air grew. Each breath only brought him more strength.

Someone stabbed through his arm, but he grabbed them by the face and threw them into the wall; another aimed for his back, but their knife glanced harmlessly against crystal. He swung without looking and connected with something; whoever was on the other end dropped limply. The red light was just another few seconds away when someone grabbed him by the ankles, and he went down.

It could've been the twin of the woman they'd caught in East City, or maybe the triplet as an identical woman appeared to his right, stabbing at him from above. She sliced at his arm, but he was ready, the tip of the blade turned aside, and she seemed to vanish, a shadow moving away from where she'd been. Kirin grabbed her ankle once she was solid again and threw her, freeing one of his own feet to kick the one who'd stabbed at his head. She let go and vanished herself, a shadow creeping to his opposite side.

They attacked at once, in sync, and Kirin simply dropped, their attacks missing him entirely. They collided with each other instead, harmlessly, but in their confusion, Kirin pulled them down and ripped the masks off their faces, and within moments, they were unconscious.

He made it to the door. It was wrapped in wire, evidently set to detonate if anyone made it all the way down unharmed. But he didn't need a door.

Kirin stabbed his arm through the wall, slicing through concrete like it was butter, carving out a new opening. The red light bathed him, and he heard new footsteps filling the tunnel behind him, more than before, and more frantic too. He worked faster, pulling brick after brick out of the wall, the sight of a chair bolted to the floor making him speed up. He shoved his way into the room, and his breath caught.

Phoenix was staring back at him, tears rolling down her face. Ifrit was next to them, his head lolling backward and his face slack. Even the red light couldn't hide how pale he was, and for a moment Kirin couldn't do anything but stare, terrified that he might be too late. But then he was thrown backward, Ifrit's face shrinking as he careened back through the opening, Phoenix screaming after him.

His head hit the wall of the tunnel with no protection, the crack sounding distant. There, standing over him, was the woman in white.

"You are tenacious." Her voice was as clear as it'd been on the feed, though he couldn't see her mouth move from behind her flat mask. Aether members spread out behind her, separating him from Ifrit and Phoenix. Dimly, Kirin could hear the frantic tugging of chains, as Phoenix tried to break free. "And no respirator. That's interesting."

Kirin couldn't talk, his jaw still crystallized to hide his face. He just glared, trying to assess the situation as best as he could while his vision swam. There were at least six members of Aether, not counting the head herself. Kapre might be able to sense the attack and try to help, but Kirin had run so far since they'd separated, and if they'd headed toward the surface, he was likely out of their reach. This he would have to do alone. He got to his feet shakily, the woman not even attempting to stop him.

"You're not yet a hero, my friend. I'm afraid you can't do much." She tilted her head. "After all, you're trained to weigh lives, are you not? What are two compared to the oh so many you could save once you graduate?"

The words made his blood boil more than anything else she could have said. What were two? Phoenix, running themself ragged to keep their classmates safe. Phoenix, apologizing to Kuafu, trying so hard to fix the mistakes they'd made. Phoenix, scared and ashamed, sitting in the doorway to the dorm, waiting for Ifrit to come back to make sure he was okay.

And Ifrit.

The Aether members were spreading out around him, warily.

Ifrit, who struggled to verbalize his emotions and instead cooked them food every night. Ifrit, who was working so hard to prove that he wasn't a demon like everyone thought he was. Ifrit, who liked action movies and terrible romance books, who swore with almost every breath, who hated making promises he couldn't keep, whose hands shook when he tried to offer comfort.

Ifrit, who Kirin was not leaving without, one way or another.

"What are they worth, hero?"

Kirin let his mien fall.

"Everything."

He moved so fast he hardly felt it, flying at the first person on his left, ripping the mask from their face and onto the next before anyone noticed. He didn't see the faces underneath his hands, didn't feel the blades that were thrust toward his side, his arms, his back; all he knew was that they were *right there*, and he wasn't going to fail now.

The first two were down, but the third was fast, inhumanly so. They were behind Kirin and suddenly there was a knife to Kirin's throat, him barely hardening in time to avoid being sliced open. He reached over his head and grabbed them, even their speed not enough to get out of the way when they were in such close quarters. He threw them into one of the approaching villains, but that left two to surround him.

One detached their torso from their waist and began attacking him on two fronts, while the second morphed into an enormous snake and began squeezing him tightly, in an attempt to choke off his air. Even the special material of his costume wasn't enough to save them from shredding themself against the crystallized skin once they pulled too tight, and they reverted to human form, bleeding. The dismembered man proved harder, as no hit seemed to hurt him. When he latched his arms around Kirin's neck, Kirin slammed back against the wall and smashed his head back into the man's, hearing the mask snap and the pressure around his throat faded.

That still left the fast woman and one other, a hulking person nearly Kirin's height.

"You'll have to kill us, you know, to keep us quiet."

Kirin ignored the woman in white, since she had made no attempt to join the fight, instead focusing on the two still left. The small woman was fast, but Kirin had dealt with fast enemies before, all that time practicing with Aïcha and Ifrit put to good use. In the end, her speed helped him, for when she charged, he stepped to the side and kept her momentum going right into the wall.

That left the large person and the woman in white.

"You're willing to kill, then?" The woman sounded amused. "If all heroes are as ruthless as you, we are in trouble indeed. Do you think that you can hide what you did down here by only using half your strength? You're doomed dear, and you've burned a bridge with us. We would've welcomed someone like you, had you just not fought back."

"And yet you're the one who seems scared." The doorway was just to his left; he'd managed to switch places with them without anyone noticing. His dodging had seemed random, but he'd slowly made his way back to this side. He could even see Phoenix now, see Ifrit, and there was just one person left.

"You have no weapon; they'll know what you did." There was something off about how she kept trying to get him to talk instead of trying to fight. The large figure next to her seemed just as reluctant, which Kirin didn't understand until he took in the scattered bodies across the floor. How many now had he taken out? His mind refused to count. There was just one more, just one more and Ifrit would be free.

"Who said I had no weapon?" Kirin hardened his hands and cut off his hair.

The large person charged at last, reaching for Kirin and met with a stake through the hand, pinning them to the wall of the tunnel, Kirin's hair hardened into an unbreakable rod. Though they couldn't move, they managed to grab Kirin's head and smashed him into the wall, repeatedly, until blood ran down his face. He couldn't tell if he was holding himself up or if they were, hands scrabbling around their throat, their shoulders, trying to reach for the mask around their mouth. He dimly heard a crash behind him, but his vision was going dark around the edges, grappling there in the doorway just a meter away from the person he was trying to save.

"You chose wrong, hero."

His attacker's face swam and suddenly it was his father, watching him with sad, detached eyes. Kirin opened his mouth to apologize, and blood trickled in, the metallic tang bringing his gaze back into focus. No, his dad wasn't there. He didn't need to ask for forgiveness. And he was *going* to save his friends.

The strength of his conviction brought clarity to both his thoughts and his sight. No, that was wrong again. He felt a weak grip on his ankle and looked down to see Phoenix, Ifrit's chair having been tipped over and dragged across the floor until they could just reach. Their hand fell away a moment later, their eyes fluttering with exhaustion.

With renewed strength, Kirin wrenched the hand off him, kicking his attacker in the chest forcefully enough that he felt something crack. They stumbled back, eyes widening, blocking Kirin's first punch, his second, but *retreating.* Their fatal mistake was turning to look for guidance, and Kirin shattered their mask with one final blow.

They didn't drop immediately, fear turning to anger as they charged back at Kirin recklessly. They were holding their breath, hands outstretched to reach for Kirin's throat, and he let them get close. So close that with their next step he had to look down to see them, to see his own blood drip onto their face. Kirin grabbed their head this time and picked them up, slamming them down onto the floor as quickly as he could. They didn't move anymore, and Kirin hoped it hadn't hurt in the end.

That left only her, the woman behind it all, who even now wasn't trying to attack.

He tossed the remaining stake to his left hand, his palm and fingers crystallized around it to stop from slicing himself open as he rushed forward, the woman falling back lazily, almost aimlessly. She nearly floated away, like gravity had no purchase on her.

"It seems that you think you've won, but unfortunately for you, you're a mite too slow." She was suddenly in his face, the mask so perfectly flat and shiny, though it didn't show his reflection at all. "What a fine grave this will make for you."

And then she vanished, like she was never there to begin with.

Kirin didn't care. He ran back to Phoenix, who was still sprawled on the floor, arm twisted violently where the chain pulled her back toward Ifrit. Their mien was trying to fix it desperately, the muscles writhing under their skin.

"What did she mean by a grave?" Phoenix asked as Kirin helped them sit up, a delicate operation since they couldn't risk Phoenix losing contact with Ifrit. They'd ripped up their pants to keep a skin-to-skin connection, their ankle pressing against one of the cutouts in Ifrit's costume.

"It's gas. Toxic gas." Kirin hated it, but he couldn't get the chains off either of them yet. The chance that they'd spark if they broke was high, and then it would all be for nothing. He'd run a long way from where he'd first entered the tunnel, and he suspected it was only the original imbalance of air that had let Medusa and Kapre walk away. "They've turned this whole tunnel into a bomb, with this room at the center."

"How..." Phoenix turned to look at Ifrit.

The open windows at night. Being so afraid when people came close. A human flame thrower, or at least the fuel source for one.

"He doesn't control fire." Kirin whispered. "He creates and controls *carbon monoxide*. But he isn't immune to it either."

Why were the three of them paired together alone on the top floor? To make sure that no one was hurt when he was asleep and couldn't control it.

"We need to get out, we need to..." Phoenix was pacing, or trying to, but the metal linking her to Ifrit was short. "How are they going to ignite it?"

"Doesn't matter. If we wake him up, he can control it."

"He won't wake up! I haven't stopped healing him, and even that's just keeping him from... from..."

"It's okay, Phoenix." The chair that Ifrit was chained to was wood, and Kirin broke it apart piece by piece as quickly as he could, fearing they'd hear the rush of fire any second. The chains slid free, still wrapped around both Ifrit and Phoenix's wrists, but no longer attached to the miserable box they'd been held in. Ifrit felt cold to the touch as Kirin lifted him, his head falling heavily against Kirin's neck. They stepped through the destroyed wall and into the corridor, the red light reflecting off Phoenix's skin as they looked at Kirin with fear. "I'm going to need you to hold onto my neck, and when I say to, close your eyes."

Phoenix did as he asked, but Kirin didn't fail to notice how frail their grip was, and though he hadn't said to yet, they buried their face in his shirt, like they couldn't bear to watch.

Kirin had to adjust how he was holding Ifrit, one arm wrapped around his back and hugging him to Kirin's side, the other extricated from Phoenix to reach out and touch Ifrit's face. He lifted Ifrit's chin, trying to quiet the thundering in his ears, ignoring the ghastly cast the light gave to his skin.

"Please work." Kirin whispered.

And before he could question what he was doing, Kirin covered Ifrit's mouth with his own.

He summoned all the carbon in his body and crystallized his back, his legs, his arms, the top half of his face too, breathing out and forcing oxygen into Ifrit's lungs, praying— to who or what he did not know— that he could just give him air, let him *breathe*. He held there, five breaths, ten, forcing himself to keep his exhales deep and steady, even as his hands started to shake. Thirty seconds. Forty. Tears were building behind his eyelids, thinking that it wasn't enough, they weren't going to make it, before, suddenly, he felt the slightest gasp.

Kirin released his mien on his face so he could open his eyes, greeted with the sight of Ifrit looking back at him, disoriented but *awake*. Ifrit reached up as if in a daze, touching the side of Kirin's face like he wasn't sure Kirin was real. Kirin opened his mouth to explain, to say that Ifrit needed more, but Ifrit already knew, pressing their lips back together and sliding his hand into Kirin's hair.

Tears fell on Kirin's face, and he knew they were a mix of Ifrit's and his own, his hand sliding to the back of Ifrit's neck, his fingers running through Ifrit's hair, pulling him closer, savoring the fact that he was there, right *there*. Ifrit's other hand found Kirin's jaw, tugging Kirin down, their noses bumping, the rough edge of Ifrit's lips scraping against Kirin's; it all said that Ifrit was real, that he was in Kirin's reach. He'd found him. A laugh bubbled up in Kirin's chest, happiness despite the impending danger, the sound captured by Ifrit's mouth.

Kirin would move mountains, would fight until he fell, to have a moment like this again. Ifrit, here in his arms, a missing piece slotted into place.

Ifrit was gaining strength, the air around them starting to churn, the taste of charcoal filling the back of Kirin's throat as the air grew denser, heavier, compacted beyond anything natural.

"Ready?" Ifrit asked, his mouth moving against Kirin's.

"Ready."

Kirin held them both as Ifrit snapped his fingers, and the world turned to flame.

28

Sacrifice

THE COLUMN OF FIRE burned straight through the metal above them, the force of it spewing the steel into the sky; Kirin curled his body around the other two as they were shot out of the ground with explosive speed. The moment they hit the open air, Phoenix gasped, coughing as they breathed for the first time in days, their tears mixing with the pouring rain. Ifrit sagged against Kirin, energy spent, and it was only through sheer luck that Kirin was able to direct their fall and avoid plunging straight back from where they came.

They crashed into the ground hard enough to hurt, even with Kirin's mien active, rolling over several times before they came to a stop. Now out of the metal prison, he could hear his classmates actively yelling in his ear.

"We're heading to the location of the fire!" Aïcha was yelling to be heard over the sounds of gunfire.

"Goldhorn, any sign of Dulu, Ness, or Clidna?" Naddāha's voice sounded desperate.

"Antaeus is injured, moving him back to the jet, need someone to cover the civilians at the corner of five and twenty!" Wyrm said, panicked.

"I'm coming, Wyrm." Adlivun's voice was a calm island in the midst of the chaos.

"Ad?" Phoenix spoke up in a croak, hand going to their ear. Even with all the background noise on the comms, Kirin could hear the sharp inhale from Adlivun.

"We'll go to Antaeus, you go to them." Aïcha came through again, sounding breathless but quieter.

"Kuafu, Lilin, you too." Pressure was on the line, confident and authoritative. "The enemy is converging toward the explosion. Kirin, you have about one minute until you're surrounded. Move."

Kirin ripped the chain connecting Ifrit and Phoenix apart, throwing Ifrit over one shoulder and Phoenix over the other. Pressure had said one minute, but he saw someone flying toward them already, gun in hand and aimed for Kirin's head. Without a thought, Kirin ripped a sign out of the ground and threw it like a javelin, hitting the villain square in the chest and sending them spiraling off into the air.

A blast of fire came from the right, and he was thrown to the side, but it was only Ifrit, pushing them out of the way of someone attacking from behind. They had no weapon and instead held out their hands; Kirin elbowed hard them in the face, starting to run before he knew if they'd fallen.

Adlivun was suddenly there, emerging from around a corner, Naddāha just behind. Kuafu and Lilin came from a different street as Phoenix wriggled out of Kirin's grasp and threw themself into Adlivun's arms. They buried their face in Adlivun's shoulder, bright orange hair mixing with black as Adlivun let out a strangled cry, hugging them back with all her might. But Kuafu and Lilin were staring horrified at something behind Kirin.

He turned, putting Ifrit down since it was now too late to run, and together, they saw the wave of villains approaching, an insect plague filling the sky. Weapons were drawn, laser sights all appearing on Ifrit's skin. Then— darkness.

Kirin grabbed Ifrit at the same time as Ifrit reached for him, but then a smaller hand grabbed Kirin's wrist and Kuafu appeared, shining behind the living shadow that was Lilin. He created a bubble in the darkness, lighting a path around buildings and rubble, their group starting to sprint again.

The darkness moved with them, rain appearing out of pure black clouds, Lilin keeping them out of sight for one block, two. Shades flickered in and out of existence, mouthing words to Adlivun who would then correct their course down different streets, avoiding groups of fighting on the ground. They hadn't been running long, but both Phoenix and Ifrit were starting to lag, the days of torment catching up to them, Kirin increasingly pulling Ifrit along by his hand instead of running beside him.

Kirin had just paused to lift Ifrit again when Lilin screamed, thrown backward into the darkness of her own making. The shadows lifted almost immediately, revealing her crumpled on the ground, blood dripping from her temple, a villain with a wicked knife staring Kuafu in the eyes. Kuafu didn't hesitate, shoving his burning palms toward the man's face, the knife abandoned as the villain rubbed at his now blind eyes.

Phoenix tripped and fell as they went to Lilin, reaching her just as the first of the airborne villains found them again. Guns were cocked and aimed again, Kirin wrapping his body around Ifrit and crystallizing, bracing for the impact as bullets began to fly. But then Naddāha stepped forward.

There was fury in her eyes, like Kirin had never seen before, and she *screamed*, the sound echoed a moment later by dozens of voices, filling the sky like thunder.

People fell from the air, clutching their chests, their heads; some shot off in random directions and hit the sides of buildings, glass blending with the rain as it fell. The wind whipped Naddāha's hair out behind her as the few remaining enemies trained their weapons at her, as she merely raised her head in defiance. Kirin only had just enough time to jump in front of her before the shots went off, feeling one hit the soft tissue inside his elbow as he stretched his arms out to cover her face.

As he hit the ground, more gunshots went off, and some part of his brain knew he couldn't make it in time, knew that there was no way, watching the bullets fly in almost slow motion. Still, he shoved himself up, hoping, praying that somehow, he could get there, but then the ground ripped itself straight upward, the bullets bouncing harmlessly off a thick meter of stone. The wall erupted farther upward still, Kapre covering them as Ifrit grabbed Kirin's hand and they ran, Adlivun leading the charge.

Someone leapt out from a side alley— an Aether agent judging from the hover pack— but before anyone could react, the metal started twisting itself together, forming a metal snake. The villain was pulled backward by the throat, abandoning them entirely. Yantra, where was Yantra?

As they broke into another side street, they were met with the final obstacle, a wall of powers ranging from electricity to technopathy blocking their path. There were police sirens in the distance, but what help would that be? They were as good as villains to the authorities now, the evidence scattered throughout the city. Even then, what could their exhausted group do against fresh-faced enemies?

"Don't look." Medusa's voice came through clearly, Kirin only catching a glimpse of her dragging Kapre's body before he forced his eyes to the ground. After a few moments, he snuck a peek at the villains, finding them frozen in place, even the electricity sparking between one of their fingers stopped midway through its arc. They could leave now, but that would mean leaving Medusa behind, for either Aether or the police to pick up.

"What do we do?" Adlivun had come to the same conclusion,

warring desires crossing her face as she looked at Phoenix, who was barely able to stand.

"Stand down." Pressure's voice found them twice, their headset repeating the words that filled the air behind them. Despite Medusa's warning, Kirin turned, watching as villains trailed in Pressure's wake as she appeared between buildings, flattening anyone within ten meters into mush upon the ground, the concrete cracking with the force of it. Still more came, shooting, flying close, any attempt to stop her, but she was unstoppable, anyone close reduced to dust in seconds. She almost seemed to be taking her time with them, toying with those around her, smashing them into each other, shearing others apart. Many were fleeing, but they didn't get far. They did, however, draw Pressure's attention to the group of her students staring up from the ground.

Everyone attacking Pressure was blown backward, the force of the blast shattering all the windows nearby. She was on the ground and in front of them faster than Kirin could see her move, and her hands trembled as she reached for Ifrit, pulling him into a hug. She was crying; not the cold, detached crying they'd seen in her office, but full body-wracking sobs as she held him.

"It's okay, I've got you."

A memory flashed through Kirin's head from the same city, a decade before. Under a post, barely conscious. The brightest blue. *It's okay, I've got you.*

"What did you *do*?" Ifrit's voice came in a hard whisper. While Pressure's face was a mask of relief and joy, Ifrit's was a study in dread.

"What I had to." She held his face tenderly, like she was studying it, and gave him a kiss on the forehead. "I told you kid, right? I was always going to come back for you."

"But—"

"It was worth it." She said it resolutely, her eyes absolutely sure. Even through her tears, she smiled, and if Kirin had to put a name to her expression, he would've said she looked at peace. She rose back in the air, though there was no one left to fight. "It was worth every second. Kirin, get him back to Shifter for me, no matter what he says."

Ifrit lunged to go after her, but Kirin caught him around the middle, holding him in place.

"We need to get you safe." Kirin held him as gently as he could with Ifrit fighting so much, reaching out after her and trying to summon enough of an explosion to get off the ground.

"No, you don't fucking understand!" Kirin tried to walk away, but Ifrit was struggling too much, seeming more desperate than when he'd woken up, more desperate than Kirin had ever seen him before. "She can't fight!"

"It's okay, she's just covering our retreat." Naddāha stepped forward, hands raised, but before she could say another word, Ifrit detonated an explosion at point blank range, blowing her backward into a building and knocking her out.

"Ifrit, what the hell!" Kuafu yelled.

"They're going to kill her!" He managed to get out of Kirin's grip briefly, but Kirin grabbed his ankle and brought him down again, understanding dawning slowly.

"What?" Even Adlivun was confused. Pressure was almost alone in the sky, but the few villains remaining proved to be no trouble, crushed like bugs and joining the corpses littering the ground.

"Not the fucking villains!" Ifrit got in the air again, a shade of Phoenix appearing above him and tackling him to the ground, vanishing a moment later.

The remaining Aether agents finally started to flee, realizing the fight was long since lost, leaving her with easy pickings. She didn't let a single one escape, taking them down with cold, methodical precision, until it was only her left in the air, hair fluttering in a breeze that couldn't be felt so far below.

A police car appeared in view just next to her, some of the raised magnetic lanes still functioning even after all the damage the city had taken. Another quickly joined it.

"See, it's fine, backup is here now." Lilin tried her hand at comfort, Kuafu having picked up Naddāha. "But we have to go, since she's licensed to be here, and we're not."

Ifrit wouldn't listen, back in the air and shooting for her as fast as he could. Kirin ran behind him, dread building in his stomach. How much the police had seen was a toss-up, with Ifrit having been out of the fight for most of it, but running toward them felt like an awful idea. Pressure hovered there alone, silhouetted in the car headlights, raindrops shining like fallen stars decorating her pristine blue suit, head held high. She looked down, saw Ifrit shooting toward her, and though it was too far away to tell, Kirin felt like he could see her smile from fifty meters below.

Ifrit was still far away, too far away, when the guns went off.

Pressure folded, dropping like a stone. Ifrit seemed frozen for a moment, staring at where she had been, but Kirin kept running, lungs burning, feet feeling like concrete, and he dove, her body hitting his arms instead of the ground.

It didn't take more than a single glance to know it was bad. There were several holes in her chest, one in her throat, and a dozen others, though the blood was washed away by the rain. She still smiled, though.

"He deserved better." Her eyes were to the sky, where Ifrit was dropping, wreathed in fire. "What a... ridiculous kid, huh?"

Her eyes closed.

"Phoenix!" Ifrit screamed as he reached the ground, shaking hands touching her face. But as they looked up, Phoenix and the rest of their friends were surrounded by police, Phoenix trying to shove their way through, half jumping over the officers surrounding them, screaming wordlessly as they were held back.

"Come on, don't do this to me, not here." Ifrit's eyes were filling with tears, looking like there might be something nearby that could help, could heal her, but the blood was already slowing. "Not here."

"Phoenix!" Kirin couldn't stop himself from yelling too, even though he knew— he *knew*— it was too late.

Pressure didn't respond, the small smile on her face still there. She looked satisfied.

"Please don't leave." Ifrit whispered. "You said that I could stay with you. You said that you'd keep me safe. How can you do that now?"

She didn't respond.

Ifrit took her hand in both of his and bowed his head like he was praying.

"Please... please don't leave me here alone."

But she had already gone.

29

Goodbye

Kirin refused to leave Ifrit's side.

Not when they pulled him away from her body, not when they were all piled into police cars, not when they were pushed into interrogation rooms. One officer tried to separate them, but Kirin had nearly sent the man flying, until Shifter appeared and said something to appease the cop. They'd stopped trying to pull the pair apart since.

Time passed. Kirin didn't know how much. If asked, he couldn't have even remembered what he told the police, arms aching from holding so tightly to Ifrit, like he was going to disappear any moment. Ifrit, he could recall, didn't say a single word.

There was paperwork to do, lots of it. It wasn't for him. It was for Ifrit, as Pressure's designated next of kin. Her body was considered government property, and he had to sign it away, the paper almost illegible from the water spilled on it. For the first time, Kirin considered that when he died, his mother would have to do the same. It was only after the documents were signed and sealed that they were allowed to join the others, back in the lobby.

Everyone was lying there, wrapped in thick blankets, covered in dirt and ash and blood. They started when Ifrit appeared, Kirin still holding his hand. A moment later and they were swarmed, the whole class hugging them. Ifrit made a choked sound, and suddenly they were on the ground, a pile of bodies and tears with nothing needing to be said. When the first wave passed, Kirin noticed that there were only fifteen.

"Where's..." His throat felt raw, and he had to clear it a few times before the words would come out. "Where's Ness? And Clidna and Dulu?"

Shining eyes greeted him, Yantra still crying silently, tear tracts clearing the ash off her face. No one spoke, and his heart plummeted even further, looking around again, hoping beyond all hope that she was there, somewhere, just hard to spot, like always. But try as he might, he couldn't see a tell-tale blur anywhere.

"They're not..." He couldn't say it. He stared at each face that greeted him, hoping that one of them would tell him no, he was mistaken. They were already on the plane; they were just waiting for everyone else. They couldn't be... Not Dulu. Not Clidna. Not *Ness*.

Shifter appeared from one of the hallways, more disheveled than usual, eyes rimmed red. Kirin looked at him, hopeful, but he didn't meet any of their eyes.

"We're all set to head back." His voice was quiet, the edge of anguish present. Absently, Kirin wondered how he'd explained his presence to the police here. "The school has been informed of the situation, and you've all been granted pardons for your participation. But we do need to head back quickly, so they can start doing damage control."

"Damage control?" Naddāha was the one to speak up, usually so level-headed, but sounding furious now. "I don't give a damn how the world sees us, I just want my friends back, and I'm not leaving until we find them. We came here to get two, we're not leaving with three still missing!"

A chorus of voices joined hers, Kirin too numb to add his own.

"We're not giving up." Shifter never raised his voice, so the volume was effective now. "But we can't do anymore here. We need to get all of you back to campus where you can clean up and *rest* and we can let the local heroes continue the search."

"But how long will that take?" Goldhorn sounded close to tears themself.

"I'd say just a few moments more. We *tried* to get here as fast as we could, but it's hard when you don't have a map." A voice spoke from the doorway.

Kirin almost couldn't believe his ears, and turned to face the voice's owner slowly, half thinking it was a dream. But there were Ness, and Clidna, supporting a very pale-looking Dulu between the two. They were filthy, covered head to toe in grime, Dulu's wings almost as dark as his skin with soot, but very, very much alive.

Kirin might not have recovered from the shock, but everyone else did; Ness was practically buried under Yantra and Wyrm, Phoenix rushing to Dulu but closely followed by Naddāha and Goldhorn, and Clidna tackled to the ground by Medusa, quickly lost to view as the rest of the class gathered round. While they all hugged, Kirin helped Ifrit to his feet, still refusing to let go even for a moment.

"Kirin." Shifter was at his elbow, and on instinct Kirin crystallized the whole side of his body. If Shifter was offended, he didn't show it, offering a mask out instead. "There are press outside. Make sure to cover up."

Kirin took it silently, but Ifrit resisted the one he was offered.

"Your own mask's destroyed." Shifter reminded him.

"I don't want that on my fucking face." Ifrit's voice was even more gravelly than usual, since it'd been hours since he last spoke.

"It'll just be for a minute." Kirin squeezed his hand, touching the side of his face lightly. "If it's too much, I'll just shield you instead."

Ifrit pressed his cheek against Kirin's hand, a silent thank you, and when he pulled away Kirin found the tips of his fingers were damp.

Now that the joy at their missing classmates' return had died down, it became obvious who was still missing.

"Wait," Clidna said. "Where's Pressure?"

Silence took over, Adlivun lowering her eyes. Some didn't though, looking at Ifrit and Kirin with the faintest trace of hope, like maybe the reason they'd been held so long was because they were checking in on her, instead of confirming that she was dead.

"She's gone." Ifrit swallowed hard. "She's... she's gone."

"How?" Ness's eyes were wide, taking a step forward almost involuntarily.

"She didn't have a license." Shifter stepped in before Kirin had a chance to, neither of them wanting to make Ifrit explain.

"But—"

"How did she—"

"She lost her fucking license because of me." Ifrit pushed Shifter out of the way, nostrils flaring as he breathed in to avoid crying. "She was supposed to kill me, the first time, and she didn't."

The taut muscle in his jaw and suspicious brightness of his eyes kept anyone from asking further questions. Even if they'd wanted to, Shifter was already pulling open the door to the precinct, and they were drowned in shouted questions and flashing lights. Officers began bringing them out to waiting cars, two at a time, which left Kirin space to find his own words.

"I'm sorry." He whispered. "I should have stopped her."

"You couldn't do shit." Ifrit wasn't looking his way, but his voice sounded thick, all of a sudden. "She was a stubborn old bitch when she wanted to be."

"Still, I should have—"

Ifrit turned around sharply and headbutted Kirin. It wasn't hard enough to make him move, but it did force him to look at Ifrit's eyes. They were red, and this time it wasn't only from his irises. Kirin still thought that was the most beautiful color he'd ever seen.

"I got to live with her for ten years. Trust me, there's nothing—" His voice caught. "There's nothing any of us could've done."

Kirin didn't know what to say to that. Luckily, Phoenix did.

"Come on." They reached out to both of them, standing just before the door. "Let's go home."

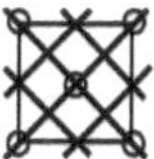

The world is still in shock after the events that unfolded in Satol, a city attacked not once, but twice. The biggest blow was perhaps not that the city was targeted again, but that the foremost hero in the world, and the one who saved the day the first time, Force, was struck down not during the conflict, but after it, and by the police, no less.

"I understand that they say now *she had no license, but she's been doing good work for a decade, apparently, without one, so why did they kill her? Seems unfair to me."*

"This woman managed to save a city twice *before the age of forty, and they murder her for it? How can we expect heroes to help us when the thanks they get is murder at the hands of the police? She was even working to help reduce these incidents— the only person I've heard of working to make her own profession*

redundant— and yet we're treating her like she's the villain."

"I know what she did was illegal, but if anything, that makes me respect her more. She knew what the consequences would be and yet she still chose to do the right thing. I have family that lives in Satol, and I have no doubt that they're alive today because Force was there when we needed her."

While some are angry that such a prominent hero was killed, others maintain that the police did the right thing.

"She had no license and killed, if the numbers are correct, hundreds of people. What end could she have expected? She deserved it."

"I just can't believe they let that woman teach the next generation of heroes. What have they been learning this whole time? Why was she allowed to hold a position if she had no license herself? To me it says that she was so used to getting away with whatever she wanted she thought she could get away with this, too."

"As far as I'm concerned, she was just as terrible as Aether is, and it's a good riddance we found this out before we had to face both of them together."

Whatever might be thought of the now controversial woman, her students have garnered nothing but praise. Told that their licenses had been advanced, they still showed remarkable restraint in using their miens in the city, and indeed, the locals on the scene reported that the death toll would have been much worse had the students not been present.

"They worked tirelessly and determinedly, and I, for one, am glad that they were on our side. We couldn't have stopped this without them, and if I had to give credit to only a few for the city still standing, it would be those kids," local hero Mesmer stated.

While we'll have to wait another year to know the names of our rising heroes, one face, certainly has risen to the top.

This student, captured for the second time by Aether, can be seen in this footage channeling all the destructive force that would have leveled the city into the air, nearly killing himself and two classmates. It seems that only sheer luck saw them land safely, or rather, luck and a powerful mien indeed. It is this network's professional opinion to keep your eyes not only on this fiery newcomer, but also his large and silent classmate who was able to withstand the force of ten combustion engines and a fall from nearly twenty meters.

Whatever your thoughts might have been on Force, she has certainly paved the way for more discourse surrounding miens and how they're perceived, and the world will absolutely be watching those set to follow in her footsteps.

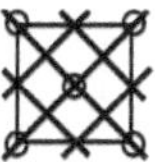

There would be no funeral, not officially.

Pressure had broken every law ever set for heroes, and so she died in disgrace. It'd been her plan all along, knowing what would happen if she set out for the city. Shifter had told the police a story that had elements of the truth, but not all of it. It left everyone free of blame except her, everyone else safe but her.

He'd been kidnapped from the hospital and forced under duress to tell her where he thought Ifrit and Phoenix might have been taken. The class was told their licenses were granted early, due to the extenuating circumstances. All their actions were made under the assumption it was legal, not knowing that Pressure was operating for her own means. She had, after all, told no one that Ifrit was her adopted son, taken in after his own parents refused to take him back.

It was only right, then, that Ifrit was the one to speak about her.

"She always said there was power in appearances," Ifrit said hoarsely, tears falling freely. His nose was red both from the cold and emotion. "When the whole world knows who you are, they can't really do much to you. They needed her to put on a show, couldn't dismiss the most famous hero, so they let her come here. And whatever she might have done wrong before, she started trying to put it right."

They had no body to bury, the police in Satol incinerating her body as they did for all criminals. Ifrit had picked a photo, one of her smiling, looking carefree, not staring at the camera but off to the side, the joy in her eyes clear to see.

"I'm not going to pretend she was perfect, because she fucking wasn't. Who the hell teaches a ten-year-old kid to swear? But she was a damn good teacher and a damn good mother when she didn't have to be." Ifrit's hands tightened, struggling to keep going. Kirin put a hand on his back, and he took a breath. "I wouldn't be here today if she hadn't looked at herself, looked at the world and said 'something's wrong here.' She lost her whole life because she wanted to take a chance on me."

He took a few more shallow breaths.

"I wish she didn't." His voice cracked. "I wish she were still here, because I think this world was a better place with her in it. But she was always going on about how you can't control what other people do, only what you do about it. So, I'm going to do my best to live, and live in a way that I think would make her proud."

With that, he wiped his face with the back of his hand and placed the photo in the hole they'd made, dropping the first handful of dirt on top. He turned away quickly, as if he couldn't bear to watch her fade from view as Kapre filled the ground back up, Pressure's smile vanishing forever.

Shifter was watching from the back door of the house, his own eyes far from dry. When Ifrit passed him, he ruffled his hair, Ifrit's shoulders hunching as he started to sob.

The rest of the class stayed outside a little longer, maybe not ready to say goodbye, maybe just trying to find the words to say something themselves. Kuafu, perhaps unsurprisingly, was the one who found his first.

"Pressure found me at the worst moment in my life." The hair falling across Kuafu's eyes failed to hide his tears, though his voice was steady as ever. "I'd just had everything stripped away from me, found out everything I'd ever known was a lie. I still don't know why she was there, since this would've been after she'd lost her license, but it's always felt like she knew I needed someone to believe in again.

"Force was the most popular hero in the world, and I'd never heard of her. She'd walked into the room and didn't even bother introducing herself, just started talking to me. When I finally asked who she was, she started laughing so hard. It hadn't even crossed her mind that I wouldn't know."

Goldhorn squatted in the grass and pricked their thumb, a small drop of blood falling into the soil. A bloom of flowers appeared through the snow, all bright blue.

"That was when I got to meet Pressure, instead of Force. Even though we'd been talking for a while, there'd been this... distance. Like I needed to be kept at arm's length. But then it was gone, and for the first time since I'd been captured, it felt like I was a person again. That I was someone deserving of kindness again." Kuafu's voice broke and he took a breath before continuing.

"I didn't trust her at first. I didn't trust anyone, and she never held that against me. She didn't get angry, she didn't ever raise her voice even when some days I wouldn't talk to her at all. She just kept coming back, checking in on me. She kept asking me if I would consider joining the hero program, to learn under her. I told her I didn't think they'd let me. She promised me, if I wanted to, that she'd make it happen."

Goldhorn stepped back and rested their head on Dulu's shoulder, tears dripping down their nose.

"I couldn't understand then why she was so insistent that I join. But I get it now. They are going to ask us to do things that are wrong. They are going to ask us to hurt people who don't deserve to be hurt. She didn't want heroes to be like she was, to just follow orders. She wanted heroes who would stop to think about whether what they are doing is *right*." Kuafu cleared his throat. "She might be gone, but we're all still here. Which means what she wanted for the future is still possible. I don't know how we'll manage it, but I think the best way to honor her is looking to the future, as she was, and trying to make it better."

"I'm willing to at least try." Lilin said softly.

"Do any of us even know where to start?" Aïcha hugged her elbows. "People will be far less likely to trust anything that *we* do, since they know we are... were her students. We know the coalition *exists*, but we don't even know who's in it."

"I think we all knew this was going to be an uphill battle from the start." Kirin was surprised by the sound of his own voice. "Most of us never even thought we'd get in. We didn't know that we had someone on our side, so in a way, things haven't changed that much. Except she had plans. She had ideas that we can make a reality because *we're still here*. She deserved better, it's true. But we all do. And we know no one is going to do it for us. The world doesn't trust us now, but did they ever? Their anger will fade, because at the end of the day, we stopped Aether. A lot of people are alive today because of us, which— cover story or not— is the real reason the police couldn't touch us.

"It'll take time, but we've got it. I didn't know how I wanted to see things change when I came here, but I think she did, and all we need to do is keep going. She wasn't upset when she died." Kirin swallowed down the lump in his throat. "I don't think I'd ever seen her so peaceful. You're right, Kuafu, that she just wanted to give us a chance. We were her big play, people who know firsthand what it's like to be beaten, to be hated, because until you live it you don't know how bad it really is. For kids who look different, for kids who don't have support— that's power. *That's* where we start. We have a year before we're on our own, and then the world is ours to change."

"And of fucking course we know someone who's in the coalition." Ifrit was back, leaning against the doorway. His hair had grown long in the past month, but in the aftermath of everything he'd managed to dye his hair black again without the school complaining. It reflected the fire that now circled the top of his head like a crown, making it shine. "The amount of time this fucker spent with her; you think he doesn't know anything?"

Ifrit was pointing at Shifter, who'd been standing quietly by the door the whole time. As the entire class turned their gazes to him, he held up his hands.

"We've had enough legal trouble for a lifetime. Licenses *first*, then we'll discuss the coalition." He stepped back and gestured inside the house— Pressure's house, which would, after graduation, pass to Ifrit. "But before that, rest."

They filed back inside, some taking an extra minute to say their own goodbyes. Kirin felt obligated to be the last one there, though he felt Ifrit's gaze on the back of his neck. When Adlivun headed inside, she patted his arm, and he was almost alone.

"I was too scared to be remembered as who I used to be, so I never asked if you always knew who I was. I'll never get to now." He cleared his throat, fighting the urge to talk quieter, knowing Ifrit was just behind him. "If I had, I would've wanted to say thank you. You rescued me in more ways than one that day. I knew I wanted to be someone like you, if I could. In the ambulance, I don't know if you remember holding my hand, telling me that I did good. I held onto that for so many years, even when things got bad. And…"

Kirin hazarded a glance over his shoulder, Ifrit meeting his gaze.

"I have to thank you for bringing us together again." He looked back down at the dirt. "I don't… I don't know what I'd do without him."

He could hear Ifrit fidgeting in the doorway, which brought a smile to his lips. Ifrit hadn't gotten any more patient, at least that hadn't changed.

"I'll take care of him. Not that he really needs me to. But I want to." Kirin hesitated. "And I'm sure he never said it, but he really did love you."

With that, Kirin turned away from the flowers and the frozen dirt, greeted with Ifrit's nervous gaze. They hadn't really had any time alone in the past month, everyone still on edge as if Ifrit might disappear again. Kirin couldn't blame them, since he was just as guilty as they were.

"You can ask." Kirin sighed.

"Do you blame me?" The words came out in a rush.

Kirin frowned, having expected Ifrit to want to know what he'd just said, nosy as he was.

"Blame you?"

"For your dad." A muscle in Ifrit's jaw clenched. "He wouldn't be dead if it weren't for me."

Kirin took Ifrit's face in his hands gently, making the other man look him in the eyes instead of at the ground. When crimson met black, Kirin slammed their foreheads together, hard.

"Ow, what the fuck?" Ifrit stumbled back, eyes wide in shock, not anger.

"You're a dumbass." Kirin laughed out loud, the sound of it filling his chest, and then he wrapped Ifrit in a hug, laughing harder when the fire went out in a puff of smoke. "You're *such* a dumbass! Of course I don't."

Ifrit grumbled to himself about Kirin being the real dumbass, but he still burrowed his face into Kirin's jacket.

"She said you'd say that."

It was the first time he'd mentioned Pressure without seeming like he was going to cry.

"Because it was never your fault."

"Mm." Ifrit relaxed against Kirin's chest, Kirin resting his chin on Ifrit's head. "She was right about a lot of things."

"Yeah?"

"Yeah."

Kirin just wanted to stay there, like that, and so the two of them just stood in silence for a while, looking at the flowers in the backyard. It was cold, and their breath puffed in the air, mingling into one cloud. Kirin watched the mist dissipate, suddenly thinking of another time their breaths were shared, a time that had been pushed aside and hidden in a corner by the enormity of grief, of things they still hadn't spoken of, feelings that Kirin wasn't sure he fully understood yet. When he pretended to stretch to peek at Ifrit's face, he found Ifrit watching him, almost too knowingly.

"Aren't you going to ask?" A smirk was tugging at the corner of his mouth, enjoying Kirin's rising blush.

"Well—"

"What the *fuck* are you still talking for?" Phoenix appeared in the doorway, doing a terrible impression of Ifrit's voice. He'd even attempted to pin his hair into Ifrit's new circlet shaped ring of fire, with medium success, his dark and brooding impression only marginally worse than the attempt at Ifrit's voice. A moment later, he dropped back into his normal tone. "Seriously though, Aïcha did bring cookies, and I *will* finish them all if you don't come back in here."

Adlivun appeared, steering Phoenix away and muttering an embarrassed sorry. The second the pair disappeared from view, Kirin dissolved into laughter again.

"I hate him." Ifrit said resolutely, which only made Kirin laugh harder. Only his arm around Ifrit kept him upright.

"I know, I know, he's terrible." Kirin wiped tears from his eyes, sliding his hand down into Ifrit's. "We can talk about this later, yeah? We've got time."

"Yeah," Ifrit agreed, interlacing their fingers as he led them inside, "we've got time."

X
Plotting

THE BASE WAS QUIET at night, not that it was much different during the day now. The defeat at Satol had greatly depleted their numbers, though recruitment was picking up nicely. Something about the hero of the hour being shot down by police after she'd rescued them all left a sour taste in most people's mouths.

She'd lain low, for the most part, in the prior month, not wanting to remind anyone that it had been entirely her idea. The operation was thankfully not considered an entire failure, but close enough to one that she was licking her wounds and healing before daring to suggest anything more. The mask that she'd suggested in the beginning to keep her own identity safe now meant that she was easily replaced, a fact that she was all too aware of.

Once upon a time, she would've walked these halls with her head held high, no one daring to look at her twice or question where she was going. But now, she was skulking around in the dark, slowly making her way to her own office like she was doing something wrong.

They wouldn't even be *anything* without her. Just some angry people arguing over how to best enact change. *She'd* tripled their numbers, even accounting for their recent losses. *She'd* brought them into the global eye, given them information and technology and *direction*. And yet, all they saw were her failures.

She slipped into her office and pulled up the screens, knowing that if she was caught in her task, she would be running from not only Aether— and the name had been *her* idea even— but from East Tech as well.

The heads were correct in saying that trying to break into the servers of East Tech was incredibly irresponsible, that they had far better cybersecurity than most *governments* these days, but she was done with being cautious, and she wasn't even looking to change anything this time. She just needed to see.

The hours ticked by as she poked and prodded, combing through files to see if she could find what she was looking for. There was precious little that they kept on the server, which was alright with her. She didn't need much at all, just one tiny piece of information that shouldn't be as well guarded as it was. They must've tightened security again. Oh dear, Force *had* done a number on their confidence, hadn't she?

Despite the frustration with her task, she allowed herself a small smile. Backups were always necessary, and the plan at Satol had, in her mind, multiple ways to succeed. There was the obvious way, the bomb detonating and taking Futurus and their bloody research into the high heavens. But that was always a stretch, always bordering impossibility. The difficulty with transporting materials into the city had been all but eliminated with the discovery of the boy, but that had left so much up to chance. How much carbon did he put out? How far had the little healer's powers gone? They hadn't known at the start and could've hardly guessed how far that blast would've reached. With the levels they'd measured near the end, they would've lost all those stationed in the city anyway, had the plan been seen to fruition.

But that uncertainty had given them more ways than one to succeed. When she'd been in the police files, she'd dug deeper. Very deep, in fact, decades deep. She'd found the reports from when the Satol child had been brought to East City, from when his guardian had to keep reporting neighbors for harassing the boy. She'd dug deeper still and found the report from the original attack, detailing how the hero Force had refused to kill the child, had stuck her neck out, only to be barred from service ever again.

Yet the police and the hero system at large could not contain the clamor for *her*, for the hero who'd saved what was left of the city and the boy himself, and so a petty agreement was struck. She was used as a figure head, an icon of the heroes, while not being able to be one herself because of an act of mercy.

Oh, how she *loved* Force. No matter which way the story ended, she won. Both the woman and the child— now a fledgling hero himself— dead, the grief of a mother destroying the world, or a son grieving his mother, who had already stopped the worst from happening *twice*. It mattered not that Aether's actions created the situation, because the public only knew who died and who had killed her, and they were angry because of it.

She could hear the whispers already.

She saved us, and yet look what happened to her! What's to say they won't do the same or worse to us?

She had allowed herself the luxury of skimming through forums here and there, wanting to see how well the seeds were sown. Undercurrents churned, the perfect kind of dissatisfaction that led to action.

But there was one thing that bothered her.

She'd somewhat counted on the heroes under Force being discredited, disbarred. The monster class, they were mocked as in the private chats of school staff. They threatened her beautiful web, a statement of commitment to change, of progressive action. Hope needed to be extinguished for action to occur, and there was one in that group that she particularly wanted gone.

That had led her here, sitting at the screen, her eyes trailing across lines of code as she pulled and pushed her way through slowly, meticulously. She knew what he looked like, had seen his face unmasked, but the image in her brain wasn't enough to work with. She needed a photo.

Like magic, the seals broke, and she was in. A smile stretched across her face as she found what she was looking for, though he was much changed from when she'd seen him, dark where now he was light. The image she stole and brought elsewhere on the web, following the trail wherever she could find it, pulling the information she sought from less guarded sources. Just one photo, and a map was spreading out in front of her, a plan of action forming in her mind.

She'd thought the plan before was her masterpiece, but she'd looked too narrowly it seemed. She hadn't thought they would have someone so powerful in their arsenal, nor had she expected that he would stop at nothing to return those taken. Force was supposed to be the one to do it, not him.

But now she had an adversary, someone worthy to be called a true challenge. There was strength left in him, and she could work with that.

An image was pulled up on her screen, a photo taken over ten years before. A sweet family with four kids, two just babies, not yet missing a piece.

"Come now Kirin," she whispered to herself, "let's see what it takes to make you break."

Acknowledgements

Where to start?

Firstly, I feel like I must give a huge hand to my beta readers, who put up with me and my bullshit far more than they needed to. Thank you to Sam, Jennifer, Erin, Trick, Mini, Quinn, Monty, Jai, Reid, Vi, Janna, Geo, Mira, Steph, Spencer, Jude, Duda and everyone else who was forced to read a snippet when my brain decided to stop processing words. Truly this book would not exist in its current format without you, and your feedback and comments has made all the difference.

I would then like to add an extra shout-out to Quinn and Steph for being my official/unofficial editors. Thank you for pointing out my sometimes egregious use of commas, especially when they aren't necessary. I'm sure I've misused some in here but I wanted this to be a surprise, so I'll let the typos stand as a testament to how the book would have looked without your invaluable expertise. I also have to thank Quinn for the very first fanart that I received, and want you to know that I will never, ever remove it from its place of honor.

Speaking of art, I cannot fail to mention Mini. Thank you for surprising me with random doodles of my boys and the rest of the class, it made my day every time and helped me keep going when I felt like I was drowning with other work. Knowing my characters lived rent free in your head gave me the courage to believe that perhaps these characters could mean something to other people too.

I would also be remiss to not give a heartfelt thank you to Irene Te, and all your incredible tips and guidance through the self-publishing process. While it was still a harrowing and daunting task, it felt so much less overwhelming knowing I had someone as kind and genuine as you in my corner. I'm glad the Instagram algorithm worked for once and brought us together; I couldn't imagine tackling this without your expert guidance!

And lastly, I do need to thank my wonderful partner for dealing with all the late nights I kept him up typing or proof-reading or editing in bed. Thank you for bearing with me when I got stressed or frustrated, for bringing snacks to my work desk when I forgot to eat for hours, for rubbing my shoulders when I would go full shrimp after writing all day. I love you so much and I couldn't have done this without you.

(I also need to say thank you to Chomp for eating all my bad drafts and not eating my proof copies for that one day I left them on the floor.)

About the Author

J is far less interesting to talk about than their adorable rabbit, Chomp. They have kindly provided a photo of him below for your viewing pleasure. *Warm-Blooded* is their debut novel, the first of the Carbon Chronicles trilogy.